Praise For SEASON OF LOVE

"[This] love story is by turns heartbreaking and delightful."
—*Library Journal*

"SEASON OF LOVE is holiday romance perfection. Warm and cozy, emotional and swoony, Greer has expertly crafted a delightful queer, Jewish holiday story that will easily steal your heart and leave you longing for a weekend away at Carrigan's."   —Rachael Lippincott, #1 *New York Times* bestselling co-author of *She Gets the Girl*

"If you are like me and completely obsessed with Hallmark and holiday movies, then you don't want to miss Helena Greer's debut novel, SEASON OF LOVE. This book hits on all your favorite Hallmark tropes as it weaves a beautiful journey from hate to love for Miriam and Noelle. A cozy, queer, heartfelt holiday romance that will have you grabbing a blanket, a cup of hot chocolate, and snuggling down to read this charming book."   —Rachel Van Dyken, #1 *New York Times* bestselling author of *The Godparent Trap*

"A heartwarming and inspiring story about letting go of the past to find your joy and being open to love."
—Abby Jimenez, *New York Times* bestselling author of *Part of Your World*

"If you need the cozy feel of a Hallmark holiday movie in book form, visit Carrigan's! SEASON OF LOVE has all of the warm, queer, Jewish holiday vibes you could possibly want. It's a cup of cocoa with the perfect amount of marshmallows, it's a sweet kiss under the mistletoe. Helena Greer creates characters and settings that I never want to leave behind."

—Jen DeLuca, *USA Today* bestselling author of *Well Met*

"Satire and romantic holiday magic in equal measure, SEASON OF LOVE is a sly, big-hearted book that will have you laughing even as it makes your heart grow three sizes."

—Jenny Holiday, *USA Today* bestselling author of *Duke, Actually*

"SEASON OF LOVE is a warm and witty romance with characters that leap straight off the page and a setting so cozy readers will ache to visit Carrigan's for real. Greer's writing is vibrant and she handles grief and complicated family dynamics with tenderness, treating her characters with the utmost care and affection. Readers will be absolutely smitten with Noelle and Miriam!" —Alexandria Bellefleur, bestselling author of *Count Your Lucky Stars*

"A warm, cozy holiday romance, SEASON OF LOVE is a vibrant exploration of embracing that which is most unexpected in life...and in love. Best read under the glow of rainbow twinkle lights with a cup of cocoa."

—Ashley Herring Blake, author of *Delilah Green Doesn't Care*

"SEASON OF LOVE uses the magic of the holidays to do what romance novels do best: convince its main characters (and its readers) that the healing power of love is something every single person deserves. This heartwarming debut has everything you

want in a holiday romance—and I can't wait to recommend it to my friends."   —Therese Beharrie, author of
And They All Lived Happily Ever After

"Greer has crafted an idyllic setting I want to whisk away to for Christmas (but then stay all year) and a charming cast of characters I want to befriend. Readers are going to lament that Carrigan's isn't a real destination they can jet off to."
—Sarah Hogle, author of
You Deserve Each Other

"One of the most unique and uniquely queer things I've ever read, SEASON OF LOVE is more a place than a book: Carrigan's Christmasland's heart beats just as strongly in these pages as all of its loving, messy, large cast of characters, all of whom are looking for home in their own ways, even if they're already there. By the last page, readers will feel as if they're part of this special family, too."
—Anita Kelly, author of *Love & Other Disasters*

"Greer's debut simply sparkles. It's so easy to get lost in the magic of Carrigan's with Miriam and Noelle, and a stellar secondary cast that includes a fat cat named Kringle. This delightful Christmas Chanukah mashup will have you braiding challah by a Christmas tree."
—Roselle Lim, author of *Sophie's Lonely Hearts Club*

SEASON OF LOVE

HELENA GREER

FOREVER

New York Boston

Copyright © 2022 by Helena Greer

Cover design by Daniela Medina. Cover illustration by Cathy Arnold. Cover copyright © 2022 by Hachette Book Group, Inc.

Forever
Hachette Book Group
1290 Avenue of the Americas, New York, NY 10104
read-forever.com
twitter.com/readforeverpub

First Edition: October 2022

Forever is an imprint of Grand Central Publishing. The Forever name and logo are trademarks of Hachette Book Group, Inc.

The publisher is not responsible for websites (or their content) that are not owned by the publisher.

Library of Congress Cataloging-in-Publication Data
Names: Greer, Helena, author.
Title: Season of love / Helena Greer.
Description: First edition. | New York : Forever, 2022.
Identifiers: LCCN 2022019461 | ISBN 9781538706534 (trade paperback) | ISBN 9781538706541 (ebook)
Subjects: LCGFT: Romance fiction. | Novels.
Classification: LCC PS3607.R4726 S43 2022 | DDC 813/.6—dc23/eng/ 20220422
LC record available at https://lccn.loc.gov/2022019461

ISBNs: 9781538706534 (trade pbk.), 9781538706541 (ebook)

Printed in the United States of America

LSC-C

Printing 1, 2022

For KOS, my North Star, my ride or die.
There is no Carrigan's, or me, without you.

Content Guidance

This book contains discussions of past emotional and financial abuse, the death of family members both suddenly and from prolonged illness, grief, parental estrangement, and 12-Step recovery from alcoholism, as well as passing mention of being the adult child of alcoholics. It also contains a brief mention of online trolling, including antisemitism and homophobia, and a brief mention of unspecified harm to animals.

Please treat yourself with care if any of these topics are sensitive for you.

SEASON
OF LOVE

PART 1

Sukkot to Thanksgiving

Chapter 1

Miriam

When Miriam Blum's life changed forever, she was holding a chain saw in both hands, a bottle of glitter glue between her teeth, and standing in an empty warehouse over an antique bed frame.

The warehouse was mostly dust, painted concrete, and fluorescent lights, but soon it would be the flagship store-front for Blum Again Vintage & Curios, her online antique upcycling business. The old naval shipyard of Charleston was the perfect spot for its first ever physical space. As part of the up-and-coming arts destination, it would be a place for people to find, as her window promised, "What You Never Knew You Always Needed."

She'd just flown back to Charleston this morning from a whirlwind trip to spend Sukkot with some friends, and to check in on her network of Old Ladies who owned antique and junk shops. They kept her supplied with weird vintage things she chainsawed, decoupaged, and hot-glued into art pieces that were shockingly popular on Pinterest. At the moment, she was waiting on a potentially haunted doll for a client in Huntington and some brooches she was going to make into the skirt of a life-sized ballerina.

Her phone played a dirge from the pocket of her dress—her mother's ringtone. Setting down the chain saw, she walked outside to take the call, not wanting to get her mother's energy in this space. The dread that always accompanied speaking to her mother coalesced uneasily with the realization that it wasn't their designated time to check in. Miriam couldn't handle more than one phone call a month, which her mother knew—even if she never acknowledged it. If the schedule had changed, something bad must have happened.

"Mom, what's wrong? It's not our Friday," she said, instead of hello.

"Well," her mother said primly, "if you would accept my calls any time other than Shabbos . . ." She trailed off, her guilt trip hanging heavy in the air. Miriam didn't feel guilty. Her mom knew why their relationship was relegated to fifteen carefully curated minutes a month.

"Mom. Why. Are. You. Calling?" Miriam asked, again. She kicked an acorn across the street, watching it skitter.

"Cass died, sweetheart. I'm so sorry." Her mom's voice broke on the last word.

Miriam gasped, her heart clenching.

Despite not having seen her in ten years, Cassiopeia Carrigan was the North Star in Miriam's life, her role model and hero. Her mother's aunt was the gray sheep of her family. She'd walked away from the family's booming bakery business to open, of all things, a Christmas tree farm. More than that, the property was a Christmas extravaganza, with a tree farm, a Christmas-themed inn, and a two-month-long festival full of every Christmas tradition ever invented. An immersive Christmasland experience.

"I'm still Jewish," Cass would explain. "I just couldn't find another job where I only had to talk to people two months out of the year." Cass was An Eccentric. Every winter break, her parents had taken Miriam to Carrigan's Christmasland for the world's least traditional Hanukkah.

"Miri? You still there?" Her mother's voice cut through her memories. She sounded exhausted and broken, two things Miriam would have said her mother was incapable of feeling.

"How?" Miriam asked, trying to wrap her mind around the idea of anything taking out the human tornado that had been Cass Carrigan as Miriam knew her.

Her mother took in a sharp breath. "She was sick for a long time, Miri. Years. We thought she was getting better, but she had a relapse, and she was gone fast."

Cass Carrigan, her Cass, had been sick and no one told her, so that she could say goodbye. In the lifelong list of her mother's betrayals, this one was worse than most.

"When is the service? I want to sit shiva. I'll be there, even"—she tried not to choke on the words—"if Dad is coming." Her mother was silent for a beat.

"I'll text you all the details," she said, finally.

Just like that, it was settled. Miriam would fly back to the place she'd been avoiding for a decade. She told the voice in her head screaming in panic that it would be fine.

She'd spent every Christmas, and some summers, at Carrigan's. She'd thrived under Cass's love—a heat lamp compared to the frigid conditions of her house—running wild through the trees with her cousin Hannah and their childhood best friend, Levi. Being safe, for little pockets of time, from the worst of her father's behavior. Until her dad finally went too far, and she'd stopped going anywhere near her family—anywhere he'd ever been. There hadn't been goodbyes or any explanation for the people she'd left behind.

Miriam had kept in touch, sort of, with a happy birthday text here, a letter there, sometimes sending a flower arrangement for the High Holy Days. Nothing that went past the surface. She'd never meant for her absence to be permanent. She'd just needed some time.

"Next year, at Carrigan's" was her tiny private version of "Next year, in Jerusalem." She'd always thought, *Next year, I'll have the courage. Next year, I'll stop running, and go home to my family.* But she'd always seemed to have a good reason to put it off, and now it was too late. Now, the only thing left was to say the goodbye she hadn't said ten years ago.

Miriam locked up the warehouse and began walking home, hoping the long meander through the old city would help sort out her thoughts. Her mind raced as she tried to figure out how to fit a trip to New York into her current life. The storefront's grand opening wasn't until New Year's Eve, but she would have to be back in Charleston as soon as shiva ended to prepare.

On top of the store opening, her fiancée, Tara, hosted or attended a seemingly never-ending stream of social events. Miriam was expected to appear at them all and schmooze.

She didn't know how Tara would react to her having to leave, even for a short time. Probably not well. Tara's life was impeccably planned, and any variation perturbed her.

The tight schedule was good. No matter how nuclear things went at Carrigan's, she had reasons to come back to Charleston immediately. An escape plan. At worst, she would have a really bad week dealing with everything she'd left behind, but it would only be a week.

Charleston's Historic District was a town of ghosts, held at bay by the haint blue painted around doors and under porches. Horse-drawn tourist carriages clogged narrow streets, winding past the market that stretched for blocks, where you could buy artisan goods, Gullah-Geechee baskets, and so much food. Master builders renovated historic homes, churches older than the country flew Pride flags from their wrought iron fences, restaurants did molecular gastronomy takes on shrimp and grits.

It was a city full of people trying to tie their roots to their futures. Miriam, who had severed nearly all her roots and was making her future up as she went, was drawn to that. Charleston was a perfect place to lick her wounds, hide out, build a new version of herself that none of her family knew. The polar opposite of Carrigan's, which had built her and knew all her secrets. Charleston wasn't home, exactly, but it was a hell of a lot safer than Carrigan's.

Yet just around that corner, there was a port with many of the country's worst sins written on it, and you couldn't walk a block without bumping into living, thriving injustice. Charleston's charming gentility was a beautifully painted mask on hundreds of years of pain, its safety a facade.

Speaking of places that were not home, exactly—when she opened the door of the home she shared, marginally, with Tara, the wall of humidity off that same port surrendered to an assault from the air-conditioning.

Tara's Single House was a showcase. Always full of light, but rarely noise, it was the perfect set piece for the lesbian debutante daughter of one of Charleston's oldest families to entertain. Tara wore perfect Southern gentility like armor in battle, wielding her manners and the legacy of her family's power as weapons in her crusade to radically change South Carolina's criminal justice system. This house was her command center.

There was a place inside for Miriam's purse, jacket, shoes. There wasn't a place for her art, but she had the warehouse. Miriam had never had a home that reflected her or made space for her. She caught herself, sometimes, dreaming of vibrant walls and kitschy clutter, but asking for it felt beyond her. She'd been too well trained as a child not to intrude.

Miriam dropped her keys in a hammered silver bowl on a carved teak stool in the foyer, listening to them echo. Her foot connected with something heavy, wheeling it away. She looked down, dazed, to find her carry-on. She'd left it there earlier today, arriving home from the airport before heading straight to the warehouse to get work done. It made the house feel like an Airbnb she was checking out of. *At least I won't have to unpack*, she thought a little hysterically.

At the end of the polished wood hallway, a blonde bob peeked out of a doorway.

"Babe! I'll be off this conference call in five minutes. I have dinner being delivered any moment." Tara didn't yell, just projected her honey drawl down the hallway, by force of will. Her hair swung, shiny, back into her office.

Miriam pulled her own dark curls into a messy bun. Unlike Tara's willowy frame, Miriam was very short, just over five feet, although the halo of her curls gave her the appearance of another three inches or so. She usually wore it long and big and untamed. With her small, pointy face and very large features, she resembled nothing so much as an illustration of a Lost Boy. She felt lost, now, as she sank down into a chaise longue, set adrift by the idea of returning to Carrigan's. By the loss of Cass's existence, somewhere, in the world.

She was ordering a Lyft to the airport when Tara sat down next to her, bumping her with a shoulder. "Hey, you."

"Hey, you, back." Miriam tried to move her mouth into a semblance of a smile.

"There should be barbecue on our doorstep any second," Tara began, looking at her phone and not noticing Miriam's mood. "I made sure there's no hidden pork in yours. I'm almost done with trial prep for the day."

"Tara," Miriam interrupted, "I have to go to New York. Today. My great-aunt Cass died."

Tara slowed, softened. "Oh, Miriam. Oh my gosh." Miriam found herself being pulled into a hug. "Do I know who your great-aunt Cass was?" Tara asked, puzzled.

Miriam almost choked on a sob of surprise. She'd never told Tara about Carrigan's. Of course she hadn't.

Carrigan's was the thing that had most hurt to give up when she'd cut ties with her family. The place closest to her heart. She never talked about it now, if she could help it, and Tara had met her in the time After. And if Miriam never talked about Carrigan's, she never talked about Cass, because Cass *was* Carrigan's.

Besides, she and Tara didn't have a relationship built on sharing their deepest secrets. Tara had needed an interesting wife as an accessory to throw garden parties, and Miriam had needed a place to land with someone safe. Tara was often thought of, by Charleston's old guard, as a bit of an icy bitch, partly because she challenged them and partly because she was prickly as hell. Miriam helped her project a softer public image, and Tara took care of Miriam's needs even as her prickliness kept Miriam comfortably at a distance, where she preferred to be.

They were friends, lovers, and co-conspirators, but they were not in love. They had a pact: Miriam helped Tara create a faultless life, and Tara gave Miriam stability to build her career.

Neither their souls nor their pasts were a part of their arrangement. Miriam would never have agreed to marry Tara if she'd thought there was any danger of falling in love with her.

"I've mentioned Cass," she insisted nonetheless, crossing her arms. "She owns a Christmas tree farm in the Adirondacks. My cousin Hannah works there? My family spent our vacations there when I was a child, and Cass was very important to me. Carrigan's was very important to me, once."

"I'm sure if you had mentioned that to me," Tara bristled, "I would have remembered."

"Maybe?" But Miriam knew she was unfairly picking a fight. Tara never forgot anything.

Tara hummed. "Well, we were supposed to be at a party for

my firm, but we can make it up. The firm will understand that
you were pulled out of town for a family funeral. Although for
a great-aunt you haven't seen in ten years, perhaps you could
send a floral arrangement?" Tara was slowing her Southern
cadence down even further, in that way she did when she
wanted to give the listener time to change their answer.

Tara was very effective in front of a jury.

"I need to go be with my family. I need to go home to
Carrigan's," Miriam told her.

Tara stared back. "Miriam. One: Carrigan's is not home, it
is a place you spent vacations. I've never even heard of it until
today. Two: You are estranged from your family. Three: You're
Jewish, and Carrigan's is, apparently, a *Christmas* tree farm."

Tara always argued in numbered lists, without giving anyone breathing room, so that by the time she got to point five,
you'd forgotten what point one was. It was a great lawyer
trick, but a less charming girlfriend trick.

Miriam took a deep breath, though a tsunami of grief threatened to swallow her. She stuffed it down, as she'd done with
all her feelings for so long now, and tried to be fair to Tara.

Tara wasn't fixating on law firm dinners for nothing. She'd
built her criminal defense practice to ensure fair trials for
those victimized by the very systems her family had upheld
for generations. But to reform those power structures from
within, she needed to maintain access to them. To keep
herself from being ostracized, especially as a lesbian, she was
always skating a fine line. She skated it beautifully, gracefully,
from years of practice—but with enormous effort.

Miriam couldn't be mad at Tara for panicking a little, even
if her grief wanted someone to lash out at.

She jumped off the couch and wiped away tears.

"I'll be back right after shiva. I promise. I'll do all the rounds with you, be the perfect fiancée," Miriam said, grabbing her scarf and coat, then the forgotten carry-on. "I need one week, then we can go back to pretending my old life never existed. Believe me, I'll be ready for that after seven days with my mother."

"Let me meet you in a couple of days," Tara said, her voice softer. "I need to rearrange a few things, because I'm supposed to be at trial, but I can make it work. Then we can come home together."

Miriam couldn't stomach the idea of managing Tara's almost certain dislike of the eccentric, cluttered chaos of Carrigan's, introducing her parents, being present for Tara while also trying to get through the week herself. It was kind of Tara to offer, but Miriam didn't want Tara to be a part of this. She wanted her Before and After lives to stay very, very separate.

"We both know you can't, Tara." Miriam shook her head. "There's no way they can spare you from your trial, and you can't have your phone at shiva! Your client is relying on you, and my family is going to be as much as I can handle."

Tara never let down a client, which Miriam admired immensely. It also allowed Miriam an easy out.

Tara bit her lip. "I'm sorry I would be something else to handle."

Maybe not such an easy out, then. "Thank you for offering. I have to go to the airport, like, right now. I will be back in a week. I just. I have to deal with this."

Tara followed Miriam out the door, as etiquette demanded.

No emotion ever got between Tara Sloane Chadwick and proper etiquette.

Miriam was already regretting leaving things this way, but she couldn't figure out how to fix this chasm right now. She had far wider chasms to worry about.

"I'll call you a car," Tara offered, a little stiffly. She always got formal when she was upset.

"My Lyft's already here. I'm sorry I'm missing the takeout you ordered. I owe you a dinner next week."

One week at Carrigan's to say goodbye. It would be over before she knew it.

Chapter 2

Miriam

The car had barely turned off her block when her phone rang, again, this time with a Britney Spears song.

If she didn't answer, Cole would just keep calling. Cole had been her best friend since college, and while she loved him more than life, he was a lot. She wasn't particularly ready to deal with him, but then again, she wasn't ready to deal with anything. She might as well start somewhere. "Cole."

"MIMI, WHERE ARE YOU?!" he demanded. "You never answered my texts I need you immediately."

"Cole, breathe real deep." Miriam rubbed her hand over her face. "I'm on my way to the airport. I need to book the next flight to New York." She stretched out her booted legs, belatedly wishing she'd stopped to change her socks. Her entire world had just crashed, but she would rather focus on her eighteen-hour grungy socks.

"You just got home," he whined. "What, is there an antiquing emergency? Do the Old Ladies need you?"

"I'm not going for work," she said, dragging in a breath. "I'm going to Carrigan's."

"Carrigan's?" His voice lit all the way up, nearly screeching. Cole had a long fascination with the idea of Carrigan's, which was most of the reason she'd never taken him there. When they'd met in college, she had still spent every winter break on the farm with Cass, Hannah, Levi, and the rest of the Matthewses, but she'd always found an excuse to leave him behind. By the time she stopped going for good, they'd been living in different states.

"Wait, you don't go to Carrigan's. Ever. What happened?"

She braced a hand against the side of the car, grasping for purchase against the wave of grief as she said, "Cass died." She heard him suck in his breath. "I have to sit shiva."

"I'll meet you at the ticket counter."

"What? You can't just hie off to upstate New York." She couldn't ask him to come keep her company in a place he'd never been, to mourn a woman he'd never met. Although she ought to have expected him to offer. It was like him to drop everything for her.

Her sweet, loyal boy, her platonic puzzle piece.

"I'll meet you at the airport, Mimi. I'm buying your ticket! I've been trying to get you to take me to Carrigan's for years." Cole hung up before Miriam could tell him no.

* * *

By the time she saw Cole in the ticket line, she had stopped shaking. Mostly.

Cole was huge—very nearly six and a half feet—and built

like a rower, with shaggy sand-colored waves of hair and guileless ocean-blue eyes. He'd played lacrosse in college and sailed a yacht. He was a quintessential Southern Bro, hiding a progressive heart behind clothes embroidered with lobsters. When he showed up at the airport in a too-small ugly Halloween sweater over a pink button-down with a popped collar, she felt herself start to breathe a little bit. Cole coming was good. He would distract her from falling apart, and he would pick her up if she did.

"I know you're going to have an opinion about the sweater." He held her hands tightly, curling his large body protectively around her very small one like a big brother— or a daddy penguin. "But I'm here with my credit card to whisk you away to your ancestral homeland, so don't give me shit."

"I never lived at Carrigan's, Cole. I'm from Scottsdale. In Arizona?"

"Shh." He shook his head. "Don't ruin the magic. I'm ready to immerse myself completely in the Spirit of Christmas. I'm going to be Father Christmas! No, Brother Christmas. I'm too young to be a father."

He pulled away, bouncing on the balls of his feet. His suitcase, a vintage piece Miriam had bedazzled, threatened to roll away from him. Miriam knew that part of him was exhilarated about finally going to Carrigan's, but part of it was an act for her. He was giving her an opportunity to fall into their comfortable, playful banter so she could get through the terrible mundanity of the airport intact.

"Also, Mimi. I'm so, so sorry. I know Cass meant the world to you." He dropped his backpack and wrapped her in a painfully tight hug. "I'm so glad I invited myself. You need me. You can't face your parents alone."

Miriam decided to sidestep this mention of her parents. She was going to let Cole's performance sweep her away for a few hours, before she had to face a Carrigan's without Cass. Instead, she focused on the rest of what Cole had said.

"You're thirty-five, Cole. People our age have kids who are in high school. You're past old enough to be Father Christmas. And I think you are overestimating the Carrigan's experience."

"It's basically the set of a Hallmark movie, right?" His eyes were those of a kid waking up the morning of a Disney World vacation.

She tried to temper his excitement and her own anxiety at the same time.

"I mean, that's not wildly inaccurate. But remember, I haven't been back in ten years. And the Christmas festival doesn't start until November first, which isn't for a couple of weeks. It might not even be Christmas-y, yet. I don't know what it's like now, especially with Cass gone."

"My body is ready. My faith is going to be renewed. I'm going to find true love." Cole gestured wildly. "I'm prepared. I packed my candy cane boxers. I can't wait to meet the real Santa, thinly disguised as a large white-bearded man named Kris."

She laughed a little, but it threatened to turn into a sob. He put his arm around her shoulder, shuffling them both up to the ticket counter.

"You're Miriam and Cole," the woman at the computer said, her eyes wide. "Oh my gosh. Can I take a selfie with you? I always hope I'll run into you around town, this is so exciting. Are you going on a buying trip for the new store?"

Miriam winced. *Not a Bloomer, not right now.* The fandom for her online store, and its associated Instagram and Pinterest, was big enough that her followers had given themselves a name. She was used to getting recognized by Bloomers in public, but she couldn't put on her Bloomer Face today.

Her carefully cultivated persona was for her own privacy. She was incredibly grateful to her fans for making her artwork a viable career, but they wanted to know her, and she barely wanted to know herself. Having that Bloomer Face to slip into had helped her avoid spending too much time in her own brain over the years, but today, when her past was at her doorstep, it was an ill-fitting costume.

She was grateful when Cole took over the conversation, snapping a selfie with the woman while he handed her both their IDs. He steered Miriam meekly to the winding line for TSA. She could barely feel her feet touching the floor. He continued their conversation as if she was responding. It was how he'd been talking to her, basically without stopping, for seventeen years.

"Isn't Tara freaking out that you're not helping her prepare for some terrible rich-people party her parents are throwing?" he asked as they put their shoes back on past security.

"Your parents are friends with her parents," she pointed out. "You're richer than she is. You took Tara to cotillion."

"Yes, so I'm uniquely qualified to pass judgment on their parties. They're terrible." He swung his arm around her as they walked, and she let her body relax against his.

"She's freaking out, a little. She doesn't think I really need to go. But someone needs to help my cousin Hannah mediate all the cousins. Plus, my parents," she added, grimacing. "And I need to do it, for Cass. It's important."

"Well, I do love sitting shiva," Cole said. "I could eat a hundred hard-boiled eggs. I'm basically Gaston. And, if need be, I can always kill your dad for you." He shrugged, as if he were joking, though Miriam knew he probably wasn't. Underneath the yacht bro exterior was a hacker with a feral sense of loyalty to the people he considered his, one that could sometimes supersede his morals. The only reason he hadn't already wreaked havoc with her dad's identity was that Miriam had asked him not to.

On the plane, Miriam toyed with the corner of her drink napkin. When Cass was younger and still traveled the world, she would jot down little letters, sketches, and observations. Cass wrote in sharp, uppercase letters of various sizes, with unexpected capitalizations and a great number of exclamation points. She would tuck the napkins into cheesy cards and send them to Miriam from Kathmandu and St. Petersburg and Cairo. Miriam had a box full of them under her bed.

After Miriam stopped coming to Carrigan's, Cass's napkins kept arriving. When Miriam least expected it, an envelope would arrive filled with cutting observations and cynical but loving gossip. She checked her purse for a pen, thinking she would do a drawing to keep up the tradition.

Instead, Cole's conversation sucked her in.

Cole was not an introvert. He'd been known to opine that introverts do not exist. He had trouble understanding that other human beings did not, necessarily, want the gift of his running commentary on the world around him. Miriam found him oddly calming to tune out to.

He was giving their poor, polite seatmate a monologue, describing Carrigan's with the zeal of a promotional brochure, only not quite accurately, having never been there.

"Mimi's aunt bought the farm with money she inherited from her father, who started a greengrocer business from nothing as a Polish immigrant.[1] She was some sort of scandalous vaudeville dancer in the twenties[2] and her family cut her off,[3] so to piss them off she bought a Christmas tree farm!" He clasped his hands to his heart as he said this, as if it were the most delightful thing imaginable.

"Then, she turned it into a whole Christmas Festival that runs from Halloween to New Year's. There are sleigh rides and hot cocoa tastings, barn dances, gingerbread competitions, cookie swaps, and something at midnight with reindeer. They even put real candles on trees and have a big ceremony to light them. It's a walking, talking Christmas card owned by an old Jewish lady," Cole continued. "It's literally the best place on Earth—sorry, Disneyland."

Miriam decided to rescue the stranger. She laid her head on Cole's shoulder.

"Distract me, bashert." Miriam said. Cole, blessedly, left the seatmate alone, and turned his body, squished into a middle seat, fully toward her to better regale her with the emergency he'd called her about earlier.

---

1   He was a Ukrainian baker.
2   This part was mostly true.
3   She remained very close to her family all her life. While they thought she was eccentric, they were proud of her for building her own business.

Once again, he had ghosted a perfectly nice girl. She wasn't convinced this was an emergency, but he needed to talk out what tiny thing he'd found wrong with her. He met lots of wonderful women and always seemed to like them a great deal, until he found a problem, got bored, or forgot they existed. Miriam wondered if he just hadn't met anyone yet who made him want to be serious. As she ribbed him comfortably about his dating habits, her stomach settled into their well-worn dynamic.

They landed at LaGuardia, Cole once again physically moving her through the packed crowds. She didn't know how she would ever have gotten out of the airport without him. The only thing her brain had room for was terror at the prospect of going back home. They took the train upstate, to Advent, the closest station to Carrigan's Christmasland. Advent was the kind of small town that went all out and then some for Christmas, although Miriam wasn't sure if that was because of their proximity to Carrigan's, or if Cass had chosen the land for Carrigan's because of its nearness to an already-established Christmas destination.

Stepping off the train used to mean seeing Aunt Cass, in high-heeled boots, turban, and fur coat, climbing out of her beat-up farm truck with mud splashed up to the windows. Now, it meant anonymously boarding the Carrigan's shuttle and bouncing along the winding road through the trees. The absence felt like a vacuum had opened inside her.

All of the Adirondacks was riotous in autumn reds, lush and

crisp and overdressed. There were glimpses of lakes and flashes of moose. Then the Christmasland came into view over the curve of a hill. The house and its immense lawn sat at the front of the property, with 160 acres of evergreens growing behind it. Little-girl-Miriam had taken enormous pleasure in spending Hanukkah at the Hundred Acre Wood.

Carrigan's Christmasland was the velvet Elvis version of a Thomas Kinkade painting. They entered through giant double wrought iron gates, in curling filigree C's. Miriam had hoped every inch would be draped in greenery and winking colored lights (Aunt Cass was of the immovable opinion that tiny white lights were for suckers and the only correct Christmas lights were the giant colored glass bulbs). But instead there was a dark, empty lawn, like the whole farm was wearing mourning colors. The Christmas Festival started in two weeks, and they hadn't decorated yet.

Miriam dragged her feet, walking up the front porch. Dilapidated and rumored to be haunted, the original Victorian mansion had been on the property when Cass bought it in the 1950s. Cass had lovingly restored the turrets and balconies and white cake trim while adding large, rambling wings for guests. It wasn't massive, not a true hotel. There were twenty-five guest rooms, staff quarters, a top floor where Cass lived, and an attic full of strange treasures. Behind the house sat a barn that was mostly for housing hay, reindeer, and tractors, save for the occasional dance. Next to it were stables for the horses, a carriage house, a couple of small guest cottages, and a work "shed" the size of a three-bedroom house.

Miriam hadn't been inside the inn for a decade. Standing before the front door, she steeled herself against the onslaught of emotions she'd organized her life around running from. Until now, she couldn't be anywhere that reminded her of her father, even this place that should have been a haven. She brushed her fingers over the mezuzah for strength, expecting any moment to freeze in terror.

But the terror didn't come. Just grief and the feeling of coming home she'd always experienced standing on these steps.

The front door opened into a hallway that, in any other year, would be draped in garlands. To one side was a massive kitchen, to the other, the great room they used as an event space. From there rose a curving staircase. The ceilings soared up to the second floor, and a fireplace stood in the center of one wall, topped by a massive carved mantel. Carrigan's wasn't ready for the Christmas Festival, and it made everything feel so much more real. Cass's absence hung over every empty spot that used to hold a stocking.

The staircase led to the guest rooms, which surrounded a central landing that had been made into an entertainment area, with comfortable couches and a flatscreen TV. Down the stairs sauntered a tortoiseshell cat the size of a pony with ear tufts as wide as a human hand. It wound its way around Cole's legs.

"Kringle!" Miriam exclaimed.

"Hello, pretty girl." Cole knelt down to rub the cat, whispering absurdities about its glorious size and fluffiness.

"Kringle is a boy. He's a Norwegian forest cat who wandered in one day from the snow." As she crooned gently to the animal in question, he rolled onto his back, exposing four feet of belly floof.

"All tortoiseshells are girls," Cole argued.

"Most tortoiseshells are girls," Miriam corrected. "The ones who aren't"—she pointed at Kringle—"are magic."

"I hesitate to ask how much he weighs," Cole said as he lifted Kringle up to get an estimate—and was engulfed by the monster.

"I'm going to take you home," he whispered.

"Cole! Do not steal the cat!"

"Did I hear 'Cole'? Miriam, have you finally brought us the Infamous Cole?"

Miriam's cousin Hannah came down the stairs, darting in for a quick, hard hug. Her hair was the color of dark honey and looked sun-burnished even inside. It was braided down her back, reaching to her waist. Her eyebrows winged over dark eyes, olive skin, and soaring cheekbones. Miriam's heart, which she'd thought was already as broken as it could be, shattered into tiny shards at the sight of her.

Hannah, her entire childhood in a person, one-third of the trifecta of trouble that made up every happy memory Miriam had from before she'd left her parents' house. Her first real friend. Hannah, who she'd relegated to likes on social media posts and rare, stilted phone calls. She'd sacrificed so many relationships to be free of her father, and she'd pretended she didn't miss Hannah like a hole in her heart, but she couldn't now.

Hannah turned to Cole. "I'm so excited to *finally* meet you!" She threw her arms around him, and Cole, never a man to turn down a hug, picked her up.

"Mimi, your cousin Hannah looks like the Jewish Mae West? I'm very angry that you've withheld this vital information from me for seventeen years." Cole grinned.

Miriam elbowed him. "I think Mae West was the Jewish Mae West."

Hannah stepped back and scanned Cole. "You, however, look like Dick Casablancas got put through a Froyo machine."

"I'd be offended if that wasn't the exact vibe I'd been cultivating. Is there a room for me, or do I have to sleep on the floor in this miscreant's room?" Cole asked. "Or in a manger?"

"I think there's room for you at the Christmasland Inn," Hannah said, already moving. "C'mon, Casablancas, I'll put you in Miriam's childhood room. It still has some of her old Baby-Sitter's Club books tucked into the back of the closet."

"Oooooooh." Cole followed Hannah up the stairs. "I'll see you in the morning, my love! Claudia Kishi awaits me!"

Hannah looked back over her shoulder at Miriam. The Business Boss mask that Miriam hadn't known Hannah was wearing slipped, and her face fell for a moment into agony. Realizing she no longer knew how to read her cousin's face pierced her. Miriam wanted to hold her but didn't feel she had the right. All the bridges between them were either burned or long neglected and in terrible disrepair.

"Will you be okay finding your room?" Hannah asked. "I put you in the old Blue Rose room."

Miriam nodded. "I need to go find the Matthewses, first."

Aside from Cass, the Matthewses were the people who had loved Miriam the longest, and best, of anyone in her life. Mrs. Matthews was the cook at the inn, and Mr. Matthews handled general maintenance for all of Christmasland. Now in their sixties, they had been born in Advent and gotten jobs at Carrigan's as teenagers. They'd fallen in love and stayed, caring for Miri and Hannah alongside their son Levi and their younger twins, Esther and Joshua.

Miriam's parents hadn't been parents but jailers. Hannah's were documentary filmmakers who traveled the world, home-schooling her from far-flung locations until she convinced them, her sophomore year of high school, to let her live full-time at Carrigan's. The Matthewses always had room for all of them.

Miriam found Mr. Matthews sitting on a tall stool at the kitchen island, drinking a cup of tea and watching his wife roll out cookie dough. The blue delft tile was the same as it had been all her life, a crack in one corner of the island where she'd dropped a heavy pot when she was twelve. Behind Mrs. Matthews was the pantry door where she'd marked Miriam's height every holiday, and past that was the mudroom where Miriam and Hannah had taken off snow boots a thousand times.

When Mrs. Matthews looked up and saw Miriam, she dropped her rolling pin to the counter with a clatter, and Mr. Matthews turned around. In a moment, they had surrounded her in a hug.

She thought she would have to walk on tiptoes to avoid being decimated by memories of her father's abuse, with tiny trauma landmines scattered about, still active after so many years. There hadn't been any, yet, although she wasn't letting her guard down. What she hadn't expected was how much more deeply she could breathe here, seeing these beloved faces.

"Finally," Mrs. Matthews said, putting her hands on Miriam's

cheeks and looking into her eyes. "You owe us a sit-down."
Miriam nodded solemnly. She owed them more than that.

"Soon. I promise. I'm not going anywhere," she told them.

Part of her wished that were true, that she wasn't leaving in a week, that she had all the time in the world here.

Chapter 3

Noelle

Noelle Northwood woke up the morning of Cass's funeral to a pit of dread in her stomach and a crying hangover. It wasn't as bad as the drinking hangovers she used to get, but it wasn't great. She wasn't ready to go to a second funeral for a second mother. Burying one in a lifetime had been plenty.

From the time she'd lost her parents to the day she'd shown up on Cass's doorstep, she'd been adrift. Then Carrigan's had opened its doors and heart to her. Noelle felt she and the farm belonged to each other. The trees were her salvation, and Cass had given them to her.

She wasn't ready for this funeral, but she never would be, so she got dressed. She freshly buzzed her undercut and put on her carefully constructed Dealing with Funeral Visitors outfit, black slacks with a black button-down, the sleeves worn long to hide her tattoos, in deference to the Orthodox side of the Rosensteins. Her tie and suspenders were black matte with embossed black stripes. It was a look Cass would have approved of.

On her way out the door, she patted the head of the elephant statue that sat next to her fireplace. Like much of the art at Carrigan's, it was inexplicably decoupaged and covered in glitter, of unknown provenance, and decidedly odd. Noelle loved it very much.

In the kitchen she started laying out pastries and little quiches Mrs. Matthews must have spent all night baking. When Noelle found carafes of hot cocoa waiting on the kitchen island, she wondered how late Mr. Matthews had dragged his wife to bed. Today they would all three be walking the tightrope of having been family but not relations. Mrs. Matthews was handling it by making sure everyone was fed. Mr. Matthews was, Noelle suspected, handling it by fixing things that didn't need fixing, and trying to make his wife rest. She would have to check on them both. Along with Cass they were the chosen parents of her heart. She needed to make sure they weren't left adrift this week.

The door to the kitchen swung open. A tiny woman who looked exactly like a very young Cass walked in, barefoot, wearing a puke-green reindeer sweater and leggings with a T-shirt wrapped around her head like a pineapple.

The woman blinked at her. Noelle blinked back, her mind racing. Who was this elf?

She must be a Rosenstein cousin Noelle hadn't met yet. She was far too beautiful, far too early on this particular morning, for Noelle's comfort.

Noelle saw the woman do a surreptitious perusal of her body, her eyes lighting in interest. She felt a little fizzle in her stomach. She would have absolutely sworn five minutes ago that the morning of Cass's funeral was the last time and place on Earth she would ever feel a spark of interest in a woman, but that was before this elven person had walked into the kitchen.

"Is there coffee—" the elf asked, her voice still fuzzy with sleep.

At the same time, Noelle said, "I'm sorry, this is rude, but what on Earth are you wearing?"

The elf huffed out a little sound that could have been a laugh. "I'd just come back from a trip when I got the call about Cass, I left my house in a hurry. None of my clothes are even clean, much less suitable for sitting shiva," she explained. "I took the sweater from my best friend. It used to light up, so I guess small blessings?"

"Very small. Hot cocoa?" Noelle offered, as the woman settled warily on a stool, looking behind her like she was bracing for something unpleasant.

The elf raised her eyebrows and scowled. "Is there... espresso... in the hot cocoa? Because otherwise, definitely no." With her face scrunched up, she looked like a grumpy cat meme. Noelle found it oddly charming.

"There isn't currently, but I think I can make it happen." Noelle flipped a kitchen towel over her shoulder. Espresso, she could do. Espresso was mindless, and let her turn her back on the strange, interesting woman interrupting her grief.

"You're my new favorite person," the elf said happily, before laying her head on top of her folded arms. God, she was cute. Noelle told her brain to pipe down. This was a Rosenstein, here to mourn. She didn't even know the woman's name. She should be hospitable, and not a creeper, even if the elf had looked at her with stark interest.

"Bagel? Muffin? Croissant? I have about fifteen freshly baked carbohydrates available for consumption." She pointed to a serving platter covered in choices. "Or, if I know Mrs. Matthews, there will be challah French toast in the dining room soon."

"Are they from Rosenstein's?" the woman asked, perking up. Cass's family had made their money and reputation in a bakery that was now famous for traditional Jewish baked goods. Noelle had learned fast that all the extended family tree was fiercely loyal about their pastries.

She pretended affront. "Would they be anything else?"

"I will have a muffin now and also some French toast later," the woman announced, as if she were deciding something of grave import. Noelle handed her the cup of hot cocoa containing two perfectly pulled shots of espresso, and an orange cranberry muffin.

The elf sighed happily. Noelle's stomach flipped.

Then Hannah walked in.

"Oh! I'm so glad you're both here. My first best friend and my forever best friend." Hannah draped an arm over the elf's shoulder. "Noelle, this is my cousin Miriam. Miri, this is Noelle, the farm's manager, my number one best ever person."

The flip in Noelle's stomach turned to a dive.

The elf was Miriam Blum. Miriam—the woman who

had abandoned Carrigan's and broken Cass's and Hannah's hearts—was in their kitchen, looking beautiful and vulnerable and devastated, making Noelle want to wrap her up in a blanket. She'd thought this day couldn't suck more.

"I have to go deal with the cousins, Miri," Hannah said, already walking back out the door, "but please don't feel you need to talk to them before coffee. I'll leave you in Noelle's very capable hands."

Noelle could read Hannah's face, and it said, "Please take care of her right now, I have too much else to deal with."

Hannah was an Organizer. She'd been running the Christmasland Inn for years, taking care of Cass as her health declined, and organizing all the Christmas Festival events. She was an unstoppable force with a clipboard and color-coded spreadsheets. If Hannah was delegating, it was because she was desperate for an assist.

For Hannah, the best friend she'd ever had, Noelle would continue to be pleasant to this woman. But Noelle had seen how the residents of Carrigan's pined quietly but inexorably after Miriam, continuing to speak of her glowingly all these years after Miriam abandoned them, and she wasn't interested in getting close to her. She had enough heartbreak for a lifetime, without chasing more.

"What are you doing awake?" she asked, her voice colder than it had been. She couldn't believe she'd been flirting with Miriam Blum. "Didn't you come in late last night?"

Miriam took a long drink before she said anything, not seeming to react to Noelle's change in tone. Noelle waited, resting an elbow on the counter, popping a mini quiche into her mouth.

"I heard my mom is here," Miriam finally managed.

This did not answer the question of why Miriam was awake, but it did bring up several more questions.

"You knew she was coming, right?" Noelle didn't know all, or even most, of the story of Miriam's mysterious long absence, but she knew something had happened with her father. Ziva, Miriam's mother, was Hannah's dad's sister. She sometimes came to family events, though rarely with her husband, whom Cass and the extended Rosensteins all hated.

"One is never prepared for Ziva," Miriam said, draining half of her gross chocolate coffee in one gulp. When she pulled the T-shirt off her head, a cascade of curls fell out. They were mesmerizing.

Noelle tried to avoid thinking about how soft Miriam's hair would be to touch. "Your dad isn't here. Your mom said he's not coming," she said, taking a guess at what Miriam was so wound up about.

Miriam's entire body deflated into the stool. So Noelle had been right. What the hell had her father done to make her hold herself like prey hoping to go unnoticed by a predator at the hint of him?

Never mind. This woman was not her problem.

As if she'd been summoned, Ziva's voice filtered into the kitchen. Miriam sighed, pushing off the stool, her shoulders slumped. Noelle followed her out to the dining room, curious against her better judgment.

Ziva Rosenstein-Blum swept into the nearly empty dining room in her athleisure clothes. Her hair was up in a high ponytail, perfectly straightened. Her yoga pants were designer. Her eyebrows were newly microbladed.

"Miriam," Ziva said without preamble, "I stopped to get you a dress for the funeral, so you don't have to rip up one of Hannah's."

Noelle noticed that Ziva and Miriam did not touch, and that neither mentioned Mr. Blum. She'd met him a couple of times, but he never deigned to notice her. He mocked Cass's tendency to collect lost souls (never in front of Noelle, whom he considered The Help, but to Hannah, who told Noelle everything), calling Carrigan's the Island of Misfit Toys. He spent all of his short visits looking itchy, as if the entire Adirondacks were an ill-tailored suit.

Mr. and Mrs. Matthews appeared from their apartments off the kitchen to embrace Ziva stiffly. Complicated though their relationship seemed to be with the Blums, it stretched back before Noelle had been born, a hundred thousand memories tying them together.

But she wouldn't let Ziva, or Miriam, who had been gone for a decade, make her feel like an interloper. Everyone else might be happy to welcome the prodigal daughter back into the fold, but she had no happy memories of Miriam and no reason to make space for her. This place was hers. Ziva and Miriam would leave after the seven days of shiva while Noelle and Hannah would stay and try to get through their first Christmas without Cass, and everything would be...well, not normal, not ever again. But at least there wouldn't be beautiful careless women in ugly sweaters asking her for cups of coffee.

Throughout the day, Rosensteins from around the country trickled in, along with families who had spent Christmas at Carrigan's for years, sometimes generations. Cass Carrigan had been an eccentric aunt to uncounted lost souls in need of no-nonsense love.

She was buried in the closest Jewish cemetery in the middle of the drizzly afternoon. The crowd of mourners shuttled out in the big Carrigan's van, and back again, clothes torn in grief.

In the great room, Miriam sat stiffly as if she might shatter. Miriam's friend Cole lounged on a settee, though Noelle still wasn't clear on why he was there. She'd asked him if he had a job to get back to and he'd changed the subject. Hannah was leaning against the fireplace, and Noelle fretted that her friend's legs were close to giving out. Noelle rose, wrapping an arm around Hannah's shoulders to lead her into a corner.

"What's wrong?" she asked. "What can I do?"

Hannah shook her head. "You can't help. I was just wishing Levi Blue were here."

"That's the worst thing you, or anyone, has ever said to me," Noelle replied.

Hannah laid her head on Noelle's shoulder, and Noelle patted her hair like a child. Levi, the Matthewses' eldest son and Hannah's evil ex, was Noelle's least favorite human being on Earth. He should be here, he'd grown up here, but Noelle was grateful he wasn't. She could protect Hannah from a lot of things, but if Levi were here, he would break her heart again, and Noelle would be powerless to stop it.

"Breathe," Noelle whispered. "What would Cass tell you?"

"Cass would tell me there were too many fucking people in

her house, and to stop letting them eat all her deviled eggs," Hannah whispered back.

"Well I can't fix Cass being gone or heal the damage that is Levi, but I can fix one problem. Let's go get some deviled eggs," Noelle said, grateful to have a plan of action instead of floundering around feeling useless and sad, "and then, fortified, we will rejoin the madding crowd."

"An egg-quisition plan!" Hannah announced, her voice brave if wobbly.

Noelle walked behind Hannah, shielding her from being intercepted by relatives. She would get Hannah fed and keep her from collapsing. That was a thing she could do.

Guests from years past who hadn't made it to the funeral wandered in over the next few days. Each carried food and memories. They told story after story, giving Noelle back pieces of her heart. The cousin Cass had taken on joyrides on long summer nights, the friend's business she'd quietly financed, the one-woman show she'd run for a week in Paris before she got bored. Nine decades of eccentric, joyful, idiosyncratic life.

Noelle had needed this. When her parents died, she'd been alone, and all she'd been able to do was get up in the morning, stay sober, and go back to bed. This process was good. She watched Miriam and Hannah say Kaddish, a minyan around them, and felt for the first time a tiny hope that someday, maybe, she wouldn't be drowning in this grief.

But she kept her own stories of Cass hoarded like pearls. In some ways, she'd been just another of Cass's collected souls; in others, she'd known a Cass no one else saw. The grouchy, misanthropic introvert as well as the cutting wit and

the larger-than-life performer. The Cass who snuck downstairs in a silk caftan in the middle of the night to steal snacks
from Mrs. Matthews's refrigerator while smoking a forbidden
cigarette out the back door of the kitchen. The Cass who
refused to talk about money for farm expenses because it was
"simply too boring, and anyway, that's why I pay you!" The
Cass who hid out for months in the off-season, refusing to
speak even to her or the Matthewses because she needed to
"rejuvenate."

That Cass was hers. She'd been a real pain in the ass, and
Noelle treasured that secret truth.

Shiva marched on. They ate casseroles, cried, and gave themselves space. Hannah kept the guests busy with the help of
Cole, whose presence was still a mystery, but who proved
surprisingly useful. Miriam spent time with the Matthewses.
Noelle walked past her telling an animated story that involved
an island off the Washington coast, a sledgehammer, and a
bottle of epoxy. Mr. Matthews had his head thrown back in
laughter, and Noelle grimaced. What the hell did Miriam *do*
that was more important than being here? Miriam caught her
eye and smiled, a flush on her cheeks, and Noelle turned
away. She spent a lot of time with her trees after that.

When the week ended, Cole went back to Charleston, the
family all left, and only the Carrigan's crew stayed—except
for Miriam, who was scheduled to fly out of the city the
next day.

But before she could leave for the airport, Cass's lawyer

arrived. Mr. Elijah Green, Esquire, was a tall, thin Black man with a short afro and frameless glasses. He was one of Noelle's favorite people in all of upstate New York, or maybe the world. He was dryly hilarious, endlessly welcoming, and the driving force behind whatever queer community she'd managed to find in these mountains. She pounced on him, and he squeezed her tightly.

"How is Jason? How are the twins? Is your mom feeling better?" Noelle was ecstatic to see her friend—and also talk to someone she hadn't spent the week with.

"Jason is currently negotiating a truce between the twins because one wants to have a twin Halloween costume, and the other does not. My mom's hip is healing really well, probably because my sister is on her every day to do her exercises."

"She's killing me at Words with Friends, with all her spare time," Noelle said, and Elijah laughed before adjusting the sleeves of his argyle sweater carefully. All his movements were precise and measured. Noelle knew him as her rad gay friend who always had a gathering going, the guy who made pub quiz and karaoke and book club happen, but she'd never seen him lawyer before. He cleared his throat.

"I'm so sorry to have missed the funeral—" he began.

"If you had missed your grandmother's ninetieth birthday for her funeral," Hannah said, "Cass would never have forgiven you."

He nodded. "I realize this is absolutely not an ideal, or even reasonable, time to talk about Cass's will, but I needed you three in the same room. I wasn't sure if Miriam was staying past the seven days, or I would have waited. My mom sent a casserole," he added, as if by way of apology. "I put it in the fridge."

All of this seemed ominous. Why did they need to talk about the will? For years, Cass had said she was leaving Carrigan's Christmasland to Noelle and Hannah, to continue to run it as they'd been doing. Maybe Cass had left Miriam something as well, some small remembrance?

Hannah ushered them from the great room into the library and waited for everyone to settle.

"We need to discuss the property and business of Carrigan's Christmasland. Up until last year, her will had, for some time, reflected that she wished to leave the business and land in equal parts to her niece Hannah Rosenstein and her general manager, Noelle Northwood."

The hackles on the back of Noelle's neck rose. All her muscles tensed.

"However, recently Cass amended her will to split the aforementioned assets in four equal parts, leaving the third and fourth portions to her niece Miriam Blum and Levi Matthews. It's my understanding from my last conversation with her that she had not made any of you aware of these changes. Is that true?"

"I'm sorry," Miriam squeaked, "she did what?!"

Noelle was half out of her chair, her face slack. She looked to Hannah for some idea how to respond. Hannah's entire body seemed to have frozen into a cartoon version of shock, eyes as wide as plates, hands half raised to her mouth. Noelle scrubbed her face, pulled the ends of her hair straight up, sat down and crossed and uncrossed her arms, stood back up, and leaned against the back of the chair. None of it helped.

They all stared at each other.

"Okay, this is easy, right?" Noelle asked, breathing in and out slowly, trying to stay calm. "Miriam can sell us her portion, and we'll go on with our lives. Levi doesn't care what we do."

Hannah made a little sound in her throat, and Noelle winced. She never knew when the sound of Levi's name was going to gut Hannah.

"Miriam, you don't want to be part of running Carrigan's, right?" Noelle asked before getting up to pace.

She could fix this. She and Hannah wanted to spend their lives running this place. They'd planned it, talked about it, dreamt of it. They were good at it. Great, in fact. They could just go on running it, even if Cass had had some last-minute terrible idea.

"What on Earth was she thinking?" Noelle asked the room.

"I know what she was thinking, as I was present when she amended the will," Elijah answered, though the question had been rhetorical.

"Although Cass was a decent, if idiosyncratic, businesswoman, traffic had dropped off sharply in the past few years," Elijah explained. "More people are buying artificial trees, fewer are heading out into the country to have a Christmas experience. The recession happened and Cass dragged her feet on creating an internet presence for the farm. Carrigan's used to subsist on Christmas tree income and returning annual holiday guests, but that's not viable anymore. She was forced to take out a second mortgage, and she'd fallen quite far behind. The members of the bank board knew Cass for decades, but with her gone, they're no longer able to honor the, uh, somewhat unorthodox verbal repayment agreement she had with them. Because Carrigan's is an important local institution, they're willing to work with you on repayment *if* you can present them with a viable plan, but there's no way around it: the farm is in real financial trouble. Cass believed the four of you, as a team, could right the ship."

In her shock, Noelle dropped onto the couch with a thump, startling Kringle. *Cass believed what?*

"She loved the ship metaphor," Elijah continued. "She said she had a dream that Carrigan's was a ship. Miriam was the sails, the creative wind. Noelle was the anchor that kept everyone from blowing off in wild directions. Hannah was the captain, Levi was the map to unknown lands, and she, Cass, was your North Star."

Everyone was quiet a moment.

"She changed our entire lives based on a dream about a ship?" Hannah asked, sounding stunned.

"This is Cass we're talking about," Noelle murmured, and Hannah nodded slightly. It was a very Cass move.

"How am I supposed to help make any of that a reality?" Miriam asked, incredulously. "I don't have any real money anymore, not the kind you're talking about. I spent any savings I had renovating my store, and that's sunk cost even if I wanted to get it back. But I don't. I'm about to open my dream shop, I have a fiancée and a *life* in Charleston. Besides, I don't know shit about trees. Or hotels."

Noelle's brain stuck on the word fiancée. It was bad enough that she'd flirted with Miriam Blum, but an engaged Miriam Blum? This week kept getting, impossibly, worse.

"She didn't want your money, Miriam." Elijah pushed up his sleeves, smiling. "She wanted your brilliance."

"What could I possibly contribute to Carrigan's?" Miriam snorted. "Ruined antiques?"

"I'm trying to think like Cass," Hannah said slowly. "What would Miriam bring to Carrigan's, if this were her home base? There's room for a studio and a shop in the carriage house, maybe. She could bring traffic in during the summer months..." She trailed off at Noelle's glare and shrugged. "If this is what Cass wanted, shouldn't we at least have a conversation about it?"

Noelle didn't want to have a conversation about it. Miriam had been handed this magical place on a platter, and she'd thrown it away. She'd left Cass for ten years and never came back, even when Cass was dying. She had no place in Carrigan's present or future.

"Elijah," Noelle asked, "leaving the rather serious question of Levi aside for a moment, walk me through what it would look like if we bought out Miriam." She tapped her short, buffed fingernails against the wooden back of the couch, the sensation helping her think.

"Well, the first question is, do you have the money to do that?" he answered.

Hannah shook her head. "I certainly don't. My parents had Rosenstein money, but making documentaries is expensive. And I've been here since college, getting paid, well, the family rate."

She pulled her cardigan closer around her, and Noelle shook off her own panic enough to realize that her best friend was terrified, with much more right to be. To Noelle, Levi was an annoyance, and Miriam a problem to solve. To Hannah, they were the other two legs of her stool, and they'd left her here alone to wobble desperately before she'd miraculously found her own balance. Now, she had to rely on the same people who'd proven themselves unreliable to do right by the only home she'd ever had.

"Wait," Miriam interrupted. "I should sell it to you both. And I probably will, cheap, so it's not a hardship on you and I can go back to my life. But Cass must have left it to me for a reason. I'd like to think about that before I make any final decisions."

She looked around but Noelle refused to meet her eye. "I just found out this was happening, and I can't even process it. I need some time, Noelle. Hannah. I'm sorry. Can you give me a little while?"

"How much time?" Noelle growled. Some better angel deep in her consciousness told her she was being unreasonable and unfair to Miriam, who had been taken by surprise as much as anyone. She told her better angel to shut it.

Hannah reached across their chairs and squeezed Miriam's hand. "You don't have to know right now, babe," she sniffled.

Noelle lost the battle with her temper and slammed out the door.

She loved Cass, but how could she do this to them? How could she have hidden that the business was on the brink of bankruptcy? Noelle knew traffic had slowed down, but why hadn't Cass trusted them with the full picture?

Noelle didn't care if she inherited a half or quarter share, but she did care that her home now belonged in part to Miriam the Absent and that little fuckhead Levi. All that had been getting Noelle through losing Cass was the belief that she and Hannah would be carrying on Cass's work into a new generation, and now that was gone. The woman she'd thought had loved and trusted her had pulled the rug out from under her.

She stomped through the trees to her work shed, which by God was still hers—Levi and Miriam be damned.

Chapter 4

Miriam

Miriam caught up to Noelle in the work shed, a massive building that housed fertilizer, saplings, and the huge variety of implements it took to successfully raise award-winning evergreens. It smelled like growing things and winter, crisp and pungent.

"Can you leave me alone for five minutes until I don't want to murder anyone?" Noelle asked through her teeth. "Please? Can this not be about you for five minutes?"

"Why are you so angry at me?" Miriam tried to put her hand on Noelle's sleeve.

"To clarify," Noelle snapped, jerking away, "I'm angry at Cass and livid at Levi. You barely matter enough to warrant being mad at, and I'd love to keep it that way. In fact, I've done everything I can to *not* get to know you this week, and if you leave now, I won't have wasted that hard work."

Miriam didn't realize Noelle had been deliberately avoiding

her, and she didn't understand how Noelle could already dislike her so much. Their only conversation was when Miriam had walked into the kitchen and been knocked back on her heels by the sight of a blistering hot fat butch in suspenders—all broad shoulders and hips a wide revelation. She'd asked for coffee because her brain was too scrambled to think of what else to say. It shouldn't even bother her that Noelle didn't like her, but it did.

All week, she'd been observing Noelle, because shiva was long and slow when it wasn't hurting like hell. Her extended family was pleasant but distant, and Hannah was always running. Cole and the Matthewses were the only people who really talked to her. Drifting off, out of her body, and watching Noelle was easy, admiring the way she rolled her flannel over her strong forearms or flexed her thick thighs inside her worn-out jeans. It was simpler than facing the battering ram of grief trying to break down Miriam's walls. And she was curious about this magnetic woman who had become so much a part of Carrigan's while she was gone.

She'd seen Noelle's easy way of being in her body, her humor, the warmth and care she showed everyone, but she hadn't noticed Noelle's distaste. Miriam sort of wished she had. Maybe it would have shut down her sudden, intense response to the woman. Lusting after a stranger while she sat shiva was unnerving and totally inappropriate. Especially since she was engaged to someone else.

Maybe Miriam's emotions were coming back online after a decade of disuse, rusty and miswired. She couldn't remember the last time she'd cried before this week. Maybe her grief was simply coming out sideways. But she didn't think her interest had been obvious or the reason for Noelle's animosity.

"Okay, I don't know what you're mad at Levi for, but I've met Levi, so I'm sure you're probably justified." She shoved her hands in her back pockets. "And I don't know what you have against me, since as you said, we don't know each other. I didn't know anything about this. This is exactly something Cass would do, though. This is like, peak Cass Carrigan."

"You don't know what I have against you?" Noelle scoffed. "You left Cass here to die without you, and Hannah to deal with it. You never came back, the whole time she was sick. What am I supposed to think of you? And now you're telling me exactly what Cass would do?"

Noelle's accusations were like a punch. Miriam's body folded in on itself. All that worrying about land mines from her childhood, and words from a stranger were what hurt her.

Noelle was right, she'd never come home. She'd thought she was protecting herself, but she'd been hurting everyone she loved. And now she couldn't look herself in the mirror, and she didn't know how to make it up to any of them, let alone Cass.

From somewhere outside herself, she watched herself heave a sob.

"I didn't know," she choked out. "I didn't know Cass was sick. No one told me."

"If that's true, whose fault is it?" Noelle asked, her arms crossed over her chest. "No one can rely on you. You are the last person anyone would call in an emergency. And if we're about to lose the Christmasland, we sure as hell have an emergency on our hands."

"You can hate me, but you have no right to judge my ability

to be a part of Carrigan's. I do have a lifetime of memories here." Tears still ran down her face, but she mirrored Noelle's stance, her arms crossed and her feet rooted. "I know what goes into creating a Carrigan's Christmas season." Noelle's anger had called up her own, and for once, instead of fleeing or folding, she wanted to fight.

"I have every right!" Noelle snapped. "It is my business, Miriam, it's literally my actual business. You know nothing about Carrigan's Christmasland. You were a child when you were here for the season, with no awareness of how much labor goes into making Carrigan's run smoothly." Noelle was pointing at her, and it made Miriam want to bite her finger. "You're in no way equipped to take any of this on. Based on what I know of you, you are the opposite of equipped for real life."

"What possible evidence do you have of that?" Miriam demanded, screwing her hands to her hips. When people bigger than her yelled, usually Miriam shrunk, but not now. She stared Noelle right back down.

"You're all over the country, making some bullshit fake art for Instagram and avoiding the people who love you. Where were you when Hannah broke apart?"

When Hannah broke apart over what? Miriam wondered but didn't ask.

"You are totally unavailable to do any heavy lifting in your relationships. That's fine! That's a choice you've made! But we have people whose lives and meals depend on Carrigan's running smoothly. You've never paid anyone's paycheck. I don't even know how you pay your own! We need dependable, and you've already proven no one should trust you."

She looked at Miriam, and Miriam found that she couldn't

break away from the absolute certainty on Noelle's face. That certainty was really pissing her off, and it felt great. She'd been sad, scared, and shut down for so many years, but now she was only afraid that her anger was going to light her hair on fire—even if some dark part of her worried that Noelle's words were true. She needed to prove to herself that Cass was right to trust her. And she wanted to prove it to Noelle, so she could shove it down Noelle's throat.

"And you're some dependable angel, here to save the poor denizens of Carrigan's Christmasland from the evil Miriam Blum?" She was shaking, she was so angry.

Noelle's feet widened a little farther, and her shoulders went back. "When someone I know is in trouble, I'm the person they call. When someone needs money, or a ride, or their car jumped, or tile grouted, I'm the person they call. I have intentionally built my life so I am that person. I am *steadfast*. You're frivolous."

Miriam knew then how she could prove herself and make her absence up to Cass and everyone else. She couldn't believe what she was about to say, but it felt completely right.

"Well," Miriam snapped back, her hands balling into fists at her hips, "this frivolous knockabout is about to save your damn farm. Do you, or do you not, need help getting through the Black Friday rush?"

"What does that have to do with anything?" Noelle threw up her arms.

"I'm going to be your seasonal help. I'm going to stay here, and work the Carrigan's Festival, which, you're right, I've never done. For free, because Carrigan's can't afford to pay me. I will get us through Black Friday weekend, and by the time I leave, I'll have a plan to take to the bank. Literally. Then you can eat your words."

Holy shit, what had she just committed herself to?

Staying here through Thanksgiving was absurd. She had no idea what would convince the bank that they were a good business risk. But she knew she had to do this.

"Why the hell would you do that?" Noelle demanded.

Miriam rose up to her face, or as close as she could considering their height difference. "If you're right and I let Cass down, what better way could I make that up to her but to fulfill her dying wish? Should I just blow that off, too? What would that say about me?"

"You'd better clear this with Hannah," Noelle growled, stepping back. "And call your fiancée."

Fuck, Noelle was right. She was going to have to call Tara. Which was going to suck.

"Thank you for your input. And, just FYI, Cass knew exactly why I wasn't coming home, and she understood." Miriam headed toward the door.

"Did Hannah?" Noelle called after her.

Miriam flinched, but she didn't answer. Instead she extended her middle finger up above her head as she pushed outside.

She stomped back to the inn, letting her adrenaline drain as she went. Inside, she found Hannah sitting stiffly on an antique chaise that would look better as a moose statue. *Maybe Hannah would give this to me to rehab*, Miriam thought idly. This was the first time she'd seen Hannah truly still all week.

She sat down next to her cousin and twisted her hands in her lap. "I'd like to stay until Thanksgiving, if you'll have me. If there's any possible way I can help with creating a plan to present the bank, I owe it to all of you to try. And I would love more time with you and the Matthewses."

Hannah cocked her head, started to speak a couple of times, and stopped herself. Eventually she said, "I don't know if I want you to stay long term, yet. I missed you so much, but it hurts to have you back. Still I can't ask you to leave, not without trying to see if Cass was right." She blew out a breath. "Maybe none of this matters. I'm going to call the cousins and see if they can help with the bank mortgage."

"The Rosensteins? Why would they bail us out?" Miriam had never gotten any support from them, even when she'd badly needed it. They'd never even bothered to check on her when things were at their worst with her parents.

"Do we have other mutual cousins I don't know about, who also own a large national business and might want to invest?" Hannah asked, lifting an eyebrow. "They would bail us out because we're family and they love us."

Miriam was skeptical of this, but Hannah's parents were closer to the larger family. It was worth a shot.

Hannah paced the room while making the call. While Miriam waited, she checked the massive backlog of Bloomer messages from having her phone off for a week. She deleted dick pics and antisemitic tirades with resignation.

Ah, the internet. How she'd missed it.

Hannah's shoulders drooped further and further as she listened. *I was right*, Miriam thought.

Hannah sank back down.

"They want to help. But they just sunk a bunch of money into the West Coast expansion," she said, her eyes off in the distance, "so they don't have the funds for a big cash infusion."

"I'm sorry. I know you were hoping," Miriam said, trying not to add, *I told you so.*

"They didn't completely say no. They would be willing, and happy, to invest a smaller amount in whatever plan we present to the bank, if we can show them it's viable." Hannah twisted and untwisted her hair on top of her head anxiously, and Miriam wished she knew if her support would be welcome.

"So if we can get them on board, the bank will look much more favorably on our business plan," Miriam said.

Hannah nodded.

"Now we really have to come up with a plan." That was terrifying, but also a tiny bit...exciting?

"I guess you're staying until Thanksgiving." Hannah laid her head back, staring at the ceiling for a moment before looking over at Miriam. "As for you moving here to fulfill some sort of prophecy of Cass's...let's make sure there's somewhere to move to, first."

"Speaking of Cass's prophecy, where's Blue?" Miriam asked.

Miriam had done a better job keeping up with Levi Matthews than she had with anyone else from Carrigan's. The three of them had grown up running together, an inseparable trio. Hannah and Miriam had started calling him Blue when they were little, since he shared a name with the world's most famous blue jeans, and it had stuck. He was irascible, difficult, mischievous, and obsessed with cooking from the time he could walk. He'd gone to Le Cordon Bleu and had grand plans to transform the inn into a culinary destination. He was, in many ways, a hometown legend around Advent.

Then he'd run off on a cruise ship to be a chef.

The beautiful, angry boy who left.

"I mean I know where he's been, we talk," Miriam clarified, "but... why wasn't he home for the funeral?"

Hannah stiffened beside her. "I told him never to come home," she said quietly.

Miriam reeled back. *What?* She'd clearly missed something crucial. When she'd left, Levi and Hannah were best friends, pieces of a whole who fought as much as they talked but who always circled back to each other. She knew, from her calls with Levi, that something had caused an estrangement, but she couldn't imagine Hannah ever telling Levi to leave Carrigan's and not come home. How had his parents felt?!

"We were engaged," Hannah continued, picking at an invisible thread on her blouse, "more in love than I thought was humanly possible. When we broke up, it didn't go well. It's my fault he's not here."

What the hell?

Miriam's entire world had just blown open. Her eternal compasses had not only fallen in love, but also had a catastrophic breakup, and no one had told her. They'd planned to get married, and no one had asked her to be in the wedding. She talked to Levi at least once a month. He told her about life on a ship, seeing the world.

He had *not* told her he was in love with her cousin. *What the hell?*

"How?" was all she could say.

"The first year you didn't come for Christmas, it was just the two of us, and we ended up under the mistletoe." Hannah shrugged, as if she were merely reciting facts, but a tear leaked down her cheek. "That was it."

Miriam frantically did the math. She left ten years ago, and Levi four years ago. So they'd dated for six entire years, and no one ever mentioned it? How was that possible?

"We were soulmates, I thought," Hannah continued. "And then he decided he needed to leave, and I couldn't. I couldn't let things fall apart, I couldn't risk being gone if Cass got sicker. So, he left without me." She chewed on her lip, not meeting Miriam's eyes.

"I told him, if he left, he should never come back. I didn't mean *never*. His parents live here. This is his home. But apparently he took me seriously, because it's been four years. And he didn't come home for Cass." Hannah shook her head, her tears falling faster.

"I'm going to kill him," Miriam muttered. "This is *not* the version he told me about why you weren't speaking."

Hannah brushed tears off her chin and smiled. "I'm sure the version he told you makes him look better."

It hadn't, particularly. Blue was nothing if not self-deprecating. But it had been remarkably short on details. They were, if she remembered correctly, "temporarily at odds about his life choices."

"Why didn't anyone tell me?" Miriam buried her face in her hands, suddenly overwhelmed by how much her family had fundamentally changed while she'd been pretending they were all in stasis without her.

"At first, none of us knew if you wanted to hear from us,"

Hannah explained, "and then it was weird because it had been going on so long…and then he was gone, I guess. I assumed he'd told you."

"I didn't mean to break your trust so badly that you would keep this a secret from me," Miriam said, the weight on her heart feeling like it might crush her. "I wish you could have trusted me to talk to me about it. Or Cass's illness."

"I wish you'd trusted me with whatever happened with your dad," Hannah said, somewhere between resigned and bitter. She was squeezing her hands together, her knuckles turning white.

The words stung, and some of her hurt turned to anger. "That's shitty, Nan. I was doing the best I could. I didn't mean to hurt you." She dashed tears from her eyes. Had she, though, done the best she could? She and Hannah and Levi had been each other's closest friends for so long, and she'd shut Hannah out a long time before Hannah returned the favor.

"I was doing the best I could, too, Miri, and I was drowning," Hannah said, throwing up her hands. "I fucked up. My feelings were hurt, and I fucked up. I didn't mean to keep you from Cass. She made me promise not to tell you how sick she was. I should have done it, anyway."

She'd told herself for years that her secrets only affected her, but it had been a convenient lie.

"I want to tell you, about my dad. Someday," Miriam said. "I just can't, yet." She needed to gather the courage to make that leap.

"Well, I can't handle one more big emotional reveal today, so let's table that and circle back to it. I love you, I'm glad you're here, and I would like for you to help Noelle and I figure out how the fuck to dig ourselves out of this mess that Cass made." Hannah smiled weakly. "Come on. We're going to nap, and hydrate, and then we'll come up with a plan."

Miriam nodded and wondered if Hannah could come up with a plan that involved her never having to talk to Noelle again.

⁂

"Miri, is everything okay? Did your flight change?" Tara asked when she picked up the phone.

"Hey, so—" Miriam started.

"I need you to change at the airport—"

"Tara—" Miriam tried again, but Tara kept talking.

"I'm sending a car to take you to this restaurant, we've been asked to have dinner—"

"Tara," Miriam interrupted more forcefully, "I'm not flying in tomorrow. I had to change my plans."

"You had to?" Tara asked, suspiciously. "You promised that you'd be home the second shiva was over. That you couldn't stand to spend more than a week with your mother."

"Oh, my mom won't be here. She never stays when there's hard work to do. And I know I promised, I'm sorry. Something's come up and I . . ."

Shit, how could she explain so Tara wouldn't argue? If Miriam told her the whole story, Tara would come up with a hundred solutions, want to look at the will, and give a grand jury–worthy argument as to why Miriam should come home.

So she simply chose not to explain. It wasn't her finest moment, but she told herself there would be time, later.

"I need to stay through Thanksgiving. After that, we should have everything wrapped up."

"Thanksgiving?!" She could hear Tara's panic starting to rise, her voice squeaking, then her deep breaths. "Okay. You've spent countless hours dealing with my terrible family, I can spare you for a while for you to deal with yours." Miriam noticed that Tara didn't offer, again, to help her deal with her family, but she was glad. She wasn't ready to share this.

"Do you need anything? Can I send you some clothes? What are you doing about commissions?"

Tara pivoting to action was so comforting. They didn't have to talk about their feelings. "You can send some clothes, that would help. I'm not in the middle of any commissions, because of the store opening."

"What are you going to do about the store, Miri?" Tara sounded exasperated. She had a right to, since it was her money paying the lease on Miriam's dream project, now on hold.

"Just hope I can get everything together in time, I guess," Miriam said, chewing on the side of her thumb.

"Well," Tara drawled, "don't be a stranger."

And she hung up.

Miriam stared at her phone. She would have to call Cole, too, before he talked to Tara and got cranky that Miriam hadn't told him first. He would probably be thrilled and try to move in to Carrigan's full time. And she had to call the Old Ladies, to tell them she would be postponing her check-in visits.

An alarm rang on her phone, reminding her to post to social media. Being a full-time self-sustaining artist didn't allow for weeks off to figure out her life. She had a brand to maintain.

That, she could do. She couldn't yell at Cass for not telling Miriam she was sick, she couldn't fix the years she'd missed with Hannah, and she couldn't convince Noelle to stop hating her, but she could make content for her fans. She knew how to turn her real self off and put her Bloomer Face on.

Pointing her phone camera at herself, she started a new video.

"Hi Bloomers! Welcome to my family farm, Carrigan's Christmasland!" Her voice sounded hollow to her ears. "You all are always asking for more insights into my life, and I can't wait to show you one of my favorite places..."

She smiled at the camera, back on steady ground. With internet strangers who never asked her hard questions or accused her of failing her family.

Miriam and Noelle spent the next very unpleasant week trying everything in their power to not speak to each other. While Noelle transformed the front lawn into a winter wonderland and Hannah trained seasonal workers, Miriam was put in charge of the in-house decorations. This was work Miriam excelled at. She knew what Carrigan's was supposed to look like at Christmas. When they were done, the half-abandoned ghost of a hotel was once again the Christmasland Inn of her memories.

It was magnificent.

As visitors drove through the gates, animatronic cherubs with horns blasted "Carol of the Bells." A cacophony of trees, decorated in every theme imaginable, stretched out on either side of the lane, taking up the whole lawn. There were trees with giant bows, trees with popcorn and cranberry garlands, trees dripping with cut glass icicles. Among them were statuary—elves, reindeer, snowmen.

Inside, evergreens hung off every surface, punctuated with holly berries, clusters of white LED candles, and smaller statues in gold and silver. There were more Christmas trees in every size, grouped improbably into corners, under stairwells, on verandas. Wreaths hung from the staircase, mistletoe in every door frame.

The mantel in the great room was now home to a collection of antique nutcrackers. As a child, Miriam had named them all Steve. Big Steve, Little Steve, One-Armed Steve, Ballet Steve. Even the TV was draped in tinsel.

On day three of their week of preparations, Miriam was carrying an armful of vintage white plastic reindeer past the kitchen, thinking about ways to advertise "cut your own tree" packages to day tourists, when Mrs. Matthews stuck her head out the door.

"I have cookies."

"Tell me about Joshua and Esther!" Miriam said, as she settled onto a chair. She avoided asking for updates on Blue.

Mr. Matthews swelled with pride from his perch on his favorite stool. "Well, you know, Joshua is with the philharmonic now." He was a cellist. "And his son, Grant, is in the first grade."

Miriam's heart ached, for the loss of this easy camaraderie with the people who'd raised her, for never having met Mrs. Matthews's grandson, for everything she'd missed while she had her head stuck up her own ass.

"And Esther is in charge of her own lab," Mrs. Matthews chimed in.

"Gosh, all your children are such geniuses," Miriam said, "and I just destroy antiques for a living."

"Nonsense," Mr. Matthews grumbled, crossing his arms. "You have the Bloomers."

Miriam's jaw dropped. "You know about the Bloomers?"

Mrs. Matthews smiled mischievously. "That little dustup last week in the comments of your Green Goddess fountain was really something, wasn't it?"

They talked about the wild things the Bloomers did and said, and Miriam couldn't get over that these warm, loving, wonderful people with three accomplished grown children took time out of their lives to follow her Instagram drama.

Being back at Carrigan's in its holiday glory was both easier and much harder than she'd feared. She'd expected this trip to be awful because of the memories of her dad it would bring up, but his presence was nowhere in sight. Every day that passed without his poltergeist jumping out at her from corners, she had to ask herself why she'd been gone so long.

She thought she couldn't stand to be here, and she'd been wrong, and she'd missed everything. She'd missed that her two oldest friends were in love.

She'd missed that Cass was dying.

The more being at Carrigan's didn't suddenly spring flash-backs on her, the more she started to let down her guard and enjoy being back. Everywhere she turned, though, Noelle was there, an impossible-to-ignore presence, a discordant note in her reclamation symphony. They hadn't spoken since their fight in the work shed, moving silently around each other as much as was possible. Miriam was still determined to show Noelle she'd been misjudged, but she didn't know how to do that if they weren't speaking. Additionally, annoyingly, impossibly, that magnetic pull of attraction remained even while Miriam wanted to shriek in frustration every time they were in the same room.

One afternoon, Miriam went to get a cup of coffee and sit in the breakfast nook, hoping to read *Jane Eyre* quietly away from Hannah's intense organizational zeal. Noelle burst in.

"Mrs. M, Hannah wants to know if you have—" She stopped when she saw Miriam behind the counter with the coffeepot in hand. "Oh. You're here."

"Coffee?" Miriam offered. Noelle growled.

"I'll make my own." She glanced at Miriam's book. "Fucking asshole Rochester."

How was that fair? What was sexier than a woman who hated Edward Rochester?

"Where the hell is Mrs. Matthews?" she asked, and Miriam shrugged. Noelle harrumphed, and left.

It felt, to Miriam, as if Noelle were always reasserting her right to this space, always silently reminding Miriam that she didn't belong here anymore, but Noelle did. That these people were hers now. Finders, keepers.

Chapter 5

Noelle

T his isn't where the bows go," Noelle said, snatching a bow from where Miriam had just affixed it. She had been trying to deal with this woman invading her space and her life, but the sight of her putting all of Cass's decorations in the wrong place threatened to drown her in grief, and she didn't have time for that right now.

"I'm sorry, are you decorating now, as well? A renaissance woman!" Miriam snapped, yanking the bow back and putting it back where she'd had it. "Why are you here? I thought you were avoiding me. Can you return to that?"

"I *am* avoiding you except when you are doing something the opposite of the way Cass did, and I need to fix it. Influencer 'artist' can't even decorate for Christmas," Noelle said, putting finger quotes around "artist."

"I'm sorry, do you have a problem with my job?" Miriam asked, wheeling on her. "Also, what the hell do you know about where bows go?"

"I have a problem with the fact that you don't have a job, you just make money selling people weird junk and taking pictures of yourself around the world. Famous on Instagram is not a job. And I know where the bows go, because while you were throwing Carrigan's away, I was here, holding it together," Noelle said through clenched teeth.

Miriam cocked her head to the side. "Do you actually know what I do for a living, Noelle?"

Noelle shifted, a little uncomfortable. "No. And I don't need to. All I know is, you travel everywhere but Carrigan's. And now you're here, and you can't even put the bows where Cass did, probably because you didn't talk to her FOR A DECADE."

"How about I make things pretty, you grow trees, and oh yeah, I give you free labor you need? And you keep your judgments about my career and my bows to yourself?" Miriam shot back. Her hair was standing even taller than usual around her head, and it was really cute, which made Noelle even grouchier.

"It's not free! You're getting room and board!"

"No one else is staying in those rooms!" Miriam pointed out, loudly.

"I'M CALLING AN INTERVENTION!" Hannah shouted over them, and they both startled. Noelle hadn't even heard her walk up. "Noelle, I sent you in here to ask Miriam what she wanted for dinner, and you're yelling at each other where guests can hear you! Meet me in my office in ten minutes. I have plans for you both."

When Noelle arrived, neither Hannah nor Miriam was in the office. She settled into a chair, getting her thoughts together. For Hannah's sake, she was going to be nice and try to put this animosity behind them. She heard their voices float through the open door, Miriam's voice sending a shiver down Noelle's spine, and she grimaced at herself.

They walked in together, and Noelle's stomach gave a traitorous dip. All of her nerve endings became raw when Miriam was in the room. She didn't like it. When Miriam's inner lights were turned on, when she was present, she was sparkly and fascinating, and Noelle wanted to collect her like a raccoon collecting treasure. When her lights were off, when she went away from herself and seemed to almost leave her body, Noelle wanted to find out why and turn them back on. It annoyed her. She didn't need attraction, and she didn't do that kind of emotional connection. It was too risky, especially with an engaged woman.

Noelle leaned forward, her elbows on her spread knees and her hands clasped, bracing herself. Hannah sat behind her desk, her bookshelves at her back making a throne. When Noelle took a breath to speak, Hannah held up her hand.

"You have said enough, missy," her best friend told her. Oof. She'd told Hannah about her fight with Miriam. She'd tried to be honest about her own part, because it was important to her sobriety, and Hannah had told her she was being an asshole. Moving Hannah from being steadfastly Team Noelle was hard, but this had accomplished it.

"I'm going to talk," Hannah said, "and you're both going to listen. When I'm done, you are going to figure out a way to work together until Thanksgiving, because you're making it impossible for me to do my job."

"But, Hannah—" Miriam started.

Hannah stopped her.

"Miri, Noelle said some untrue, unkind things about you, and she had no right to. I won't make excuses for her, but we were having the worst week of all our lives. You may not be able to forgive her, but maybe you can understand we're all low on grace at this point?" Hannah asked Miriam gently.

Miriam just looked defiant.

"We can't build a new vision for Carrigan's together if she bites my head off every time we're in the same room," Miriam said, an edge to her voice.

"Noelle, do you have anything to say for yourself?" Hannah asked.

She crossed her arms over her chest. "I don't trust her, and I'm not thrilled about being on the Save Christmasland group project with her."

Hannah groaned. "You're not helping, Noelle."

Noelle shrugged. Damn. She'd meant to be conciliatory when she came in the room, and then she'd gotten her hackles up, again, like she always did when she had to look at Miriam's face. Noelle should just let her pretend she was helping. There was no way in hell this woman was going to make it all the way through the opening of the Christmas season. She would quit within the week.

They did need a plan for the bank, though, and they were wasting time catering to Miriam's whim to play homecoming.

"Tell me one thing that would make me think you're ready to come up with the kind of plan we need, and then execute it," Noelle said to Miriam. "No, not even that. Tell me one time you've shown up when someone needed you. Give me one good example." She sat back, feeling sure Miriam couldn't.

"The Old Ladies," Miriam said smugly, and Hannah laughed in delight. Noelle scowled. She was missing something.

"Miriam has this national network of little old ladies—and men, I assume—who own antique shops," Hannah explained. "She buys from them, but she's also sort of their surrogate daughter, checking in on them, making sure they're doing okay and not isolating, that sort of thing. She's like the social coordinator for a vast underground web of junk collectors."

"Not just their social coordinator," Miriam said. "I'm the person who schedules their doctors, sets up their meal trains when they get hurt, sometimes I'm their power of attorney." She fluttered her eyelashes, her voice syrupy. "I'm happy to give you all their numbers, if you want to call for references."

Noelle stared. That was the first weighty thing anyone had told her about Miriam Blum. "Why would you do that?" she asked.

Miriam waved dismissively. "You know how it is; your dad is an abusive monster and your mom is an emotionally unavailable ice cube, you find parents wherever you can!" she said, her voice a little too bright.

Noelle did not, in fact, know. Her parents had been complicated, but not monsters. Noelle wondered again exactly how bad Miriam's childhood had been, and how that had led to her running away from Carrigan's. Not that it was any of Noelle's business, because she wasn't trying to figure this woman out. She'd lost her best argument for why Miriam shouldn't be here, and Hannah was trying to murder her with only her eyeballs, so Noelle gave up.

"Fine. You win. Operation Save Carrigan's, welcome aboard," Noelle ground out. "You'd better not fuck it up."

"In order to make this work, you will be civil," Hannah said with an iron voice. "You will not avoid each other, and you will not make everyone else's lives miserable. We have to find a solution, or Noelle and I will be out on our asses. That means you play nice. Are we all agreed?"

They both nodded. Noelle assumed they would shake on it, but Hannah typed out the agreement, then printed it and made them sign it. She then insisted they follow her to the second-floor lounge, where she tacked it to the wall and hung one of Miriam's ugly plaid bows over it, for emphasis.

"Great," she said, standing back from the bow and admiring her handiwork. "Now that y'all have gotten on your adulting pants, we're going to cement our new agreement with a Bonding Activity."

"Halloween is tomorrow," Miriam reminded her, slumping onto the sectional, "which means Opening Day is in two days. Don't we have to, I don't know, open up the festival, cut a ribbon, start welcoming tourists? There must be a million last-minute details."

"Please, as if all that hasn't been planned for months. You must know I can multitask better than the average person can task." Hannah held up her clipboard, as if in proof. "You decorated, Noelle cut trees, I organized seasonal workers. We have time for forced bonding."

She produced sheet masks from under an end table, and Noelle complained that hers was tingly.

"Shut up and mask, Noelle," Hannah said. More seriously, she added, "Be nice to my cousin or I will personally harm you. This animosity is unacceptable."

After their masks had been pulled off and Noelle had scrubbed the snail slime from her face, Hannah disappeared back to her office to do more work, and Miriam went out onto the porch. Noelle thought about wandering into the trees to get some time alone, since the past several hours of interpersonal interaction were far over her comfortable limit, but the Old Ladies had her curious, and she was willing to pretend civility if only to pacify Hannah. She found Miriam bundled up on the porch swing.

"I brought you some cocoa as a peace offering," Noelle said, sitting down next to her. Miriam glanced over from inside her blanket cocoon, only her wild hair and hazel eyes showing. She scrunched her eyebrows at the mug of cocoa.

Noelle smirked. "It has three shots of espresso in it."

Miriam snaked one arm out of the blankets to grab the cup. "That's very kind. Thank you."

Noelle rested one arm across the back of the swing and stretched her legs out, trying to figure out how to begin building a bridge between them.

"Are you here because Hannah told you to be nice to me?" Miriam asked, looking ethereal as the steam from her cup coiled up around her face.

"Yes," said Noelle. "I thought I might try the unheard-of tactic of getting to know you before I decide if I hate you or not."

Miriam chuckled. "You should spread the word of this tactic to the internet."

They fell into silence for a few minutes before Miriam spoke again.

"I didn't know about Levi and Hannah."

Noelle wasn't sure why Miriam was telling her this. "Why did you think he wasn't here? Being an asshole? Didn't care about his parents' grief? Stuck on a boat?"

Miriam blew out a breath. "You know how they make cake pops? Cake scraps and frosting smooshed together in someone's hands and then covered in a pretty coating?"

She nodded, waiting to see where Miriam was going with this.

"I'm kind of like that, right now, except made up of trauma and grief instead of cake and frosting. I knew he wasn't here, I just hadn't processed how strange that was. Everything is strange, right now."

"That description of yourself does not inspire confidence in me, as a potential business partner," Noelle said, without animosity. She understood trying to hold the little bits of yourself together when you lost people you loved.

Miriam held her hands up. "I'm not going to lie to you to get you to like me."

"Does finding out about Levi and Hannah change anything for you?" Noelle asked, wondering if Miriam was angry or jealous to be on the outside of what had always been a triad.

"No, it just makes me sad they never told me. And I get why you thought I abandoned Hannah when she needed me. I didn't know. I wish I had." She shrugged.

Noelle didn't point out that it was Miriam's fault she didn't know. Besides, she'd promised Hannah a truce, and she was too hollowed out by grief to keep trading barbs. "Let's talk about something that's not . . . any of this."

Miriam nodded, staring out at the night, her blanket wrapped around her. "What's it like to be the lone lesbian out here in the wilderness?" she teased.

"How do you know I'm a lesbian?" Noelle countered.

Miriam cut her eyes over. "Could it be the framed commemorative Melissa Ferrick poster I can see peeking out from behind your door? The well-loved copies of *Rubyfruit Jungle* and *Oranges Are Not the Only Fruit* on your office bookshelf? The fact that you dress like the December cover girl for *Dapper Butches Monthly*? I'm a queer from Arizona, one of the reddest states in the nation." Miriam shook her head and the swing moved underneath her. "I am a finely tuned divining rod for subtle clues and low-key signals that a lady might like other ladies. Also," she pointed out, "literally no one has ever met you and not known you're a lesbian."

Noelle snorted. It was very annoying that Miriam was funny.

"Good to know my queer coding is working as intended. Is *Dapper Butches Monthly* real, because I need to fire every gay on Earth for not telling me about it."

Miriam giggled.

She turned toward Miriam before quickly looking away again. No one should be that beautiful.

"I'm not the *only* one," she explained, getting back to Miriam's question. "Elijah and his husband have been amazing about building a crew and have graciously let me in. But it's true that there's a distinct lack of sapphic companionship. Which is fine." She kicked Miriam's feet with her boots, when Miriam looked skeptical, and rubbed her hands along her thighs.

"My love life hasn't existed for a long time, and that's my preference. I decided to stop dating years ago, and it's worked out for the best."

To change the subject, Noelle said, "So uh... what *do* you do for a living? I know you're famous on Instagram, and you do something with antiques? I probably should have checked your account. I maybe made some assumptions based on wanting to dislike you." She cleared her throat around that admission. "Cass made it sound like you were an international jet-setting antiques dealer, but that's probably not a thing."

The night was deepening. The world had dropped twenty degrees, it felt, in the span of a few sentences. The farm was quiet. It made the porch feel like a miniature world that only the two of them occupied.

Miriam sipped her cocoa before she answered. "It's probably a thing. But not my thing. I do some restoration for clients with specific needs, who trust me. Most of what I do is using discarded, damaged, or low-value antiques as the basis for art pieces. And you should not feel bad about not looking at my Instagram," Miriam assured her. "I'm not even famous, I'm... well-known in a very small circle. Although I'm kind of famous by Pinterest standards." The wind whistled through the trees, and Miriam burrowed further into her blanket.

"Like, you make sculptures?" Noelle was intrigued now, in spite of herself. The idea of turning unloved antiques into art pieces appealed to her, keeping the past but reinventing it.

"Hmm, sometimes, but more often I decoupage a piece with interesting paper I think relates to it in some way, or I disassemble things and make them into shadow boxes, or take furniture with very classic silhouettes and paint it neon eight-ies colors," Miriam explained, moving her arms as she spoke. "I'm not sure what these gestures are supposed to mean— maybe 'I glue this weird thing to this other weird thing, then voila I sell it!'

"Plus a lot of kitschy, craft show kind of stuff. Aunt Cass used to have a bunch of them actually. There was an elephant lamp I covered in pages from *The Jungle Book* and old tracts I found about the Indian Independence Movement and modern indictments of Orientalism." She looked over at Noelle. "It was pink. It used to live in the front hallway, years ago. Cass sent me pictures."

"You did Dumbo?" Noelle was stunned. "I love that thing."

"It's actually the first-ever Miriam Blum original, from before I started doing upcycling as a career." Miriam tucked a curl behind her ear, looking sheepish. "I took a lit class in college where the prof taught Kipling without any context, and I turned it in as my final project. I called it 'The Elephant in the Room.' The professor was unamused, but Cass loved it. You really like it?"

Noelle nodded. "I stole it. It's in my room. Is all the stuff up in the attic yours, too? The haunted doll maypole statue?"

Miriam hid her face in one hand and nodded. She took an embarrassed sip.

"Ah yes," Miriam said, "some of my earliest work. Back when I was just messing around, before I became the Manic Pixie Dream Bisexual of the estate sale scene." She vogued her hands around her face, and Noelle bit back a laugh.

"Your stuff is awesome," Noelle said truthfully. "I'm really into the detail work you put into everything." Noelle had loved Miriam's art the whole time she'd lived here. She'd asked Cass about the pieces, but Cass had been cagey about where she'd gotten them.

"An up-and-coming young artist I want to support," she'd said.

Knowing that Miriam had made all those pieces forced her to re-evaluate her assumptions. The flighty, thoughtless Miriam of her imagination who wasn't serious about anything could not be the same person who had made that art.

Damn it, she was going to have to admit she'd judged too quickly.

It stung, but fair was fair. She still didn't want to get to know Miriam better because being attracted to someone who was engaged and leaving in a month was a bad idea. But she'd promised Hannah, and now she felt she owed it to Miriam. Maybe art could be a space for them to negotiate a peaceful acquaintance. They could find this one piece of common ground and be pleasant to each other in that context. That would be safe.

How turned on could you get talking about glitter, after all?

"I want to go up to the attic with you, before you leave," Noelle offered, "so you tell me about all those pieces." This felt like a good olive branch. Maybe the gesture would make up for some of her earlier animosity. Which she did still feel justified in, given the information she'd had, but she didn't have to tell Miriam that. She could be magnanimous. "And you should take whatever you want back home with you. I mean, you gave it to Cass, and Cass..."

Miriam shook her head. "I'm not going to take the inn's

art, unless you don't want it. I gifted that to Carrigan's. Besides, I would never willingly take pieces from someone who gets my work."

"You're famous on Instagram," Noelle teased, a little sheepishly, nudging Miriam with her shoulder. Why hadn't she looked Miriam up in the first place? "Lots of people get your work."

"No." Miriam shook her head, not taking her eyes off the night sky. "They like to *have* it, but most of them don't take me seriously."

"Doesn't your fiancée like your work?" Noelle asked. She shouldn't feel defensive of Miriam, but damn it, she was really talented.

"She likes the idea that I make art more than my actual art, I think." Miriam said, without rancor, which Noelle didn't quite understand. Why wouldn't Miriam want her fiancée to like her work?

"Anyway," Miriam continued more briskly, "to your original question, I do travel to pick out pieces. It's mostly road trips down the Atlantic seaboard, or weekends at interesting estate sales. I go to Berkeley every couple of months for the Alameda Flea Market."

Noelle watched Miriam first get excited and then even out her face, like she was trying not to seem too enthusiastic. Noelle was almost glad for the respite because Miriam geeking out was so luminous, she could hardly look. Miriam had every right to be passionate about her work, but some self-preservation instinct in her seemed to click on whenever she showed too much feeling. Noelle had wondered what caused Miriam's internal light to go on and off, and now she was watching Miriam turn down her own dimmer switch. Had her dad ingrained that in her, that unwillingness to show deep interest in anything? Is that why Miriam had called him a monster?

"I've been to the Alameda Flea Market! That place is wild!" Noelle didn't know why, because half an hour ago she'd hated this woman, but now she felt compelled to show Miriam that nerding out with her was safe. Miriam didn't need to dim herself for Noelle. "Hey, do you ever road-trip through rural parts of the Midwest and stop at tiny junk shops in the middle of nowhere? I've always wanted to do that."

"I do, with Cole," Miriam said. Noelle wondered why Miriam wasn't taking those trips with her fiancée. "It's one of my favorite adventures."

They made eye contact, and Noelle almost smiled. Looking away awkwardly, they sat quietly watching the night.

Chapter 6

Miriam

Noelle was talking to her now, and it was *not* better than being ignored.

Instead of avoiding her, Noelle was sitting close to her, smelling like Old Spice and citrus shampoo, talking to her about art. Miriam felt herself letting her guard down without even noticing. Being around Noelle felt like pulling on a new pair of jeans that unexpectedly fit perfectly. Miriam had to stop herself, several times, from leaning in to bury her face in Noelle's neck. She liked women—a lot—but she rarely wanted to nuzzle them within a few days of having met them.

Running her fingers along the arm of the swing, where she and Blue had carved their initials so long ago—they were almost invisible now—she let her brain play leapfrog. From Noelle's curves and warmth and interest in her art to Tara's calming no-nonsense steadiness. Miriam and Tara had been texting over the past few days. Brief check-ins about minutiae,

"The cheese guy at the farmer's market said hi, do you want a cheese tray for the shop opening?" and "Do you need me to pick up a dress for my parents' party or do you have one?"

Nothing that touched her heart or gave her butterflies. Nothing that exposed the pain she was processing or that bittersweet mixture of joy and deep regret at coming home only to realize she'd missed all those years for no good reason.

To be fair, she wasn't talking to Noelle about those things, either, but she could imagine it. She'd shared a lot of secrets on this porch, once, and Noelle fit there so perfectly that it was easy to picture. It should have scared her, how tempting it was to let Noelle close. She spun her engagement ring until it bit into her palm.

Dating Tara was easy, in a lot of ways. They had their agreement: they lived their separate lives and showed up for the other as needed. The sex was good, if not world-changing, and the company was pleasant. Miriam could travel to her friends' shops all over the country, shut herself in the workshop with podcasts for three days, spend the weekend with Cole, and Tara never asked for specifics. Miriam played the interesting trophy fiancée, a part she'd been groomed for all her life, and got to use that training for good instead of evil, which was a nice fuck-you to her dad. She had the financial backing to build a career for herself, and a place to land if it didn't launch.

Maybe Tara never said, "I miss you," but she often asked, "Do you need anything?" She liked Tara precisely because she knew she would never be in danger of falling in love with her. Out here in the quiet Carrigan's night she could almost hear Cass's voice, telling her that was baloney and to get it together. Cass believed in love writ larger than life, which was rarely comfortable, it seemed to Miriam.

Maybe she'd been comfortable for too long.

In the old days, Halloween at Carrigan's had been a three-day masquerade extravaganza culminating in the opening of the festival, and the Carrigan's season, on November 1. Guests would stream in for the start of the revelry, and leave with a tree and a hangover on All Souls' Day. This year, none of the staff was ready to do the event without Cass. Instead, on Halloween day they made sure every last item was in place for the festival tomorrow.

And that night, they put on animal footie pajamas, opened giant bags of miniature chocolates into a bowl, and talked about what they wanted to do for Halloween next year.

If there was a Carrigan's next year. There was going to be. Miriam was going to make sure of it, so that she could say, "Next year at Carrigan's," and mean it.

"What if you had a spooky burlesque show?" Miriam asked, lying upside down on the sectional on the landing, her legs over the back and her hair hanging over the seat. "Or one of those trunk-or-treat events that churches hold, but for adults." She waved the candy bar in her hand, thinking about the possibilities. "There could be hard cider from local breweries, and we could put a screen up on the inside of the barn and project horror movies, or *The Rocky Horror Picture Show*. It would be such a great way to connect with other merchants—" She cut herself off when she saw Noelle and Hannah staring at her.

Noelle took the bowl of candy away. "I think you're drunk on Butterfingers," she chided playfully.

"I was imagining something small," Hannah said from where she was starfished on the floor, "maybe inviting local kids for a costume party. Elijah told me it's hard to find a place in driving distance to take the twins to show off their costumes since trick-or-treating is so spread out among the farms, and we could be that place. It would be helpful to remind the townspeople of their childhood nostalgia, both around Carrigan's and Halloween in general. People are open to collaborations when they feel warm and fuzzy."

"I don't remember Halloween being a warm fuzzy time," Miriam said, sitting up and tucking her knees underneath her. "My dad only let us do things that looked good for his business, so we were always in expensive tailored costumes at a company party. But I assume for people not raised by abusive narcissists, it's a happy childhood memory."

She bit her lip. She never talked about her dad, especially not blithely about his abuse, but something about the two women—the cousin who was almost a sister and the stranger who already didn't like her, even if they *had* geeked out about art together—felt like they had given her permission to open the floodgates. The two certainties, that she could neither lose Hannah's love nor win Noelle's regard, set her free.

Noelle handed her back the candy bowl. "Never mind, you earned these," she said, a line between her brows, her voice a low grumble. "I vote burlesque."

"I finally get you two to agree on something and it's naked women?" Hannah groaned.

Miriam and Noelle looked at each other, and a tiny corner of Noelle's mouth lifted. Miriam found herself suddenly very interested in her candy.

On All Saints' Day, they officially opened the Christmas festival to business. The animatronic cherubs played "Joy to the World," while the lights in the trees out front flashed in time to the music. Ziva reappeared, just in time to preside ostentatiously over the proceedings. A line of townies stood outside, wanting first pick of the trees as soon as Miriam's mother ceremoniously flung the gates open. Most families would buy on Black Friday, but the people who lived nearby knew to avoid the tourists and snag the best trees early.

Miriam livestreamed all of it for the Bloomers, who were starting to ask uncomfortable questions about why she was still in New York. She tried to distract them with pomp and circumstance, since she definitely wasn't planning to give them any real answers.

It was Miriam's first taste of working Carrigan's, talking to people about the attributes of various fir trees, taking payments, directing customers to the seasonal workers. Business stayed slow but steady (and grueling) in those first few weeks. She often found herself working shoulder to shoulder with Noelle, usually while Noelle picked up a giant tree like it was made of air and carried it to a customer's car.

Miriam absolutely did not swoon every time, even if

Noelle's shoulders bunched under her flannel and her tattoos rippled where her sleeves were rolled up. They were sniping at each other less since their conversation on the porch swing, but they hadn't had any more authentic interactions. Noelle grouched about having to help the newbie learn the ropes but also smiled at her a few times—a miracle. Miriam wanted to believe Noelle was being nice for her own sake, although she suspected it was to avoid Hannah's wrath.

Hannah might be the organizing force behind Carrigan's Christmasland and the Matthewses might be the backbone, but Noelle kept all of them from working until they collapsed. Miriam kept catching Noelle forcing bottles of water into Hannah's hands or shooing Mrs. Matthews out of the kitchen or showing up just when Mr. Matthews needed a second pair of strong hands. She wondered who was taking care of Noelle. Not that she wanted to volunteer, since she had her caretaking hands full fielding emergencies from the Old Ladies even from here.

But she hoped someone was making sure Noelle hydrated and slept and felt looked after.

As the days wore on, Miriam became increasingly convinced that Noelle and Hannah had conspired to show her how hard a Christmas season at Carrigan's was to work. She didn't know if they were testing her or trying to drive her off, only that they were keeping her so busy she collapsed into her bed every night with very little energy left for scheming about visions of a New Carrigan's. She'd taken to carrying a little pocket notebook in her work apron, and she wrote down ideas as she walked around the farm, listening to tourists talk about their plans for winter break. Wine tasting and local chef pairings? Carrigan's could host that. Holiday craft market? That would be easy to add to one of their existing events.

Most days saw Miriam stationed out front when business opened, welcoming people as they came off the shuttle. Her resemblance to Cass was a blessing and a curse, as it both put people at ease and brought their grief to mind. It seemed that anyone who'd ever so much as spoken to Cass in passing loved and missed her. Miriam got used to hearing, several times a day, how startlingly like her aunt she was.

After two weeks of this, her head was too full of the farm, and her ideas, and her feelings, so she ducked into the kitchen to call Cole.

"Babe," she said, "I have terrible news. I need you to help me process some emotions."

"Gross! We don't have those." Cole laughed. "Hit me, I'll see if I can remember how feelings work."

"Everything here is so *much*. All these people who've known me all my life, who loved Cass, all these memories, all these regrets. Even the wallpaper feels like it's heavy with memories. I feel like I'm being rubbed raw."

"And it makes you want to come home to hide again?" Cole guessed.

"No, that's the part I don't understand. It makes me want to stay." Miriam sighed, laying her head down on the kitchen counter, the phone wedged under her. "I have this carefully constructed life in Charleston, I have my shop, I have you and Tara. I never have to deal with anything that hurts or is hard. Why would I want to abandon that to try to save a dying business, alongside a cousin I barely know anymore and a woman who kind of hates me? Please explain to me why my heart keeps whispering to me to stay."

Cole hummed, and she strained to hear him over the street noises from wherever he was. "You've been successfully running from this most of the time I've known you. Now that these feelings are coming up, they're probably going to keep surfacing until you work through them. Cass and Carrigan's were the center of your life in a lot of ways, and then they suddenly weren't, and you never processed that loss. You'll have to do that, even if you're in Charleston. But you could do it at Christmasland! I don't really want you to move to New York, but I don't want you to miss a once-in-a-lifetime adventure. Follow your heart!"

"What if my heart is making unreasonable and irrational demands?" Miriam whispered.

"It's probably about time it did. Okay, I love you more than life, but I was actually on a date who I've now abandoned inside a bar, so I have to go."

"Cole!" Miriam chided, horrified. "You didn't have to take this call while you were on a date!"

"Eh. It wasn't going well anyway. Speaking of dates. Have you talked to Tara about any of this?" As protective as he was of Miriam, he and Tara went all the way back to birth, and he looked out for her in his way.

"You know how she is, Cole." She was still slumped on the kitchen stool, but she'd lifted her head off the counter to gesticulate. "If I manage to get her on the phone, instead of her declining with a 'can't talk now, text me if it's urgent!' response, it's all business. Besides, what am I going to tell her? I'm kind of sort of thinking about moving to the Adirondacks?

What is she going to do with that? It's not fair to talk to her until I know what I'm going to do."

"That is some very twisted logic, my love. Who on Earth is better at thinking through all the logistics of complicated situations than Tara? She could actually help. Oh shit, my date is looking for me. I adore you, call your fiancée, talk to you soooooon." He trailed off and hung up.

Miriam looked up from her phone to find Mr. Matthews watching her, an eyebrow raised. He gestured her toward the door to the Matthewses' back apartments. He didn't say anything, although he must have heard at least part of the conversation, and she was grateful that he always gave her space when she needed it.

Mrs. Matthews was setting up shabbat candles, just as she'd always done on Friday nights when Miriam was little. She used to hope for an invitation into their little family space, with the Matthews kids, for this ritual, and felt so special when she was.

She'd forgotten about that, until now.

Her eyes welled up. Of course Mr. Matthews would know that she needed some time to rest and pray right now. It tore at Miriam that in running from Carrigan's because there was a chance it might remind her of her dad, she'd missed years of shabbat prayers with her real family, the people who actually wanted to stand as her parents.

While she was here, she could make some of that up to them—and herself.

She left the Matthewses as the final rays of dusk were fading from the sky, with a sense of peace. She had Cole at her back and the Matthewses supporting her. Whatever she decided, she would be loved and have a place to land. The peace lasted exactly thirty seconds, before her mother intercepted her walking up the stairs to her room.

"Oh, Miriam, I've been meaning to come find you," Ziva effused.

Miriam flinched while her mom air kissed both her cheeks. "That's not necessary," she said through a tight smile.

Refusing to take the hint, her mom gripped her elbow and propelled her forward, forcing Miriam to walk with her or make a show of pulling away where guests might see them. Miriam had learned very young not to make a show, and her mother knew it.

"I wanted to talk to you about this terrible joke of Cass's, leaving part of the Christmasland to you. And the Matthews boy, what was she thinking? The help's child?!" Miriam's blood started to boil at her description of Levi. She began to speak, but her mother kept talking.

"Obviously you can't keep the shares." Her voice was the one she used to get people to do what she wanted, where she was so reasonable no one dared argue, and she was walking a little too fast for comfort. "You have a perfect thing going in Charleston. That woman you're marrying is a catch, you wouldn't want to do anything to jeopardize that kind of security, especially since you insist on playing with glitter instead of getting a career."

It was funny how her mom sounded exactly like her own inner monologue, but somehow when Ziva disparaged her work, Miriam wanted to lash out. She also wanted to tell

Hannah and Noelle she was definitely staying, because anything her mother thought was a terrible idea must have some merit. She hadn't rebelled as a kid, because it wasn't safe, and her dad had brutally shot down her early forays into rebellion in her twenties.

Now, at thirty-five, she felt herself itching against the audacity of her mother giving her an edict she expected to be followed.

"Thanks for the input, Mom," she managed, trying to rein her anger in. "I'll be sure to add it to my own calculations."

Her mom stopped and looked at her. "Miriam, I know you will never believe this, but I love you and I want the best for you. How are you going to have that up here, playing hotel?"

That placating tone, and that shameless lie—that her mother had ever, for an instant, wanted or even thought about what was best for her—broke the dam of her anger.

"I have had half a life for years because Dad took everything from me, while you watched. He burned down my career, destroyed my life financially, drove me from my family, and you were complicit in that." Her voice grew louder. "Was that what was best for me, in your twisted mind?" Miriam had never, in her life, shouted at her mother, but she couldn't—and wouldn't—stop herself now.

"I won't talk to you about this when you're being irrational." Her mother huffed and walked away.

If the worst her mother had to throw at her was that she was being irrational, she'd won that round. She could tell, because Ziva had felt the need to swoop off dramatically.

"Why do you even talk to your mom?" Noelle asked, appearing from behind Miriam and startling her.

"Were you listening to us?" Miriam demanded, angry at her mother and Noelle's intrusion.

"You were shouting in the hallways of my home," Noelle pointed out, her arms crossed defensively.

That was hard to argue with. Now that her mother was out of sight, and it was just her and Noelle in an empty, musty hall, her anger bled out, and she was tired. "Moms are complicated, you know?" Miriam leaned against the wall, and Noelle leaned next to her.

"Oh, I know so, so well." Noelle smiled sadly.

Miriam wanted to know what was behind that smile, but she was sure Noelle didn't want to tell her. "I still talk to her generally because it's easier than dealing with the drama she would kick up if I tried to cut her off. Today, specifically, she ambushed me. I don't know. She's a victim of my dad's abuse too, even if she could have left more easily than I could. She was the only person who was in our home with me who might ever be able to understand how bad it was, if she would ever admit she was being abused. It's..."

"Complicated," Noelle finished for her.

Miriam nodded.

"She seems to be trying to repair things, in her own un-skilled way," Noelle observed.

"She would like people to believe that, certainly," Miriam snorted. "She and I both know she just let yet another Yom Kippur go by without making any attempts at restitution. It's all for show."

"If you grew up with that kind of mom, it might be hard to trust your own instincts," Noelle said quietly.

That was exactly it. It was so hard to trust her instincts

when all the adults in her family, except Cass, had told her that what she was feeling and experiencing wasn't real.

She felt way too exposed by Noelle's insight. Her brain yelled "Danger! Retreat!"

"I'm sorry," Miriam said. Dumping her family's bullshit on Noelle was unfair and wouldn't get her anywhere. It's not like Noelle cared. "I shouldn't shout in the hallways."

Noelle propped one booted foot behind her on the faded wallpaper. "You know, you don't have to forgive her for all that, even if she was abused, too."

Suddenly angry again, Miriam pushed off the wall, balling her fists hard enough to dig her nails into her palms. How condescending for Noelle to act like Miriam couldn't handle her mom on her own or had never considered cutting her off. "Thanks for your unasked for input, strange woman who hates me! I'll file it right next to my mom's unwanted advice," Miriam replied.

"Whatever," Noelle said behind her, as she walked away.

The next day, driven by spite at her mother, she called a meeting with Hannah and Noelle. Instead of Hannah's office, she asked them to meet her in what she thought of as neutral territory: the library. Tucked into an architecturally improbable room at the back of the inn, the library was so filled with memories that walking inside felt like being punched in the solar plexus. Built-ins lined the walls, jammed with all sorts of books people read on vacation and then left behind to make room in their luggage.

The books were not organized in any perceivable way, instead piled, jammed, and inserted wherever there was room. Discovery by a reader was left entirely to happenstance. This was the room Miriam had spent all her winters curled up in. This was where she'd met Miss Marple and decided to be her when she grew up. It was the place she went to in her head when nothing felt safe in her life. Her parents never ventured there, which was how it had become her go-to childhood haven.

Her little pocket notebook was full of ideas, and they had coalesced into a plan—or at least the start of one. She needed the others to finish rounding it out. She had sketched out a calendar on butcher paper on the wall in her room: Twelve Months in Christmasland, and pinned it with cards she'd gathered from area artisans, tiny renderings of social media ad runs, and printouts of other event destination farms with details about how much they charged.

When Hannah and Noelle arrived at the meeting, she handed them each a sheet of bullet-pointed ideas.

"Wow, you really are Hannah's cousin," Noelle observed.

"I have the beginning of a plan, maybe," Miriam said, standing nervously as they sat down. "Not a whole plan! That has to be all of us together. But hear me out. I know I have a lot to learn, and some of these ideas might not be workable or might make things worse instead of better. That's why I'm bringing them to you, the experts."

Hannah and Noelle had a silent conversation with their eyebrows, which Miriam couldn't interpret. Noelle gestured for her to keep talking.

"Okay, I know this is a terrible name, but my idea is

basically Carrigan's All Year. Make this a tourist destination in spring for Easter egg hunts or a fancy-dress Matzo Ball for Passover. A food truck festival in June and a Fourth of July carnival—no fireworks near the trees, Noelle—a Purim parade, weddings, bachelorette weekends. We need to be an event destination."

"Where are we going to have all these events, that I assume I'm going to plan?" Hannah asked, sounding unconvinced.

"In the barn?" Miriam ventured.

"Where are the tractors going to live, if we have weddings in the barn?" Noelle said.

"I don't have all the answers yet! But given Elijah's explanation of Cass's vision of a new Carrigan's, and the downturn in Christmas business, I started thinking about ways to get people up here. I thought about classes local experts could offer, and seasonal experiences we could host, ways to partner with businesses in Advent. We have so much to offer, it doesn't have to just be Carrigan's *Christmas*land."

"You're talking about a complete overhaul of everything we've ever done, our entire relationship with the town of Advent, and moving our whole focus away from growing and selling Christmas trees." Hannah began chewing on the end of her braid thoughtfully.

"No," Miriam disagreed quickly, trying to keep them both from immediately dismissing the idea, "the trees are crucial. I just want to add things during the other ten months of the year. I know it's a huge departure from what we've always done, but it's a pretty normal business model."

Hannah scrunched up her nose. "This feels really risky, Miri, and the Rosensteins and the bank want a feasible plan.

We don't have any experience planning an event calendar on this scale. And by we, I mean me."

"You love work," Miriam pointed out. "You're happier the busier you are. Think of how many things you could be in charge of! How many people you could boss around! The spreadsheets it would require!"

Noelle cleared her throat. They both turned to her.

"First, look, I hate the name, but that's neither here nor there," Noelle said, her arms across her chest. Miriam's heart sank. "Otherwise, it's a solid start. Some kind of all-year event destination is probably what we need to pivot to, even if it's going to mean so many more people in my damn woods. If we can get the Rosensteins on board as investors, and give the bank numbers, we might be able to sell them on it. But there's something you're missing, Miriam."

She was pointing at the paper, and Miriam looked at it, trying to figure out what she'd missed.

"We need to get people here. And of the three of us, only one of us has a fandom. Ugh, I can't believe I'm saying this." Noelle scrubbed her hands over her face. "The best way to attract tourists would be for you to be here full-time."

Miriam blinked at her, her mind blank. She couldn't do that. And Noelle couldn't really want her to.

Hannah looked thoughtful. "We could do a lot of stuff targeted around art if you were here, really carve out a niche as a destination. Art classes, local artist collaborations, week-long artist retreats, antique auctions."

"DIY ruin your own antiques," Miriam said, seeing it in her mind.

Noelle was scowling at her, which didn't seem fair, since

she was the one who'd brought up the idea in the first place. She must really love Carrigan's, if she was willing to broach the idea of Miriam staying to save it.

"Could you leave Charleston? Logistically?" Hannah asked. "Have you thought about it?"

She *had* thought about it. She'd done all the math late one night. Just in case, she'd told herself. What it would take to close up the store, move all her materials here, and set up a permanent workspace. How much it would cost, and what part of Carrigan's she could take over without disrupting the entire business.

The day Elijah told them about the will, Hannah had mentioned the carriage house. Miriam had snuck away from customers to do a walk-through during those long, busy two weeks when they'd first opened. It wasn't a bad option. With the right conversions, it could be perfect. She would need to add a filming space, with a lighting setup, but it was doable.

She nodded. "Logistically, I could." Emotionally, that was more complicated math. She would have to give up Charleston and Tara, who would never move here. It was more risk than she'd taken in, well, a decade.

"I think this is a plan we can take to the Rosensteins," Hannah said. "First, we need specifics, projections, concrete ways we'll get ourselves through the first year..."

"I've started cost analysis, although I need some numbers from you on Carrigan's expenses," Miriam assured her. "Except I didn't write myself into the plan."

"We need to know if you're onboard, before we talk to them," Hannah said. "Because it's a whole different pitch."

"Do you want me here?" Miriam asked. She wasn't even

going to think about whether or not she wanted to be here, herself. One step at a time. Noelle was silent, but Miriam already knew her answer. She was watching Hannah. If Hannah wanted to do this with her, maybe...

"I do." Hannah smiled, and that smile was a part of Miriam's happiness she'd forgotten she needed. "I want you here. I want to do this wild idea with you. Cass wanted you here. The Matthewses want you here. Do you want to be here?"

The idea of making a decision that would alter the lives of everyone she loved made Miriam want to run back to her warehouse and hide. In that space, she made all the rules, and nothing she did impacted anyone but herself.

She breathed through a rise of panic.

"We said I would stay through Thanksgiving and then we would figure things out, and that's in a week. Can I still have that week? To try to sort out my brain?" she asked, pleading with Hannah with her eyes to understand why she couldn't make this decision on the spot.

"You've had a decade, woman," she heard Noelle grumble under her breath.

Hannah nodded, though. "Let's all sleep on it, I'll do some more finessing to the parts of the plan that don't hinge on you, and we will talk about this in a week." Hannah hugged her, hard, and she held on tightly.

"I need you to know that it means the world to me that you asked, Nan," she said, a couple of tears falling into Hannah's hair.

"Whatever," Hannah said, wiping away her own tears. "Anything for Carrigan's. Now let's get back to work. We can't sell trees from the library!"

Chapter 7

Noelle

T he weeks before Thanksgiving were busy enough for Noelle to feel her introversion stretched, but even as she lost herself in the hustle, she couldn't turn off her brain. She missed Cass, she couldn't ignore how hard Miriam was busting her ass, and she worried that Hannah was burning herself out. She was itchy with stress about things she couldn't fix or change. She found herself more than once out in the back acreage, taking care of trees she could mostly control.

There was a stand of young saplings she was coaxing into full health after a scorching summer. During the off-season, she read and spoke to botanists around the world about the effect of global warming on pine tree growth. She was trying various ways of adjusting the planting season to meet their new reality. Still, if she lost this crop, there would be a very lean year soon, so Noelle was doing everything she could to get them through.

The day after Miriam presented her plan, Noelle patted one particularly scraggly little tree on the top. "Good girl," she whispered. It never hurt to remind the trees that you loved them.

Shoving her gloved hands under her arms for warmth, she looked around. It was almost laughably perfect outside, crisp and cool but not the biting cold that would come as winter set in. The air smelled like woodsmoke, wet earth, and pine. At the very back of the property, she could hear the stream that ran down from the mountaintop snowmelt, bubbling happily in the background. She breathed deeply and felt every muscle in her body relax, for the first time since Cass died.

Nothing about losing her was easy, and her choice to leave part of the farm to two people who'd walked away when they had been needed the most still irked Noelle. She didn't want to be mad at Cass, but she couldn't help it.

Admittedly, Miriam wasn't as bad as Noelle wished she was. She also fit better at Carrigan's than Noelle would have liked.

Noelle noticed, and didn't want to, how naturally Hannah and Miriam fell into a lifelong secret language of sideways glances and half thoughts. She noticed Miriam and Mr. Matthews riffing goofs at dinner, and how the light from the Christmas trees caught in Miriam's curls.

She noticed Miriam.

Noelle had been up late the last several nights scrolling Blum Again Vintage & Curios' Instagram feed. She might have looked at every picture Miriam had ever posted, which was . . . many. If Miriam was going to disappear again, rather than stay and be part of the new Carrigan's, Noelle wished she would get it over with. Noelle needed her equilibrium and sleep to return. Where was Miriam's absentee fiancée, and why hadn't the woman come to swoop her back South? If Miriam were hers, she would be there for her in her time of grief, standing by while she made an impossible life decision, acting as a guard for when Miriam didn't feel up to dealing with Ziva.

But Miriam wasn't Noelle's, she was someone else's. Noelle couldn't start wanting to take care of her.

Everything about Miriam was a puzzle. Noelle knew parts of her. The girl Cass talked about glowingly, whom she was jealous of, and the swath of heartbreak that girl's absence had left behind. She knew the sad, adorable elf who had shown up on her doorstep and drunk all her coffee. She knew the art she lived with every day and felt a connection with. And she knew the woman who, when asked about her mother, started to unravel. It was clear that somehow, Miriam leaving Carrigan's was rooted in trauma; she hadn't woken up one day and decided she didn't care about her family. That didn't undo the harm her absence had caused, but it forced Noelle to re-evaluate her initial judgment that Miriam was flighty and unreliable. Miriam was spooked and running from something. For whatever reason, Carrigan's had gotten caught up in that.

She had to figure out the whole picture of Miriam Blum, whether she could trust Miriam to be a part of this place Noelle needed for her own survival—and if she could work with Miriam, without combusting in ill-advised lust.

Since the shit had hit the fan, hard enough that even her trees couldn't talk her off the ledge, Noelle did the only thing she knew how to do: she went to a meeting.

Her normal meetings were at night, after work. There was a different crowd at a noon meeting in the middle of the week—a crew of little old lady alcoholics who'd been sober as long as Noelle had been alive, and who'd been up in each other's business just as long. Noelle knew them, because being sober in the Adirondacks meant you knew every other sober person in driving distance. They had great recovery, but she usually avoided them because they were always trying to con her into helping out with an event.

Her usual haunt, the alano club in Mt. Pleasant, had meetings all day, cheap bad coffee, and always a few alcoholics up for a card game. They also had alcothons—twenty-four-hour meetings on Christmas and New Year's, so people without family had somewhere to go in case they had the urge to drink. At the first sign of weakness, Noelle would get suckered into providing a tree, bringing a ham, and welcoming newcomers. She didn't even know where she would cook a ham. Certainly not in Mrs. Matthews's pork-free kitchen.

Seeing the little old lady alcoholics made Noelle think about Miriam's Old Ladies. Noelle had overheard Miriam on the phone, checking up on them. *How did the surgery go? Did you get the grocery delivery I sent? I told so-and-so to get in touch with you about that piece, if she doesn't give you a fair price you let me know.* She was like a mother hen clucking over her chicks, except all her chicks were over seventy.

After the meeting, the ringleader of the old lady alcoholics cornered her.

"You didn't listen to a single share, kid," the woman said. "Your head was a million miles away. Get your ass in the car, we're going to lunch, and you're going to tell us about it."

Noelle wanted to protest that she had her own ride, but she just yes ma'amed and got her ass in the car. She was taking her life in her hands, as the woman drove like a bat out of hell, but she would also have been taking her life in her hands if she'd said no.

When they were all settled on the patio of an old beat-up diner, long menthol cigarettes lit, coffee cups filled and rimmed in red lipstick, they turned to her.

"We've been worried about you since Cass died," the ringleader said.

"If you hadn't come down off the hill soon," another added, "we were going to come up and get you. Did that woman leave a mess behind her? Is that what's got you all twisted up?"

"No," said a quiet, ancient woman who looked like she might have played pro ball in her youth, "she's got girl trouble."

Noelle choked on her coffee. "Cass did leave a whole hell of a mess," she said, feeling disloyal. Still, if you couldn't tell the truth at the meeting-after-the-meeting, you were in real trouble. "And there is a woman who's complicating my brain. But nothing's going to happen with her."

"Why not?" the ringleader asked, waving her cigarette. "When was the last time you dated?"

Noelle sighed. "Before my parents died," she admitted. "I've been focusing on my sobriety. But!" she raised a hand, as one of them started to speak. "Even if I wanted to date, I couldn't date this woman. She's not staying at Carrigan's, and she's engaged. Although there's something weird happening there. She never talks about her fiancée."

"Girl," said the quiet, ancient woman, her white curls bobbing as she shook her head, "if you can't get laid and stay sober at the same time, there's something wrong with your sobriety."

The others nodded, taking long drags of their cigarettes and long sips of their lukewarm coffee.

"The fiancée is a different matter entirely," said the ring-leader. "If she's off-limits, it's simple, she's off-limits. So what's the tangle?"

Noelle sighed. "I prejudged her, pretty badly, and I was unkind, and she thinks I hate her. I made her feel unwelcome at Carrigan's, which is not what Cass would have wanted."

"It's good you came here today, and you're not trying to figure everything out in your own head. It's not safe up there alone," the quiet woman said.

Tears came up, ones she'd been stuffing down since the funeral just to get through. Before she knew it, Noelle was weeping into a polyester tracksuit while the woman closest to her held her and rubbed circles on her back.

"I was so angry," she choked out, "and scared and sad, without Cass. And this woman, Miriam, she got in the path of that. Somehow all my anger at Cass got pushed on her. Because I would have done anything to have another ten years with Cass, and she could have but she didn't." She was speaking around big, wracking sobs, and the old women were nodding. One handed her a crumpled tissue from the bowels of an alligator purse. "I didn't know how to be fair and everything hurt so much, and now I hurt someone else. And I do like her, and I do wish she didn't have a fiancée, and I do want to date again maybe eventually, and I don't know what to do." Her run-on petered out, and she took a deep breath before blowing it out. "I've been trying to hold it in and be strong for everyone, and it came out sideways."

"You need to make amends, first of all." The ringleader put out her cigarette and pointed a neon pink nail at her. Noelle nodded. She really, really did. "And then, you need to pray. You'll figure it out. But not alone, and not all right now. One day at a time."

She could do that. She could make an amends, and pray, ask for help, and take it a day at a time.

* * *

When she got back to the inn, Noelle found Hannah trying to teach Cass's byzantine paper registration system to Miriam. It amounted to them never having kept records of anything.

"There wasn't a set rate," Hannah was explaining. "Cass charged you based on her own calculations of how much she liked you, and how much she thought you could afford. She definitely hosed some people and gave other people their rooms for a song."

"You do realize that all these people are about to show up here, expecting to pay whatever they've always paid, and you're not even going to know what to charge them, right?" Miriam's voice rose in pitch as she spoke. "We need a filing system. We need an account book!"

She was cute when she got her serious business face on,

and even cuter when annoyed. Miriam's intensity about their financial structure (or lack thereof) surprised Noelle. She herself hadn't cared how Cass charged people, as long as they paid something and she, in turn, was paid. She knew a hell of a lot about growing trees, but almost nothing about book-keeping. Miriam's obvious knowledge about the subject took Noelle aback. She knew now Miriam ran her own business but hadn't really thought about the financial logistics it would include, just the art-making and social media pieces. She kept underestimating this woman and being proven wrong.

"Okay breathe," Hannah said, putting her hands on Miriam's crossed arms. "I'm still the manager of inn operations, I have a whole degree in hospitality management, and I will figure this out."

Noelle smiled a little at her best friend, who was extremely territorial, no matter how much she wanted Miriam here. "Miriam, let Hannah do her job. She's good at it, I promise. Scary good, really," she said, laying a hand on Hannah's shoulder.

"Of course you're taking her side!" Miriam said.

At the same time, Hannah said, "Stay out of this, NoNo, I'm handling it!"

Noelle raised both hands and stepped back.

"Sorry," Miriam said sarcastically, "my fault for trying to help at all, I forgot that Queen Hannah never needs any assistance. I saw visions of an IRS audit dancing in my head. I'll let you deal with this clusterfuck." Miriam stomped out of the room.

Noelle watched her go, annoyed by her impulse to soothe Miriam's bruised feelings. She turned back to Hannah.

"What the hell was that? I thought you two were ecstatic to be reunited?"

"Oh, you know," Hannah said with the sort of loving nostalgic exasperation reserved for family you loved even when you didn't like them, "leftover hurt feelings, old buttons getting pushed. Miriam and I have been butting heads since we were born. She thinks I'm controlling, and I never let anyone else be in charge."

Noelle secretly thought Miriam was kind of right.

"I'm grateful to Cass for bringing us back together, but why did it have to be to clean up this gigantic mess she made?" Hannah chewed on the end of her braid, a sure sign she was processing something. Noelle waited for her to finish. "There's no money, there's no paper trail, there's no system for contacting past guests! There are sticky notes that predate the invention of the sticky note!"

"I miss her, too," Noelle said, and Hannah put her head on Noelle's shoulder.

"Miriam's right. This is a clusterfuck. I don't know if even my supernatural powers of organization can save this farm." Hannah blew out a breath.

"You can't, alone," Noelle reminded her. "But you don't have to. We're a team."

Chapter 8

Miriam

The decision about whether to stay at Carrigan's should have been an easy one. No matter how much Miriam had loved it as a child, Carrigan's was her past. She had a beautiful, ambitious woman at home waiting to build a life with her, and a store she'd dreamt into being. Maybe she and Tara would never be in love, but they were an ironclad team.

Here, she had an unwanted attraction to a woman who didn't like her and a mountain of emotional baggage to unpack. True, she had her family back, and a big, fascinating project she was collaborating on with her favorite cousin. Now that she had envisioned Carrigan's All Year, she wanted to see what it could become, in person. She wanted to be a part of building it.

The real problem was, whenever she thought about going home, something wild and insistent inside of her whispered she was already there.

She'd been putting off calling Tara, because every time she decided she knew what she was going to do—for sure, definitely this time—she changed her mind as soon as she picked up the phone. Cole had told her to follow her heart, but Cole loved change and was adept at making himself large. Miriam had spent all her life trying to keep things from changing, trying to make herself so small as to be invisible. She'd invented an entire social media persona she could hide behind, so no one would ever see who she really was! Including herself. She had stopped listening to her heart, because she'd been burned so badly whenever she'd tried.

Now that her heart was yelling loudly at her, without her permission, she didn't know how to set herself free. It felt reckless and unsound. Since Hannah, the Matthewses, and Noelle had all made their opinions known and she still wasn't closer to a decision, she went to visit the reindeer.

There had always been reindeer at Carrigan's because Cass preferred them to people. Miriam had been afraid they might have been sold, their upkeep too expensive as the farm tried to stay afloat. She should have known Cass would never allow it.

"Hello, my sweet friends," she cooed, pulling apples out of her coat pocket. "It's so lovely to see your fuzzy, fuzzy faces. Yes, it is. No, sir, you can keep your teeth to yourself. Now, no one around here has anything for me to do, but I suspect you are in need of skritchy-skritches behind the ears, aren't you? Aren't you, you beauties?" She snapped a quick selfie with them for the Bloomers.

She heard a throat clear behind her, and turned around to find Mr. Matthews, his hands stuffed in his pockets, and Noelle, an eyebrow raised and a smirk on her face.

"The reindeer were lonely," Miriam said defensively, her heart in her throat. If her dad had caught her being sweet with an animal, she would have had to worry forever that he would use it as emotional leverage against her. But this wasn't her dad. The reindeer were safe.

Mr. Matthews shuffled his feet and grumbled. "The barn's looking mighty ratty, and it sure would be nice if someone repainted the old mural that used to be on the side, the one with the Carrigan's logo."

Mr. Matthews was right. What had, in her childhood, been a vibrant mural done by some wandering artist trying to impress Cass was now a few sad peeling scraps of color.

Noelle looked between the two of them. "Miriam," she said, "would you like a project? You know how to paint, right?"

Miriam blinked. That was a much bigger question than Noelle knew. She hadn't painted in a very long time.

She went with the obvious answer.

"I *am* a professional artist. I could do the mural. I remember what it used to look like."

"Maybe you could add a few artistic touches," Mr. Matthews added, in his sly, taciturn way. If anyone but Mr. Matthews had made the suggestion, her stomach would have knotted and her blood would have turned to ice. She could do this. Painting a barn wasn't making a painting. This was fine. She could paint a damn pine tree and a weird vintage reindeer on the side of a barn. Weird vintage reindeer were practically her bread and butter. The Bloomers would love it.

"Alright, you probably know what you're doing," Noelle conceded. She crossed her arms, her face screwed up. She looked like it was physically painful to admit Miriam might have skills. If she didn't want Miriam doing this, why had she brought it up?

Then, she surprised Miriam by asking, "Do you need an assistant?"

"Aren't you busy growing trees?" she asked skeptically, both terrified of anyone witnessing her painting and desperate for Noelle to stay.

"The trees are pretty much growing themselves," Noelle said, her smirk back.

Miriam was ready to say no, but she kind of did need an assistant if she wanted to be done priming and sketching by nightfall.

Which was how she ended up on top of a ladder, directing Noelle. When Noelle looked up at her, the sun turned her auburn hair bronze, throwing the shadow of long eyelashes onto her cheeks.

Miriam waved at a roller brush and a bucket of paint. "The part I marked out down there needs to be filled in with white. I assume you know how to paint the side of a barn white?" she asked, turning Noelle's earlier question around.

"I think I can manage it." Noelle laughed and rolled up the sleeves of her shirt to prep. Miriam turned her eyes purposefully away from the exposed forearms and tried to remember what she'd been working on. Out here, you could see the whole farm, and the mountains rising beyond it. Every time she looked out, the sight took her breath away.

"I've never been here in fall before," she said, to distract herself from her nerves. "I didn't expect"—she gestured at the shocking reds and yellows splashed against the crystal blue sky—"all of this."

"You've never been here for Rosh Hashanah?" Noelle asked.

Miriam shook her head. "We didn't do High Holy Days with the Rosensteins. I wish we had."

"Why don't you as an adult?" Noelle asked. "Hell, they even invite me."

"Wait, you go to Rosh Hashanah with my family?" Miriam's heart hurt with jealousy.

Noelle shrugged like it was no big deal. "Hannah invited me the last couple of years. I'm a sucker for kugel. She was going through a miserable breakup with Levi, and she needed me to run interference with any overly nosy family members."

"Which is all of them," Miriam laughed. She looked down at the top of Noelle's head, watching her brushstrokes for a moment. "You really take care of her. Of Hannah."

"She's my person," Noelle said, glancing back up and meeting Miriam's eye, "and someone has to. She's always taking care of everyone else."

"And we all left." Miriam finished the part Noelle didn't say. She was glad Noelle was here, being Hannah's person, and yet so sad she couldn't breathe.

"That's not what I meant, Miriam," Noelle grumbled. "I wasn't judging you. This time."

"It's true, though. We did leave. Anyway," Miriam said, her voice cracking, "it's beautiful up here."

"It's a little overdressed," Noelle conceded. "It reminds me of Cass. I think that's why she loved it here, because the mountains are as Extra as she was."

It felt so unbelievably good to share a happy memory

of Cass with someone who had also loved her. Part of the irresistible draw she felt to Noelle was this, that Noelle loved everyone Miriam loved. She loved Carrigan's as much as Miriam did. Being with her was like finding someone who spoke a language she thought she'd made up.

"It makes me want to drive out into it and get lost for a day, hiking and napping and reading," Miriam admitted. "I've been a lot of beautiful places over the past ten years. Driven the Pacific Coast Highway, camped in Yosemite, spent a day just watching the sun move the shadows over the Grand Canyon. I've walked along pony trails on Chincoteague Island, and stood in lighthouses over the surf in Maine. But somehow I've never been here when it looked like this."

Noelle looked surprised by the regret in Miriam's voice, her expression piercing Miriam. She didn't know why she wanted Noelle to understand her so badly. It was a foreign impulse for someone who usually hid her real feelings even from herself.

"It's my favorite place I've ever been," Noelle said after a long pause, sitting back on her haunches and resting her arms on her thighs. "The place I love most and feel most at home."

"Mine too," Miriam said. This time, Noelle's face showed stark disbelief. She understood—how could she say that, and mean it, after being gone for a decade?

She tried to explain. "Have you ever loved anything so much that it made you too raw? Loved it so much you needed to cocoon yourself from it, because the loving left you unable to breathe?"

Noelle shook her head as she looked up, shading her

eyes against the sun. "I'm a big fan of experiencing my emotions, personally. I'm not always great at it, but it usually works out better when I try." Miriam would have expected condescension, but Noelle seemed to be genuinely trying to answer her.

"Lucky you," Miriam whispered. That impulse to make Noelle understand her drove her to continue. "I've kind of been in a self-imposed fugue state, like I pulled up the castle drawbridge, locked all the doors, and hunkered down. And it was hard to maintain, at first, before I was practiced at living in isolation. Anything could have breached my walls, and I couldn't let them be breached."

"And Cass would have breached them?" Noelle guessed.

"Cass, Hannah, Levi, the Matthewses. I had to keep them outside the perimeter, because if I let them close, my whole castle would crumble. I was too raw to feel that much."

"And after your wounds scabbed over, when you weren't so raw?"

"I guess I didn't want anything to upset my delicate balance? I don't know, I was on autopilot at that point, because that's what a fugue state is *for*. I didn't have to make decisions or examine myself. I could just put one foot in front of the other and survive."

She went back to painting the Christmas tree, and they fell into silence. She shouldn't have tried to explain. She never talked to anyone about this stuff, not even Cole or Hannah or Blue.

She kept trying to get Noelle to understand her, to see that her assessment of Miriam was unfair, but she couldn't tell if she was succeeding. Noelle had never mentioned their fight, and although they were civil to each other and had a few conversations where it felt like she was making headway, she didn't want to assume Noelle's opinion of her had changed. It was like Noelle had said, Miriam couldn't trust her own judgment. She was afraid if she was wrong, it would hurt even more. She couldn't read Noelle's body language, her feet always set wide and her arms crossed over her body like she was a tree, solid and dependable and incapable of being swayed.

"You have a gift for this," Noelle said, startling Miriam out of her thoughts. She looked down, and Noelle was standing back, planted, hands on her hips, eyeing the whole sketch. "Have you ever done any painting for your art, or is your heart in antique upcycling?"

"My art is as real as painting," Miriam said defensively, because she couldn't give any of the other answers to Noelle's question. That she couldn't paint, even if she wanted to, and it didn't matter where her heart was. Upcycling had to be enough.

"It absolutely is." Noelle nodded. "And you're incredibly talented at it. I just wondered. You can be good at many things at once."

Miriam chuckled sadly. "I sometimes wish I could trade some of my art and business skills for skills at being human," she said. "And I don't paint."

Not anymore, she whispered to herself.

"I—" Noelle started, and then stopped.

"What?" Miriam asked.

"You're not the worst person I've ever met at being a human," Noelle said, finally.

Wow, talk about damning with faint praise. Noelle sounded like that admission had been dragged out of her. Miriam was very glad she hadn't started to believe Noelle might like her, eventually.

"That's demonstrably true," Miriam agreed, trying to sound flippant to hide her disappointment. "You've met my dad."

Noelle tipped her head in acknowledgment. "And Levi."

Every piece of this conversation was like standing on, well, a rickety old ladder. Talking to Noelle made her yearn for things she couldn't want. She'd spent all her childhood trying to convince people who didn't love her to change their minds about her, and she was done with it. Trying to befriend Noelle was like banging her head against a brick wall. She'd done that until her head was bloody. No more. It didn't matter if Noelle spoke her secret language, she didn't need anyone to get that close to her innermost self, anyway.

"I think I'm done with the part I need your help with," she said, curtly. Noelle muttered something about soil samples before gathering her paintbrush and hauling it away with her. Miriam breathed a sigh of relief. Sexy, funny, hardworking women who liked her art were better admired from a distance.

She was in a deep painting zone when she suddenly heard Noelle's voice again, startling her.

"Okay, this is ridiculous, I need to apologize," Noelle was saying, her hands stuffed into her pockets and her hat pulled down over her forehead.

"For what?" Miriam said, lost. And annoyed. She'd just decided to be done trying to make Noelle like her, and Noelle wouldn't go away and let her paint in peace. Couldn't she leave things be, so Miriam didn't have to think about her anymore? She set her paintbrush down a little too forcefully and turned on the ladder to look at Noelle.

"For the way I hauled off on you, after the will reading. You obviously think I still believe everything I said, and I can't let that be. Besides, I'm in this program that kind of requires I make amends when I'm an asshole."

"Wait, did I know that about you?" Miriam asked.

Noelle shrugged. "I don't drink anymore. It's not a secret."

"Congratulations. On the sobriety. That's a big deal, and it's amazing," Miriam said.

Noelle shuffled her feet in discomfort. "Yeah. It's pretty great."

Miriam tried to absorb this new information about Noelle. She had so many questions. She wanted to know everything about Noelle, her whole past and what made her tick. She tried to remind herself again that, while their short acquaintance loomed large in her consciousness, she had no real claim to Noelle's secrets.

"I shouldn't be having this conversation on top of a ladder," Miriam said, climbing slowly down. Noelle waited until she was at the bottom to continue.

"Nothing I said was fair, or true. I had you pegged wrong." Noelle took her hands out of her pockets, tried to stuff them into her hair, found her hat, huffed, and crossed her arms. It was cute—and distracting.

"Over the past few weeks, getting to know you, it's become excruciatingly obvious you're a lot more than I first judged you for." She sounded gruff, and still pained, like she was uncomfortable having this conversation and couldn't quite figure out how to say what she wanted to. Miriam realized that earlier, she might not have been damning with faint praise—she might have been trying to start this conversation and not finding the right words.

Maybe she wasn't still mad at Miriam. Maybe she just sucked at apologies.

"Even if you weren't," Noelle continued, "I had no right to talk to you that way. Can I make it up to you?" She stared at Miriam and waited.

For several heartbeats Miriam stared back.

"Why are you telling me this, now?" she finally asked.

"Other than my sponsor chewing me out for not apologizing earlier? I feel like a complete monster every time you try too hard to show me you belong here. You shouldn't have to. Cass wanted you to stay. Hannah and the Matthewses want you to. You don't need to prove anything to me." Her shoulders rose around her ears.

"I need to be really explicitly crystal clear, because I don't like guessing how people feel about me. Are you telling me right now that you don't hate me?" Miriam said carefully, feeling foolish.

"I don't hate you. I don't know you that well, but I kind of understand why Hannah, Cass, and the Matthewses think highly of you. You're fine. You have several positive qualities." Noelle ducked her head, and Miriam wanted to laugh. She truly wasn't great at this, which somehow made Miriam feel much better.

"You don't think I'd drive the business into the ground?" Miriam asked.

"You know you wouldn't drive the business into the

ground. Or further into the ground. You have a killer social media marketing game, and you know a hell of a lot about bookkeeping."

Miriam nodded. She did have those skills. "You really don't mind if I stay?"

"I know you have a lot to think about," Noelle said gruffly, not making eye contact. "Your business, your life, your engagement. Whatever your decision is, don't let how I'm going to feel about it stand in your way. You might be good for Carrigan's. You should decide if Carrigan's would be good for you."

Noelle turned to leave, then stopped and turned back. "It's like Sleeping Beauty."

Miriam tilted her head in confusion.

"What you said, before. You were sleeping, in a castle. And you were behind all these obstacles, to keep yourself from waking up," Noelle said, her hands in her pockets and her shoulders hunched. She kicked at a rock instead of making eye contact with Miriam.

Miriam almost cried. Yes, that's exactly what it was like.

"And now I have to decide whether to stay awake or go back to sleep," Miriam said, lightbulbs going off inside her.

"Can you? Go back to sleep? What did Rumi say? You must ask for what you want. Don't go back to sleep."

"Noelle Northwood, did you just quote Rumi to me?" Miriam was going to swoon. Actually, literally swoon.

"I'm wide, I contain multitudes." Noelle shrugged, her face smug.

"Rumi *and* Whitman? Show-off." Miriam was grinning, and she'd been painting, and her heart was flying. Noelle was right. She didn't know if she could ever go back to sleep.

Noelle's expression sobered. "Hey, now that we're square, can I ask you a totally inappropriate question that's none of my business?"

"Ah, the Cass Carrigan special. Sure," Miriam nodded, wondering what Noelle might want to know about her.

"What is the deal with your fiancée? You never talk about her, even as it relates to moving here. Wouldn't you both be pretty heartbroken?"

"It's hard to explain," Miriam started, trying to decide how specific to get. "We get along well, and we each have things the other needs. She needs a society wife, and I need financial stability. We keep each other company and her family leaves her alone about getting married. We're, I don't know, friends with benefits, but some of the benefits are tax-deductible. We're not in love. We never have been."

"Are you aromantic?" Noelle asked. "Because that sounds like a great marriage for a lot of aro people I know. Sex, friendship, shared bills, no chance of love."

Miriam shook her head. "No. And neither is Tara, I don't think. If we were, it might have been a wonderful queer platonic partnership. But our motives weren't that healthy. We both thought if we were already together, we wouldn't have to risk the messiness and vulnerability of falling in love. Neither of us really goes in for the unpredictable."

"That sounds like something Cass would have called hog-wash, right before doing something to make your life super unpredictable."

"Oh, like leaving me one quarter of her business?" Miriam laughed. "Yeah. She wasn't a fan."

"She was such a meddler." Noelle shook her head, smiling

ruefully. "Alright, I'll leave you to painting. I'm going to go cut down some trees. Let me know if you want to come use the chain saw. I find it very meditative when I'm having trouble with a decision."

That offer was both the nicest part of Noelle's apology and strangely hot. Miriam gave an awkward thumbs-up and turned quickly back to the wall before Noelle could read her expression. Some part of her had hoped, against all rationality, that Noelle would ask her to stay. Instead she'd told her to decide for herself.

How was Miriam supposed to know what would be good for her? She never had up to now.

Now that she knew Noelle didn't hate her, the pull she felt toward the woman wanted to burst from its chains. She wanted to ask Noelle all of her secrets. She'd never wanted to swap secrets with Tara. No matter how much she liked Tara, she didn't want to get lost in her.

Feeling that way about Noelle fit together pieces in her mind like a puzzle she'd been avoiding finishing. She might never be with Noelle, but the partnership she and Tara had planned wasn't going to work for her anymore. There was nothing wrong with a friendly respectful marriage with no romance, it just turned out she wanted something else entirely.

She needed to be honest with Tara.

Like she'd been summoned by Miriam's thoughts, a sleek blonde bob wrapped in a long white coat swept around the corner of the barn.

Miriam forgot to breathe for several beats.

"Hey, darlin," Tara said, smiling at her. "Can you show me to my room?"

"I wasn't expecting you," Miriam managed, finally, a hand to her chest. Okay, so she was going to have to be honest with Tara really soon. In person. At Carrigan's.

Wasn't expecting was an understatement. She would never have imagined that Tara would come here—would be here, incongruously, in this place. She'd told Tara they would have everything worked out by Thanksgiving, and Miriam knew the Thanksgiving meal was a huge event for the Chadwicks. She'd expected Tara to call her on Friday to check in, not to show up for the holiday. What had she said to her parents?

Cole appeared behind Tara, dragging suitcases. "I tried to stop her, but she wouldn't be stopped, so I came with her to mitigate the damage."

Tara made no sign she'd heard Cole. "Why don't you show me around?"

Miriam shook herself out of her daze. "Yes. Let's go inside." She led them in through a side entrance to the great room, where they found Hannah and Noelle. Hannah's eyebrows shot up, and Noelle looked between Tara and Miriam, crossing her arms and frowning.

"This is my cousin Hannah—" Miriam began.

"Such a pleasure to meet you, I've heard such lovely things." Tara had dropped into the debutante cadence she fell back on when she was uncomfortable or felt out of place. Miriam's heart hurt at how badly Tara was trying to be polite. "And you are?" Tara's gaze had moved to Noelle.

"As you've just walked into my home, I feel I ought to be the one asking that," Noelle said, stuffing her hands into her pockets and subtly widening her stance. She looked like a lizard frilling out its neck to threaten intruders to its territory. Why was she being so rude?

"I'm Miriam's fiancée," Tara said tightly.

Miriam stepped in. "Noelle is the manager of the tree farm. She was Aunt Cass's right-hand woman. She owns part of Carrigan's now." Miriam did not add "With me." That was not a conversation to have in the middle of the foyer.

Hannah picked up Tara's suitcase. "We're so glad to meet you. I take it you'll be joining us for Thanksgiving? I'll just put this"—she looked at Miriam, who subtly but briskly shook her head—"in the back cottage! It's so twee and comfortable, Tara, you'll be snug as a bug."

Tara's eyes went from Hannah to Miriam, and her lips flattened. She turned her best Southern Belle on Hannah and said, while her eyes also cut daggers at Miriam, "Why, that will be so wonderful, I'll adore all that privacy."

"I have to say," she told Noelle as she passed, "I love this whole dapper..." she paused, as if looking for the words, "aesthetic you've cultivated."

"I call it Farmer Dyke," Noelle said, grinning a little evilly. "And bless your heart."

Chapter 9

Noelle

That night, Noelle flopped backwards onto Hannah's bed and pulled her hair into spikes. Kringle complained about his spot being disturbed but resettled next to her head. "Please remove me from this timeline and insert me into one in which I have fewer feelings."

Hannah put her head on Noelle's stomach and looked up at her.

"Are you panicking because a certain beautiful cousin of mine is supposed to give us an answer tomorrow, or are you panicking because said cousin has a real flesh-and-blood fiancée you can no longer ignore?" Hannah asked.

"Miriam's *so* beautiful, and talented, and funny. I want to hate her, but she's actually great? Which makes me really mad?" Noelle stopped for breath. "She might be good for Carrigan's? Or she might be a flight risk who disappears as soon as we all start to rely on her? She makes everything too complicated. I don't want her to stay, because I'll want to date her and I can't. I *do* want her to stay and be single and make out with my face. I think I've been doing a great job of not freaking out about this situation up to this point, but I have reached my limit!" She pushed herself up, away from the headboard, and tugged on her hair.

Her best friend gave her a level stare. "You have been doing an absolutely terrible job of not freaking out about this but go on. Wait, first, why can't you date her? Other than the fiancée?"

"What if we broke up, and we still co-owned the farm together? It would be catastrophic!" Noelle said, throwing her arms up. Miriam was obviously trying hard to sort out the tangle of her emotions, and Noelle should not even be considering complicating that. She was a terrible person, and she should not have feelings of any kind for Miriam, and she was going to stop as soon as she figured out how.

"Yes, I cannot imagine anything worse on this Earth than co-owning Carrigan's with your ex," Hannah said.

Noelle cringed. "That was thoughtless."

Hannah waved it off. "Please continue with your freak-out."

"How can she not know what she wants? How can she not want to grab Carrigan's with both hands and never let go? I don't trust that. And now this fiancée."

Hannah sighed.

"You think I'm overreacting," Noelle pouted.

"I would never say you're overreacting, because (a) that is made-up and (b) this is the biggest decision of our lives. Also I know you haven't had a crush in over a decade so this feels fatal." Hannah coiled her hair on the top of her head in a scrunchy, like she did when she was about to do Serious Thinking. It was an impressive feat because she had Rapunzel's hair.

"Do you honestly think she can make this whole plan work?" Noelle asked.

"I don't know," Hannah said. "I think so? I don't think she's as big a flight risk as she seems. She's got an interesting perspective, and she's a successful working artist. That's hard. And she did it mostly through working her butt off and very keen marketing savvy. We maybe have a better chance of saving the farm with her."

"You know who might have an idea of what she'll do?" Noelle wondered, and then stuck her head out into the hallway.

"Nicholas!" she called, and Cole materialized, all big shoulders and blond waves and neon green seersucker shorts—an interesting choice for late November in the Adirondacks.

"You summoned?" he asked, walking in, scooping up Kringle before settling himself on the edge of the bed.

"We have a question, and you know things," Hannah told him.

Cole looked cagey. "I don't know what you're talking about."

"Calm down, we don't want hacking secrets. You know things about what Miri will do, as her best friend," Noelle explained. "And we are trying to figure out if she's going to stay or go."

Cole relaxed. "I haven't known what Miriam was going to do since she called me to say she was flying to Carrigan's. It's an all-new era for Miriam Blum. Anything could happen."

The next day, they sat down to Thanksgiving dinner gently, as if their happy facade were a physical thing that might shatter at any moment.

Like Halloween, the Thanksgiving meal had been a massive get-together in years past. Now, there were a few locals who came to have their dinner at Carrigan's, but the dining room (and the guest rooms) was mostly empty. The table, however, was overfull of traditional upstate New York food, because, Mrs. Matthews argued, it tasted better than Thanksgiving food.

"I appreciate your refusal to bow to cultural norms," Cole said, surveying the dishes.

"We secretly hate Thanksgiving," Mr. Matthews whispered.

"It's not a secret," Hannah whispered back.

"Thanksgiving," Noelle grumbled, "is the darkest day of the year. It's racist, the food is terrible, and you have to spend enforced time with your family, watching grown men get serious head injuries for fun and profit. It's a perfect storm of bad vibes."

"We used to have fun Thanksgivings with the Rosensteins," Hannah said, pushing potatoes around on her plate, "but Miriam never got to come."

"I don't think we were invited," Miriam admitted, her eyes on her plate, her voice small.

"I'm sure you were," Hannah told her, "because the aunts and uncles all complained every year that you weren't there."

"I wish we'd have come. Instead we would go to one of dad's associates' houses."

"Not fun?" Noelle guessed.

Miriam huffed out a cynical laugh. "At the party, no matter where he was in the room, Dad was watching. If we did anything he deemed unacceptable—even if we'd done it a thousand times before, even if he'd told us to do it—there would be hell to pay. Driving home afterward, I'd never know what I'd done wrong, but I always knew he was going to find something. And there were going to be consequences. Sometimes, it was only the silent treatment. Sometimes he pulled money from things he'd promised or canceled my afterschool activities or threw out my favorite stuffy while I was at school. Once, after I'd worn a bow on the wrong side of my head, he sold my horse. It was always inventive.

"It would have been great to know we were invited to the Rosensteins," Miriam concluded, twisting her napkin. "I thought they didn't want us. To be fair, I didn't blame them for not wanting to invite Dad."

"If your dad was at odds with the Rosensteins, why did he come to Carrigan's? He must have hated Cass most of all," Noelle asked. She'd wanted to understand Miriam's childhood, and now she almost wished she knew less. The idea of this funny, creative, sensitive woman as a little girl in a house that tried to break her made Noelle want to cry into her gravy.

"Oh, he did. But he would never let us come up here alone, I think because he was afraid Cass would try to spirit us out of his control. We either came with him or didn't come at all. That's why I thought this place would be full of his ghost. It's not, though. It seems like Cass managed to exorcise him." Her face had fallen.

Noelle wished she could hug her. She'd known it was more

complicated than Miriam choosing to throw away an idyllic life with Cass and the wonderful Rosensteins, but it was so much more than complicated. She'd been right that Miriam was running scared, and it seemed like she might have had good reason.

They all looked around at each other, the sadness a blanket.

"So," Tara said over a forkful of chicken riggies, "Noelle, tell me about yourself."

"Well," Noelle drawled back, "I got my master's in forestry—"

"From Yale," Hannah interrupted, because she felt it was her sacred duty to brag on Noelle.

"Fine, fine, I went to Yale," she said. "It was full of people I hated and guys named Todd. But it was a good program. I had fun. I intended to go into public land management, work for the Parks Service, maybe."

She'd always wanted to work outdoors, and she'd thought a little cabin on the edge of the Grand Canyon might suit her, with just herself and her books. A meeting in Flagstaff when she got lonely. Unlike people, nature was never a disappointment.

"What happened?" Miriam asked, finally looking up from her plate. She had schooled her features back to neutral, although she was still hunched in on herself.

"My parents died suddenly," Noelle said. "And we were on pretty shaky terms at the time. I kind of ran away from my life for a while. Spent six years wandering around the world, working on sustainable development farms, being inaccessible to anyone I had an emotional attachment to, basically."

As she said this, she realized she'd done pretty much exactly

what she'd accused Miriam of doing, and maybe to a greater
degree than Miriam ever had. She shifted uncomfortably in
her seat, thinking maybe she'd been judging herself, instead
of Miriam.

This dinner had too many emotional revelations. Thanksgiving was the worst.

"How did you end up at Carrigan's?" Cole looked fasci-
nated, probably because he was imagining himself with a
manbun and a puka shell necklace, planting crops next to an
adoring vegan girl. She had only ever seen Cole in boat shoes,
so she wasn't sure he was cut out for farming.

"A college friend got married here, and I came back to the
States for the wedding," Noelle explained. "I lost touch with
the friend but kept Carrigan's."

"Basically, I kidnapped her and made her be my best
friend," Hannah said.

She'd been sucked out of her lonely life path by Hannah—
without her she might still be refusing to form emotional
attachments, like Miriam. Speaking of Miriam's questionable
emotional attachments...

"What's your whole deal?" Noelle asked Tara, feeling
prickly about how she wasn't doing anything Noelle could
see to soothe Miriam's pain. It was petty, but Noelle wanted
to see if she could get Tara's ice queen facade to break. "You
kind of live off antebellum power and money, right? What's
that like?"

Cole choked on his soda. Hannah put her hands over
her mouth.

"It's shitty, is how it is," Tara said, meeting Noelle's eyes. "I
went into criminal defense law with an idea about overhauling

the whole broken criminal justice system, and I can't tell if I'm helping at all. I keep ties to my family because I worry that giving up access and leverage won't help anyone, and it's better to try to fix it from inside, which might be an excuse. I haven't figured out what's right, yet. I don't spend my weekends assuaging my white guilt by doxxing white nationalists, like some people"—Tara looked pointedly at Cole, who was staring very intently at his plate—"but I try to take cues from the Black leaders in Charleston on how the hell to make it better instead of worse."

Damn, that was a good answer.

Noelle speared a slice of turkey a little too hard. It almost made her like Tara, which bugged her. She should have gone to Elijah and Jason's Friendsgiving and avoided this entire scene. She had to stop prejudging people and putting her foot in her mouth. At least now she'd gotten to see a glimpse of what Miriam might see in Tara, which made her less confused about how they'd ended up together. "Sorry, I shouldn't have assumed the worst."

"No, it's fine," Tara said primly, setting her silverware down on her plate with practiced manners. "I know who my family is. I would have made that assumption, too."

"What do you do, Cole?" Mrs. Matthews asked, obviously trying to turn the conversation. Cole stuffed a whole roll in his mouth, and then pointed at it to indicate that he couldn't answer with his mouth full.

Hannah started talking about a new show she and Miriam were watching. They made it to pie without anyone digging further into their family trauma.

The next day was Black Friday, and they were busy with

customers for twelve hours. Noelle saw Miriam hauling trees, with no sign of Tara, who they'd stuck at the cash register. She had no idea if Miriam had told Tara what was going on, or what her decision might be about staying.

They got to closing time with no indication of either.

Chapter 10

Miriam

At eight, they finally closed the farm to customers—hours past when they should have—and fell onto the couches in the great room. Miriam was past due to decide if she was going home with Tara, or staying here, and even more past due talking to Tara about it.

Charleston, electric with possibility, was ready and waiting. In the opposite direction, she had a half-empty inn full of ghosts she couldn't exorcise and missing its most important resident. What magnet kept drawing her to say yes to Carrigan's? Nostalgia? An opportunity to know her extended family? People who had always seen the real her—and liked that person?

Or, she thought, looking over at where Noelle had pushed up the sleeves of her hoodie and crossed her booted feet, was it simpler than that? Now that she knew that somewhere in the world, there was a handsome woman who gave her butterflies, who took her seriously and saw her, could she go back to her old life? She could hear Cass in her head, telling her that real things were always harder but that a real life was always better lived.

Before Miriam could get up the courage to pull Tara aside, Cole tromped down the stairs, declaring that there was absolutely no day like today to go Christmas caroling and see the town, and everyone was coming.

So Noelle, Miriam, Tara, and Hannah found themselves bundled up to their eyeballs against freezing gusts of wind, exhausted to the point of delirium, singing through their scarves to the residents of Advent. Along the way, they picked up Elijah, who left Jason at home with the twins, and put on a Christmas bow tie to join them. They knocked on doors hung with wreaths and mistletoe, on houses so covered in Christmas lights that Miriam wondered if you could see the tiny village from space.

Tara, who was good at everything she did—because she never did anything she wasn't good at—sung beautifully. Cole sung enthusiastically and better than he had any right to, a result of a decade in an Episcopal choir. Hannah and Miriam made up lyrics to carols they knew only peripherally. Elijah could not sing on key at all, but he knew all the words, and he could project. Noelle hummed loudly.

They did not sound good, as a group.

It felt magical. Miriam was the most present she'd been, in the moment, in her body, in maybe all her life, and she wanted to keep that feeling. She wanted to stay here, in her little Christmasland next to this strange, tiny, festive town, with these people who brought her back to herself. It would be a huge risk, and it was impractical and illogical and maybe a terrible idea, and she wanted it.

This was where she belonged.

As they walked through town, they were joined, impromptu, by people happy for any opportunity for something to do on a Friday night. Miriam could not have imagined that any of the Carrigan's team were ready to laugh, especially not to laugh until they cried and the tears froze in their eyelashes, but they were and they did. It was, she realized, the first time she and Tara had laughed together in months.

I should be streaming, she thought before shaking her head. This moment wasn't for the Bloomers, it was for her. The real her, no masks. When they all decided that caroling was not worth losing fingers to frostbite, they descended on Ernie's, the tiny dive bar / music venue / dinner hangout on Main Street.

Advent's Main Street was full of renovated historic facades, rows of clapboard stores with white trim in a rainbow of colors. Ernie's was a long skinny room with a stage at the back and a wall of local moonshine. The wood-paneled walls were bursting at the seams with punch-drunk carolers yelling over each other to order French fries, beer, and anything that might warm them up. Miriam snapped pictures and texted them to her Old Ladies, who loved a dimly lit party full of alcohol and carbs.

Cole swooped on a big corner booth, so the five of them smooshed into it. Miriam was, ironically, pressed up against both Tara and Noelle. Elijah took one look at the booth and shook his head. "No way am I smooshing these newly ironed slacks into that mess!" he shouted over the din. "Someone's starting a Scrabble game, you know where to find me."

Noelle reached her arms out to him. "Don't abandon me, my love!"

"You know I can't resist the siren call of a Scrabble board."
He held up his hands, feigning helplessness.

"Leave them with some dignity," she told him.

He rearranged his bow tie and folded his jacket over his
arm. "I can't make any promises."

Noelle turned back to the table and said, deadly seriously,
"Never let him scam you into a game of Scrabble."

"This is a scene from *Rent!*" Hannah called as the noise
crescendoed.

"VIVA LA—!" Cole and Noelle began, in unison, before
collapsing into giggles.

A young Black woman with box braids and an impeccable
red lip, wearing an apron and carrying an order pad, walked
up, eyeing them warily.

"Are your friends okay?" she asked Hannah. Hannah made
a "so-so" gesture while Miriam fought back tears as she tried
to stop giggling. "Wait"—she squinted at Miriam through
cat-eye glasses—"you look just like Cass."

Miriam came up short.

"I do," she said. "I'm Miriam Blum, I'm—"

"Ooooh, you're the long-lost Miriam. Cass talked about
you a lot."

She stuck her pad in her apron and held out her hand. "I'm
Ernie. This is my place."

Miriam shook it. "Your place is incredible. Thank you for
accommodating this last-minute deluge of ridiculous singing
people."

Ernie smirked. "Y'all aren't nearly as bad as the tourists.
What can I bring you?"

Hannah took over. "We want two of the Fried Everything

platters, Cass-style, to start with, please, while these hooligans settle down enough to figure out what they want to eat. And, a pitcher?" She looked around, shaking her head at them. "Does everyone but Noelle want beer?"

"Cole also doesn't drink," Miriam said. "Bring him anything with caffeine and sugar, he'll be fine. Wait, what's Cass-style?" She flipped over the menu, trying to find what she'd missed.

"Everything's kosher," Noelle said. "It's on the secret menu." Warmth washed over Miriam at the idea that this small-town dive bar had loved her aunt Cass so much, they had a secret kosher menu.

Noelle turned to Cole. "You don't drink, either?"

Cole was busy building an elaborate structure out of sugar packets. Ernie was watching him like he was an overgrown child who should not be allowed out by himself.

"Nah," Cole said. "Both my parents are alcoholics, seems like genetic Russian roulette tee-bee-aitch. I mean, never tell them I said that. They don't think they're alcoholics, just 'well pickled.' Anyway"—he did spirit fingers—"I make enough bad decisions without adding a lack of inhibitions. What about you?"

"I played the game of genetics and lost," Noelle admitted. "I drank my whole lifetime share of beer before my twenty-first birthday, so now I let other people drink instead."

Miriam was torn between loving Noelle and Cole bonding and dreading that she had to talk to Tara, pretty much immediately. She turned to Ernie, who was waiting for them to decide, and said, "A pitcher of hot cocoa, if you please."

Ernie went to leave until Miriam called out, "Wait! This

is very important. Is your lipstick transfer proof?" If she was staying here, she was going to start making friends, and this seemed like the place to start.

"It'll still be on when I'm buried, probably," Ernie said. "I'll write all the details on the check."

"You're an angel," Miriam told her seriously.

Ernie looked down at her beer-soaked Ramones shirt, torn-up skinny jeans, and decade-old Chucks and nodded. "I am."

"Is that why things were tense with your parents? The alcoholism?" Tara asked Noelle, sounding genuinely interested, the ice in her tone thawed. When her hair brushed past Miriam, it smelled like star jasmine, cutting through the grease and hops and musk. The floral smell was comforting, but it didn't make fireworks explode inside her the way Noelle's citrus and Old Spice did.

"Pretty much," Noelle said. "I quit drinking and they didn't. They always kind of felt like I was abandoning them." She took all the menus and stacked them precisely on top of each other, lining up all the corners.

Ernie came back with a massive platter of fried foods. Miriam coordinated with Hannah on their complicated childhood dance of mixing the side of ranch with hot sauce and testing it carefully for taste. That familiar ritual, done without thought, opened a door inside Miriam she'd forgotten even existed in the past decade.

You can be known, her heart whispered to her. *You can be at home in your skin and stop running.*

"Does anyone have functional, happy parents?" Cole asked, waving a fried pickle at the table. "I know Tara and I don't!"

"I do!" Hannah said, snagging the pickle from him and eating it. "I mean, they dragged me all over the world as a child and now I have crippling panic attacks about the very idea of leaving Carrigan's, but that has more to do with my anxiety than anything they did wrong. They were doing their best. How were they to know I'd develop a desperate need to control my surroundings?" She laughed hollowly, and then said, too brightly, "Let's change the subject. Cole! What's a movie you've watched so many times you could recite it start to finish, and none of your friends will watch it with you?"

They played the time-honored xennial game of getting to know each other through beloved nostalgic pop culture (Cole's answer was *My Cousin Vinny*, Noelle's *Drop Dead Gorgeous*).

They were still arguing about the relative merits of Madonna versus early Green Day when their meals came. Hannah and Noelle stood firm with Tara on the side of Green Day, while Miriam and Cole threatened to burst into "Like a Prayer." Cole stole half of Miriam's onion rings, Hannah stole half of Cole's sandwich, and Tara and Noelle swapped pickles for tomatoes.

"How did you guys meet?" Hannah said, gesturing between Miriam and Tara. Tara nodded at Miriam, giving her the reins of the story.

"Cole and I met the first day of freshman orientation, in college," Miriam said, "and were inseparable ever after. When I needed a place to stay after things exploded with my parents, I went to Cole's place in Charleston. Tara was at Duke Law but kept coming home for family obligations. They have all the same friends, so we kept running into each other."

She realized it was more a story about Cole than it was about her and Tara, which probably said something. But how did she explain that she and Tara had seen kindred spirits in each other, each needing a safe harbor in another person who would not press too hard on their open wounds?

While they waited for the check, Cole and Miriam went to find the bathroom, arguing along the way about the best Darcy, a fight they'd been having for years, when someone from behind the bar interrupted, "It's obviously *The Lizzie Bennet Diaries.*"

They both spun to find a short man with long, dark hair, an old-fashioned waxed moustache, and a button-down shirt covered in flying pigs, holding a bottle of whiskey and grinning at them—although mostly, Miriam noticed, at Cole.

Cole answered his smile and pointed. "Yes! Miriam, *finally* someone understands!" He moved to shake the man's hand. "Nicholas Jedediah Fraser IV. Cole to my friends, which you obviously are."

The man was dwarfed by Cole's size but seemed totally unfazed by his exuberance. He shook Cole's hand back, hard. "It is entirely my pleasure, Nicholas Jedediah. Sawyer Bright." The upward tilt of his head, and the glint in his eye, told Miriam that he was flirting. Miriam wasn't sure Cole had noticed. Cole's base interaction with all of humanity looked like flirting to most people.

He winked theatrically at Sawyer and hit the bar with his palm. "To be continued," he said to the bartender, before he swept away.

When Ernie brought them their bill, Tara, true to form, insisted on paying it.

"You should join us for pub quiz next week," Ernie said to Miriam. "Elijah and Jason run it, and it's kind of the only fun to be had in this town if you're between twenty-five and fifty."

"She won't still be here this weekend," Tara said, her drawl thick and excruciatingly polite. "She's coming home with me, to Charleston."

"Oh," Ernie said, looking at Hannah in confusion. "I thought Cass... Never mind. I'll be back later to check on you."

"What was that about?" Tara asked pointedly, her eyes cutting between Cole and Miriam. Cole ducked his head, and Tara reached over and flicked him. He looked up at Miriam, his sea-blue eyes beseeching.

He never had been able to say no to Tara, and Miriam knew it wasn't fair to make him tell her this. Miriam had to get her shit together, she'd already fucked up badly by not being honest. She didn't know if there was any way to mitigate the damage at this point. It might be too late to make amends, and Tara might genuinely not forgive her, but she could do the right thing anyway.

"Can we go outside to talk?" she asked. She knew Tara hated when laundry was aired in public.

Tara turned to face her, her blue eyes iced over and her movements precise. "Well," she began, her drawl like molasses, "I would say that since all these people already know our business, it could not possibly hurt to discuss it in front of them, as I am clearly the only person who does not know what's happening, but I would not want to put them in the situation of feeling uncomfortable, since I suspect they have done nothing to deserve that."

Tara's tone was cold enough to freeze Miriam over. She deserved it. Cole scooted out of the booth to let them out, grimacing at her behind Tara's back.

As soon as they were outside, Miriam began talking before she could lose her nerve. "Cass left me a quarter of Carrigan's," Miriam said in a rush of air. "At first I thought I'd give it to Noelle and Hannah, but Tara . . . I really want to stay here. I want to set up a shop, and help them get the business back on its feet, and lure tourists here to sell them art. I can't stop wanting it." She had wrapped her arms around her, both for warmth and in some misguided attempt to protect her from Tara's response.

They stood in silence. The dam inside Tara that kept her from yelling in public remained unbreachable.

Finally, she spoke. "You couldn't have told me this over the phone?" Her voice was quiet, and Miriam strained to hear. "Before I made excuses to everyone in my life about where you were? Before I looked a fool? What about the store, Miri? What about our life? Was I so impossible to talk to that you couldn't tell me this thing that's upending our entire future?!"

"I talked myself out of telling you because I was scared. I should have trusted you more," Miriam said, chewing on her lip. "My head was a mess, and I handled all of it poorly, and that wasn't fair to you. To our deal with each other. I was a really shitty co-conspirator."

"Did you do this so I would keep paying the lease on your studio?" Tara accused.

"No!" Miriam said immediately, horrified. "I promise, no. It wasn't that mercenary. I just didn't know how to make you understand where my heart was." Miriam ran her hands through her hair, and wondered how Tara managed to look completely, perfectly polished in the middle of a breakup fight. Probably another sign that they were wrong for each other, the fact that she couldn't ever fluster Tara.

"You're right. I would not have understood giving up our beautiful home, a fascinating city, all the good work we were doing, to live in a ramshackle dying inn with molding parrot-print wallpaper, in the middle of the woods, surrounded by nothing but trees and lakes as far as the eye can see. This would never be what my heart could want."

"Cass—" Miriam started.

Tara cut her off. "All weekend I've heard about the magical Cass." That Southern drawl somehow made her sarcasm extra sarcastic. "But you can't use her as an excuse with me, because you never introduced me to her."

"I deserve that," Miriam conceded. "I just didn't think you wanted to deal with all the baggage that came with Carrigan's."

"Maybe you're right. Maybe I wouldn't have." Tara shook her head. "I'm tired, Miri. I know we're not some great love story. It's fine if you came up here and realized you needed something different. It's reasonable to decide you want to fall in love. But we're friends. We were a team. You should have told me the truth."

"I didn't know if I would be brave enough to stay," Miriam admitted. Saying the truth out loud, to Tara, made it so real. The part of her heart that always hid from realness was screaming at her, even as the rest of her breathed a sigh of relief. It was all out there now. She couldn't take it back.

"I've never seen you happier than you are, here," Tara told her, stuffing her hands in her jacket pockets. "I didn't even know this side of you existed. I'm glad you're staying, if this is who you are when you're at Carrigan's. And maybe you didn't tell me because I'm hard to talk to about emotions, or because I would have tried to lawyer you into the rational choice, but now I'm out here in the snow getting dumped, instead of with my family for the holidays, because you were scared."

Every day since she'd arrived at Carrigan's, Miriam had been forced to confront the fact that she'd hurt people she cared about by shielding herself from reality and avoiding difficult conversations. She owed Tara better than that, and Miriam wanted to believe she was becoming better than that.

"You're right. You deserved honesty, and I was too scared to even be honest with myself. Let me try now. I love it here, and I want to stay."

Tara chuckled sadly. "God, you're a mess, Miriam Blum. I didn't even know you had it in you to be this chaotic. I'm kind of glad for you. One of us should be able to lose her shit. And to be honest, this is low in the ranking of worst Thanksgivings of my life."

"Maybe next holiday season, you'll fall in love and throw your life into chaos," Miriam said, cautiously hopeful that they might end on, if not good terms, at least not catastrophic ones.

"You shut your mouth," Tara said, sounding horrified and crossing herself. She opened the bar door and leaned her head in, yelling, "Cole, you're driving me to the train station."

Cole ran out the door, followed by Hannah. "Ooh, stealing cars at midnight," Cole said, jacket in hand. "We haven't done that since middle school."

Hannah squeezed Miriam's hand. "I'll go with them to make sure they take a farm truck instead of Noelle's truck."

Tara took one last look at Miriam. "Don't call me for awhile." Miriam nodded. It was better than she'd hoped for.

Once they were gone, Miriam slid back into the booth across from Noelle, who had been left alone, an ocean of cold leftover onion rings in front of her.

"Well, you fucked that up pretty good," Noelle said. She took a small wooden duck out of one inside pocket of her coat, and a knife from another, and began whittling, not looking at Miriam.

"You're not wrong," Miriam agreed, leaning her head back against the booth and closing her eyes.

"What are you going to do now?"

Miriam thought for a long minute. "Order more fried food and cry into the plate?" she speculated.

She was deeply regretful that she'd hurt Tara. They had been together for years, and even if they weren't in love, they had loved each other. Miriam wanted to honor that by mourning the end of their relationship. But she was also relieved, which made her feel like an asshole. She wanted to get on with her new life, let herself become giddy with possibilities. To see how she really felt about Noelle, now that she wasn't engaged.

It was a lot of feelings to try to have at once, for someone not used to having any.

"I meant more big picture," Noelle said, and Miriam picked

up her head from the booth. Noelle sat forward, looking her in the eyes. "What do you want, Miriam Blum?"

Miriam took a fortifying breath and practiced telling the truth again.

"I want you to ask me to stay."

PART 2

Thanksgiving to Christmas

Chapter 11

Noelle

Miriam was twisting her hands again, paint and glitter still caught under her short nails. Noelle reached over and put her own hands, rough and work-hardened, over Miriam's. Seeing her with Tara had made it impossible for Noelle to ignore how she felt about Miriam. Noelle's rational adult brain understood that their being together would, in fact, be a huge, potentially disastrous complication. They'd only known each other a month. Yet Noelle wanted her to stay. Even if they never got together.

Because she didn't want a Carrigan's without Miriam Blum.

She didn't know where to start, so what she said was "I need to tell you, there hasn't been anyone in my life, since my parents died. I have a really hard time trusting that people won't leave and allowing myself to rely on people. I don't know that it's going to be better, now, with Cass gone, too."

"You rely on Hannah," Miriam pointed out.

"Hannah literally stops breathing if she goes past the city limits of Advent," Noelle deadpanned. "I know she's not leaving me, as long as I'm at Carrigan's."

"That's not why, and we both know it. Hannah's a rock," Miriam argued. Noelle smiled. Hannah was that. "And I'm not. I left everyone, and you don't think you can trust me not to leave you."

Noelle ran her hands through her hair. "Look, I know you left because of something your dad did, and not because you decided you didn't care about your family anymore..." she began.

"But I still ran, and stayed running, and never explained to Hannah or Levi or the Matthewses why I wasn't coming home," Miriam finished for her. "I still seem like a flight risk."

Maybe, if she wasn't still smarting about how Cass had chosen to leave things, Noelle wouldn't be so gun-shy. Or if her parents hadn't walked away from her. This was who she was, though, this was what her sore spots were. She couldn't unprogram her buttons just because she recognized them.

Why did Cass have to choose *this* woman, who she must have known would get into every crack in Noelle's armor, to share the business? Was she trying, from beyond the grave, to push Noelle into outgrowing her old fears? It was something Cass would do, manipulating all of them because she'd decided Miriam and Noelle needed it, and that brought a fresh wave of frustration at Cass. It wasn't fair that Cass had waited until she was gone to spring this on her, so that Noelle couldn't yell at her.

Miriam sat watching her, waiting for a response.

"Can we be honest? I just watched you break up with your fiancée and you might not need one more thing to add to your mess, emotionally. You seem like you might be at capacity."

"You're not wrong," Miriam conceded. She leaned forward, her elbows propped on the table. "I'm not asking you to marry me, Noelle. I'm not even asking you to kiss me. I don't know what's going to happen with whatever this attraction is between us. I'm asking if you want my help saving this farm."

"Saving the farm is almost more serious than whatever might or might not happen between us in the future. Carrigan's Christmasland is critical to me. If I trust you to be all in on the farm, what happens if you get spooked again? Are you going to run?" Noelle held Miriam's eyes because she needed to know that Miriam had thought about this.

"I'm not running away from Carrigan's again," Miriam said seriously. "I promise."

Noelle didn't really believe her, but she was willing to give Miriam an opportunity to prove her wrong.

"You know it's going to be awkward. With the..." Noelle paused, trying to think of the words.

"Constant desire on my part to do filthy things to your thighs? Yes. I know," Miriam said. "I'll try to keep my hands to myself." She planted them on the table as if to demonstrate.

Noelle stared at her. Where had this Miriam come from?

"Sorry! That was too far. I seem to have lost my filter tonight. Blame it on emotional exhaustion." Miriam giggled. "But if I'm staying, we should have all our cards on the table, know where we stand. I'm not ready to get into anything romantic again right now. I need to get my head on straight."

"And I am going to have to do a lot of work on trust before I get involved with anyone," Noelle agreed, relieved that she didn't have to let Miriam down gently.

"Good. We're on the same page. What about your shop?" Noelle asked. "Hannah made it sound like it was everything you'd ever wanted."

Miriam's eyes filled up. "It was. It was all of my dreams," she admitted, running her free hand through her curls to shake them out. Noelle had to stop herself from audibly gasping. Miriam's curls made her think about pillows and beds and what her hair would look like spread out on them. Now was not the time.

They were having a serious emotional moment. About feelings. Not pantsfeelings, but actual heart feelings.

Miriam continued, "I'm going to build new dreams of my shop here, to help me let go of that very beautiful dream of a perfect little shop in the city."

"I'm sorry," Noelle said.

"I'm not." Miriam shook her head, her voice steady.

"Hannah needs you, to talk to about Levi," Noelle said. "I'll never understand why she loves him, so there are ways I can't help."

"That doesn't sound like asking me to stay," Miriam pointed out. "Wait, what's happening with this duck?"

Noelle looked down at the piece of wood she had been whittling to keep her anxiety at bay. "I'm making Christmas gifts for the Green twins. It's Carrigan's pine."

"That's cute. Sorry. I distracted you." Miriam looked up from beneath her lashes and grinned. "You were about to ask me to stay."

Noelle swallowed hard. "Miriam Blum, will you stay at Carrigan's and help us save Christmasland?" she asked, holding out her hand.

Miriam's face transformed with joy. God, Noelle had known this woman was trouble the first time she saw her, she just never imagined how much.

"Hell yes, I will." Miriam grinned, shaking Noelle's hand. "Let's call the Rosensteins with our plan."

"Let's have *Hannah* call the Rosensteins with our plan," Noelle amended. "You know how she gets when she's not included."

"Can we go home now?" Miriam sounded punch-drunk. She was starting to list over in her seat. "I need to talk to Hannah. And the Matthewses. Then I need to sleep a lot."

Noelle's eyes unexpectedly filled with tears. Miriam being at Carrigan's might disrupt her whole life, but it would also settle something big inside the hearts of the people she loved best. She knew the hole Miriam had left in their lives, and she hoped this really was for good.

Because it was going to be so much worse if she left again now.

* * *

With a plan in place, Hannah and Miriam spent the next week hunkered down in the office: outlining all the businesses in Advent they could partner with, building a multipronged PR strategy, researching permits they would need to file and the best places to rent tents and generators and table linens in the area. Hannah was in heaven.

Noelle felt a little left out, watching them together, but not as territorial as she had a few weeks ago. She was used to being a two-person team with Hannah, and she'd expected to feel threatened by the closeness Hannah and Miriam were rediscovering. Instead she felt mostly grateful. She had always worried that, if she ever got seriously involved with a woman again, she'd have a hard time balancing her closeness with Hannah with a romance. Miriam understood, perfectly, what it meant to have a best friend who was half of you, and she and Hannah had their own connection.

Not that she and Miriam were having a romance. They'd been very clear with each other about that. Saving the farm came first. Making out came later—or maybe never.

Noelle sometimes stuck her head in, bringing them sandwiches so they would remember to eat. At the end of the week, she told them she was heading to Plattsburgh with Elijah to take the twins to the children's museum. They glanced up, Hannah's burnished gold head nestled next to Miriam's giant halo of near-black curls, and Noelle's heart turned over. Miriam was flushed with pleasure as Hannah listened to her describe an idea, and Noelle wondered how often people took her seriously. In a flash, Noelle saw what Cass must have seen in Miriam, a brilliant mind full of too much art, constantly trying to make herself smaller so as not to attract her dad's attention, while also bursting to prove herself, to anyone.

"How are things going with the pretty interloper?" Elijah teased when she showed up at his house for their field trip.

"If you give me shit, I will not give you these cookies that Mrs. Matthews sent," Noelle warned.

Elijah grabbed the bag. "Noelle has a crush! She wants to kiss the girl!" he sang to Jason, as he walked off to make sure the twins had peed and put on all their mittens and hats. Noelle scowled. Why did she have friends? He was right though.

She really wanted to kiss the girl.

When thoughts of making out kept her up until three a.m., Noelle wandered down to the kitchen to steal treats from Mrs. Matthews's stash. Instead of cookies, she found an elf with an apron on, standing in the middle of Mrs. Matthews's spotless blue delft kitchen (in need of new appliances, only where would they find the money?), rolling out dough with an old wooden rolling pin. Noelle propped herself against the doorway, arms crossed, watching Miriam hum to herself. Her little wild soul wrapped up in this domestic scene did something to Noelle's insides.

"What are you doing up?" she asked, instead of wiping the flour off Miriam's face and then leaning her up against the counter for a kiss, which is what she wanted to do.

Miriam startled, and her eyes widened.

"What?" Noelle asked.

"You're standing under the mistletoe," Miriam choked out. Noelle flashed her a grin. She wasn't the only one thinking about kissing. She looked up, deliberately, at the mistletoe, and then moved out of the doorway toward the kitchen counter. This was where she'd first seen Miriam, but now their spots were reversed.

Miriam watched her approach before turning her attention back to the massive butcher block under her hands. "A Thing To Do," she began, "when one is trying to distract oneself from a breakup or avoid one's feelings of having failed one's family, is to bake."

Noelle noticed how she spoke like she was thinking about her feelings, instead of feeling them.

"I'm a Rosenstein," Miriam continued, as if that was a full explanation. It was, Noelle supposed.

"So you're making cookies? With...fig jam?" She looked more closely.

"These are poppyseed rugelach," Miriam gestured, "which are pastries, not cookies. From the secret family recipe that is only available in the Rosenstein's flagship storefront, and only during Hanukkah. They are made of magic, and I was craving them."

"Processing the breakup, huh? Also I know what rugelach are, please. I'm not new." She reached over the counter to where Miriam had made a pot of coffee and filled a cup for herself. Miriam dolloped the exact right amount of cream in it for her, and there were those feelings, again.

"Do you have secret breakup rituals?" Miriam asked, waving Noelle over to her side of the counter. "Here, spoon filling in this batch then I'll show you how to roll them." She scooted over bowls and carefully arranged dough, creating a second station so they could work side by side.

"I listen to Soul Asylum's 'Runaway Train' on repeat until

I'm so sick of myself that I have to get my shit together," Noelle said as she carefully portioned out poppyseed spread.

"Does it work?" Miriam laughed, leaning over to roll the pastry carefully. She watched Noelle copy her movements and nodded her approval. When their arms brushed, Noelle's heart raced.

"It's at least less self-destructive than the way I used to get over breakups, which was getting blackout drunk," Noelle pointed out. She tucked one of Miriam's errant curls behind an ear. Miriam licked her lip and ducked her head. Noelle felt a surge of victory that she was getting to Miriam just as much as Miriam was to her.

"I'm glad you've moved on to moody nineties rock," Miriam said softly. "Solid choice." She held a clean spoon with fig filling up to Noelle's mouth to taste. Noelle tried to remember what they were talking about. Oh, right, breakups—because Miriam was in the middle of a big one and didn't need Noelle to move on her, immediately after saying she wouldn't.

She was watching Miriam roll pastry, mesmerized by the movement of her hands, when Miriam surprised her by saying, "When I was fighting with my mom, you said you understood having a complicated relationship with your parents, but I didn't realize . . ." She shook her head. "Anyway, I thought you were just trying to tell me what to do. I didn't realize you'd lost your parents, without getting to reconcile. I'm sorry. And thank you, for not telling me I should reconcile with my dad, because I might regret it otherwise. I get that a lot."

"Are we really going to talk about our parents right now?" Noelle grimaced.

Miriam shrugged. "I'm trying to get to know the woman behind the suspenders. You know all about my demons."

Noelle conceded that they might be uneven in the sharing of personal secrets department. "No one cuts their parents off lightly, and I don't think we're put on this Earth to spend time with people who are shitty to us, just because we're kin. I wish I'd reconciled with mine, maybe, but I don't know what I would have done differently. I still would have gotten sober, still would have drawn boundaries. I definitely shouldn't tell other people what to do about their parents, which I was doing, by the way, because I'm nosy. I'm sorry about that."

"Honestly, I've been hoping all my life that someone would tell me what to do about my parents." Miriam laughed a little caustically.

Noelle tried to figure out how to explain something she rarely talked about with anyone. "Sometimes I wish I had more time, or more closure, just because I've spent so much time since they died trying to prove them wrong or prove that I'm not them. If they were here, I might be able to just live, instead of reacting to them."

"What do you mean?" Miriam had scooted up onto the counter and was leaning forward, listening.

"My parents did a lot of promising they would do things, be places, then not following through, because they were drunk, and that's what drunks do." Noelle kept spreading jam on pastry, so she didn't have to look at Miriam.

"And that's why you try to always show up for people?" Miriam guessed.

"I think so. And maybe part of me thinks I just wasn't a good enough daughter, but if I can be perfect for everyone else, I won't get left again." This was incredibly uncomfortable to admit. Could they go back to talking about Miriam's problems, now?

Miriam hopped down off the counter, brushing her hands on her apron, leaving big streaks of flour. "Thank you for telling me that. You seem so stable. It's nice to know you're a mess, too, in some ways. I like messy you. She's pretty great." Miriam smiled shyly.

Noelle looked down into her face, trying to receive the gift of those words. She *was* a mess, and she was always trying to hide it. Could Miriam actually like her messy side? The idea of someone seeing her poorly repaired cracks and still wanting to kiss her was . . . nearly irresistible.

Miriam Blum made her want dangerous things.

She shook her head, trying to stop from building castles in the sky, populated by princesses with giant hair. Miriam might be alluringly supportive in this middle-of-the-night tête-à-tête, but that didn't mean Noelle needed to dump all her baggage on the woman (and then kiss her in the middle of Mrs. Matthews's kitchen).

"How long do these take to bake?" Noelle asked, to distract herself.

"You have a little filling, right here," Miriam said, instead of answering Noelle's question. She leaned over, brushing her thumb over the corner of Noelle's mouth before licking the filling off the pad of her finger, never taking her eyes from Noelle's.

"That was evil," Noelle said, desire sparking all along her body, little dancing flames along her skin. She was trying so hard to behave, but Miriam was making it so difficult. "I didn't know you had an evil streak."

"I had a fiancée," Miriam said. "I hadn't started flirting yet."

"I thought we agreed—"

Miriam's eyes sparkled with mischief. "We agreed we weren't dating. We didn't agree I couldn't flirt with you. Although I'll stop, if you want me to."

Noelle did not want her to stop.

"I'm going to bed before I get into trouble." She stepped deliberately away, shaking her head and smiling a little, her hands flexing in a battle to take control from her brain and touch Miriam, everywhere. "Save me some rugelach for the morning."

Chapter 12

Miriam

Miriam did not sleep that night, just listened to Soul Asylum and watched pastry cool until the sun rose. Her skin felt hungry, and the butterflies in her stomach were starting to reproduce at an alarming rate. Noelle disturbed her life, made her think about her choices, made her be present in her body. A month ago, Miriam would have said that was the last thing she wanted, but now she couldn't stop wanting it.

She missed Cole. If he were here, he would distract her.

She'd made him go home, to Charleston, to his boat and his job (whatever that was). Cole had tried to convince her he could stay through Christmas, that he could set up an office here. She loved, so much, that he would offer to make his life wherever she was, but she couldn't let him. "I'm FaceTiming you EVERY DAY," he'd said. "If you need me, I will break the sound barrier to get here to you."

"I know," she'd told him, and she *had* known. Her heart had understood that he would always have her back, no matter what, and that allowed her to let him out of her sight. Tara and Charleston might have been temporary, but Cole was her person forever.

She called him once the sun was up, his huge face appearing on her screen.

"Miriam Blum, are you eating rugelach for breakfast?" he asked, instead of saying hello.

"I mean, it's a breakfast food," she said, defensively.

"I haven't seen you eat a vegetable since you got to Carrigan's, except for three candied carrots at Thanksgiving."

"There were potatoes with dinner yesterday!" Miriam protested. "I take a multivitamin!"

"Potatoes are a carb," he recited, a little primly.

"Nicholas Jedediah Fraser," she said, "you sound like your mother. It is not a good look." Telling Cole he was behaving like his mother was the fastest way to get him to stop doing whatever awful, WASP-y thing he didn't realize he was doing. Like food policing.

"Oh, jeez, babe, I'm sorry," he said immediately, his eyes widening with horror. "Can I start over? Are you okay? Are you hiding? Why are you still in bed? Wait, let me put my phone down." The angle changed steeply and then he was back, his chin propped on his fist.

"I haven't slept yet," she admitted. "If I tell you something, will you promise to try so, so hard not to make fun of me?"

Cole rubbed his hands together in mock villainous glee. "I will solemnly promise to try."

"I have"—Miriam grimaced—"a crush. On Noelle." She

hid her face in her hands before peeking through her fingers at Cole.

He was trying to school his face into something that resembled shock. He failed.

"Miriam, I'm sorry, did you think this was a secret?" he asked. "Your pupils dilate, your cheeks flush, and your hairline sweats. Like, the moment she walks into a room. You're basically a walking pheromone."

"She's so hot," Miriam sighed. "But you didn't say anything. You've never not said anything. Ever. About anything."

Cole shrugged. "I was waiting for you to be ready to talk about it."

"I can't really, right? Have feelings for her? It's just that I'm grieving Cass and searching for some kind of lifeboat, and I snagged on Noelle because she loved Cass, too." Miriam asked. "Please tell me I'm imagining this. I've known her for like four minutes."

"Or you've been in close proximity for a month and a half," Cole said, "and sometimes it only takes a minute to meet the right one. It's true she's not your usual type. She's not blonde *or* intense and disconcerting. I guess you might be rebounding. But I did say we were going to find love up in the mountains!"

"I do not only date intense blonde women, Cole," Miriam protested.

"No, sometimes you date intense blond nonbinary people, and there was that very ill-advised poli-sci dude in junior year," Cole said, counting on his fingers teasingly.

Miriam rolled her eyes, mostly because he was right. Especially about that poli-sci dude.

"She's handsome, and she listens, and I think I've been sleeping on brunettes," she admitted. "She's so much better than my regular type." She chewed the skin on the side of her nail. "She's so good with her hands. And so...voluptuous." She was afraid her eyes had turned into cartoon hearts.

Noelle had faced her own grief and her demons, walked through all of her personal hells to the other side. She was so brave, and competent, and—this shouldn't be such a sexy quality but somehow it was—stalwart. She loved Carrigan's as much as Miriam did and understood Miriam's ideas for it. She felt like she'd found someone who spoke a language she thought she'd dreamed.

"Well," he said thoughtfully, "I like her a lot. What's the sitch? Are you making out?"

Miriam hugged her pillow in front of her. "We baked rugelach at three a.m. There were several Significant Looks, but no smooches."

"What's the holdup?" he asked. "Are you worried you'll break up and your new life will suddenly be very uncomfortable? Hard to hide from a breakup if you live in a hotel with your ex."

"She doesn't date," Miriam said, "and I need to not date, probably. Plus she scares me. I don't think she wants to be all in, and that would be my only setting with her. If I put a toe in, I'm going to fall hard."

"Are you not going to hook up, then?" Cole asked, his face skeptical.

"That's what we agreed to. I'm not sure how long it will last." Miriam scrunched up her nose. She knew she should want to wait before starting a new relationship, instead of throwing herself in the deep end, but her hormones felt otherwise, as did the butterflies in her stomach.

"You'll be making out in a week," Cole predicted.

Miriam stuck out her tongue. "Thank you for your faith in my willpower. I'll talk to you later."

"Ziva's here," Mr. Matthews grumbled as he passed through the breakfast room.

"Your mom's here," Noelle warned, as she came in to get coffee.

By the time Hannah texted her to say, "FYI your mom's outside," Miriam knew she should probably go find her.

Ziva was standing on the front lawn in the freezing wind when Miriam trudged outside, her long coat whipping around her, looking very much like Cathy waiting for Heathcliff on the moors.

Miriam was equally amused and annoyed. "Mom, are you out here waiting for someone to come ask you what the matter is? You know you can brood attractively inside next to the fire, right?"

"But darling, it would be so much less elegant," Ziva said wryly. "I bought this coat just to look melodramatic. I haven't gotten my money's worth, yet."

"You can drop the mask, Mom. It's only me. I know you, remember?"

Miriam watched her mother's face change, rearranging all her features into something wholly different, and much more exhausted.

Miriam continued. "What are you doing out here, anyway?" Or at Carrigan's, for that matter. She was probably here to berate Miriam about ending her engagement, which would be a fun conversation.

"I was just hurting. Just out here letting the cold make me feel something," Ziva said. "I wonder, if I hadn't kept you from Cass, if you would have made this terribly foolish choice, now. Also, I heard the aurora borealis might be out tonight. I've never seen it. I thought if it appeared, I might...I don't know, get answers to what I should do with my life." She laughed at herself a little.

Miriam rolled her eyes, frustrated by her mother's ability to center herself in Miriam's life and make Miriam want to comfort her over how bad she felt about being a shitty mom. "You don't get to have my estrangement from Carrigan's to add to your treasure chest of martyrdom, Mom. Or my decision to stay. Feel sorry for yourself about all of the years of my childhood, if you need to, but you can't have my choices now."

Ziva stiffened. "I spent all of your childhood keeping you safe!"

The grief and cold finally broke down Miriam's last filters. "You let him do it!" she cried. "You let him do all of it."

"You think I let him?" Ziva sounded genuinely shocked.

"You control every tiny aspect of your whole life. Yes. I think you let him." Miriam had tried for years to find ways to excuse her mother, but she *was* angry at her, and she *did* believe Ziva had chosen. And she wouldn't keep pretending otherwise. "And I know for certain that you stayed after. You stayed all those years, through everything." This, her mother could not refute.

Ziva hugged her coat closer. "I guess I'm flattered my illusion of control is so good that even my own daughter hasn't seen through it. You're right that I didn't leave your dad. When you were little, I thought he would make it worse if we left, and when you were older, I didn't want anyone to know I'd made a mistake. It's hard to leave, when you don't have anything left of yourself to go toward."

Miriam shivered. This was the first time she'd ever heard her mom talk so honestly about her marriage. It was the first time she'd ever told her mom what she thought of her choices or even directly addressed her dad's behavior in a conversation.

It felt seismic.

Being here, with Hannah and Noelle, claiming a big messy future, was giving her the strength to have this conversation she'd intended to avoid until she died. Their entire lives had been built on a fiction and now they were looking each other in the eye and admitting the emperor had no clothes.

"Do you think we can ever have a relationship?" her mom asked, breaking into her thoughts.

Miriam thought about telling a polite fiction but decided that's not what they were doing here.

"Not while you're still married," she said, honestly.

Ziva nodded.

Miriam wanted to process the end of her engagement and the future she'd envisioned in Charleston as well as the conversation she'd just had with her mother, but Carrigan's kept distracting her. They were in the thick of the Christmas Festival now. It seemed like most of New York had shown up to get their trees. Miriam had trouble believing their business had declined by half, although Hannah assured her it was true.

There was so much to prep needed to make the guest rooms ready that Miriam wondered what they would have done if she weren't there. In between it all, she and Hannah tried to fit in brainstorming sessions about Carrigan's All Year, often during walk and talks or while changing linens. Who would they contact about hosting drag balls? Which area rabbis needed to know they were available for b'nai mitzvah parties? Should they take a break in August or offer day camps for kids who needed some wilderness time before school started?

She met with Elijah and Jason, who were the beating heart of Advent's social scene (such as it was), about what events people would show up to. She fielded crisis calls from her Old Ladies with one hand while updating cost analyses with the other. She was nonstop from dawn to midnight, and in between, she should have been sleeping.

But when she lay in bed at night, all she saw was Noelle.

In stolen moments, Miriam tried to make art. Her Instagram was full of pine trees, instead of the anything she actually sold to make money. She tried setting up at a back desk in the library but ended up reading. She tried making a space in an unused storage room in Noelle's work shed, but Noelle kept appearing there, sexy and annoying. Her ass was very distracting.

Miriam finally landed in the barn, setting up a worktable next to the reindeer pens, with a lot of half-finished concept drawings spread out on top. She told herself it would be different if she had all her pieces from Charleston. Then she could finish work she'd already planned. Those items were in limbo, because they'd been stored behind Tara's house while Miriam worked on the warehouse renovations. Tara wouldn't let professional art movers onto her property to pack anything for shipping. Miriam couldn't hold that little pettiness against her.

So, Miriam told herself, she was also in limbo—but she knew it was an excuse. The inn had no shortage of weird, junky antiques, and neither did the surrounding towns. She was just missing her spark.

A few weeks into the Christmas Festival, Hanukkah arrived. Miriam liked Hanukkah, in spite of its minor religious significance, because she liked the candles in dark windows and the joyful eating of fried food. She had so many memories of celebrating at Carrigan's. Even when the holiday didn't overlap with Christmas break, Cass would make them all eat latkes and tell the story of the oil. It was an antidote to the Christmas cheer that threatened to overwhelm them. Cass had collected menorahs from all over the world, saying she wanted a menorah from anywhere the diaspora had touched.

"We may go all out for Christmas for the tourists," she'd explained, "but when it is just our home, we will light up the sky for the Maccabees." Cass never did anything small.

The first night of this first year without her, they set out the menorahs in the windows, and every member of the family lit one. "Miri and Hannah," Ziva said, "you must say the blessings. It's what Cass would have wanted."

Miriam rolled her eyes at her mom's pretend benevolence,

but she didn't refuse. They covered their heads and entwined their fingers. "On three," Hannah whispered, squeezing Miriam's hand three times. "Baruch ata Adonai..."

Dinner after was chaos.

The Greens came, and Noelle gifted the twins their carved ducks, to their delight and their fathers' horror.

"If you really loved us," Elijah told her, "you would not have doomed us to weeks of quacking."

Noelle didn't look at all repentant. "I'll come babysit and they can quack at me."

"Mr. Matthews," Jason laughed as he picked up one of the twins from under the table and swung them around, "do you want me to get these little monsters out from under your legs?"

"Don't you dare!" Mr. Matthews said. "It reminds me of when Esther and Joshua were little. We don't have enough little people running amok around here, these days."

"Oh," Elijah interrupted, "we would be happy to drop ours off any time. You can let them run around the back acreage until they get tired out, and we'll come back for them."

"Please do that!" Mrs. Matthews exclaimed, her hands at her heart. "Only one of my children has blessed me with grandchildren, and he's in the city."

Jason was short and stocky with the face of a model, with cheekbones that could cut someone. He had midnight dark skin, shining locs, a dimple, and he seemed made of pure charisma.

"Elijah," Miriam whispered, "your husband is the most beautiful human I've ever seen in real life."

"I know," he whispered back.

She caught Noelle smiling at this exchange.

"What?" she asked, poking Noelle in the ribs with an elbow. "You have that smug little smirk again."

"Nothing. Elijah and Jason are important to me, is all. I'd like you to make friends with them," Noelle said, not quite nonchalantly.

"Because you think I might become important to you, too?" Miriam teased.

"Eat a latke, Miri."

"I *would* eat a latke, Noelle, but I am too horrified by the amount of applesauce you have put on yours, and I can't go on," Miriam said, right before putting an entire latke in her mouth.

"Excuse me, you have hot sauce on yours. You have no room to judge. Team applesauce for life."

Miriam shrugged, splashing more Tapatío on her next latke. She would not apologize for her potato genius.

Everyone let the fried food and lights of the holiday smooth over the rough edges of grief and anxiety about the business, for a little while. Not even the presence of her mother, hovering at the perimeter of the room and trying to casually insert herself as if they could have a normal conversation, was enough to dim her glow.

The next morning, Miriam invited Hannah to go into Advent with her, both to shop for extra Hanukkah presents and to get out of the house. Hannah protested that they couldn't leave during the Christmas Festival, and Miriam reminded her that Noelle, Ziva, the Matthewses, and their seasonal workers could handle Tuesday morning traffic. Hannah didn't look convinced, but she acquiesced because Miriam reminded her that they hadn't had any real time together, just the two of them, and that they needed to celebrate finalizing the plan for the Rosensteins.

The town had somehow grown even more festive since Thanksgiving weekend. Garland and twinkle lights wound up every light pole. Over the street, winking merrily, reindeer pulled Santa and his sleigh. In every window, there seemed to be a Carrigan's Christmas tree, stuffed to bursting with decorations.

"I don't say this lightly," Miriam observed, "but this is a lot."

"I like it," Hannah said. "It feels like a sort of good-natured inside joke that all of Advent is in on together." She stopped suddenly in front of a door. "Wait, let's go in here."

Hannah pulled her into a tiny diner selling cappuccinos and giant sandwiches on bread baked in-house. Framed photos of the townsfolk through the years hung on the wall, including Cass, and there were red and white checkered tablecloths.

"This place was not here ten years ago," Miriam said. "I would have remembered fresh bread and good espresso. Does this town have an endless supply of adorable local shops?"

A man who resembled a grizzly bear walked up to their table, wiping his hands on his apron. He had brilliant orange hair that probably always needed a trim and a magnificent beard.

"Name's Collin," he said, voice coming from so deep in his chest that Miriam wondered the walls didn't shake. "I'm the owner here. It's good to see the prodigal daughter returning."

"Oh, gosh, I hope you haven't heard all bad things," Miriam said, only sort of kidding.

Collin grinned, big. "Esther Matthews dated my college roommate," he rumbled. "She told me a lot of stories about you all running amok up there on the farm. That's how I found out about Advent. It sounded idyllic."

"Is it?" Miriam asked, shrewdly.

He made a "so-so" movement with his hand. "You can tell I fell in love with the people," he said, gesturing to the photos on the walls. "Cass did a lot for me."

Miriam's eyes welled up, involuntarily, and then his did, too. "Tell me." She gestured to an empty chair, but he shook his head and leaned his hand the size of a pie tin against its back.

"I came here to visit one Christmas," he started, his feet shuffling and cheeks going pink, like he was a little embarrassed. "I met a girl who owned a business here, and I kept finding reasons to come visit or to stay longer. And Cass, you know, she saw everything."

"Collin had been pining over a certain boutique owner," Hannah teased gently, winking at Collin. "What did Cass say, or do?"

Collin covered his face with his other hand. "That obvious, huh?" he asked, through his palm.

Hannah nodded, but her smile was kind.

"She told me, you can't base your whole life around someone you might be in love with. That I needed an adventure I could take on, that would help me find out who I really was and would be mine whether the romance worked out or not. When this space came up for sale, I bought it. I'd always dreamed of a diner."

Miriam's eyes welled up. This felt like a gift Cass had left for her, like she was still speaking directly to Miriam. Her feelings for Noelle had helped Miriam decide to stay, but she'd begun to find something here that was just hers. If this were the great, life-changing adventure Miriam believed it could be, then she needed to anchor it in who she really was.

The problem was, she didn't really know herself.

"But," Miriam asked, "it never worked out with the girl? Do you still love her from afar?" She winced as Hannah kicked her shin under the table. "Sorry, I'm nosy."

"It hasn't worked out yet, but Christmas at Carrigan's is magic, after all. You never know. I'll bring you both coffees?" he asked, clearly changing the subject.

"I thought this place might be up your alley," Hannah said from behind a cup the size of her head. "I've been meaning to get you over here. I keep thinking about Christmases when we were kids, when our parents put us together to play and by New Year's, we never wanted to see each other again. Now we're so busy we barely get a meal together!"

"I never wanted to be rid of you, I just wanted to stop playing hotel!" Miriam protested. Hannah had known from a very young age that she wanted to run Carrigan's and had made them all practice, nonstop, but Miriam still would have kept her all year, if she could have. Miriam's normal life, at home in Arizona, had been lonely, with no friends she could safely invite over, in case they found out the truth about her family.

"I missed you," Hannah said, simply.

Miriam cracked open, her tears welling up. (Where were all these tears coming from? Had she been saving them for ten years?) "I'm sorry. I didn't mean to be gone so long and miss so much. I thought you had your life's dream. You didn't need your mess of a cousin flailing around."

Even as she spoke, Miriam knew it sounded like a terrible excuse. All the excuses she'd used not to come back sounded terrible, now that she was here and Cass wasn't.

"I needed you," Hannah said, shrugging before splitting their sandwiches so they each had half of the other's, like they'd always done as children. Then, she deconstructed her egg salad on rye and rebuilt it with a layer of potato chips in the middle. "Especially after Blue left, I needed someone who knew all of me, I guess."

This was exactly what Miriam had been thinking about Hannah, and it pierced her. All the years she'd been gone, she'd thought she couldn't survive the scrutiny of people who'd always known her, that having no one know her whole self was a feature, not a bug, of avoiding the Carrigan's crew. But being back, she realized she'd forgotten what it felt like to have someone who had been with you for all of your past, who understood who you'd been at every point of your life. She'd robbed Hannah of that while denying herself, and she hadn't even thought about whether Hannah would miss her, really. She hadn't done it on purpose, but the damage had still been done.

"I don't know how to make that up to you," Miriam admitted.

"Just keep showing up," Hannah told her. "Don't run."

Miriam nodded. "I'm not sure I'll do that perfectly. Running is what my feet know best. I can just practice not running every day."

Hannah gave her a half smile and swiped her last potato chip. "Good enough."

Their next stop was Marisol's Boutique. Marisol had been one of many mourners to come to sit shiva and tell stories about Cass. She had long black hair she wore loose down her back and had a great dress on.

"Hey!" she yelled to Hannah. "You're here without your other half!"

"She's deeply invested in trees today," Hannah said, hugging Marisol.

"Noelle shops here?" Miriam asked, looking around at the racks of skirts and heels.

"Nah, she hangs out, getting her ass kicked at Spite and Malice," Marisol said. Miriam smiled at that picture.

Marisol had met Cass in a cafe in Zurich. Cass had stopped her and said, "I have a feeling we're meant to travel together. Do you like Christmas?" And now here Marisol was, in Advent.

"Is this Collin's love?" she whispered as Hannah looked through a rack. Hannah dramatically shushed her, which Miriam took as a yes.

"Sooo," Hannah said to Marisol, "Miriam and I are cooking up a plot to do more year-round events at Carrigan's, including partnering with Advent businesses. What do you think? Fashion show in the barn?"

"Anything you can do to bring in more tourists throughout the year, with more money to spend in town, I am on board with," Marisol said, leaning against the counter.

"Good! We'll keep you in the loop. Also, my poor cousin needs clothes. Everything she owns is for a South Carolina winter and I'm tired of her complaining that she's cold."

After sorting through the racks, Hannah handed Miriam several very soft sweaters, in flattering colors that showed off a little cleavage. Miriam suspected Hannah had ulterior motives that included matchmaking.

"These make me look heterosexual," she complained.

Hannah looked at her cuffed overalls and backwards floral snapback and raised an eyebrow. "I'm not sure that's possible," she said skeptically. "You'll end up bedazzling them in a way that somehow screams 'No one confuse me for a straight person.'"

So Miriam bought them, because her bedazzler could use some action, and because she wasn't opposed to new clothes that made her boobs look great.

Chapter 13

Noelle

That Wednesday, they sent the official business plan for Carrigan's All Year to the Rosensteins. Now they were only waiting to hear what the answer would be.

With only three weeks until Christmas, guests were arriving, sad about the loss of Cass, but looking for the full Christmasland Experience. Most of the families had been coming all their lives. Hannah was committed to making it feel like a Carrigan's Christmas, which meant all the regular activities.

"The gingerbread is fresh baked, and it doesn't behave the way graham crackers do," Miriam complained while Noelle laughed.

The Carrigan's guests took their Gingerbread House Competition very seriously. Miriam was trying to build a house, and Noelle had decided to help by offering gently mocking commentary.

"I was, once upon a time, a master of gingerbread house construction," Miriam observed, as the roof slid off her current structure and fell with a crack. "When I was eight."

The smell of the ginger was incredibly distracting, especially when mixed with Miriam's skin, so very soft and very near Noelle's own. The heat of her thigh radiated through her leggings and into Noelle's jeans. Frosting covered her hands. Noelle was concentrating very hard on not grabbing and licking her fingers.

Finally, Miriam's leaning tower of cookies had been covered in an improbable number of candies. It was not the scale model of Carrigan's Christmasland she'd proclaimed she was making, but she seemed content with it.

"This," Noelle said judiciously, eyeing it with her head turned sideways, "would be improved by trees."

"You're a farmer," Miriam reminded her. "You think everything would be improved by trees."

"I run a Christmas tree farm. Everything literally is. What in this world cannot be made better by a Christmas tree?" Noelle gestured out the window at the brilliant green acreage.

"I've never decorated a Christmas tree. Am I going to get kicked out of Carrigan's?" Miriam teased.

Noelle almost fell out of her chair. "You grew up spending Christmas at a place called Christmasland."

"I'm Jewish! And don't give me that 'they're a secular symbol that comes from paganism' line," Miriam warned her. "No one believes that."

"Oh no," Noelle shook her head, "they're definitely not.

What they are is very, very shiny. You know you would have fun making sure everything is exactly, perfectly placed."

Miriam ducked her head, but Noelle could see her tearing up a little.

"What's wrong?" she asked, alarmed. *Great job, NoNo, make the pretty girl cry.* "What did I say?"

"It's just...you see my work as art, and you like it. You think it's important."

"Your art is important to you, and you're the person who matters most," Noelle said, annoyed at everyone who had made Miriam feel inferior. Instinctively, she squeezed Miriam's leg under the table, and Miriam let out a small and very satisfying gasp.

"Keep your hands to yourself," she hissed, "or we are going to give our guests more than they paid for."

Noelle couldn't stop herself from grinning. "Sorry. Well, not really sorry. You were giving me that look, with those big eyes. What were you saying about Christmas trees?"

"Before Christmas is over, I will decorate one tree," Miriam said, clearing her throat. Noelle was sad to see the lust leave her face as she composed herself. "I promise. It will be kitschy and garish and extremely loud. And then I'll probably never decorate another one."

They did not win the contest. One-hundred-and-one-year-old Mrs. Finn won with a gingerbread Eiffel Tower that Noelle could have sworn was held together with superglue.

"I met my third husband on top of the Eiffel Tower," Mrs. Finn confided afterward to Miriam and Noelle. "He was about to propose to someone else when he looked up and saw me. He was my favorite husband, Robert. I probably should have kept him, but life is short." She paused. "Well, not my life! Mine's been long as hell!" She cackled to herself while she wheeled off to another activity.

"I've never wanted to be anyone so badly." Miriam dropped her chin into her hands.

"Are we free now? Can we go do something that isn't forced togetherness and merriment?" Noelle asked, hopefully.

Noelle needed to get out of the stifling confines of the room, which had felt perfectly big enough until Miriam sat down next to her and pressed their thighs together while they worked. Why did Miriam's mouth have to be so wide and interesting, and her lips so full? It made it impossible not to stare at her.

She fled to her trees so she could remember how to breathe.

*   *   *

The first snow snuck up on them. On Sunday they woke up to a world blanketed. It was the day they were supposed to get an answer from the Rosensteins, and everyone was tense and snapping at each other. So the Matthewses sent Miriam, Noelle, and Hannah off sledding.

Mrs. Matthews shoved them out the door, saying, "Do not come back into the house for four hours, or I am quitting. Your anxiety is giving me hives."

They bundled up in every layer of protective snow gear that could be found in the entire inn, walking around like abominable millennial toddlers.

"Oh my gosh, Nan, the snow!" Miriam cried in astonished

glee. "I forgot about the snow!" She giggled as she ran her hands under a pile of white fluff, throwing it up in the air. "Oh shit oh shit oh shit it's cold!"

Noelle doubled over laughing.

Hannah looked at Miriam and gave the sort of wicked, trouble-making grin that Noelle hadn't seen on her best friend in a long damned time.

"Oh no, I know that look," Miriam said, waving her arms in a desperate attempt to stop whatever was coming. But as Noelle knew, there was no stopping Hannah when her mischief was up.

"I declare—" Hannah paused dramatically, raising one finger high in the air in proclamation.

"Don't do it!" Miriam cried. Noelle watched them, back and forth, beginning to see how they must have been as children and teenagers. The way Miriam's presence eased something in Hannah made Noelle's heart flip over.

"—a Shenanigan!" Hannah finished. Then, all in a rush, she said, "I declare a Shenanigan!" She threw back her head and laughed at the still-snowing sky. Miriam fell to her knees in mock anguish.

Hannah put her hands on her hips, a triumphant smile lighting up her face. "You know the rules, Miriam Blum."

"I know, I know. Once a Shenanigan has been declared, no one may back down. I would never break our most sacred oath."

Noelle didn't understand the byzantine rules that governed the calling of a Shenanigan, because it had been Hannah and Levi's thing, but she did understand that she was now honor-bound to keep Miriam and Hannah from killing themselves by doing something reckless. So, as they piled onto a sled, she wound up on the bottom, ostensibly steering. Mostly, she tried to concentrate on surviving while distracted by Miriam's ass pressing up against her, Miriam's mane of curls blowing in her face.

It was like a Calvin and Hobbes strip, if Calvin and Hobbes were sexually frustrated sapphics.

All three of them hurtled down the tallest hill on the property at wildly unsafe speeds, ending up at the bottom in an inglorious heap. Miriam landed on top of Noelle, her nose inches from Noelle's own, her hair curtaining them from the outside world.

"Hi," Miriam breathed, making no move to get up. She smirked a little.

"Hi yourself," Noelle managed to grunt. She reached up to push a curl out of Miriam's face. Miriam turned her head so that her lips nuzzled Noelle's palm, for just an instant, before she felt Miriam being pulled off her.

"Miriiiiiiii!!!!!!! Our first Shenanigan in a decade! We must celebrate!" Hannah crowed, dragging Miriam back to the house. Noelle was left behind, happily, to bring the sled back to the barn. She looked ahead at her best friend, waddling around with snow under her clothes, her head thrown back in a laugh, and at Miriam, the wind blowing her icy hair into liberty spikes. It felt like they were in a snow globe, precious and fragile, and at any moment, someone might turn the whole thing over and shake it.

"Wait!" Hannah yelled, suddenly stopping. She turned back, running clumsily toward Noelle in her snowsuit. "NoNo! You have to be with us! We're the Three Musketeers now!"

She linked her arms through Noelle and Miriam's, sandwiching herself between them, and looked up at Noelle with peace radiating from her face. "When was the last time we had fun, Noelle? When was the last time we were just...happy?" Noelle saw her eyes get wet as she asked this, and she teared up in response. She always cried when Hannah did.

"I don't remember, babe." Before Cass got sick, maybe. Before Levi left. It had been a long damned time.

Mr. Matthews rolled his eyes when they wandered back in and refused to let them past the mudroom in their gear. The three of them stuffed in together, pulling off each other's boots, blowing on their fingers to make them work well enough to undo zippers, and throwing scarves over each other's heads onto hooks. When they were finally reduced to fleece-lined long johns, he admitted them into the kitchen for stew and hot tea.

That night, they all lay on their backs on the floor in the great room, with their stockinged feet propped up in front of the fire. Kringle had stretched his whole body out, belly up, to join them, and was nearly as long as Miriam. Miriam's hand was so close to Noelle's their fingers brushed against each other. It felt like high school, with all the potential of someone you liked who liked you back, trying to decide when to finally let the delicious tension break.

Except, of course, giving in would mean trusting that Miriam was staying and wouldn't run away again as soon as things got complicated.

"Do you think any moment will ever feel this perfect, again?" Hannah asked, sounding sleep-drunk. Noelle looked over at Hannah, who had basically been vibrating with stress every moment since Cass died. She was confused as hell about a lot, right now, but if she got to see her best friend this happy, it might all be worth it.

Noelle pretended to shake an imaginary Magic 8-Ball. "Outlook not so good."

"What will we do? If the Rosensteins say no?" Hannah had turned over on her side to face the two of them.

Miriam propped herself up on her elbow to meet Hannah's gaze. "Then we go to the bank without them, and we still save Carrigan's," she said, sounding more sure than Noelle felt. "I'm not giving you up now that I just got you back."

Hannah nodded, holding a fist out for Miriam to bump. "Ride or die."

Later, long after the fire went out, Noelle was still awake, remembering Miriam licking s'mores off her fingers. She pulled her blankets over her head and groaned to herself. Miriam was closer to being exactly what she was looking for than Noelle wanted to admit. If she were looking. Which she wasn't. If a romance exploded spectacularly, they could lose all the work they'd put into saving Carrigan's. But it was hard to ignore how her whole body lit up when Miriam walked into a room.

She hit herself over the head with her pillow. *Go to sleep, Noelle*, she told herself. *You aren't going to solve anything after midnight.*

Finally, under the weight of Kringle and the promise of a very early morning, she fell asleep.

When she awoke, the answer had come from the Rosensteins. They were ready to sign on—with one condition. They wanted to see an event successfully planned and executed by the new Team Carrigan's.

"We need to go to the bank *soon*. Like, before Christmas. How do we show them an event in time?" Noelle asked, pacing in front of Hannah's desk, where they'd gathered to read the email.

Hannah took a pen out of her bun and tapped it against her lips, her gaze unfocused. She materialized a yellow legal pad from seemingly nowhere. She propped herself on the corner of her desk and perched her purple sparkly reading glasses on her nose before pointing her pen at Miriam. "This is your baby. You got any ideas?"

"I actually kind of do have an idea," Miriam said speculatively, nearly vibrating with what Noelle now thought of as Miriam Geeking Out Energy. She loved when Miriam got excited about something. All her lights were on, right now. "We have the annual tree lighting on Christmas Eve to wrap up the festival. It's new, since it started after I left, so I don't know for sure, but it's mostly unveiling the tree, right? Not a lot of other stuff going on?"

"Mr. Matthews usually dresses up as Santa," Hannah said, nodding. "Other than that, the attention is on the tree. Cass decorated it every year, and you know if she was giving a performance, she wanted the spotlight on her."

"Okay, it's already happening, so we can amplify it, rather than add an entirely new event to the calendar. What if we made it a carnival, with a bunch of booths from local places. Invited everyone from Advent, have some live music. A real closing night for our Christmas season. We could livestream it on my Instagram and use photos and video from it for promo." She deflated a little, sitting back in her chair. "Is it too last-minute to get people to come, though?"

Noelle shook her head. "Oh, you've never lived in a small town where there's nothing to do. If you have a party, everyone will come. Especially if it's in honor of Cass. People want to celebrate her. It's a great idea."

Hannah already had a pen in her teeth. "It's really smart. It could work."

Noelle turned to Miriam. "*You* should decorate the tree."

"What?!" Miriam squeaked. "That's way too important a job to give to me. I've never even decorated a normal-sized tree."

"Miri, you're the artist." Noelle crouched down in front of her and took her hands. "You're the one with the vision to pull off an over-the-top fiasco of a tree worthy of Cass Carrigan. If this is going to work, we need your art at the center of it."

"Noelle's right, Miri," Hannah said. "This one has to be you."

Miriam nodded a little, and then again decisively.

"Alright, let's put on a fucking banger of a carnival," Hannah said. "We're going to get the Rosensteins on board. And"—she pointed at Miriam, and then at Noelle with her pen—"if they don't, we give the bank the plan anyway, because Carrigan's All Year is happening, and nothing is going to stop us."

Noelle whooped and pounded a fist in the air. Miriam launched herself into Noelle's arms, kissing her soundly on the cheek. She smelled like coffee and pastries, and Noelle's mouth watered.

"Let's plan a tree lighting, woman," Noelle grumbled, setting Miriam aside before she did something untoward in Hannah's office.

Chapter 14

Miriam

Hannah and Noelle were trying, with mixed results, to treat Miriam like an equal partner. Noelle was doing a pretty good job, mostly because planning the tree lighting didn't interrupt her work so she had no territory to protect. Hannah, however, kept ending up in a tug-of-war with Miriam when Hannah felt she was overstepping, which seemed to Miriam was happening every time she so much as refilled a napkin container.

Which is what she was doing, in the empty dining room after breakfast, when Hannah started walking behind her and fixing her work.

"Really?" Miriam asked. "The napkins? You're going to micromanage the napkins?"

"They have to be done exactly this way, or the dispenser jams, and then it's more work to fix it," Hannah sniped, waving the aging napkin dispenser.

Miriam could not figure out what Hannah's problem was. All of a sudden, Hannah was on high alert, and Miriam couldn't figure out what had changed.

"Why don't you teach me how to do it? Or buy new napkin dispensers that don't jam?" Miriam asked, her hands on her hips. "Oh right, because then you wouldn't be the only person who could do it right."

"The napkins aren't your job. They're my job. Like the welcome baskets for the guests who arrived yesterday, and the tour information you gave, and the pamphlet display you decided to rearrange without asking me." Hannah waved the napkin dispenser toward the front hall, where the display was, before setting it down with too much force.

Miriam was so frustrated she wanted to scream. "I was trying to help! The display looks way better now, and the guests asked me for information about the tours. What was I supposed to say?! You'll have to wait until Hannah is free and ask her, because she's the only person designated to Google things at Carrigan's?"

Hannah had *asked* her to stay here. She'd left her entire life to move here, and now she felt like she was in the way.

"Shh! The guests can hear you," Hannah hissed. "And I don't want you to help! I want you to do your job and let me do mine!"

"I don't know why we're yelling about this!" Miriam angry-whispered back. "I also don't know what my job is, so I can't do it!"

"Can I make a suggestion?" Noelle asked, coming up behind them. "We should create a specific role for Miriam, with clearly drawn parameters, so she has room to do her job, and Hannah, you can focus on being the best in the world at the part of Carrigan's that's yours."

"We probably should have a role for Miriam. We definitely should." Hannah nodded, knotting her hair on top of her head like she was ready to Take Charge. As if she hadn't already been Taking Charge of everything Miriam tried to do all week. "That would make things much clearer. What are you envisioning, Noelle? Artist-in-Residence?"

Miriam stared at Hannah. Was she fucking kidding? "I'm sorry, Artist-in-Residence? Because I didn't just create an entire business plan for us out of thin air? Thanks for this work, Miri, go put glitter glue on old stuff now?"

"You love to put glitter glue on old stuff!" Hannah protested.

"That's not the point!" Miriam said, her voice rising. "I came up with Carrigan's All Year and you won't even let me format social media blasts without redoing all my work!"

"Oh, what," Hannah said, dismissively, "do you want to be in charge of the entire project? The Christmasland Calendar manager?"

"Actually, in charge of the entire project is exactly what I was thinking," Noelle interjected.

Hannah spun to face her. "I'm the events manager! I should be in charge of planning the events. Besides, Miriam is going to have to travel for work. She'll be with the Old Ladies, not managing things."

"Do not use the Old Ladies as an excuse!" Miriam accused her cousin. "I'll be here more than enough, junk buys or not."

Noelle nodded at Hannah. "Yes. You absolutely should collaborate with Miriam on deciding which events get planned, what support you need to run them, all of that. But you are already head of guest services, which is a full-time job. If you trust Miriam to come to you for the parts that require both of you to sign off, you can focus on managing the big influx of guests this is supposed to bring us. Hell, you can make an org chart that lists all the decisions requiring two-person approval, so no one is ever confused."

"I do love an org chart," Hannah conceded, her face softening.

Miriam had a lot of feelings about Noelle standing up for her, trusting her with the business, and advocating for her to have so much responsibility. She was going to think about those feelings later, when Hannah wasn't around, because they were confusing and overwhelming—and also pretty horny. Right now, she was going to try to figure out what the hell was happening with her cousin.

She sat down at one of the tables and pulled out the chair next to her. Hannah reluctantly sunk into it.

"Nan, I thought you were glad to have me here. I don't want to keep stepping on your toes, but I don't understand why delegating some of this responsibility is pushing your buttons," Miriam asked. "Things were fine between us when we were brainstorming."

"Because that was theoretical, and this is execution," Hannah explained, crossing her arms around herself protectively. "I'm in charge of execution. I have to be, because it keeps me moving. I learned how to take care of this place without you because I had to. You weren't here when Cass was dying, when I walked away from the love of my life and it almost killed me."

Oh, no. This wasn't just about Hannah panicking when she wasn't in charge of things, this was so much bigger.

"I got good at doing everything myself. This is mine. I gave up everything for it, and if I'm good at it, then it was worth it." Her voice broke on the end. "If you don't need me, why am I here?"

"Instead of with Blue?" Miriam asked quietly.

Hannah nodded through sobs, and Miriam wrapped her up in her arms.

"Noelle's not wrong, I don't need a second full-time position. But I also really hate not being in control," Hannah said, finally pulling away. "I'll think about it." She got up and walked away, and Noelle, who had been listening silently, followed. Noelle nodded at Miriam as if to convey that she would make sure Hannah was okay.

Miriam sat in the empty dining room, playing with the shitty old napkin holders, until Mrs. Matthews entered.

"Come help me make challah," Mrs. Matthews called to Miriam. "No one is any use to me with baking. You'd think a braid was an alien object."

Miriam knew a con when she saw one, but she walked into the kitchen anyway, rolling up her sleeves and washing her hands.

"You know my challah is middling," Miriam reminded her.

Mrs. Matthews shook her head in dramatic disappointment. "I was hoping you might have improved your game, all those years living in the South, without access to quality bread."

"There's been a settled Jewish community in Charleston since the 1740s," Miriam teased. "I'm making do okay."

Mrs. Matthews handed her a ball of dough, and they worked for a few moments in silence, Miriam letting herself get back into the rhythm of something she'd known how to do all her life.

"I know you're just trying to help me feel useful," she told Mrs. Matthews. "And I appreciate it."

"I don't know what you're talking about. I was using you for labor while also looking for excuses to hang out with you." Mrs. Matthews winked at her. "Noelle and Hannah are very similar, you know."

Miriam knew better than to interrupt.

"It's what drew them together when Noelle first moved here. They were two peas in a pod who had finally found each other. Hannah has been searching all her life for what Anne Shirley called a kindred spirit. She was looking for her Diana."

"I always thought that was Levi," Miriam murmured.

Mrs. Matthews chuckled. "He was and he wasn't. You may remember that as a child, he was...intense and capricious. Hannah likes things to be rock solid."

As children, Miriam had seen Hannah's loving parents, her close relationships with the Rosensteins and Blue, and envied all the love in Hannah's life. She hadn't realized her cousin was lonely, too. Maybe hating traveling wasn't the only reason she wanted to stay at Carrigan's so desperately.

"But, you know, she's bossy. She likes to be in charge of everything. She needed someone as strong willed and territorial as she was. She and Noelle, they fit. Noelle took the farm, Hannah took the inn, and neither of them has ever had to cede any territory. It's been worse since Levi left, because work has been the only thing keeping her from drowning some days."

"I'm not asking Hannah to give up any of her work," Miriam insisted, finally seeing Mrs. Matthews's point. "I am not capable of doing what she does, and I would hate it."

She pounded the dough harder than she ought, which earned her a reproving look.

"For you to do what you're good at, she's going to have to change some of what she does," Mrs. Matthews said. "She's going to have to consult with someone else sometimes, instead of being the High Queen. I know you're feeling like you exploded your whole life to be here, but you're not the only one whose whole life was just exploded. There are a lot of moving parts." She broke off four small balls of dough and arranged them on the counter. One was in the center, and the other three circled it. "If you stop seeing yourself as the center of this story," she continued, moving the middle ball out so that all four made up a circle, "and start seeing all of you as an interdependent web, whose actions all affect each other, you'll have a better time empathizing with your cousin."

Looking down at the dough under her hands, ready to rise, Miriam reflected that a lot of the hurt of the past ten years might have been mitigated if she'd remembered to take herself out of the center of the story.

"Do you want me to come back when this is rested, to braid it?" Miriam asked.

"When was the last time you braided a challah?" Mrs. Matthews replied seriously. "It's fine. I'll braid it. You can come back and Instagram it." Mrs. Matthews shooed her away from the counter with a kiss.

"Are you done lecturing her?" Mr. Matthews asked, coming in through the outside kitchen door. "Can I come inside now?"

"Fine, fine, you can come in. Wipe your boots," she said to her husband. Miriam had always ached to have a love like theirs, with old worn-down arguments they'd had a million times. She slipped out while they were swatting lovingly at each other.

Hannah was lying in wait for Miriam in her room when Miriam went up to bed, sitting in the armchair by the fire, her knees drawn up to her chin. It was hard to have privacy when you lived in a hotel, and everyone had keys. Hannah's cheeks were tear-streaked, and the knees of her leggings had little wet spots on them. She motioned for Miriam to sit down, and Miriam didn't argue. Hannah hadn't cried much when they were kids. She had a quick temper, but she was more likely to write a list of possible solutions for heartache than cry about it.

"I shouldn't have yelled at you," Hannah admitted. "I don't know what came over me."

"You finally broke?" Miriam guessed.

Hannah hiccupped a laugh and started to cry again.

"Do you still want to yell at me?" Miriam asked. "You can, if it will make you feel better. You're allowed to have a complicated emotional response to me being back."

"Thank you for your permission," Hannah said dryly. "No. Yes. I don't know." Miriam handed her some tissues, and Hannah bunched them up in her hand, gesturing wordlessly, as if she could wave the words out of the air.

"You left, and I handled it. I missed you so much, but it

was okay. I knew you were doing what you needed to. And then Levi left. It was more pain than I knew any human could survive. But I did. I kept getting up in the morning, and I kept running the business, and I was going to make it. Then Cass got sick, and neither of you were here." Her voice broke, and she sobbed. Miriam sat in front of her, and held her hands, waiting for her to be ready to speak.

She didn't point out that she would have come, if she'd known Cass was sick. Hell, she didn't even know if that was true—she might have kept making excuses. She wished Hannah had given her a chance to find out, but they had time, hopefully, to hash that out, so she bit her tongue.

Miriam stood up from where she'd been kneeling, pacing the small room, eyes on the carpet. It needed replacing, she noticed.

Hannah reached into the pocket of her robe and pulled out a crumpled airline napkin. She handed it wordlessly to Miriam, who looked down at it in her hand.

"This came a couple of days ago," Hannah said. "It was tucked into a get-well-soon card with kittens on the front. It was addressed to you, but I recognized the handwriting, so I opened it."

It was from a budget Australian airline, with writing in blue ballpoint.

Oh, her heart. The handwriting was Levi's:

Can I come home yet?

Miriam cocked her head at her cousin. "Well? This is your call. You told him not to come back, so he didn't. What do you want to do?"

"I was going to burn it, but I thought you had a right to see it. Um. Mostly because it was your mail." Hannah looked only vaguely apologetic.

"It's a bit of a cheap shot, using the napkin trick." He would have known that writing like Cass always used to would get straight at her heart. Miriam turned the note over in her hands, trying to feel annoyed over the wave of sentimentality that engulfed her. She had been studiously avoiding feeling Blue's absence too keenly. Trying to fit into the business, mourn Cass, miss Tara, pretend she was okay taking things slow with Noelle were all the complications she needed. She didn't need another flaming sword thrown into her juggling act.

But she wasn't sure what Hannah—or what Levi, for that matter—needed. She thought about Mrs. Matthews's ball of dough and mentally tried to move herself out of the center.

"I'm not ready to see him," Hannah admitted quietly.

"We can't ignore him forever," Miriam told her. "I tried really hard to ignore my past forever. It turns out that's not how any of this works."

Hannah hissed before snuggling in closer to Miriam, who hugged her tight.

"I'm sorry you felt you couldn't go with him. Have you thought about therapy for the whole can't-leave thing? I mean, if you want. It's okay if you don't, you don't need fixing."

Hannah sighed. "That's what Rabbi Ruth keeps telling me to do."

"Maybe you should listen to them," Miriam suggested.

Hannah sniffed. "Maybe we should both go to therapy."

"I will if you will," Miriam said.

"Deal."

They sat there, holding hands in front of the fire like they had when they were little, sharing the tissue box.

"I think you should be manager of Carrigan's All Year operations," Hannah said, after a few minutes.

"Are you sure?"

"Yeah. I always thought so, from the beginning. I just get weird when things are outside of my immediate control. I shouldn't have put you in the middle of that."

"It's not like I've never put you in the middle of me getting weird."

"I have all this anger, since Blue left," Hannah admitted. "Waves of rage that overtake me, and I don't know what to do with all of it. If I have everything locked down, in order, it feels like it won't pull me under."

Miriam knew exactly how it felt to try to lock everything down so it wouldn't pull her under.

"Is it working?" she asked her cousin.

"Nope." Hannah shook her head, emphatically.

"We're gonna save this farm," Miriam said, patting their joined hands, "and then we're going to get some therapy."

"In the meantime, I'm going to work really hard on giving up some control," Hannah promised. "Because Noelle's right. Why is she always right? It's annoying."

"Speaking of Noelle . . ." Miriam began, and Hannah raised her eyebrows. "When she advocated for me earlier, it made me want Things."

Hannah laughed. "I think you already wanted Things."

"Okay, true, but I want them NOW. I don't want to wait anymore. What do you think?"

"Do you need my blessing?" Hannah joked.

Miriam shrugged. "Kind of! And I need your advice about how to get her on board."

"Well, you have my blessing, if you can convince her. She's a little gun-shy," Hannah said, standing up and gathering their crying tissues. "As to how, my best bet would be an ambush. Catch her off guard, so she doesn't have time to let her brain talk her out of a good thing."

Miriam thought about it. She could do an ambush. It had Shenanigan potential.

"Don't hurt her, or I'll have to kill you," Hannah added, as she headed for the door.

That was fair.

Chapter 15

Noelle

The week before Christmas, Noelle found Miriam helping a guest's ten-year-old daughter with her entry for the cookie ornament contest. The ten-year-old's surly older brother was complaining about his sister getting help from a professional artist, while painstakingly reproducing the Ramones Presidential Seal logo. Miriam was laughing and singing "Merry Christmas (I Don't Want to Fight Tonight)." Both kids were watching her like she was a mythical creature. Noelle knew she was adorable, but she had not been prepared for her to also be good with kids and know all the words to Ramones songs.

When Miriam looked up and saw Noelle, Noelle made an excuse about needing to check in on everyone. She went to find Hannah, so that Hannah would tell her it was a bad idea to kiss Miriam.

"What if we break up?" she said, bursting into the office

without preamble and slamming the door behind her. "What happens then? I'll tell you what. Miriam gets to keep Carrigan's. She gets to keep you, and the Matthewses, and my trees, and I get what? I get out on my ass, where I started."

Hannah stared at her, aghast. "Is *that* what you're worried about? That's fucking absurd. Also hi, please come in."

Noelle huffed. "Why would it be absurd? It's a rational fear, Hannah." She crossed her arms and scowled.

"Why would we choose *Miriam*? Over *you*?" Hannah asked, sounding truly lost. "She doesn't know shit about pine trees, and she hasn't been here for the past five years pouring her soul into this place."

"I would choose her over me," Noelle mumbled, dropping into a chair. She could tell Hannah was trying valiantly not to laugh, and she knew she sounded ridiculous, but damn it she was scared, and some of those fears were reasonable.

"Okay, back up," Hannah told her, pushing out of her own chair and coming around the desk to perch on the edge of Noelle's. "We wouldn't choose either of you and then kick the other one out on their ass. We're grown-ups who love you both, and that's not how functional families work. This isn't really about you losing Carrigan's. What the hell is going on in your brain?" She ruffled Noelle's hair, and Noelle reflexively patted it back into place.

"My brain is trying to kill me again, I think." She buried her head in her hands. "I keep remembering trusting my parents when they would quit drinking for a few weeks, believing them that this time would be different and letting myself hope. It's like a hot stove. I'm trying to fuck up this relationship before it even starts, because I know she could hurt me someday. She's left before, what will keep her from doing it again? I don't know how to stop being petrified that this is a bad idea."

"Aha! That I can help with!" Hannah clapped, because she loved to fix things. "I fell in love, and it was a truly, extraordinarily bad idea."

"I remember," Noelle reminded her flatly. "I was there."

"And I would do it again, in an instant. My love story ended about as catastrophically as it could have without anyone dying, and I would never undo it. I would fall in love with him again, tomorrow."

"Really?" Noelle asked, shocked. "Damn." Somehow, of all the things anyone could have said, this was the one that made sense to her. The idea that falling for Miriam could go horrifically wrong but might still be worth it fluttered around inside her, like a bird out of its cage for the first time.

"I think you just have to do the next thing, even though you're terrified," Hannah told her.

"Can't you tell me what the right thing is?" Noelle pleaded.

Hannah shook her head. "What would Cass Carrigan do?"

"I'm currently closed to Cass's meddling until I've forgiven her for lying to us and using her death as a dramatic reveal instead of just reconciling with Miriam like a normal person," Noelle grumbled.

"Just because you're mad at her doesn't mean she was wrong."

That night, when everyone was long since in bed, Noelle got a text. She woke up to the insistent beeping and glared angrily at her screen.

Miriam: Meet me at the snowmobiles. Dress warmly. Bring skates.

A pond toward the back of the property had been cultivated for many years by Mr. Matthews's exacting hands and was now a perfect skating spot. They drove guests out to it via snowmobiles they kept stashed in the carriage house.

Noelle thought about letting Miriam go ice skating in the dead of night by herself but decided she was curious and that she needed to keep Miriam from falling through the ice. She wrapped herself in many layers of clothing, then grabbed her ice skates off the rack in the mudroom and headed out.

"It's the witching hour, Miriam. This is a terrible idea," she whispered, stamping her feet and blowing into her gloves. Miriam was wearing a puffy coat that went down to her knees, brushing the tops of her boots. She was so cute, it physically hurt. "Why do you always want to hang out in the middle of the night?"

"We live in a crowded hotel with my nosy family," Miriam pointed out. "The middle of the night is the only time we can be alone."

Noelle harrumphed. "I hope you know which of these has

a full tank of gas, because if we get stranded in the snow, it's not going to be cute for Insta."

"Are you always like this in the middle of the night?" Miriam asked, amused, as she climbed onto the back of the snowmobile and gestured for Noelle to sit in front of her.

"You'll just have to hang out with me more in the middle of the night and find out," Noelle told her and then mentally kicked herself. She was supposed to be treading cautiously, not flirting lasciviously.

Miriam grinned back before saying, "I'm glad you came."

They rode out in silence, neither willing to shout over the engine. Noelle drove, and Miriam held on to her back, their closeness sending jolts of electricity through Noelle. By the time they laced up their skates, she wanted to strip off all of Miriam's layers to get to her skin.

"What are we doing out here, Blum?" Noelle finally asked, after they'd skated a few circles around the ice.

"Have you ever seen *Moonstruck*?" Miriam said instead of answering. She grabbed Noelle's hands and pulled her along, skating backwards. Their fingers entwined.

"Obviously. It's a masterpiece. Why?"

"I watched it a lot as a kid because Cher's hair looked like mine. It's my comfort movie."

"That's a weird movie to let a kid watch," Noelle observed.

"It was the early nineties—people let their kids watch whatever was on cable. And my parents, specifically, were not concerned about my healthy emotional growth. Anyway. I was watching it tonight, trying to sleep. Do you remember what Nicolas Cage says? When he's talking about how the stars and snowflakes are perfect?"

Noelle shook her head. "Tell me." She loved trying to follow the fascinating trails of Miriam's thoughts.

Miriam stopped, pulled her hands away, and gestured around them to the stars and snowflakes. "He says, 'We're not here to make things perfect. That we're here to ruin ourselves, love the wrong people, break our hearts.' And I thought, I've been hiding from making a mess and breaking myself for so long. I don't want to, anymore. Nicolas Cage was right. I'm ready to ruin myself if I get to do it with you."

"What are you saying?" Noelle asked, although she knew. She wanted Miriam so much, and she wanted to hear, explicitly, with no room for uncertainty, that Miriam wanted her back just as much. She needed to know they were diving off this cliff together.

"It's my birthday, and I want a birthday kiss," Miriam said, spinning out and then coming back to a stop, very close to Noelle's face. Their breath mingled, and Noelle had to fight to take her eyes off Miriam's lips.

"Your birthday is tomorrow," Noelle pointed out. "I know this because Mrs. Matthews has been fretting about your cake for three days. It's a surprise, though, so don't tell her I told you."

"It's after midnight, so it *is* my birthday, and I want to start my birthday out with kissing," Miriam whispered, somehow moved even closer.

Noelle put her hands on Miriam's hips. To steady herself, so Miriam didn't knock her over. That was all.

"I thought you agreed this was a terrible idea," Noelle said.

"It was a terrible idea, a few days after my breakup," Miriam corrected her, "when everything was ass over teakettle. But we can't pretend there's nothing happening. We've been circling around it, and it's making me twitchy. We can't avoid it forever. We'll combust."

Noelle already felt like she was combusting, right now, smelling Miriam's toothpaste and the coconut smell of her hair as it blew around them both.

"Why now? I thought we were feeling each other out?" Noelle asked, liking that Miriam was impatient.

"You stood up for me, against your best friend in the world. You believed in me. It made me want to stop waiting. Besides"—Miriam batted her eyelashes—"why feel each other out, when we could be feeling each other up?"

Noelle barked out a surprised laugh, cutting herself off when Miriam ran a finger down her arm. She growled a little in the back of her throat.

"I'm not kidding, Noelle. I can't stop thinking about touching you. Remind me why we shouldn't get involved?" Miriam grabbed Noelle's hands again. Her face, lit up by moonlight, was so beautiful it felt unreal.

"You just broke up with your fiancée," Noelle reminded her. "We are in the middle of trying to save our shared business. We live in the same building." She wasn't even sure *she* believed any of these reasons, after her talk with Hannah, but they were her only defense left.

Her hormones shouted at her to stop mounting a defense.

"Logistics, logistics." Miriam pulled Noelle close so their bodies were flush. "What if what's going on between us is real, and we miss out on it because we're scared? We've both spent so much time trying not to get hurt, and how is that living?"

Noelle disentangled them, and Miriam made a little sound of protest. God, she wanted to hear what sounds Miriam made in bed. She wanted to throw caution to the wind, but she liked Miriam, and loved Carrigan's, too much to not be really sure.

"I wanted to take over Carrigan's," Noelle said. "It was the only thing I'd wanted in a long time. When my parents died, I was adrift. No anchor, no plans, no home base. When I got here, and Cass and Hannah enveloped me into their community, I got a family and a home again." She was getting louder, as she skated in circles and gestured.

"I have dreams again now. I have a place that's mine again." Her voice cracked, and she spun to a stop, facing Miriam. "You threw out all your old dreams in an instant for Carrigan's All Year. It scares me, that we're going to be another thing you throw away. How can I risk exploding my safe place?"

"I might be worth the risk," Miriam said softly, her eyes huge and hopeful.

Noelle's heart felt ready to escape her chest and fly out over the ice.

"It's not that I don't think you're worth the risk, Miriam. I'm just not a risk-taker anymore. I left that behind when I quit drinking, and even more when my parents died." Noelle stuffed her hands in her pockets and turned toward the trees, so she didn't have to look at Miriam when she said this next part. "Besides, I told you, I don't get emotionally involved anymore. It took me years to trust Hannah and Cass, and they're the closest I've ever been to anyone. They're stable. You're not all in on your life, and I get why you aren't, but you're asking me to go all in on you. You're talking about something real, something big. That's the only kind of thing we could start right now, something with the potential for forever, and I'm not sure I'm available for that."

"What would it take to get you to take a chance on me?" Miriam asked, not sounding frustrated, just curious. "And why have you been flirting with me nonstop if you were going to put on the brakes?" Ah, there was the frustration.

Noelle skated backwards in slow circles, thinking.

"The second question is easy. I can't stop myself. You're irresistible. The first question is harder. What convinced you that now's the time? What makes you sure, with all my baggage and everything at stake, I'm worth the risk?" she asked. "Or did you get impatient and decide to damn the potential consequences?"

She watched Miriam's face blossom into a grin.

"I knew when you told Hannah I should take over the operations of Carrigan's All Year, but it wasn't only because of that. It was you loving my elephant, and protecting Hannah, and making sure Mr. Matthews is eating enough when you think no one can see you. And because when I imagine Carrigan's, in my wildest dreams, I imagine us together. What is all of this for, except making our wildest dreams come true?"

"It could get so messy," Noelle warned her. It was her final defense.

Miriam made a strangled noise. "It's already messy! Every part of this is messy. There's never going to be a perfect time, with no risk. We can't keep dancing around each other. I can't stop wanting you, and I'm dying over here. Please, Noelle, for fuck's sake, please kiss me already."

Noelle had been trying, since the first time Miriam walked into her kitchen and asked for caffeine, to stop wanting her. Instead of stopping, the feelings had only grown into a conflagration, so that every time they brushed past each other, Noelle felt it all the way down to her core. She was thinking about Miriam naked more often than she was thinking about trees, at this point.

They couldn't pretend they were just business partners anymore. It would never work.

Noelle pulled off her deerstalker and scrubbed her gloved hands through her hair. She could hear Hannah in her head, saying that she would fall in love again in an instant. If Levi was worth that much heartache, Miriam certainly was. It might be a disaster, but it also might not be, and she couldn't live with not knowing. She realized that all her fears paled in comparison to the possibility of what might be between them—to the reality of this woman.

Besides, it would take a stronger woman than Noelle to say no to Miriam Blum when she was begging to be kissed.

She shoved her hat in the back pocket of her jeans and stripped off her gloves with her teeth.

"What are you doing?" Miriam asked, giggling. "You're going to freeze!"

"If I'm going to kiss you, I'm going to do it properly," Noelle told her, skating up into Miriam's personal space and putting a hand on her waist to pull her in.

Miriam looked up at her, the millions of stars reflected in her eyes, and a little triumphant smile on her lips. Noelle tangled her other hand in Miriam's curls, bringing her face down so their noses were touching. "Are you ready?"

In response, Miriam wrapped her arms around Noelle's waist, their puffy jackets getting in the way, and moved her head a fraction of an inch to close the gap between them. They fell into each other, the center of the night, the skies circling around them. Noelle felt Miriam's knees go weak, and she chuckled where their tongues met, as she hauled her back up.

When they finally dragged their lips apart, Miriam whispered, "I don't know if I'll ever be ready."

The next morning, after a lot of kissing and very little sleep, Noelle was up early, lying in wait for Miriam in the trees. She watched Miriam walk toward her, scarf blowing behind her in the wind.

God, she was sexy.

"When I was a kid," Miriam said as soon as she was within earshot, "I loved to walk through the farm, running my fingers through the needles on either side of the aisles. I've missed them."

Noelle could understand this, as she tended to get itchy if she was away from the trees for more than a few hours. "Have you been into the back acreage?" she asked, already knowing the answer. If Miriam had been in her trees, she would have known.

"No, I've been distracted by everything else going on. I forgot how much it feels like being Lucy Pevensie to walk back into them."

It was strange, how well Miriam understood things that Noelle had never even articulated to herself.

Exhilarating.

"Hannah told me you needed me to check out a tree for the tree lighting? I trust you to choose whichever one is best," Miriam said. "But I do want to ask you about what the hell I should put on the tree."

"Oh, no, I don't need your help. That was a ruse to get you out here, because I wanted to kiss you away from our nosy friends and relations." Although she was pretty sure Hannah already knew, because she'd basically pushed Noelle out of the door.

"Well, what are you waiting for?" Miriam asked, fluttering her eyelashes and putting her fingers in the pockets of Noelle's jeans to pull herself in.

Noelle kissed her, slowly, exploring her mouth. She tasted of coffee and a Rosenstein's raspberry Danish, and it was intoxicating.

"To answer your question," she said when they broke apart, resting a hand on Miriam's ass in her fleece-lined leggings (she couldn't stop herself), "Cass used to do the decorating, so there have been some fairly wacky themed trees over the years. Elvis, pink flamingos—the lawn decoration, not the film—and cats. Flying cats." Noelle thought back. "One year it all glowed in black light. It's pretty broad. That said, you know, family-friendly."

"No dildos, you're saying. Bummer. That's totally where I was going." Miriam rolled her eyes.

Now Noelle was thinking about dildos. She was suddenly uncomfortable in her jeans. "That's enough shop talk for today," she declared, pulling Miriam back inside the circle of her arms. Now that she was allowed to touch her, she wanted to be doing it all the time. "It's your birthday, and I want to take you on a date."

"You don't need to do that!" Miriam protested. "I don't usually make a big deal out of my birthday. Besides, we already had a romantic ice-skating date, and I already got my birthday wish." She looked up at Noelle, waggling her eyebrows. "If you know what I mean."

"I may not have dated for a while, but I haven't forgotten how a butch treats her lady. I'm going to make a big deal out of your birthday, and I'm going to woo you. You planned that date last night, and I didn't get a chance to impress you." Noelle kissed her on the nose. "I'm taking you out. But just to Advent, because we have to be home in time for Mrs. Matthews's big secret birthday celebration with her cake, or she'll kill me."

They took Noelle's refurbished red 1976 Chevy pickup. The wood paneling on the door gleamed, the white leather seats oiled to a sheen. "Did you do the rehab on this yourself?" Miriam walked around the truck, trailing her fingers down the white stripe on the door.

Noelle felt herself puffing up with pride. "She's not overwhelmingly practical in the snow, but I love her. The heat is out, sorry. I haven't had time to fix it, what with everything else going on. You can snuggle up next to me for warmth." She smirked at Miriam, who rolled her eyes.

"Oh, that's so kind of you, ma'am. I don't mind if I do," Miriam drawled. She pressed her body up against Noelle's.

Noelle cleared her throat. *I did this to myself*, she thought, *and now I'm going to have to enjoy the torture.*

"Did you build this to impress girls?" Miriam asked, laying her head on Noelle's shoulder.

"Hell yes," Noelle said, suddenly nervous. "Is it working?"

"Definitely working. I love that I destroy antiques, and you restore them. Although if you want me to add some glitter glue..."

Noelle glared at her, and she grinned mischievously.

They drove into Advent with only the sound of the radio between them, their legs pressing against each other every time Noelle shifted. Noelle kept her eyes firmly on the road, hoping Miriam couldn't see her blush.

Their first stop was an antique shop. Noelle wanted to give Miriam a chance to play and show her that Noelle took her work seriously. The owner was overjoyed to see Miriam. "I've been following you on Instagram. I love that mirror piece you posted last month. Come on, I'll make you a cup of coffee while you warm up, and then I'll show you some junk I think you'll like."

They followed the woman into the back of the shop, past a wall of porcelain heads filled with plastic flowers, and plastic Christmas decorations from the sixties. This was definitely Miriam's kind of place.

"You brought me to an antique shop?" Miriam whispered to Noelle. "I'm going to get distracted by stuff and not pay any attention to you!"

"I know," Noelle said. "I'm going to watch you do it, and it's going to make my whole day. Nothing's cuter than you getting excited about art."

Miriam made that noise in her throat that Noelle was already learning meant she was about to get kissed, but the shop owner interrupted.

"Now, I think you'll love this badly taxidermized mongoose."

They left the shop with the back of the pickup full of various merchandise and a ton of shots of Miriam holding the pieces up for the Bloomers. Miriam and Noelle walked, hand in hand, down Main Street, visiting the diner and the boutique. Collin made them latte art and blushed when Miriam asked him about Marisol.

They also stopped by a tiny library in a converted old house. The librarian had worked at Carrigan's as a teen, before going away to college and coming back with her master's, determined to convince the town council to fund a library. She was excited to see Miriam back home, and Miriam was excited to have a place for new books. When warm vanilla smells wafted out onto the snow from a bakery and ice cream shop, Miriam dragged them inside to eat specialty homemade ice cream, in spite of Noelle's protestations that it was, in fact, below freezing outside. ("It's my birthday, I get ice cream," she argued.) The baker picked Miriam's brain about some of Rosenstein's vintage recipes that they'd retired. They talked for so long about local distributors of artisanal butter that Noelle ate all of Miriam's ice cream, and they had to order a second round.

Noelle loved watching Miriam connect with all the people in Advent, who were a part of her own daily life. It made this feel more real, more concrete, that Miriam was here to stay. And she found that kissing the ice cream out of Miriam's mouth warmed her up quickly, even as snowflakes began to fall around them.

As they started to make the drive back, the snow started coming down harder.

"So," Noelle said as she drove, mostly to stop herself from daydreaming about Things a Person Could Do to Another Person in the Bench Seat of a Truck, "you're the only gay girl I've ever met who only hangs out with a straight guy and a bunch of old people who own antique stores. Don't you get lonely for fellowship?"

"Let me tell you a secret about the kind of confirmed bachelors and spinster aunts who own antique shops," Miriam said with a wink. "And I have friends in Charleston, although admittedly many of them are Tara's friends. I don't know, my childhood was somewhat lacking in examples of normal affection, you know, except from Cass, so I sort of gravitate toward people who remind me of her. Besides, I often feel unwelcome in queer spaces as a bisexual, so sometimes I avoid them, so I won't have to feel like I'm not gay enough."

"You need friends your own age," Noelle grumbled, "who do not worship you on social media." She was grouchy, because she wanted to go back and make the last ten years— hell, the last thirty years—of Miriam's life less lonely.

"Well, Ms. Judgmental, I'm so glad you've volunteered," Miriam said dryly.

"I was volunteering you for Elijah's trivia team. Is friends what we're going for?" Noelle asked, raising an eyebrow in Miriam's direction. "I'm going to be very disappointed, if so."

Miriam put her hand on Noelle's thigh, and Noelle felt the sensation all the way through her body. "I'll have to be friends with someone else then."

"Good," Noelle growled before pausing. She glanced at the little clown music box Miriam had bought at the antique store and was now fiddling with. "Can I ask you something?"

"Sure?" Miriam sounded wary.

"Well, you may have noticed that I'm interested in un-wrapping the mystery of Miriam Blum," Noelle began, "and one of the many questions I have is, why the Bloomer Face? You put this weird as fuck art into the world, but then you sell it with this fake version of you."

"Part of it is that my fans are strangers I have a parasocial relationship with," Miriam explained, shifting in her seat to look at Noelle, "and there's only so close I want to be to them, for safety reasons. I am a queer Jew on the internet, so that requires some careful boundaries. But I'm also not convinced they would want to know the real, messy, fucked-up person who makes that weird art."

Noelle shook her head. "If they don't want to, they're missing out. You have a deeply strange soul, and it's pretty incredible."

She tried to keep her eyes on the road while also gauging Miri's reaction. She could see out of the corner of her eye that Miriam had blushed all the way up to her hair.

"Pull the truck over," Miriam said, in a strangled voice. Noelle did as she was told. She put the truck into park and looked over at Miriam, who was already throwing a leg over her lap. Before Noelle knew what was happening, she was being straddled by a tiny elf, curls enveloping her head, hands in her hair, and Miriam's lips on hers.

"I'm not complaining, but what are you doing?"

"You just said the nicest thing anyone's ever said to me," Miriam said, kissing her harder.

"That you're weird as fuck, and I'm into it?" Noelle asked, against her mouth, confused but not complaining.

There was no response, except a little squeak of lust and Miriam pressing her body closer.

Noelle let herself sink into the kiss, wrapping one hand around Miriam's hips and bracing the other against the dashboard to give herself leverage. They frantically explored each other's mouths, tongues and teeth and hands everywhere. When Miriam leaned back to unbutton her shirt, her back hit the horn on the steering wheel. A tiny piece of logic entered Noelle's lust-addled brain. Beyond the fogged-up windows of the truck, the snow was falling even harder.

"Babe, we are going to get ticketed for public indecency and stuck in this snowstorm overnight, neither of which is a way to spend your birthday. You would miss Mrs. Matthews's cake." She pushed Miriam's curls away from her face, dragging a thumb over her kiss-plumped lips.

"It sounds like the best way I can imagine spending my birthday," Miriam said, grinning, "but I'll behave myself."

She resettled herself in the seat next to Noelle, and Noelle kicked herself for being way too rational for her own good.

"Did you find any inspiration for the tree at the shop?" she asked, to distract herself.

"I think all the inspiration I need is already at Carrigan's," Miriam said, cryptically.

The snow kept falling, and they only made it inside by following the Christmas lights to the front of the house.

Cole opened the front door, to her surprise. "I was worried you died in the snow," Cole whined.

"What are you doing here?" Miriam squeaked, throwing her arms around him.

"It's your *birthday*, Mimi," Cole said, picking Miriam up and swinging her around. "Mrs. Matthews baked a *cake*. Also, you need help with the Christmas tree lighting."

"Well, you can help me go up to the attic to find more materials," Miriam said. "I think we're going to be snowed in up here for a couple of days, so I should have plenty of time to finish all the decorations before the carnival."

"So," Hannah drawled, peeking into the bags, "do you know what your theme is going to be, yet?"

"I do," Miriam laughed, snatching the bag back, "and it's a secret! Cole?"

"To the attic!" They linked arms and skipped up the stairs. At the top, Miriam looked back down at Noelle and winked.

Shit, she was a goner.

Chapter 16

Miriam

I have never seen this many Miriam Blum originals in one place," Cole said, circling the attic.

"I gave them to Cass over the years. She's the one who pushed me to make a career out of turning mild-mannered antiques into kitschy wonders," Miriam said, half-lost in memories of the girl who'd made them, the woman who'd collected them, and the one who treasured them now. She ran her hands over a rocking horse with cellophane, sequin-covered dragon wings, and giant, mirrored reptile eyes. "I went through a weird dark phase where I made a lot of creepy animal mash-ups."

"You have a lot of potential money up here, Mimi."

Miriam surveyed the attic. "Yeah," she agreed. "Especially if I parceled the pieces out and sold them over a couple of years." She touched pieces she hadn't seen in a decade, parts of her past she'd thought were gone forever. "It could help keep Carrigan's afloat."

"But you wouldn't have all the pieces you gave to Cass that she kept all these years," he pointed out. She should have known he would see how hard that choice would be, even if it were the rational one.

This attic felt like another message Cass had left her: "I never stopped loving you or supporting you." If she sold all of it, she would lose another string tying her back to Cass.

"I can always make more art." Although it wouldn't be art she'd made for Cass, where she'd pulled a part of her heart out and gifted it to her favorite person, the only way she had known to show her gratitude.

"Can you?" Cole asked skeptically. "You haven't actually made any art you're happy with since you got here, I notice." Damn Cole. He chose the least opportune moments to be perceptive.

"I can," she said, picking up a miniature Ferris wheel covered in spikes. "I can feel the inklings of that creative itch with this tree project."

"What do you think the block was?" Cole sat on a trunk that was too short for him, his knees up around his ears. "Was it like a walking and chewing gum thing, where you could either experience deep emotion or make art, but not both at once?"

Miriam wandered around, picking things up and blowing the dust off as she went. "That was part of it. It's going to take some practice getting my feet underneath me." She hadn't realized that her walls being so low made her much more vulnerable when she went into her art zone. "I feel like I have a sunburn I keep forgetting about until I bang it up against something. And until this tree project, nothing was clicking. I couldn't quite drop into that mental place." She held up a three-headed cat statue and hmmed at it. "But it's also, you know, the farm's been in danger, I've been grieving, reconnecting with Hannah..."

"Connecting with Noelle," Cole interrupted, his look pointed.

"Sure, that too." Miriam laughed.

"How are you adjusting, really? You've had a tornado of stuff happen in the past couple of months, and your life is completely different than the last time I saw you a few weeks ago. You seem like you're breathing easier, or standing up straighter? Something's different." Cole set his chin on his knees, his tone turning serious.

She held her hands up in a show of ambivalence. "I'm still terrified I made the worst decision of my life and it's going to explode in my face any minute, and I still have to pep talk myself every morning about the fact that I'm taking this big risky adventure, but at the same time, all these fears I've had all my life are gone. I'm not afraid of facing my past anymore, and I feel really proud of myself, you know? I faced so much and I'm here, making a new life for myself."

"I'm proud of you, too," Cole told her seriously. And then he winked dramatically, so that the moment didn't get too emotional.

"So, to address the elephant in the room," Miriam said, "my ex-fiancée, your lifelong friend? How's Tara?" Tara, who apparently had stolen cars in the middle of the night with Cole during their shared, misspent youth. She guessed they'd both kept secrets.

"You know," Cole said, his face thoughtful, "I think

she's doing well. She asked me to go dancing at Dudley's last week."

Dudley's was the gay bar in Charleston, and not usually Tara's scene, since it didn't fit in with her country club image.

"Good for her!" Miriam said, meaning it. "Okay. I need to decorate a tree, and you need to help me find stuff for it."

She blew the dust off the top of a box and opened it. "Oh, vintage *National Geographics*!"

"You're the only person who has ever said that sentence." Cole shook his head in horror.

Miriam ignored him. "I'm going to start making a pile for you to carry downstairs, so we can get started. I hope I have enough glue..." She trailed off as she disappeared behind an armoire that hid a life-sized paper diorama of a tapdancing pig, cut in intricate detail, and which popped up when the doors were opened.

Behind the diorama, resting against the wall, she saw an unmistakable shape wrapped in brown paper. She must have made an involuntary noise because Cole came up behind her.

The package, several flat surfaces unevenly stacked together, had Cass's distinctive handwriting sprawled across its front.

Mimi Roz

"Is that what I think it is?" Cole asked, putting an arm around her to steady her.

"You know about the paintings?" she whispered because the noise in her brain was too loud to think anything else.

"I do, baby. I'm sorry, I snooped."

She would be mad, maybe, later, when she could think again.

"What do I do? Do I open them?" She turned to him, feeling wild, terrified. "What do I do?"

He put both hands on her shoulders. "You don't have to decide right now, and I will support you no matter what. So what we're going to do is go downstairs and eat cake. You're going to kiss your new girl and spend your birthday with your cousin and your surrogate parents for the first time in ten years. And you're going to give yourself as much space as you need to decide."

"I love you," she said, looking into Cole's eyes, her voice breaking.

"How could you not?" Cole asked, waving her off, pretending flippancy. "Come on, kid. We need cake."

Miriam stayed up all night, working on the decorations for the tree lighting, supergluing and glittering as she thought. She worked with intensity, Mod Podge in her cleavage and feathers stuck on her arms. She had a vision for the tree lighting, and it was going to take everyone's breath away.

Making art she was really excited about felt electric. Like she was breathing again, after having held her breath since the moment her mother called to tell her about Cass.

And all the while, her brain was a locomotive.

How had Cass gotten her paintings, and why had she hidden them? What the fuck was Miriam supposed to do, knowing they were sitting there, where she could open them at any moment? Part of her wanted to leave them there, a sleeping viper that couldn't bite if it weren't awakened, but she wasn't sure she could. Still, she needed to complete the tree installation, and if she wasn't willing to go back to the attic quite yet, there was only one other place to get the materials.

"We're cleaning out Cass's closets," she announced to the dining room when she went for breakfast, which was, this early in the day, just Hannah, Noelle, and Mrs. Matthews.

"*All* of them?" Noelle asked in horror. "Do you know how many clothes Cassiopeia Carrigan owned?"

Hannah cleared her throat. "That's, um, a big job." Miriam watched her fiddle with her teacup handle and then actually sit on her hands. "Are you sure you want to take the lead on that project?"

Miriam came out of her panic-driven productivity haze enough to recognize how big of a step this was for her cousin, letting her be in charge of this.

"Let me rephrase." She sat down next to Hannah. "I connect to people through their belongings. Seeing what people left behind as little discarded treasures is so much a part of my work. I missed a big chunk of Cass's life, but I think going through her things might help me feel close to her again. And, I might be able to use some of her stuff for the tree lighting, which would give us a chance to share her with our community one last time."

Hannah took a conspicuously long time chewing her breakfast sandwich.

Noelle winked at Miriam and stepped in. "You know, her stuff is taking up the entire top floor. If we started clearing it out, eventually we could rent out that floor and get a lot of guest space back."

Miriam watched as Hannah absorbed this information. "That's true, and I don't have time to do it," she said, finally.

"Take Noelle with you, or you'll get trapped under a pile of feather boas and we'll never find you again."

The top floor, which Cass had kept as her personal domain, looked like the inside of a fortune teller's tent from a silent film.

"Cass always did regret that she never ran away with the circus," Miriam said appreciatively.

"Too much sustained human interaction, not enough closet space, is what she told me." Noelle agreed.

Wooden beaded curtains sectioned the rooms off into various spaces. Cass's California king mattress, on a massive brass filigree bed frame draped in tulle, took up the entire center of one room. Tiny white twinkle lights ("That hypocrite!" Miriam gasped) hung haphazardly from every post.

Seamstress dummies stood in one corner, hats and ancient mink coats piled seven or eight high on each. Framed photos spanning nine decades covered another wall. One room was filled with clothes racks, from which hung pristine dresses, wool slacks, cashmere sweaters, and more scarves than Miriam had known currently existed on the planet.

One entire room was just shoes.

"Shit," Miriam said. Kringle meowed in agreement next to her, having apparently followed them to help. "What are we going to do with all this stuff? Some of it has tags from 1957."

Noelle was picking up and modeling turbans. Miriam surreptitiously took a picture of her in a lurid pink silk with a two-foot ostrich plume drooping over one ear, then couldn't resist pulling on the feather to bring Noelle's mouth down to hers.

"Gosh, well," Noelle shrugged dramatically, after breaking the kiss, "it's too bad we don't know anyone whose only friends are old theater people who now own consignment and antique shops."

"Hey," Miriam protested, wrapping herself in an avocado-green robe, embroidered with orange and teal dragons, "I'm also friends with Cole."

"Do you think any of your Old Ladies would want to carry any of this?" Noelle gestured to a bookshelf stuffed with purses.

"We should ask Marisol first," Miriam said, "because people in Advent might want something to remember Cass by."

Noelle held up a yellow and turquoise paisley trench coat, clutching it to her nose and burying her face in it. "I remember the last time she wore this," she said, tears in her eyes. "She was too sick to go down to yell at the Advent town council about something, so she made them come here, and she wore this. She said it was good luck."

Miriam caught her breath, unable to imagine Cass so sick she couldn't travel a couple of miles to yell at someone.

She walked the perimeter of the room, touching tchotchkes and the mismatched jumble of furniture, trying to imagine all the lives Cass had lived before any of them knew her. She stopped short in front of a mirrored vanity covered in gold leaf and decked in perfume bottles. Tucked into the mirror frame was a snapshot of three kids in snowsuits. She, Hannah, and Blue had to be six or seven, their cheeks red from joy and wind. They had their arms around each other, a sled at their feet, and they were glowing. Miriam pulled it gently out.

On the back, Cass had written *The Heirs of Cassiopeia*. Miriam must have made a noise because Noelle came over to see what was wrong. She wrapped her arms around Miriam's shoulders, and Miriam relaxed back into her.

"I've never seen this picture before," Miriam whispered.

"Do you remember when it was taken?" Noelle asked.

"Oh yes," Miriam said. "Blue decided he was going to sled to Canada, and we wouldn't let him go without us. Our entire childhood was him dragging us into Shenanigans. There was a big storm forecast, and our parents were livid we'd been out so far from the house, but we were having so much fun, we couldn't even pretend we were sorry. I didn't know this picture existed. I wonder why this is the one Cass kept?"

Noelle smiled softly. "None of the three of you were particularly happy children, from what I've heard, but here you all are, together and joyous, hooligans throwing away the rules for a moment of pure bliss? She must have been so proud, and so hopeful."

Miriam sat down on the bed and crossed her legs underneath her. Noelle's shoulders were bowed, her hands stuffed into her pockets. She looked...uprooted. "How are you really doing," Miriam asked, "without her?"

Noelle brought her hands up to cover her eyes, and there was silence for a long moment. Miriam patted the bed next to her, and Noelle sank down.

"This is not how I intended to get you in bed for the first time," Miriam said gently.

Noelle laughed a thin, watery laugh. "I'm not doing well,

I'll tell you that. I keep getting my grief for Cass all tangled up in stuff I thought I'd put away or gotten over about my parents. I didn't get to see them in their last months, or even years, but I got to see Cass. I got to see Cass every day until the morning I woke up to her gone." Miriam gasped out a sob, and Noelle laced their fingers together.

"I'm glad you got that," Miriam said, leaning into Noelle's warmth and solidness. "I'm a little jealous. I wonder how I'll ever get the chance to make up for missing the last ten years."

"You just stay," Noelle said, putting both arms around Miriam and kissing her curls. "You take care of what she built. You make a wild, hooligan, joyous life that breaks the rules, in her honor."

"She must have loved the hell out of you. I wish I could have seen that."

"Why do you say that? Maybe she thought I was good with an evergreen," Noelle said.

"Look at who she left the farm to. The two nieces she helped raise, the son of her best friends, whom she lived with since the day he was born, and you. She loved you like you were one of us."

"I think that's why I was so mad at you, after the will reading. Because I knew I didn't fit, with the three of you. Some part of me thought you deserved Carrigan's and I didn't, like I didn't have an equal claim."

"You belong to this place, and it to you," Miriam said, squeezing her hand. She couldn't imagine Carrigan's without Noelle, like the Christmasland had always been saving a seat for her.

Noelle nuzzled her hair. "Thank you. For saying that. When I got here, it felt like Oz, you know? Like it was too good to be true, and eventually I was going to accidentally click my heels and end up back in Kansas," Noelle admitted.

"Dorothy wanted to go home," Miriam pointed out.

"Yeah, I never understood that. Why wouldn't you want to stay in the fantastical world with the talking lions?"

Kringle chirped at this.

"Do you want me to put ruby-red glitter on your Docs?" Miriam teased.

Noelle moved away in horror. "Her slippers were silver in the book, and you wouldn't dare."

"Are you sure? I have a lot of silver glitter."

Noelle laughed, and Miriam had a moment of fierce, pure joy. Here, surrounded by the detritus of a life lived to its absolute maximum, she knew she needed to stop keeping secrets if she wanted to be an heir of Cass in any real way. She couldn't really be settled here, for good, if she didn't start building bridges from her island to the Carrigan's mainland.

"I have to tell you something," she said. Noelle must have heard the gravity of her tone, and she turned her whole body to Miriam, all her attention focused. "I found some paintings in the attic, yesterday. Some Mimi Roz paintings." Her voice stuck. She couldn't figure out how to continue.

"Who's Mimi Roz?" Noelle prompted.

"I am. Or I was. I, wait, I'm starting in the wrong place. I have to tell you more about my dad." She took a deep breath, rubbed her hands on her legs to center herself. "He raised me to follow him into business, marry well, be a jewel in his crown. He started out owning a car dealership, then bought rental properties, invested in local businesses, served on a bunch of boards." She waved dismissively. "He's a big name in Scottsdale but not a national presence. Don't tell him that, though. He likes to imagine himself as a power broker.

"During college, I started painting," she continued. "I didn't show anyone at first. I was so scared of how much I loved it." She swallowed. "When you grow up with someone who has a very specific idea of who you are supposed to be, it's terrifying to have anything that's all yours. After college I moved to New York for a couple of years, ostensibly to work for a friend of my dad's and gain some business experience, but really to try to make it in art. I was pretty good, I thought, and I had a friend from high school who was interning at a gallery in New York. My friend agreed to show some paintings to the gallery owner. He loved them and gave me a spot in a show."

"That's huge, Miriam. You must be incredibly talented, which isn't surprising, considering your other work," Noelle told her, squeezing her hand.

"Thank you." She squeezed Noelle's hand back. "I submitted the paintings under the name Mimi Roz, after Cole's nickname for me and my mom's maiden name. I thought if I didn't tie it too closely back to my father, he couldn't be too angry with me, and maybe he wouldn't interfere." She kept her eyes unfocused. Noelle brought their grasped hands up to her lips.

"Maybe he wouldn't have, either, if I hadn't gotten such good press. The show got written up in the *Times*, with pictures of me and my paintings. There were interested buyers for every piece. We sold a couple to collectors. And then, suddenly, they were all bought, by one 'very generous patron,' the gallery owner put it."

She paused to acknowledge Noelle's sharp intake of breath.

"We went out to our house on Cape Cod for a weekend, and my father was terrifying. Jovial, almost gleeful. He opened a bottle of wine, built a bonfire, served lobster. And then, he started talking. Not yelling. He was calm, almost pleasant."

She'd started shaking. Noelle rubbed her thumb in circles over Miriam's shoulder.

"He explained that he'd been telling his friends for years about his brilliant daughter who was going to come join him in business as soon as she graduated. He said that he couldn't simply have me run off to paint silly fairy-tale paintings and play boho. What would it look like to his business associates? They would all judge him if his own daughter didn't want to come work with him. It would make a fool out of him."

She breathed in, sucking air into her lungs like she was drowning.

"I can still hear him in my head. I've been hearing him, every day for ten years. I could see, couldn't I, why I couldn't be allowed to continue this delusion I had of choice. I wasn't even talented. I wasn't even using the name he'd so graciously given me. It looked like I wanted to distance myself from him."

"Miriam," Noelle asked, sounding sick, "what did he do?"

"He took the paintings out, one by one," Miriam said. "He'd bought all of them, except for the two we'd already sold. He fed them all into the bonfire. I should have stopped him, I know, but I was frozen. I thought, if I lunge at him, he'll just throw me in the fire, too." Tears streamed down her face, and she swiped at them.

"So I sobbed, and I begged him to stop. And he laughed, and they kept burning."

She could still smell it, the kerosene and the ocean, like she was back there. There was a reason she'd done everything she could for ten years to forget that night. Noelle stroked Miriam's hair until Miriam stopped shaking from the effort of telling this story for the first time.

"He thought he had left me with no options except to meekly join the family business," Miriam continued when her voice was steady enough. She wanted to pull herself into a little ball, but she let Noelle hold her instead. She wasn't sure she'd get to the end of this without that warmth. "When, shockingly, I was disinterested in working for him, he threatened to cut me off from any family funds. I took him up on it. He thought I had nowhere to go, but I had Cole's couch."

"Your dad underestimated your support network," Noelle said.

"He doesn't love anyone, so he never takes into account that people might help me because they love me," Miriam said. "Cole let me stay, and never asked why or pried. It was the only thing that kept me alive. I owe him . . . everything, for that time."

"He's a good egg. Strange, but good." Noelle's voice was warm. Miriam loved that Noelle understood Cole. "And that's when you stopped coming here?"

Miriam nodded, a bubble of grief rising in her throat. "I was barely making it through every day. I felt like I was being held together by worn-out tape. I thought if I came here, I would have to talk about it with Cass and Hannah, Levi would try to make me process it...I couldn't face any of them. It doesn't make sense, but it felt like, if I came to Carrigan's, my whole house of cards would collapse."

"We don't always make logical sense when we're responding to trauma," Noelle observed wryly, and Miriam laughed a little wet laugh. "If he hated you painting high-end gallery art so much, doesn't he hate your new work even more, especially with your real name attached? How did you get him to leave you alone and let you have a career?"

"I knew that I needed to make art, to live," Miriam said, "but I couldn't paint. I would sit in front of the canvas and cry. I needed to do something else. I spent a lot of time wandering in and out of antique shops in Charleston, making friends with the owners, trying to fill my days. Eventually, I started buying things, little tacky trinkets. They reminded me of Cass, you know?"

She gestured around them, at the room filled with small forgotten shiny things. "I would decoupage them, put them up on Pinterest. Cass loved them, and she kept buying them from me. When my dad found out, inevitably, because he hires a PI to keep track of me, he threatened to put me out of business. Cole suggested I threaten him back."

"Did you threaten to cut off his balls and deep-fry them in a vat of hot oil in front of him? Because that's kind of my response," Noelle said, her whole body puffed up in anger.

It was so freeing to have someone else be righteously indignant on her behalf. She'd never given herself the space to feel that anger. Somehow, Noelle doing it let her move out of the flashback into a more neutral space.

Miriam chuckled. "No, I threatened the only thing he cares about. His name. There had been rumors for years that he was running high-end drugs through his car imports. Bored society wife kind of drugs, nothing he'd think of as 'low-class.' He'd built this reputation as a big Community Hero, appearing on telethons and donating giant checks to shelters for homeless children, that kind of thing. He wouldn't be able to stand losing face. His ego won't let him be exposed. He needs adulation."

"Wow, so wealthy white dude playing with what he sees as 'high-class' drugs and being totally unconcerned about prison?" Noelle asked, sounding disgusted.

"Oh yeah, it's some deeply fucked-up racist privilege in action," Miriam affirmed.

"What the hell is he getting out of it that's worth the risk?" Noelle asked. "Just getting to playact as the Big Cool Drug Boss?"

Miriam nodded. "Basically. I told him I had proof of what he was doing, and that if he ever came anywhere near my art or my career again, I would release the evidence. I can't actually release the proof without someone finding out that Cole got it illegally, but it spooked him. He hasn't come anywhere near me since. I assume, as I've built a platform, he's gotten less willing to test me. If he tried anything, I would release his info to the Bloomers, and, like all fandoms, they have the capacity for vicious violence."

"You know, if I were you," Noelle said thoughtfully, "I think I'd yell at my mom a lot, every time I saw her."

"I was trained not to yell from a pretty early age." Miriam shrugged, and Noelle wrapped her up in a bear hug.

"So, now there are Mimi Roz paintings in the attic. Which I assume were stashed there, somehow, magically, by Cass," Noelle said.

Miriam nodded into Noelle's flannel, where her face was still buried.

"And you feel... elated? Terrified? Shell-shocked?" Noelle asked.

Miriam nodded again. "Yes. All of the above."

"What are you going to do with them?"

"I don't have the faintest clue, yet." Miriam pulled away to look at Noelle's face. "I haven't even unwrapped them. I don't know which ones they are. I just—I found them, I freaked out a little, then I ate cake and made a lot of art, and now we're here."

"I'll support you, whatever you decide. We all will."

"I know. But I need to focus on the tree lighting and getting the Rosensteins on board and the bank figured out. Make it to the other side of this crisis, and then I'll deal with them. They're not going anywhere."

"My brave girl," Noelle said quietly, and Miriam's dam finally broke. She wept, and Noelle held her. They sat there, rocking together, surrounded by Cass's smell and tulle and hypocritical twinkle lights, for a long time.

Chapter 17

Noelle

The night before Christmas Eve, they held an anniversary celebration for all the couples who had been married at Carrigan's over the years. Miriam was helping Mrs. Matthews finish off the dinner rolls when Noelle walked by with a stack of wine bottles in her arms.

She'd thought she had a solid grip, but one of the bottles shifted and slipped out of her hands, shattering, slow motion, on the floor. The smell of merlot filled the kitchen.

Noelle coughed. "Well, that smell takes me back to the bad old days." She smiled ruefully as she headed for the broom to sweep up the glass shards.

Mr. Matthews shooed her away from the mess. "You know I would have taken care of the wine."

"You were busy fixing the tractor, and we have to get ready for tonight, Ben."

Mr. Matthews swatted her with the broom until she went to see if Miriam needed help with the rolls.

"You call him Ben?!" Miriam whispered to her. "I've never called him Ben in the thirty-five years I've known him!"

"You're jealous that they love me more," Noelle teased, nudging her shoulder as Miriam stood at the kitchen island working.

"I'm glad they love you so much," Miriam said quietly. "You deserve it." She scooted over a tray of rolls. "Do you ever talk about them? The bad old days?"

Noelle took the basting brush from her and dipped it in the butter, watching the bristles drip but not brushing the rolls. Kringle sat under her feet, watching her intently and waiting for her to drop butter on the floor. She didn't want to give Miriam a drunkalogue of every afternoon she woke up hungover with an answering machine message from the school about truancy that her parents would ignore, every girl who she went home with from a party when she was too young for parties or girls.

But she wanted to be honest.

"They were a very long time ago, so long that sometimes I forget that I'm the person it happened to," she finally said. "I started drinking when I was ten, drinking hard when I was thirteen. I drank everything I could get my hands on all through high school." And it was easy to get her hands on whatever, because her parents were happy to have her drinking with them.

"Then senior year, I had a crush on a girl who went to young people's AA meetings, so I started going to impress her. We didn't get together, and she didn't stay sober, but it stuck for me. I worked my ass off to retake my SATs and send out my college applications. I had a great school librarian who went way out of her way to help, and by some miracle, I got in." *Without any help from my parents, who could only complain that I wasn't fun anymore,* she thought.

"I quit for good, I hope, when I was eighteen, then spent a few years trying to catch up to everyone else, emotionally. I barely knew what it meant to be human at that point. I'd been basically feral for a long time."

Miriam looked up at her, all big hazel eyes, and Noelle's heart somersaulted. "I'm so glad. That you're sober. That you're here. That you're you."

"Me too. I'm really glad to be me, and here, and sober right now," Noelle agreed, dropping her forehead to Miriam's.

Mrs. Matthews, Mr. Matthews, and Hannah all sought her out at some point during the dinner to rib her gently about how she and Miriam were finally, as Hannah put it, "dealing with the incredibly annoying sexual tension that's making it difficult to get any work done around here."

Noelle almost wished they'd hidden their new relationship for a little while, until she realized that every time they passed, they reached out for the small of a back or the crook of a neck, like magnets. Until she looked up in the middle of a conversation to find Miriam watching her, and she knew her face must have transformed with wanting, because a blush rose immediately on Miriam's cheeks. Noelle wanted to run her fingers over that pink skin, to see how much pinker she could make it, how much of Miriam's body blushed. She realized there was no hiding this.

Goddamn it. All her bullshit talk about how she couldn't fall in love and she was already three-fourths gone for this woman. They'd only just started kissing.

She was so screwed.

Now she had to hope like hell she really could trust Miriam with her heart.

Christmas Eve morning dawned brilliant, with piles of snow glinting in the sun that had finally come out. Mr. Matthews had valiantly plowed the roads through to town, and the Carrigan's shuttle was running nonstop.

The front lawn had been transformed into a bazaar, with booths packed in where decorated trees had once been. The humane society was selling roasted chestnuts and locally made wreaths. The music store had kazoos, penny whistles, harmonicas—all good things to put in stockings and then hide by the end of Christmas Day when the noise got over-whelming. There was a paperback book swap tent, where everyone dropped off the romances and mysteries and sci-fi they had accumulated over the year and took away new-to-them treasures.

Mr. Matthews was in his traditional Santa suit, taking last-minute gift requests (to the panic of parents) and photos. Cole, dressed as an elf, directed traffic. The costume had been around for decades, and the green velveteen was worn at the knees. One of the Velcro tabs had come off the back just as Cole was supposed to be out front, and the fabric was currently safety-pinned together. Since it had been designed for someone shorter than Cole's six foot five inches, it stopped at his calves. He had added on knee-high red socks with a snowflake pattern (an early stocking stuffer from Hannah) and a pair of fur-lined boat shoes that he had ordered via overnight delivery.

He proclaimed it the happiest day of his life.

Mrs. Matthews ladled out her famous homemade eggnog from her booth. Hannah was by the carriage house, bundling couples into the sleigh for romantic rides through the pines. Joshua Matthews had taken the train up that morning with his family and was driving the sleigh while seven year old Grant "supervised." Esther Matthews had brought a surprise boyfriend, improbably named Rocket, whom she hadn't told her parents about.

Mrs. Matthews didn't like him.

Miriam had deputized Esther to run the livestream on Blum Again's Facebook page, and she was wandering around charmingly describing the festival for the Bloomers and the Rosensteins who were watching to judge the success of the event.

Ziva had arrived that morning (but not, Noelle had noticed, in time for Miriam's birthday). She was holding court among the long-term returning families, telling fully orchestrated dramatic renditions of Carrigan's Christmases of Old, with plenty of haggling over details from the people who had also been there. Fisticuffs nearly broke out over the origin of the reindeer races.

A bluegrass band played Christmas carols from the porch, where they had set themselves up. Ernie was at the upright bass and the librarian was burning up banjo solos. "I'll Be Home for Christmas" on bluegrass fiddle was a soul-altering experience. Everyone was moving, everything was glowing.

After lunch, Elijah and Jason were trying to corral the

twins, who were flitting from booth to booth and begging for a second Christmas tree.

"There are two of us!" they argued. "We should have twin trees!"

Noelle swung little Jayla in a circle, while her brother, Jeremiah, pulled on Noelle's pants for a turn. "Where are you going to put two trees in your house, my sweet babies?"

Before they could answer, Miriam took each twin in one hand. "What if," Miriam said, leading them toward the trees, "we go pick out a sapling for each of you, that can be your tree forever, as long as it's growing?"

"I owe you!" Elijah called after her.

Noelle grinned, hoping Miriam and Elijah would become real friends.

Marisol and Collin had booths next to each other in front of the porch, between the roasted chestnuts and a caricature artist, Marisol selling brooches and trinkets and scarves—more stocking stuffers—while Collin peddled mincemeat pasties and peppermint mochas. Marisol was quite obviously flirting with Collin. His face had turned as red as his hair and he was at a complete loss for words. Noelle suspected, watching them, that by the end of this night, Marisol might "accidentally" drag Collin underneath some mistletoe and demand tradition be kept.

She found the old lady alcoholics wandering as a pack through the late afternoon light, haggling over prices, collecting trinkets, smoking like chimneys. They poked Noelle good-naturedly about Miriam.

"You did good, kid," the ball player told her. "Don't screw it up."

And through it all, Kringle lurked through the snow, winding through people's legs, begging for scraps and attention. Toddlers, unused to seeing a cat larger than themselves, chased him gleefully.

Noelle's heart was full of how much she loved this damn place, and all these people.

As dusk fell, she climbed up onto the stage and took the microphone. Her bomber jacket ruffled in the breeze, and the puff ball on her snowflake beanie bobbed a little. The murmurs of the crowd faded.

"Friends and family, I'm so honored to welcome you to Carrigan's Christmasland for the annual tree lighting ceremony," she said. "As you're all aware, this year is not like any previous one at Carrigan's."

There was a mournful susurration through the crowd. Noelle pushed on, trying hard not to let her voice crack. "For the first time in its sixty-year history, Cass Carrigan is not here doing emcee duty and did not decorate our tree."

The past few weeks had been a whirlwind of distractions, and now, grief almost overwhelmed her again, the absence of Cass rolling over her in a wave that threatened to suck her under. She wanted Cass to be here, so Noelle could yell at her for not intervening in Miri's childhood, for leaving them scrambling to stay afloat, for putting Hannah in such a terrible position. She wanted Cass here so she could show off Miriam, and to have Cass tell her that she was proud of how far Noelle had come.

She wanted Cass here, period, but if Cass were still here, Miriam wouldn't be, and she couldn't imagine that.

Hannah, standing on the wings of the platform, caught her eye and nodded. Noelle could hear Hannah telling her they were in this together, and besides, no one was falling into a pit of despair while there were still guests on the premises. Miriam stood next to her cousin, one arm through Hannah's, and her face lit up from within. She smiled at Noelle encouragingly, and Noelle knew, with her girls behind her, she could do anything.

"Losing Cass has left a void in our lives and our community that we may never truly fill. However, we're so lucky to have so many Carrigan women here to carry on the traditions. Mrs. Matthews, the glue that holds all of us together. Hannah, my amazing co-manager; Ziva, Cass's niece; and Miriam, Cass's great-niece. You may know Miriam better as the incredible artist Miriam Blum." A few people in the crowd whooped.

"Miriam graciously agreed to decorate our tree for the ceremony this year. And I'm ecstatic to bring her up to announce the theme and unveil the tree." The crowd applauded as Miriam walked up the stairs.

Noelle hugged Miriam, hard, and whispered in her ear, "I'm proud of you."

Miriam teared up, then faced the crowd and grinned.

"Noelle mentioned four Carrigan women here tonight, but truly, we have five. None of this would have happened without Noelle."

The audience applauded louder. Noelle dashed her own tears away. Miriam, this woman, calling her a Carrigan. It felt so right, all of them together. The future of Carrigan's was this team. She hoped to hell the Rosensteins saw it, because her heart was going to break, again, if they had to give up this magical, perfect dream.

"I've never decorated a Christmas tree before," Miriam admitted, "and I'm not certain I've lived up to Cass's precedent. The only theme I could possibly have used this year, the only way I could pay tribute to sixty years of Carrigan's, was a history of the woman herself." Miriam gave a signal, and Mr. Matthews threw a switch to turn the lights on. "Without further ado, the theme of this year's tree is... Cass Carrigan!"

The giant screen Noelle had custom built to hide the tree was rolled away.

Miriam had promised that the tree would be the tackiest, kitschiest tree Noelle had ever seen, and she had lived up to her promise. To truly represent everything Cass had been—fake eyelashes, sequins, the whole package—Miriam had created a series of baroquely decorated boxes, each one with a scene or doll or other object inside. There were little marionette dancers in tiny glittering bras, miniature gleaming challah in perfect braids for Rosenstein's, a 1963 Austin-Healey model that Noelle didn't even know the story behind.

In between the boxes, she had hung shoes. Seventy years of high heels strung in pretty silver and gold ribbon dangled from pine boughs. Winding through it all in place of a garland were feather boas.

Next to her, Noelle heard Hannah gasp. She turned, and Hannah's hands were on her cheeks, tears streaming down her face. Her own tears welled up. How had Miriam managed this, this tree that was the quintessential celebration of all of Cass's eccentricity and verve? She could almost hear

Cass, throwing confetti at people and cackling in delight at herself.

It was a triumph of Miriam's art, and it was a gift to all of them. She'd wished for Cass to be here, and Miriam had made her wish come true.

After the unveiling, everyone in the crowd surrounded the tree, picking up the ornament boxes to look at more closely and exclaiming to their loved ones. They trickled home as slowly as they could, as if the lights of the tree had caught them in a spell, slowing down time and making everything warm and a little fuzzy around the edges.

When the final guests finally wandered back to their trucks, she went and put an arm around Miriam's shoulders, resting her chin on the top of Miriam's head.

"Not bad," Noelle said, pulling back so she could look down into Miriam's face.

Miriam looked up, and their eyes caught. Inevitably, their foreheads touched, then their cold noses. They stood without moving, breathing each other in, letting the moment linger. Miriam giggled, and Noelle grinned even wider. Satisfaction surged through her when Miriam shivered against her. By the time their lips met, time had stopped completely.

"I would say that qualifies as a damn great job," Miriam agreed after they pulled apart. "And now I'm freezing."

They walked together into the inn, the dark quiet around them. They found the rest of the Carrigan's crew waiting in the kitchen, with hot spiced cider.

"I'd like to make a toast," Hannah said, holding up her mug. Her eyes met Noelle's, and all their love for each other, all the dreams they'd built and the lives they'd intertwined and secrets they'd only shared with each other, passed between them. Hannah's mouth quirked up, and Noelle's heart soared. She knew, even before Hannah finished saying anything.

They weren't going to lose Carrigan's.

"I heard back from the Rosensteins, and they thought the event was a huge success. They're ready to sign on to the plan we present to the bank. To Carrigan's All Year!" Hannah shouted, and the room erupted.

"To Carrigan's All Year!"

Chapter 18

Miriam

Miriam walked downstairs the next morning grouchy, hoping to hide out in the kitchen and avoid all the festivities. She got to a point in every holiday season when she was Christmased out and ready to graffiti dreidels on random Santa displays.

She stopped at the bottom of the stairs and looked into the great room. The guests were gathered in their Christmas pajamas, wrapped in blankets and snuggling in front of the fire. Outside, the wind was whipping the trees into song, the ice crackling on the roof. The cold had become sentient overnight, the kind of cold that made you whisper out of fear that it would steal your voice along with your breath.

Around the tree, piles of presents in bright metallics reflected the lights.

In the center of the room, Noelle sat criss-cross apple-sauce with a giant bow in her hair, in tree-patterned long johns that left little of her curves to the imagination. Her hair was sleep-mussed and she was laughing at something Mrs. Matthews had said.

On a table along the wall, there were piles of cinnamon rolls, carafes of mimosas, and—Miriam noticed, shining like a beacon—multiple pots of coffee. As she walked in, Noelle saw her and waved wildly.

"I love Christmas morning!" she shouted happily.

Miriam blew her a kiss. She was tempted to lean into Noelle's warmth, but through the kitchen doors she saw Mr. Matthews sitting at the blue-tiled island, reading the newspaper and drinking a cup of coffee. That was what her mood needed. Miriam took a moment to look him over, since she so rarely saw him in stillness. His hair was grayer, his wrinkles deeper, which was to be expected after a decade. She poured herself a coffee and slid in next to him, clinking her cup against his in wordless cheers.

Mr. Matthews grunted.

"Can I sit here with you? I'll be quiet, I promise."

"When have I ever not wanted your company?" He raised a bushy eyebrow at her. "All my kids are always welcome in our kitchen."

She teared up at him calling her one of his kids. They sat, warm and quiet and comfortable, for a long time, listening to the sounds from around the tree.

While everyone was re-creating all of Cass's favorite Christmas Day traditions (she thought Cole might perish from excitement over the reindeer races), Miriam went looking for her mother. She was standing just outside the action, watching.

"You know you're allowed to have fun, right?" Miriam asked her.

"I don't remember how," Ziva admitted, sitting stiffly on the same chaise that Miriam had wanted to turn into a moose.

"You realize how depressing that sounds."

"Yes, poor sad rich woman with the shitty husband, please pity me." Ziva held her hand up to her forehead in a vaudevillian gesture. "I'm sorry I missed your birthday."

Miriam rolled her eyes at her mom managing to make Miriam's birthday about herself.

"You've missed all my birthdays since middle school, Mom. I wasn't expecting to see you. I'm impressed that you managed to get away, now." She leaned back against the other end of the chaise, really looking at her mother, trying to figure her out. For that matter, trying to figure herself out. What was driving her, now, to try to find common ground? Was it just Carrigan's, making her defenses low?

Maybe if she could decode her mom, she could start to heal the mountain of hurt that had been suffocating her for so long.

"I'd like to stop missing them. I'd like to stop missing all your life, eventually." Ziva looked over at her, and Miriam cocked her head, considering this.

It was a wild request. She didn't hate the idea, which surprised her.

"I meant what I said, before. I'm not sure we *could* ever build something, but I know we can't while you're living with him.

I'm not asking you to get a divorce so we can maybe, some-day, possibly be closer. However, I will point out, you could get a divorce to stop being miserable." Her mother nodded, acknowledging this. Miriam pushed herself to standing. This was about as much Ziva Drama as she had emotional space for. "I'm going to go see who won the reindeer race."

Eventually, everyone retreated to their rooms for naps. Miriam was snuggling into a blanket pile when Noelle knocked a little melody on her door and called, "Come on. Put on your coat."

Miriam yanked open the door. "I've been going all day, Noelle. I'm going to introvert now. Look, I have this copy of *The Secret in the Old Attic* that outdates Carrigan's itself. I crossed out every mention of Ned Nickerson in it when I was twelve. I shipped Nancy and George."

Noelle leaned against the doorframe, and Miriam was briefly hypnotized by how her forearms crossed over her breasts. "I have a Christmas present planned."

"I'm coming, I'm coming," she grumbled.

Outside the front doors, the sleigh waited, drawn by the farm's grumpy middle-aged horse team. Mr. Matthews sat in the driver's seat, and he winked at her. Noelle lifted Miriam up beside her. She smoothed a big faux-fur rug over their laps and held one of Miriam's hands in both of hers, under the blanket. They stole sidelong glances at each other as they whooshed deeper into the woods. Miriam's heart sped up along with the sleigh runners.

Icicles hung from branches and glinted in the dusk, refract-ing the evening like crystals. It felt like a place out of time. A chickadee chirped, the only sound beside the wind tinkling through the ice and the horses' snorts. Even their hoof falls and the sound of the sleigh were muffled by the snow.

Miriam thought again of Narnia. In some ways, all of Carrigan's was a portal world, where joy and laughter and light in the darkness was the steadfast rule.

"Tell me something nobody ever thinks to ask you about yourself," Noelle asked quietly.

"You have to give me more specifics," Miriam replied. "People don't ask me all that much about myself. Or, I guess Bloomers do, but they definitely don't want anything real."

"Okay," Noelle paused. "What Avatar tribe are you?"

"Earth. Easy. Why be anyone else when you can be Toph?" She stomped her foot for emphasis.

Noelle laughed. "What DnD alignment are you?"

"Chaotic good *obviously*. Ask me a hard one." Her curls were blowing around her head, her cheeks were wind-chapped, and she was grinning so hard it hurt.

Noelle leaned back against the seat and tapped her finger against her mouth, pretending to think hard. Miriam followed the movement of her finger and thought about Noelle's lips.

"You're bi, what does that mean to you?" Noelle asked finally. "There's no universal 'this is what bisexuality looks like.' What is it for you? You don't date men? It doesn't seem like?"

"I mean, not to get too deep into queer theory—" Miriam said.

"That's the sexiest thing anyone's ever said to me," Noelle interrupted, and Miriam laughed. She snuggled in closer to Noelle, letting herself relax into her warmth and scent.

"If Josh Jackson or Timothy Olyphant showed up at my

door, I would probably faint from lust, but romantically and emotionally I rarely meet cis men I can connect to. Also, I have Cole, you know. He's one of the great loves of my life, one of the cornerstones of my happiness. I haven't often found that cis men can find room in their lives for my relationship with Cole, and it's nonnegotiable."

She looked out at the glinting world, then back at Noelle. This space they'd created compelled her to go deeper, tell more of her truth. "But also, there's this Ocean Vuong quote about how being queer saved his life, and in a bigger way, that's what being bi means to me. If I'd grown up in my house and I'd not had this piece of me that refused to bow to expectations, that grew wild in the cracks of all my attempts to be like everyone else, I don't know if I would even have been able to do art. To see that art was a possibility. It gave me the option to be something other than what I was told I had to be."

"It freed you," Noelle said, nodding. "Being butch felt that way, for me. This immense freedom."

Carrigan's had opened the dam of Miriam's feelings, and now, she was always talking through them out loud to someone, trying to describe them to herself as much as anyone else, cataloging them as they came pouring out of her. Noelle understanding her was a revelation and a relief. All her life, she'd blamed herself for her parents not understanding how she felt. She'd thought she must be terrible at explaining herself, so she'd stopped trying until she got here.

Maybe she'd always been perfectly fine at it. Her parents just hadn't been listening.

"I love your butchness," Miriam said dreamily, overwhelmed

by how grateful she was that Noelle was here, with her, sharing these inner pieces of themselves. "I want to start a Butch Appreciation Society."

"I would prefer you stick to appreciating one butch," Noelle said seriously.

"I'm satisfied with that." Miriam's gaze dropped to Noelle's mouth and she dragged her eyes away. Mr. Matthews did not want to listen to them make out like teenagers. "Okay, it's my turn to ask you questions!"

Noelle spread her arms, as if to say, *I'm all yours.*

"I don't even know where you grew up," Miriam said.

"Santa Fe. My hometown is Santa Fe." The way Noelle said Santa Fe had a certain lilt to it, a softness that Miriam didn't think Noelle knew was there. Was she homesick? Did she wish she were in the Sangre de Cristos instead of the Adirondacks?

"That's some culture shock. I love things about here, but I miss the Southwest sometimes," Miriam admitted. "The beauty, and the history, and the traditions."

"I get lonely for the mesas sometimes," Noelle said. "I miss the city itself, you know? Well, maybe you don't. Nobody misses Phoenix."

Miriam laughed out loud. It was true. She might miss the desert, the saguaros, the food, but she had never once, in all her life, missed Phoenix.

"Some cities have a soul," Noelle continued, "and I miss Santa Fe's. But my life is here now."

She wanted to know more, everything, all the pieces that had shaped the woman she was now. But she also wanted to parcel the knowledge out, find out a little at a time so she never ran out of morsels.

And for the love of Sappho, she wanted to have some fun. All the time they'd known each other, they'd been learning each other's trauma histories, existing in crisis mode, living at high alert. So, she made a mental note to come back to Santa Fe, and said instead, "Hey. I have a serious question I've been meaning to ask you."

"Shoot."

"You have a much better reciprocating saw than mine in the work shed. Do you think I can borrow it to work on a piece?" Miriam batted her eyelashes.

"I don't know if we're at the sharing power tools stage of our relationship, Miri," Noelle said, her expression surprised but delighted.

"Pleeeeeease? I'll let you play with my good chain saw when it gets here from Charleston. It's so choice. You're going to be jealous."

"I own a tree farm," Noelle reminded her. "I have many, many chain saws. But, because a beautiful girl holding a reciprocating saw was a teenage fantasy of mine, yes, you can borrow it."

Miriam grinned and snuggled in even closer.

The rest of the ride was quiet, as they let the world go by and just existed together.

An ASMR video was playing softly on the phone next to Miriam's head that night, dimly lighting the pillow and her curls, when someone knocked on her door.

"Come in," she called out, sitting up to turn off the sound.

Noelle peeked in, her hair pointing in every direction. She slipped inside.

She was wearing men's flannel pajamas, pink and covered in flamingos that were—Miriam squinted through the dark— snowboarding? She loved Noelle's collection of weird pajamas. She also loved Noelle's breasts pushing against the buttons on her pajama top, creating a gap that Miriam very much wanted to slip her fingers into.

Miriam scooted over on the bed, patting the spot next to her. Noelle propped herself against Miriam's pillows. "This is an abundance of pillows," she observed.

"Did you really sneak into my room in the middle of the night to judge my pillows?"

"I couldn't sleep. I kept thinking about you all alone, lonely, in this big bed down the hall from me," Noelle teased. "I thought you might need someone to keep your feet warm." While she spoke, Miriam's hand crept up her hip, under the fabric of her pajama top, and onto her stomach.

"That's so altruistic of you," Miriam whispered as her fingers danced up Noelle's ribs. "I can't imagine how I could ever re-pay you for your thoughtfulness. Maybe I could help you fall asleep? I hear massages are good for that. Also orgasms."

Noelle's stomach muscles jumped involuntarily when she said *orgasm*, and Miriam laughed. Noelle caught her hand, bringing it to her mouth. She kissed the palm and then nipped the pad of the thumb. Miriam gasped, not feeling as in control of this seduction as she had a moment before. Noelle rolled smoothly over so that she was holding Miriam's hand above both their heads.

Poised on top, her thigh thick and warm between Miriam's

legs, she met Miriam's gaze and grinned cockily, and Miriam wasn't sure why she'd ever thought she was in control.

Noelle dropped her forehead to Miriam's and whispered, "I certainly think orgasms are going to help someone fall asleep tonight." Her mouth dropped to Miriam's neck, and she breathed lightly into the crook there, then bit gently. "I really, really, really want you tonight. I mean, every night, and also all day, but...Do you? Want to?"

"Holy shit yes," Miriam said. "Please, now."

Chapter 19

Noelle

Noelle woke up in Miriam's bed, with Miriam tracing the tattoos on her arms.

"Tell me the stories of these," she said, her voice sleepy and sexy. "Medusa, Clytemnestra—who is this with the axe? Lizzie Borden?"

Noelle nodded.

"What's with the deadly women? You're not very scary, you know."

Noelle shivered under her fingers. "They're my protectors," she explained. "When I got sober, I kept hearing that I needed a Higher Power, but when I prayed, I imagined these badass women who would kill to protect their own." She ran her hand over her arm, where Miriam just had. She wanted to keep this woman in bed forever, she realized.

They looked up at the distant sound of the doorbell ringing downstairs.

"Are we expecting guests today?" Miriam asked.

"Nope," Noelle said. "Ugh. I'll go get it, I guess."

"Bring me back coffee?" Miriam asked. Noelle kissed her on the nose.

She found Elijah in the kitchen, where Hannah was taking his coat.

"Aren't you supposed to be eating breakfast with the twins? I thought they said something about Christmas pajamas, and your mother-in-law making pancakes?" Noelle asked, beginning to worry.

"Welcome to our happy chaos!" Hannah bussed his cheek before he could answer. She ushered him into the kitchen and set hot cocoa in front of him, including homemade marshmallows and a candy cane stir stick.

"We have such wonderful news, Elijah," Hannah told him. "The livestream of the tree lighting got so many views, and people are clamoring to buy the ornaments Miri made for the tree. I think, with her here selling from the farm and the Rosensteins' support, we have a really strong case for the bank."

"I thought I heard your name, Elijah!" Miriam said, coming in from the dining room. "We're glad to see you, but shouldn't you be enjoying the break with Jason and the kids?"

"Miriam, I'm glad you're here. Can someone find Ziva? I'm afraid I'm not here with good news." He wrung his hands nervously. Noelle had been friends with Elijah since she moved here, and she'd never seen him this visibly worried.

"I'll go get her," Hannah said tightly.

"Why would you want my mom? What could she possibly have to do with—" Miriam cut herself off, cursing under her breath. "My dad. What did he do?"

"What could your dad possibly have to do with anything? I thought he washed his hands of Carrigan's and you?" Noelle put a hand on the small of Miriam's back. She wasn't sure if she was reassuring Miriam or herself.

"Am I right?" Miriam asked Elijah.

He made a pained face. "You're not wrong," he said, "but let's wait until everyone's here."

Once everyone was together—the Matthewses at the counter stools, Ziva pacing, and everyone else huddled into the big semicircular booth in the kitchen nook—Elijah began by apologizing.

"I know you're still celebrating your wonderful success with the tree lighting, and I hate to bring terrible news." He was fiddling with a pen, something Noelle had never seen him do. His movements were always spare, precise, and calm. Something had to be very wrong. "The plan you all have readied for the bank is incredible, especially given the time-frame in which you've put everything together. Normally, I think the bank would be very happy to go forward with it, in the interest of supporting the larger town economy." He cleared his throat, and Noelle braced.

"Unfortunately, a buyer has offered to purchase Carrigan's. He has investors interested in razing the farm to build luxury vacation cabins. The bank is seriously considering it because it's a cash offer for the full amount. They are giving you an opportunity to present a counteroffer. But they need it by the first of the year."

At this, everyone began speaking over each other.

Hannah was asking how they could possibly be expected to come up with that kind of capital. Cole, who had somehow ended up in the meeting despite not being invited, pulled out his phone, saying he would call and yell at the bank. Noelle wanted to know exactly how much money they were talking about and if they needed to come up with the full loan of half a million dollars in a week.

Ziva stopped them with a heavily jeweled hand in the air.

"This mysterious buyer is my husband, isn't it?" she asked.

That had been Miriam's first reaction, too, and it burned in Noelle's stomach. Why were neither of them surprised?

Elijah nodded. "I'm afraid so, Mrs. Rosenstein-Blum." Hannah made an involuntary sound. Mrs. Matthews growled from her perch, and Mr. Matthews looked as close to committing murder as Noelle had ever seen him.

Cole caught Miriam's eyes. "There's a lot of my art in the attic," Miriam said, chewing on the side of her finger and tapping her foot. "Maybe a quarter million worth? That's an estimate. Hard to tell, with these things. But we should sell it all. We can have an online auction. Fast."

Noelle protested. "That's every piece you ever gave to Cass. I love that art, and it belongs here." She and Miriam wove their fingers together.

Miriam looked at her helplessly. "What are our other choices?"

"Cole, do *you* want to invest a half million dollars in a failing business that we may or may not still have a year from now?" Hannah asked.

Cole looked down at the table. "I would love to. If I had the money. Which . . . I don't," he admitted, not looking up.

Miriam blinked at him, and Noelle felt her shock in the lines of her body. "You don't . . . what?"

"I don't have access to my trust fund until I'm forty," Cole said, carefully, seeming to choose his words with a great deal more care than he normally did. "There was an incident when I was seventeen, and the terms were changed. My parents also refused to pay for any of my college expenses, and I hadn't saved anything, because, you know, outrageously rich." He squirmed under the stares of everyone at the table. "I lived off student loans, and now my income mostly goes toward paying just enough of them to stay afloat."

"So this whole rich boy brand you have going on is . . . ?" Miriam prompted.

"My parents financing just enough of my lifestyle that I don't embarrass them in front of Charleston society."

"Why didn't you tell me?" Miriam whispered.

Cole's face fell into complete seriousness for maybe the first time since Noelle met him. "Sometimes we're too ashamed of our secrets to tell them to the people we most want to love us."

Miriam wrapped her arms around herself, nodding a little. Noelle could tell she was starting to fall apart at the seams, and she didn't know how to fix it.

From the end of the banquette, Hannah asked, "You have *no* money? How are you buying plane tickets at the drop of a hat?"

"My parents aren't super great at checking specifics of the AmEx Black. They don't have a strong idea of what's normal business travel, so I push that to the absolute outer limit." He continued, "I could take out a loan contingent on my getting my full trust fund in five years, or...put it on credit. I mean, eventually I *am* going to be outrageously rich, I just might not have a credit score left by then."

"I'm not putting you in that position," Miriam said stubbornly.

"Alternately," Cole offered, "I could divert Richard's bank accounts to ACT UP NY, and then he couldn't buy the farm."

"Why haven't you already done that?" Noelle demanded. If Cole, Miriam, and Ziva had all known Richard was still a threat, why hadn't they already dealt with him? Why was everyone just sitting around waiting for him to ruin their lives?

"Miriam told me not to. Something about it being 'illegal.'" Cole did finger quotes. He looked unconvinced by this argument and, at the moment, Noelle was, too.

"As your lawyer, I advise against it," Elijah chimed in.

"Caveat," said Cole, "you're not *my* lawyer."

Elijah glared at him. "My point stands."

"Can we go back to the part where there was an 'incident' that led to your trust fund terms being rewritten and your parents refusing to pay for your college?" Hannah said, and Noelle could hear the frustration she was trying to keep out of her voice.

Why were they still talking about this? If it wasn't a solution, Cole's antics were just a distraction. They needed to fix *this* problem.

Cole scooted his chair back and crossed his arms defensively over his chest. "There was lighter fluid, and a golf course, and then there wasn't a golf course. Anymore."

The stares around the table intensified.

He cleared his throat. "Tara and I tried to write *Eat the Rich*, in fire, on the ninth hole. It didn't go as planned."

"Tara...Chadwick? Our Tara?" Miriam asked, her eyes glassy with shock.

Noelle was flabbergasted, her rising panic temporarily interrupted. "Tightly Wound Tara? Lit a golf course on fire?"

"More like, burned it entirely to the ground," he said. "Also the country club next to it. There was no one in it, thank God. That's how she got so tightly wound, by the way. She went all the way in the other direction. Anyway, there's a lot more to the story, but I am probably not your plan B on this one. I wish I could be."

He looked at Miriam for a long moment, moving a curl off her face before blowing out a breath. "You could sell the paintings. Undiscovered Mimi Roz paintings would bring in a hell of a lot of interest."

The color drained from Ziva's face. "There are paintings left?" she choked out.

"In the attic," Miriam confirmed, as if in a daze. "I found them a couple of days ago."

"You can't make them public," Ziva said, her knuckles white where she was clasping her hands. "He'll retaliate. You know that, Miriam."

Noelle felt Miriam flinch, and the fear she'd been feeling started to harden into anger.

"And do what, Ziva?" Noelle snapped. "Threaten Carrigan's? Oh wait." That anger unfurled something awful in her gut. A suspicion that felt like poison worked its way up her throat before she could stop it. "Miri, did you know he would do this? Did you know he would threaten Carrigan's, and you came here anyway?"

"Can someone tell me what we're talking about?" Hannah asked.

At the same time, Cole grabbed Noelle's arm and said, "HEY. Back off. She would never do that."

Noelle immediately wanted to snatch the words back out of the air.

Next to her, Miriam had started shaking, looking up with wild eyes.

"I didn't know, but I should have. If I'd just thought... I'm so sorry. This is all my fault. I should have known that he would find out I was happy, and he would come after me." Her words came out small and rushed, with no breaths in between.

Noelle wanted to dam them up, but she couldn't stop the flood. She hated that she'd said anything. She knew Miriam better than that. She might hurt people accidentally by being insular and wrapped up in her own pain, but she would never knowingly put any of them at risk.

"That's what he does—my mom's right. I'm sure he's already planning to pay her back for even being here, with me. He's been monitoring my social media, I *know* that. I should have been careful. I didn't think there was anything else he could do to me, because he already took everything. I should have remembered he could still come after my friends."

"I shouldn't have—" Noelle said, trying to hold on to Miriam, but she wrenched her body away.

"I have to go. I have to leave Carrigan's, and then he'll leave you all alone. You'll be safe if I go." Miriam tried to get out from where she was sandwiched in the middle of the booth, pushing at Cole to move.

Noelle felt something inside her fracture, her panic and anger crescendoing and crashing to shore.

She'd asked Miriam what would happen the next time she got spooked, and Miriam had promised she wouldn't run again. She'd told Miriam that she couldn't handle another person leaving, and Miriam had begged for a chance to prove herself.

"I don't know what else to do, Noelle," Miriam said, finally freeing herself and standing. "I can't take Carrigan's from all of you. I won't be the person who takes the only thing you love away from you."

"I don't want you to fall on your sword, Miriam," Noelle protested, furious. "I want you to fight for this."

"Elijah," Miriam said quietly, firmly, "please draw up paperwork to give my shares to Hannah and Noelle. It's what I should have done from the beginning."

Before Noelle could object again, Miriam fled, outside, into the snow. Noelle grabbed a jacket to push out after her.

"I'll go," Cole said, starting to get up.

Noelle held out a hand. "I'm going."

He scowled but nodded.

She found Miriam outside, shivering, with the snow swirling around her. She was staring off into the back acreage, concentrating hard on something Noelle couldn't see. Noelle slipped her jacket over Miriam's shoulders, and Miriam turned her face up to Noelle's. Noelle had never seen her so pale.

"I'm going to miss the trees," Miriam said. "I was trying to memorize them."

"You aren't going anywhere," Noelle said. "This is ridiculous. We are all going to fix this. The entire team is in there, ready to fight for this. We're not going to give up."

"We can't fight him. He always wins," Miriam said, sounding exhausted and resigned. She rubbed her hands down her jeans. "I was right. All those years, I was right. He must have been so mad, about the Bloomers, and he was just lying in wait like a spider for me to have something worth destroying. And I fell for it! I let you and Hannah convince me to let down my walls, and now there won't be a Carrigan's! Do you know what that would do to me, Noelle? All those years, I survived, knowing somewhere out there, Carrigan's still existed. I can't be the reason it's destroyed. I can't survive it!"

Noelle paced in the snow, her boots crunching rhythmically.

"So you're going to leave us, leave Cass's vision that you fought so hard for, leave everyone here who needs you. You're going to run, again, instead of fighting."

Noelle shook her head, her brain buzzing with angry bees. She hadn't even started to dig herself out of the grief of losing Cass, and now the threat of losing Carrigan's and Miriam, too, filled her with stark terror. Some part of the back of her brain was telling her that her anger was just her fear coming out sideways. She told the back of her brain to shut the fuck up. "I know you're scared, but that's bullshit, Miriam. If you run now, he knows he'll always win. Stand and fight."

"You don't get to tell me how to respond to him," Miriam cried. "It's not your life."

"It *is* my life!" Noelle yelled. "You made me believe in a

future with the two of us together, you made me fall for you, and now you're running the instant it gets hard. I told you I was scared of ever trusting anyone again because everyone leaves, and now you *are* leaving. How is that not my life?"

"I'm doing this to protect you," Miriam yelled back, her hair whipping into her mouth in the wind. She angrily pushed it back. "Because I love you! If I don't, he'll never stop coming for you. At least this way, he's only coming for me!"

"That's a lie, Miriam," Noelle spat out, her whole body rejecting Miriam's words. "The only person you're doing this for is you. And it's going to hurt you more than it hurts anyone. You're a coward."

Noelle stalked back to the house, her hands stuffed into her jacket, her head down. In her peripheral vision, she could see Miriam had sunk down on her knees, sobbing.

Noelle left her there and just kept walking.

PART 3

Christmas to Tu B'Shevat

Chapter 20

Miriam

Miriam spent the next hour packing her clothes robot-ically. Everything she'd bought since coming here wouldn't fit in the little roll-on suitcase she'd arrived with back in October, and her brain couldn't process what to do about it.

She was staring blankly at a pair of jeans when Cole knocked on her door. As soon as he was inside, his huge frame wrapped around her, his warmth surrounding her. The smell of him, ocean salt mixed with bergamot and vetiver, was one of the safest smells in her world. It pierced the fog that had enveloped her when her panic had risen up. All of the fight or flight drained out of her body.

"What the fuck am I going to do, Cole? I'm in a nightmare."

He pulled away and looked down at her. "Your dad wants you to run. He wants to keep you thinking he's the bogeyman and he's going to pop out any minute. So you should stay put and fight for this. Tell him you're not scared of him and he can go fuck himself."

"I *am* scared of him, Cole," Miriam reminded him. "Very scared."

"Fake it until you make it, baby." Cole did sad little jazz hands.

Miriam hugged herself, feeling her ability to reason instead of just run slowly returning. "If he really will pull the offer if I leave, I have to go. I can't put myself before Carrigan's again."

"But Carrigan's All Year won't work without you, Mimi. You're the linchpin. If you go, there's nothing to take to the bank. Staying and fighting is the only thing that might work."

He pulled her back into a hug, leaning over to rest his head on her curls. Miriam anchored herself to him.

"I'm sorry I didn't tell you about me and Tara and the golf course," he said, finally. "I was worried that if I wasn't the fun friend, you might do a runner on me, too."

"Well, considering my behavior today, you were probably not wrong," she said, squeezing him back. She'd told herself all her life that she wasn't running, just strategically retreating, but she'd been lying to herself. "I freaked out. So badly. I saw white and heard buzzing and I couldn't breathe. I don't even know what I said."

"We can probably fix it. If you stay."

"I want to stay," she whispered, "but I don't know if they'll still have me."

Her mom knocked in the open doorway. Cole left them alone, squeezing her shoulder as he went.

"I called Richard," her mom said, sitting on her bed, her hands clasped in front of her.

Miriam cocked her head, preparing for the final blow to her time at Carrigan's, the ultimatum that would cut her off forever. She expected Ziva to say that her dad had offered a deal: he'd leave Carrigan's alone if she stayed away.

"He won't pull the offer," Ziva said instead. "He's going to go ahead with it whether you stay or go. I'm sorry. I thought I might be able to stop him. Whatever you need from me now, Miri, I'll do it."

Miriam sank down in her chair and dropped her elbows on her knees. "Fuck."

She felt like a bucket of ice water had been dumped over her head, all of the fog finally gone. She looked around, really seeing her surroundings. She'd given her dad's terror ten years, and she'd almost just given him the rest of her life too. She'd panicked, and she hadn't thought.

She hadn't thought about what it would be like, trying to make a life after this. She also hadn't considered how much it would hurt Noelle if she ran, after promising she wouldn't. She hadn't imagined living with that regret every day, putting her emotions back on autopilot. She remembered Noelle quoting Rumi to her and knew, without a doubt, that she couldn't go back to sleep.

Miriam looked up at her mom, who was watching her cautiously.

"Okay," she said, bracing herself. "We annihilate him. Gather everyone. We need a war council."

"We could hire an assassin on the Dark Web, so your mom would get the life insurance money," Cole offered.

"That's very, extremely illegal," Elijah deadpanned before continuing. "You could do a GoFundMe. I mean, you do run a business for the kind of people who have enough disposable income to spend an extended Christmas vacation at a full-service inn every year." He paused and then pointed out, "Also, GoFundMe is legal."

"Y'all definitely could ask these people for help. All the old families and the Bloomers." Cole had leaned forward on his forearms. "They would want to help you. And, Miri, it would serve your dad right for once again assuming that you have no support."

Hannah ran her hands through her hair. "What if we don't make the money? I'm not ruling it out, because it's a lot of people's livelihoods at stake. I don't want to gamble the rest of our careers on the hope that the Bloomers would make it happen. I think we should do a GoFundMe, and also something else."

"I'll sell the paintings," Miriam said. Cole was right—it made sense. Even though she wanted to hoard them and not let them out of her sight, if she sold them now, it would be her decision, her agency. The idea that it might piss her dad off was also, admittedly, delightful.

"*You will not!*" the rest of the kitchen chorused back at her.

Elijah looked startled to find that he had joined the response. "Sorry, that's not legal advice. I simply think your dad is a shitweasel and you should keep your paintings."

"I'm sorry, I told them," Ziva explained. "I know it's really your story, but I felt they could make better choices with more context. I should have asked you first."

Miriam shook her head. "I'm relieved that I don't have to explain it, honestly." It was freeing not to be guarding that secret anymore.

They all looked at each other for a long time. The enormity of the situation was sinking in. Miriam kept trying to get Noelle to meet her eyes, but she just stared down at her hands, her face a stone mask.

"I have an idea," Noelle said finally, her arms crossed protectively. Miriam looked up at her hopefully, but Noelle was looking at Hannah. "Since Miriam is intent on donating her artistic talent to this problem"—her voice was so cold when she said Miriam's name, and Miriam's hope died—"we could have a New Year's Eve party. A big, fancy shindig. There would be an auction. Enough old and new stuff to get people interested."

Mrs. Matthews nodded, and Hannah started to take notes. "Expand this vision for me, NoNo."

Noelle started to pick up steam, counting on her fingers. "We'd livestream the event, and items would be available for internet bids and in-person bids. Miriam could auction off a series of personalized art pieces, made specifically for the auction winners."

Miriam shifted forward in her seat. She'd never thought about offering personalized commissions. It could make a lot of money.

"The final item would be one, and only one, Mimi Roz painting, the one Miriam likes the least," Noelle continued. "We would have to let the guests know what's going on. Not all of it, obviously, but enough to know they're supporting the future of Carrigan's. With an accompanying GoFundMe for people who just want to donate."

"That's brilliant," Hannah told her. Everyone nodded. "But it's only five days until New Year's Eve."

"I'm on Bloomer duty." Cole saluted. "They love me."

"I already told them I was going to have a big live event on New Year's Eve, back when I thought I was launching the store," Miriam said, "and I never actually remembered to cancel because I was so caught up in everything. Which works out great! Now I'll have a slightly more panic-driven New Year's Eve live event." She managed to sound only a little hysterical.

"No, you know what," Noelle said, hitting the table for emphasis, "we *will* be launching your store. This isn't just the way for us to save Carrigan's short-term, but to kick off Carrigan's All Year in a big way, for the future."

"YES!" Miriam picked up Noelle's thread, excited at the picture taking shape in her head. "We'll have every Bloomer in the country on a livestream. We lean hard into the next chapter of Blum Again. Studio space, storefront, and vacation packages where art lovers can come visit the artist's residence and see where I get my inspiration. Day trips to visit Advent and Carrigan's, including a shopping tour. Pop-up events at the diner and the bar."

"We're going to be announcing a whirlwind of new, and we'll kick it off with the biggest sale of Miriam Blum art in history. This isn't panic. This is opportunity," Hannah finished and fist-bumped Miriam.

Miriam's eyes welled up, her last emotional dam cracking at Noelle putting all their hopes for the future of Carrigan's in her art. She wanted to believe this meant that Noelle understood that Miriam had just temporarily panicked, but when she tried again to catch Noelle's eye, to let her see how much it meant to her, Noelle still wouldn't look up.

"This idea is amazing," Elijah said, "and absolutely has a chance of being wildly successful. But…" He paused, spreading his hands.

"But we can't do this ourselves," Hannah said, nodding. She looked at Mr. and Mrs. Matthews. "Do you think Esther and Joshua will help save Christmasland? Again?"

"It's their home, too." Mr. Matthews nodded. "They'll be here."

Miriam looked between Hannah and the Matthewses. "If it's really all hands on deck and every Matthews, do we call Levi back?"

Hannah blanched, then nodded. "I don't know where he is or whether he can get here in time, but if you can find him, you can ask him."

"You can't." Mr. Matthews shook his head, his eyes sad. "I do know where he is, and it's on an Australian cooking competition. He's unreachable. His phone was taken away until he gets eliminated."

"Which he won't," Noelle grumbled, "because he sold his soul to a crossroads demon for his culinary talent."

"We are going to talk about the utterly wild information you just gave me at a later date," Hannah told Mr. Matthews, shaking her head as if to clear it. "Right now we have less than a week to plan the biggest party of our lives."

"Okay," Cole said, practically bouncing in his chair. "Let's do this. What's next?"

"There's a bunch of New Year's decorations somewhere," Hannah said. "Mr. Matthews, can you help me find them?"

"I can do that." He popped up from his seat.

"Call me if the apocalypse is coming for Carrigan's, again," Elijah said, bussing their cheeks goodbye. Hannah shuttled him out the door, with a gift bag of cookies and a promise not to interrupt his holiday with their business any further, at least until New Year's Eve.

Miriam looked across the almost empty kitchen at Noelle, furious and hopeful, grateful and sad all at once. More than anything, however, she felt ready. Ready to be done living a life defined by her fear.

She'd spent the last ten years in an emotional stasis. Now that she was back at Carrigan's, facing down her father, and surrounded by the art of her deepest heart, she was ready to fight instead of fly.

Freaking out at Noelle, getting ready to leave...this was why Tara and Cole had never told her about the trauma that had changed the course of their lives. Why Hannah and Blue had a desperate love story they'd kept a secret from her. No one in her life trusted her to support them when emotions got hard, and she was done.

She was ready to be planted.

"Thank you," Miriam said to Noelle. "No one's ever done anything like this for me."

Noelle stared back, no light behind her dark brown eyes. "I'm not doing this for you, or us. I'm doing this for Carrigan's. There is no us."

Chapter 21

Noelle

W hat are you talking about?" Miriam protested. "I'm
staying, I'm fighting. Like you wanted. I gave up
everything in my life, to be here with you."

Noelle stood up, rocking back on her heels and crossing
her arms, trying to get some protection from Miriam and
those big, sad eyes. She needed to make it clear, to Miriam
and to her own heart, that they weren't going to be together.
She needed to draw the line painfully enough that they would
both walk away.

"All I asked of you was to not run, Miri. You couldn't even
do that. You asked for a chance, I gave it to you, you ran. It's
over. You can stay for Hannah, or the Matthewses, or Cass's
memory, but don't stay for me."

"I'm staying because this is what I want for my life,"
Miriam cried. "I'm in love with you!"

"If you loved me, why didn't you trust me to fix it? Why,

when the shit hit the fan, was your first impulse you and not us? That's not love, and I can't live waiting for the next time it happens. I can't do this, Miri. I mean it, I physically can't. I'm hanging by the tiniest thread. I can't live waiting to lose you."

Miriam's fallen face made every instinct in her body want to protect her and hold her, but she knew she couldn't. So she lied. "You don't love me, and more importantly, I don't love you. I might have, but now I never will. I'm glad I realized now, before it was too late, that you'll never be trustworthy."

"You're a liar, Northwood!" Miriam accused her, standing up out of the booth, her hands planted on the table. "Who's the coward now? You say you try to be perfect so no one will leave you, but you expect everyone else to be perfect, too. And when they mess up, you take it as proof, so you have an easy out and you can leave them first. Which, PS, you accused me of something pretty horrific, so I'm not the only one who messed up here, Miss Self-Righteous. It's a fucked-up self-fulfilling cycle—people always leave you because you can't let them make mistakes!"

Noelle whirled on Miriam, her conscious pricked, some part of her worried that Miriam was right. "That's bullshit. Cass wasn't perfect, and I knew it. She was petty, and capricious, and self-centered. I loved all of her. Hannah's controlling and short-tempered and she can be a real asshole."

"Yes, but those are the things you *like* about them. You can pat yourself on the back for loving people as they are because none of those flaws threaten your security. They're just seasoning!" Miriam banged her palms on the table, her hair flying and her eyes sparking. She looked electric and beautiful, and the sight broke Noelle's heart. "I react to one really fucked-up situation in a way you don't like, and it's all over. I'm not your parents, Noelle!"

She might not have been able to protect herself from the pain of her parents not showing up for her over and over, but she'd been a kid then. Now, as an adult, Noelle could damn well choose the people she loved, people who wouldn't put her through that same hell again.

"This isn't about me, Miriam. Don't try to make this my fault. And leave my parents out of it."

She couldn't stay here and have all the most vulnerable parts of her stripped bare for examination. She stomped out of the room.

But this time Miri didn't follow her.

The week between Christmas and New Year's, traditionally the perfect slice of liminal space out of time, was frenetic with constant movement, the inn a perpetual motion engine.

Mrs. Matthews was cooking tiny puff pastry shells so fast, Noelle thought there might be witchcraft involved. Mr. Matthews was making sure no part of the farm was in need of repair, no project left undone. Joshua and Esther Matthews had been tapped by their parents to aid in the rescue effort. Esther had sent Rocket the Boyfriend back to the city, after the third or fourth time he whined about being asked to do work.

Joshua's wife, Lydia, had worked for a party planner through grad school and was helping Hannah by getting permits and making playlists. Joshua was on kid-wrangling duty, making sure Grant and all the guests' children were happily occupied, far away from the hub of activity.

The great room had been transformed into command central.

Miriam was livestreaming every day to build up momentum, and the grand fireplace—complete with the Nutcracker Steves—had become her backdrop. Noelle couldn't stop watching her, no matter how many times she told herself to walk away, to start breaking this spell between them for good.

"Hello, Bloomers!" Miriam began, three days before the auction, her smile not quite her own. "I'm so excited to see so many of you on the stream tonight! A quick recap for everyone who's just tuning in to this project: My beloved great-aunt left her extremely cool Christmas tree farm to myself, my cousin, and two other amazing friends. We're so excited about all the art, music, and family time we are going to host here in the years to come, not to mention Bloom Togethers! But a developer is trying to buy the farm out from under us to turn it into luxury cabins. Damn the Man! Save the Carrigan's!"

At this, a flurry of little hearts rose on the screen.

Noelle rolled her eyes offscreen at Miriam's Revolution Barbie act, but she was impressed. She didn't know anyone else who could channel all their panic and pain into a performance like this, making everyone feel like they were the only one being talked to. She'd called Miriam a coward, but what she was doing right now took a hell of a lot of spine.

She whispered to Cole, "Do they really call their get-togethers 'Bloom Togethers'?"

Cole snorted. "It was my idea, but I swear, I was kidding

when I said it. I did not know they were going to run with it. Miriam makes sure they don't start calling themselves a 'tribe' or anything that approaches 'namaste,' but there are still a lot of middle-class white ladies in the Bloomers, and they have to let that energy out somehow."

In front of the camera, Miriam's spiel didn't miss a beat. "Tonight, I'm giving y'all a sneak peek at the Miriam Blum originals that will be available via web auction all night on New Year's Eve. This is a great opportunity to buy some earlier pieces you may never have seen before, some new custom pieces I'm making exclusively for this auction, and maybe get a great deal on a piece you couldn't normally afford. But remember, the fate of my family farm is in your hands, including a lot of people's jobs and health insurance, so open your hearts and your wallets.

"I know some of you are making travel plans to be here and y'all—" Her voice cracked, as the Blum Again persona slipped and the real, scared Miriam shone through.

Noelle felt the strong impulse to gather Miriam up, build them both a blanket fort, and let her find some space to deal with everything that had happened. She shook her head, trying to clear it. That wasn't fair, to herself or Miriam. She'd ignored her own judgment and given in to Miriam's magnetic draw once, and it had turned out exactly the way she'd feared: Miriam had gotten spooked and done what she always did— or tried to, anyway, even if she hadn't gotten very far.

Noelle wasn't going to make that mistake again. Maybe the old ladies had been right, and she couldn't use Carrigan's and sobriety as an excuse to avoid dating forever, but that didn't mean Miriam was the right person at the right time.

No matter what Noelle's heart said.

The sound of Miriam's voice penetrated her thinking and made her want to listen to nothing else, forever. But Miriam was still talking to the Bloomers, still wearing that practiced mask that didn't let anyone close.

"I cannot even believe the lengths to which you will go as a community to support me and mine," she was saying. "I love you all *so* much, and I can't wait to see you up at Carrigan's. I'll be doing special tours for any Bloomer who makes it up here on such late notice, and we'll have a Bloomer Breakfast on New Year's Day, complete with Rosenstein's breakfast pastries and Mrs. Matthews's famous coffee."

Miriam was known among her fans for being private. For her to open up her family home to special tours, one-on-one time, and a Bloom Together breakfast was unprecedented, and many fans were throwing out their New Year's Eve plans to book last-minute flights to New York.

"Ride or die Carrigan's!" Miriam said, signing off.

"Ride or die Carrigan's," Noelle repeated wryly. She wished she could believe that Miriam actually felt that way, and it wasn't just a cute catchphrase. "We should put that on a T-shirt. I bet the Bloomers would buy them."

"I'll be right back," Cole said, startling her. She'd forgotten he was standing there. "Gonna call my T-shirt guy."

With two days before the event, the barn had become a sparkly, shining gala venue. Hannah and Miriam had their heads together in Hannah's office, printing pamphlets to advertise Carrigan's All Year, selling family reunions and girls weekends. Cole had been pushing the event across social media, reaching out to his parents' contacts with more money than they knew what to do with. Even Tara, when she saw the hype on Twitter, offered to get her network watching.

Everyone had a job to make this auction a success—this auction that had been Noelle's idea—except for Noelle. She didn't know anyone with money; most of her friends were broke alcoholics. She didn't think the party needed bad coffee and dirty jokes, which was their primary skill set. No one needed Christmas trees, except the ones she'd already grown. Miriam was working herself to the bone, as if she somehow thought she could fix all this if she just never sat still (what *was* it with the Rosenstein girls?), and Noelle couldn't step in to make her rest, because that wasn't her place anymore. So she hauled things for Mr. Matthews, kept everyone caffeinated, and tried to talk Cole out of bad decisions.

"Okay," he began, bursting into her room that afternoon, "I know Elijah vetoed the assassin thing but I don't think we can take killing Richard Blum off the table."

"Look, we all want to do him bodily harm," Noelle agreed, "and I have more right to be angry than anyone. He's trying to take my life's work away. He broke the girl I wanted to spend the rest of my life with—"

Cole started to interrupt, and she held out a hand.

"Do not tell her I said that, and I'm not going to talk about it with you. What's important is that Miriam is entirely capable of winning this fight. We need to give her the chance to be in the lead on this. So we will provide the help she's asked for, and no help she has not asked for. Including assassins."

Noelle understood how Cole felt, the fierce protectiveness, the urge to hurt anyone who hurt Miriam. Except she'd hurt Miriam, too. Was hurting her right now. But she couldn't stop herself from rooting for Miriam, wanting to see what she could do when she fully came into her own. She did think Miriam could win this fight, and any other one she chose.

So why, a little voice asked inside her, wasn't she giving Miriam a chance to fight for *them*?

Cole scowled. "I just want to be doing something to take him down."

"You are doing something, Cole," Noelle said, patting his hand. "You're doing whatever Miriam tells you to do."

She felt good about the decision not to ruin Richard Blum's life, until she found Miriam sitting on the floor in the library, curled up and crying. She knelt, and Miriam looked up at her with puffy eyes and mascara running down her cheeks.

"What happened?" she asked, unable to stifle her impulse to protect this woman, no matter what they were to each other right now. "Tell me what's wrong."

"I got an email from GoFundMe customer service," Miriam said. "Someone reported us for fraud, and they are shutting us down while they investigate. We'll get the money eventually," she breathed raggedly, squeezing her eyes shut, "but not by the first. And we can't raise any more while they investigate."

"Richard?" Noelle asked, feeling her blood pressure skyrocket.

"Who else?"

Noelle took Miriam's face in her hands, gasping at the skin contact.

Damn it. This wasn't what she was here for. "Hey. Look at me. We still have the auction. Hannah was right that we needed a two-pronged plan. We are going to be okay. We just have to kick ass, which we are going to do."

She stood up, flexing her fingers in a failed attempt to get her palms to stop tingling from the feel of Miriam's cheek against them. Miriam fixed her ponytail, wiped her ruined mascara on her T-shirt, and nodded forcefully.

How was she even more beautiful like this?

Noelle stuffed her hands in her pockets and went to find Hannah.

Hannah was surrounded by Bloomers and, unexpectedly, Miriam's Old Ladies. They'd known the Bloomers were coming, so Miriam had activities planned for them, but the Old Ladies were a surprise. Antique and junk dealers from all over the country had rolled in, suitcases full of small, strange gifts for Miriam.

A woman named Annie, who reminded Noelle of an aging sea witch who had mostly retired from evildoing, looked Noelle up and down and declared, "They don't make women as hot now as they did in my day, but there are some lookers."

When Noelle pulled Hannah aside to whisper the news about the GoFundMe, she let out a string of curse words that would make a sailor blush and went to try to fix it, after appointing Noelle the Old Lady wrangler.

Noelle took them into Advent to meet her own pack of little old ladies and eat at Ernie's, where the non-alcoholic ones got quite drunk and a few ended up in each other's beds. Miriam had been right about the sort of confirmed bachelors and spinsters who bought antique shops. Each one of them told her a story about Miriam, how Miriam had shown up for them, checked in on them, reconnected them with lost nephews or lost treasures.

She reminded Noelle so much of Cass.

Noelle had thought of Miriam as a lost soul, without purpose, trying to heal from the damage her dad had done, yet everywhere she'd touched down, she'd planted a seed of a relationship and tended to it. She had a forest of people who loved her, just like Cass. What they said, over and over, was that she never let them fall through the cracks. It was another piece in the puzzle of Miriam Blum, and it made Noelle's heart ache.

If Miriam could show up for all these people, with only the sliver of herself she'd been living with, what would happen if she decided to show up for the two of them, with her whole self? Could Noelle trust her enough to let her try?

o˚ * ˳●˳ ⁙ ˳✳ *●˳⁚✦ * ˳ * ●˳⁚✳˳ ● ●˚⁚ ✳˳

The day before the event, Noelle went looking for Ziva at breakfast, wanting to pick a fight. Ziva had been in her element all week, as orchestrating galas was one of her areas of expertise. She flitted around, attached to her phone, seemingly everywhere at once.

"You're angry with me," Ziva said when Noelle plunked down next to her.

"You're perceptive for a woman who never listens to anyone." Noelle shoved a bite of Danish in her mouth.

"We've known each other a long time, Noelle. I thought we could have a conversation about this without your acting like a child."

"Hey, I had a mom," Noelle said, swallowing hard. "I don't need another, shittier mom telling me how to behave."

She wasn't just angry at Ziva, she was furious. Richard might have been the monster, but Ziva had been an accomplice.

"*I* never stopped speaking to my child," Ziva said.

Noelle gritted her teeth. No fucking way was she going to let this woman judge her parents, after everything she'd failed to do. "Don't even think about addressing things that aren't your place. And you may not have stopped speaking to her, but because you refused to disrupt your precious life and leave the man who abused her, you cut her off from her whole family."

"You're right, that was a terrible thing to say," Ziva admitted. She fiddled with her bracelet. "I made the wrong choice for Miri, over and over. I won't pretend I didn't."

"Did you think you were doing the right thing?" Noelle asked, exasperated. It shouldn't matter, because she was done with Miriam, but she wanted to understand what would drive someone to make the choices Ziva had. Noelle could barely leave Miriam alone when she needed to, and Ziva, her own mother, had left her to the wolves.

Ziva shook her head. "I was mostly worried about getting myself through, every day."

"You should have made Miriam safe."

Ziva smiled without warmth. "Have you never made

decisions out of your worst fears instead of your better instincts?"

Fuck. Of course she had, so many times since Cass's death, and she'd asked for Miriam's forgiveness, for a chance to do better, which Miriam had given her.

When Noelle didn't speak, Ziva continued, tapping her perfect manicure against Cass's favorite chipped Spode. "The thing is, I had a choice, but I didn't really understand that. Miriam didn't have a choice, and she was excruciatingly aware of it. What she tried to do the other day was to take some agency, to do the opposite of what I did. To save you from Richard, the way I didn't save her from him. It was misguided and hurtful, I'm not denying that, but she did something I never did. She tried to protect the people she loved at great cost to herself."

The idea that Noelle might have judged Miriam too harshly—again, exactly like she'd done when they met—had been creeping like a kudzu vine into her stubborn mind. She was starting to suspect she might be the one of them using any excuse to run because she was afraid.

"Why are you so angry about this, Noelle?" Ziva asked, looking pointedly over her coffee cup. "Is Miriam yours to protect now?"

"Miriam is her own to protect," Noelle growled, pushing back from the table, "and the rest of it is none of your business. You gave up any right to know anything about Miriam and me years before you met me."

Chapter 22

Miriam

Unwrapping her paintings restored a missing piece of herself, and it felt strangely like having her heart broken and handed back to her all at once. The paintings were from a time before she'd cut herself off. They had been made by a Miriam who still felt deeply, hoped for things, took risks.

She laid the five canvases out on the floor of the carriage house. Seeing them now crystallized her resolve. She'd given up painting because of her father, given up Carrigan's and Cass, Hannah, Levi, the Matthewses. Given up nearly every component of who she was, and now she was losing Noelle, too, because of *him*.

Miriam felt the urge to destroy him—and knew with absolute clarity that she would never again make her own life small for Richard Blum.

Winter light fell on the paintings from the floor-to-ceiling windows. This space would be the perfect workshop, as soon as she could move everything from Charleston. Every other space she'd tried had been a not-quite fit, like Goldilocks. Maybe because she'd been thinking of herself as an intruder, only finding places to work where she wouldn't be taking up anyone's territory. But the carriage house was hers entirely to claim, and inside it she could expand to be as big, as visible, as messy and destructive and glittery as she needed to be.

She'd lost the store she'd dreamed of, but maybe this space could be more. More personal, more vulnerable, more truly hers rather than a storefront on which she'd projected a polished version of herself for public consumption.

It could be, if she let it.

Miriam was deep in thought, staring at the paintings, when she heard Cole come up behind her. She knew his tread without having to turn around. When she finally looked up, she found him watching her, his head tilted in concern.

"We haven't seen you in hours, even to steal into the kitchen for food and steal out again without speaking," he said, walking around the paintings. "Do you know which one you're going to auction off?"

"I think this one," Miriam said, gesturing to a bright, more pop-inspired piece. "The others are more personal."

The rest were dark, whimsical portraits.

"I sort of love this one," Cole said, pointing to one of Baba Yaga, posed like an old king, her shoulders back and her hand on her chicken leg house like a globe. "Although I'm not sure I really get it. Noelle says your pieces have a wry political commentary underneath them, like they're winking at the viewer, hoping they get it."

Miriam almost broke again. Noelle understood and respected her work, and she'd destroyed that precious, once-in-a-lifetime connection. She kept quiet at first, not wanting to drag Cole into her emotional mess. But if she was going to learn how to be present and vulnerable, who better to start with than Cole? She knew he would love her through anything, if only out of sheer stubbornness.

"I don't know if she's going to forgive me," she said, quietly.

"Baba Yaga?" he joked.

She rolled her eyes, and his face got serious.

"I don't know either, pumpkin. Do you want her to? You spent an awful lot of time and effort making yourself that cocoon. Are you really ready to burst out of it?" He threw an arm over her shoulder.

"Isn't that what cocoons are for? So we can become butterflies?" she asked. "All that time I was gone, I told myself I was healing. If that's not true, if I'm not different, then I was always just running and hiding."

"You asked her for a lot of trust, and she gave it to you. She took all her walls down, went way outside her comfort zone," Cole said. "And then it looked like you weren't doing the same for her. That's what her parents did: they cared less about her than she did about them. They didn't fight for her or choose her."

Cole put his hands on her arms, gently, when she began to protest. "I know why your instinct was to run, and why you stayed. I see the huge changes you've pushed yourself to make since you got here. But she hasn't known you as long, and her fear is really big. She might need something more than words to see that you're fighting for her."

Miriam threw her hands up in the air, knocking away Cole's hands. "What would that even look like? How do I fight for someone who's told me she doesn't love me and doesn't want to be with me? Who accused me of knowingly bringing this down on our heads?!"

"Okay, that was shitty, and she was wrong, and you have every right to still be angry about that. If you want to fight for her anyway..." Cole sat on the ground with his elbows propped up on his long knees. "I don't know for sure, because I've never met anyone I'd consider taking all my walls down for, but I think if I *had* taken my walls down, I would need a pretty big sign from them that they were ready to do the same for me."

"How can I prove to her that I'm not going anywhere again?"

Cole brought his hands up in a shrug. "What if it's not about where you're going? What if it's about what you're willing to face right here? She faced her worst fear, being left, for you. Maybe she needs to see that you'll face your worst fear for her.

"Again, I know nothing about love. And this is only if you actually want to fight for her. Which you need to be sure of. Don't make some grand gesture if what you want, in your heart of hearts, is a safe, quiet love like what you had with Tara. Don't try to get Noelle back if you're not absolutely, one hundred percent all in. That would be the worst thing you could do."

Miriam didn't even have to think, she didn't hesitate. "I do. I want that wild, terrifying, unexpected, untamed love. I want what Cass wanted for me all along—to live a big messy risky life. I'm so tired of keeping myself small so I can't get hurt, when all it does is hurt all the time anyway. I want her, forever. She's it for me."

Miriam looked at the painting of Baba Yaga and had an idea that her brain immediately told her to run away from, so she knew it must be the right thing to do.

"I'm going to need you to get me some supplies," she said. "And keep everyone out of here for the next twenty-four hours."

Cole watched her for a long time, then nodded. Unfolding from the floor, he took her face in his hands and locked eyes with her.

"I've never believed in anyone the way I believe in you. You have my sword, Mimi Blum."

She jumped up so she could throw her arms around his neck, and they stood together while she inhaled his smell for courage. No matter what happened in this world, she was never going to be alone, because Cole would never let her fall. That thought rang through her head, clear as a bell, as he literally held her up in the air.

Once he was gone, she dropped deeply into her art zone. While making the ornaments for Cass's tree, she had immersed herself in the process, losing track of time and going into a meditative state of Mod Podge and sparkle to channel the spirit of Cass.

This was different.

As Miriam gessoed a canvas for the first time in a decade, her soul relaxed into her body in a way she'd forgotten was even possible. She thought she'd been present—at Cass's shiva, at Hanukkah, in bed with Noelle—but laying paint down on a canvas required her to exist in her body so fiercely and completely that she finally understood why Noelle thought she was always on the verge of flight.

She had been, without even knowing. She'd never even met Noelle with her whole self present.

As day turned into dusk, Miriam settled into the corners of herself she hadn't used in so long she'd assumed the locks had rusted shut. The painting, both the act and the subject, were instinctive. They came from the parts of herself that existed without intellect or distance, and to access them she had to let herself simply *be*.

As dusk turned to darkest night, she finally let herself feel everything she had been scared of feeling for Noelle—every dream for their future, every ounce of yearning. She poured her adoration into her paint, her lust and her hope and the electricity she felt every time they touched.

More than how *she* felt, much more, she poured who Noelle was into the painting. Her sensitive love for her trees, the way she cared for Hannah and the Matthewses, how she always showed up without having to be asked. She painted Noelle's confidence and swagger, her ownership of her own body, her smolder and her comfort in who she was and wanted to be. She painted Noelle's sly humor, her raw surprised laugh when something tickled her. Noelle's commitment to Cass and her grief, still so big and unwieldy, at losing her.

Miriam painted her own regret that they'd never met before, before Noelle was mad at her for abandoning Carrigan's— and, underneath her fear and her rage at Richard, she painted her anger and disappointment that Noelle couldn't see that her knee-jerk trauma response wasn't who she was as a human being. It wasn't a set of character flaws she could overcome by sheer determination.

She painted what Noelle deserved and what Miriam wanted to give her, which was the world and everything in it, someone to stay and choose her every time. She also painted what *she* deserved and wanted Noelle to give her, which was the space and grace to become herself without always being afraid that she was doing it wrong.

At four o'clock the next morning, covered head to toe in paint and with every part of her insides now on the canvas, she lay down in the path of the moonlight coming through the carriage house windows and stared at the stars. She didn't know if she and Noelle would make it. She didn't even know if they'd get a chance to start again. She didn't know if they could save Carrigan's, if they could make a success of the business, or how they would hold her dad at arm's length forever.

What Miriam did know was she'd done something she thought she'd never be able to do again. She'd painted.

* * *

The morning of New Year's Eve, Miriam dragged Hannah into Advent, back to Marisol's boutique. Nothing she had with her was suitable for the party, and she didn't have time for Tara to send her something (nor did she think that phone call would go well). Now that Miriam had painted her entire soul for Noelle, she was moving on to phase two of her plan to fight for her girl: buy a slinky dress and make Noelle swallow her tongue with lust.

Marisol took one look at her and ushered her toward the vintage section at the back of the store. "I have something for you. It's real short and real shiny." She pressed a dress into Miriam's hands. It was liquid silver, original 1970s, and composed of very little fabric.

"I don't have shoes for this," Miriam said, smoothing what there was of the dress over her thighs, exhilarated at how it felt against her skin. She was going to look hotter than she'd ever looked in her life.

If she could find the right shoes.

"I have shoes!" Marisol exclaimed. "So many shoes!"

"I hate to throw a wrench in your perfectly planned and color-coded schedule for the day," Miriam said to Hannah, "but I also need your help with a surprise."

"What are you cooking up?" Hannah asked skeptically.

Miriam grinned. "I hereby officially declare a Shenanigan."

Chapter 23

Noelle

The ceiling of the work shed needed to be power-washed. Noelle knew this because she was lying upside down in her chair, feet on the back and head hanging off the seat, as she stared up at the ceiling. She was thinking about her conversation with Ziva, about everything she knew about Miriam's past and about trauma triggers in general. Mostly Noelle was thinking about how profoundly poorly she had treated the girl she loved.

A long dark blonde braid swung into her vision, haloing a face bathed in late winter light.

"You're taking this 'too gay to sit in a chair correctly' thing a bridge too far," her best friend said.

"How did you find me?" Noelle sounded petulant even to herself.

"Well, (a) I know you, and (b) Mr. Matthews ratted you out."

"I'm going to get him. Meddling old man trying to fix my life," Noelle grumbled, knowing Hannah understood that Mr. Matthews trying to fix her life was maybe her favorite thing.

"Why aren't you dressed yet?" Hannah asked. "Everyone else is ready, and it takes you one actual thousand years to do your hair."

"I think I fucked up," Noelle said instead of answering, swinging her legs off the chair and rearranging herself so she was upright. "With Miriam, I mean."

Hannah squatted down, her hands on Noelle's knees. "Oh, I knew what you meant. And I am absolutely certain that you fucked up. Big big."

She'd been hoping Hannah would tell her she'd been entirely right and justified and had not, as Noelle feared, possibly thrown away the only person she'd ever wanted to spend the rest of her life with. But Hannah never lied to her.

"I super unfairly accused her of something really shitty. I got mad at her for a completely natural reaction to the abuse she suffered all her life. She was standing there telling me all the reasons she is the way she is, and I couldn't even see how much courage that took. What did I expect, she would magically overcome twenty-five years of abuse because she tried hard enough?"

Hannah nodded sadly. "She got all her old buttons pushed, some of them by you, which pushed all your old buttons, and it kind of set off a chain of dominoes. Neither of you was acting out of your higher selves, just old toxic fight-or-flight patterns. You fight, she flies."

Noelle hung her head, and Hannah ran her fingernails

through Noelle's hair, scratching her scalp in slow circles and grounding her. Fuck. What would she do without Hannah?

"I didn't trust her, and I chose not to see all the ways she's already changed. I got scared and blew up." Noelle felt like she'd been running a marathon, trying to get her compassionate brain to outrun her fear and distrust.

"I mean, yes, but also, you are in the middle of incomparable grief, and not reacting the way you might otherwise," Hannah pointed out. "Neither is she. We did just lose our North Star, and none of us is over that."

"I gotta do something so I don't act like this again."

Hannah nodded. "There's a pack of little old lady alcoholics who probably have some ideas. But yeah, none of us can just muscle through losing Cass and pretend it's not affecting every single thing we do, or that we'll be okay if we just keep going."

"I can't cry about Cass right now," Noelle said, shaking herself off. "I will be all blotchy faced for the party, which I'm already going to be late to because of my hair. What am I going to do? About Miriam?"

"Talk to each other, like two grown-ups. Remember that there's a gray area between 'We had a fight' and 'We can never be together as long as we live.' Schedule sessions with a counselor or a rabbi. I know a great one. Tell her you were wrong and listen to her."

"You make it sound simple."

Hannah threw back her head and laughed. "It's going to be hard as hell. You've both got scars that go all the way down. You make each other better, and you set off each other's landmines. It's not going to tie up in a neat little bow. But if there are any two people I'm an expert in, it's you and Miriam Blum, and I believe you can do it, and you'll both be fools if you don't try."

If Hannah was going to make her talk about her feelings, it was only fair to return the favor. "Since you've apparently solved my love life, are you ready to talk about how the love of *your* life is apparently on an Australian TV show right now?" Noelle asked.

"NOPE." Hannah shook her head so hard her braid whipped Noelle in the back. "I want to get you into a tux, save the farm, and get you back your girl." She pulled Noelle out of the work shed, into the cold.

"We're going to talk about this. Don't think you can avoid it forever," Noelle said, following her back up to the house.

She was already late. There was an alarming number of audaciously rich people in sequins milling around looking at her trees. She hoped this meant the auction would be a success. For an event they'd planned in five days, Noelle could barely believe how many people had arrived, and how totally the inn's regular guests had embraced the party. New Year's Eve at Carrigan's had never been quiet, because Cass never let an occasion for excess pass unfulfilled, but this year, the mood was frenetic.

All the Christmas trees in the main house had been replaced by displays of Miriam's art. Guests were being shown through the first floor by Mrs. Matthews before being escorted to the party in the barn. Hannah had disappeared to play hostess.

Noelle slipped past everyone, trying to get to her room without being waylaid by too many well-meaning well-wishers. She was on a mission, and that mission was: look hot enough to distract Miriam into talking to her for however long Noelle needed to apologize, grovel, beg forgiveness, and vow to do better.

And also save the farm. Probably somewhere in there, they should save the farm.

In her room, Noelle found herself taken back to the morning of Cass's funeral. Like that day, she freshened up the buzzed side of her hair, fastened her cufflinks, slipped into dress shoes.

That morning, she'd thought a part of her life was ending and nothing would ever fill the void Cass had left. When she'd tucked a comb into the back pocket of her funeral slacks, Noelle hadn't known that she would meet an infuriating, mesmerizing elf who would change her entire internal landscape. Somehow, in the midst of one of the saddest and most difficult times in her life, she'd become lit with hope for the future, excited for every tomorrow in a way she'd never thought she would be again.

Tonight, as she folded her pocket square and tied her bow tie, she was prepared. Noelle knew that the next time she saw her wild-haired chaos elf, her life was going to change again, for better or worse.

God, she hoped for better.

If getting to her room had been a minefield of distractions, getting to the barn was a labyrinth of people she couldn't avoid, no matter how much she needed to find Miriam before the auction. Once it started, the Bloomer Face would be on, all her performative defenses up, and she would belong to the crowd. Noelle needed to get to her first, so Miriam knew how loved she was, that she wasn't facing this all alone.

As she crept past the kitchen, Mr. Matthews appeared carrying a tray loaded with apps, startling her.

"You going to fix things with my girl?" he grunted at her.

She couldn't ignore Mr. Matthews. "I'm going to try, if I can get to her."

"You'd better. I already have one kid who ruined things because he couldn't get his head out of his ass. I don't need two of you."

She blinked at him. She didn't know if she was touched that he considered her one of his kids or horrified that he'd compared her to Levi. Before she could decide, he shooed her off. She was almost at the doors to the great room when a pack of Old Ladies, made up, confusingly, of both Miriam's antique dealers and her own alcoholics, surrounded her, delaying her again.

"We heard you don't date," said Annie the possible witch. "Were you stringing our baby along?"

"We told you not to be a fool," added the eldest of the sober ladies. "Do we need to spell out for you how that looks? Because you seem to have misinterpreted it."

"How do you all know so much about my love life?" Noelle wailed, throwing her hands up.

"That Cole boy can't keep his mouth shut," another one of them said.

She gritted her teeth. She couldn't kill Cole, not when she needed Miriam to forgive her. "I'm trying to make things right, but you are literally standing in my way. I need to get to her if I'm going to fix things, which means you need to move."

They parted before her, Furies with their rage abated, and she finally made it to the barn doors.

As guests walked into the barn for the auction, they passed racks of Cass's hats and boas for sale. Anyone who had fallen in love with the ornaments at the tree lighting could purchase their own Cass Carrigan accessory. Women in designer party dresses strolled around in vintage cloches and leopard-print capes.

Joshua was charming many a visitor into signing up for updates from the new Carrigan's site, courtesy of Cole. Sideboards had been set up all around the perimeter, with giant platters of hors d'oeuvres and endless flutes of champagne, donated by a longtime Carrigan's guest who owned a winery. A vanload of Rosenstein cousins had arrived (with another vanload of pastries) and were mingling with the Bloomers.

Noelle saw Cole huddled in a corner talking to Sawyer Bright. Sawyer was twirling one end of his mustache and looking up at Cole, who was blushing. Noelle definitely couldn't kill Cole right now, as Sawyer was about to run for mayor of Advent and he'd be mad at her if witnessing a murder got in the way of his campaign. She kept scanning, trying to see the tops of Miriam's curls over the crowd, since there was no way she'd be able to see the rest of her.

"Noelle!" came a voice behind her. She winced, but when she turned, she saw Elijah and Jason and breathed out a sigh. She loved her friends, they were at an important party she was hosting, and she was not going to yell at them for wanting to greet her. She was not *that* uncivilized, even if she felt that way right now.

Next to Jason was a stately woman with skin as dark as his and a dimple she recognized. Her white hair was piled elegantly on top of her head in a chignon. At the sight of her, Noelle did genuinely smile.

"Jason! You finally brought your mom around! I thought you were ashamed of us."

"Oh, I was," Jason assured her.

"Elijah's mother is always bragging to me about how she's friends with all of their friends, and I couldn't let her one-up me," the woman said, holding out her hand to shake Noelle's. "I'm Vaunda Green."

Noelle reciprocated and said warmly, "Ma'am, it is an honor. Can I get you something to eat?"

"I hear a rumor you might be having girl trouble," Mrs. Green said, and Noelle scrubbed a hand across her face. Apparently, everyone on the East Coast knew. "I won't bother you for a plate while you're trying to fix things. She's right over there, if you want to talk to her."

Noelle's eyes followed to where she was pointing, and she caught a glimpse of sparkling silver.

"It was such a pleasure to meet you, ma'am! I hope you'll join us for brunch tomorrow and bring the twins. I gotta go!" she called out as she went toward her new destination. Though now that she could see Miriam, she felt a new panic.

She had absolutely no idea what she was going to say.

Miriam was standing under the disco ball Cole had insisted on hanging, its glow bouncing off her curls and her dress, making her look like the brightest source of light in the room. Her tiny silver dress showed every inch of her legs all the way up and dipped in the back almost to her butt. She could not possibly be wearing a bra underneath it.

Noelle short circuited. Her first thought, when her brain

came back online, was that Miriam was wearing that dress to fuck with her.

Immediately afterward, she was terrified Miriam wasn't wearing it for her at all.

She realized, belatedly, that Miriam was surrounded by an impenetrable pack of people she thought might be famous on Instagram. Her palms started to sweat. Noelle grabbed a glass of sparkling cider and an hors d'oeuvre from a passing high school student. She chugged the cider (a mistake, she got bubbles in her nose) and stuffed the phyllo-wrapped cheese in her mouth.

She was starting to think there was no way she was going to get to Miriam before the auction started if she didn't bring in reinforcements, and then she passed Hannah wearing an electric blue bandage dress and chatting to a Rosenstein cousin.

"Hannah, I need you to create a diversion for me," she said, pulling her best friend away from her conversation. "For love."

Hannah rolled her eyes. "Really? Shenanigans? Who are you, Blue Matthews?"

"Why do people keep saying that to me?" Noelle wailed. After this, she obviously needed to seriously reevaluate her life so people would stop comparing her to Levi.

"I will do this for you," Hannah said, "but only because I am tired of the two of you swanning around my hotel pining after each other."

"Also because you love me more than your own breath," Noelle reminded her.

"Yes, also that. Be ready when you see the wolf pack

disperse; you don't have much time. I hope you have a plan for what you're going to say."

She did not.

"It will be fine," Noelle reassured Hannah—and herself. "It's totally going to be fine."

Hannah patted her on the shoulder before shaking her head, muttering how she should have gone to college for sapphic feelings management as she walked purposefully toward Miriam.

Chapter 24

Miriam

Miriam was surrounded by a cadre of famous internet crafters, who were trying their hardest to get her to spill personal details about her breakup with Tara. She was ecstatic to see Hannah walk up.

Hannah smiled brightly at the group. "Miri, love, I have an absolute emergency," Hannah said, as she hauled Miriam away.

When they were safely behind the food tables under the hayloft, she continued, "I don't, actually, but I thought you might need a rescue. Also, two dozen people have asked me about sale prices on some of the items for display. You could probably attach ludicrous prices to them tonight. Then we could stash the money in a nest egg. These people are extremely happy on champagne and ready to spend money like it's their job. Well, maybe it is their job."

"You can sell them, but only at five times their normal

asking price," Miriam told her. It wasn't worth keeping them, if there would be no Carrigan's to keep them in. "Get with Cole for estimates. Also, check in with Noelle before you promise anything to anyone. I know she has a few pieces she's madly in love with, and I don't want to sell any of them without her go-ahead."

"Aye aye, Captain." Hannah walked off toward a buyer who was eyeing a sculpture.

Students from the local high school drama club, dressed all in black, had been pressed into acting as waiters by Jason Green, their drama teacher. They were doing a remarkably flamboyant job. Even Cass would have approved of the flair with which they were throwing themselves into their work. At least one was wearing a fake mustache. As several of them parted, carrying trays of apps, she caught a glimpse of Noelle's hair.

"How are you holding up?" Elijah asked, coming up behind her.

She gestured to his tuxedo. "Elijah, I'm not sure lawyers are supposed to be this hot."

"Weren't you engaged to a lawyer for years, Miriam?" he asked, raising an eyebrow.

"Yeah, but she didn't look this good in a tux." Miriam laughed. Although, in Tara's defense, lack of hotness had never been one of her faults.

"You're dodging my question. How are you holding up?"

"My father tried to burn down my life, take everything I love, and he may have forced me into this transformation, but I am transformed, and I'm going to show that asshole he should have left well enough alone."

She stopped, realizing she was monologuing.

"Well, I'm into this Dark Phoenix energy," he said, putting an arm around her shoulder for a squeeze. "Let's use it to sell a lot of art for a lot of money."

"Carrigan's Home for Gifted Youngsters?" she joked.

"It has a ring to it."

She left Elijah and climbed the stairs to the hayloft to get a better view of the crowd. And maybe, a little bit, to try to catch a glimpse of Noelle before she pulled off her big surprise.

There, by the makeshift auction podium, stood her heart. Miriam tried to remember how to breathe. Noelle was in a perfectly tailored tuxedo and tails, in a rich navy that made her skin glow. The tux hugged her curves and accentuated her broad shoulders, strong arms, and thick thighs. Her undercut was freshly shaved, her hair waxed into a pompadour.

She was the hottest fat butch dream of Miriam's most secret fantasies, and the jolt of lust she felt almost knocked her over.

She shook herself. This was a professional party, for the business they co-owned. She needed to schmooze art patrons, not beg Noelle on her knees to take her back and then drag her into a corner to undo her bow tie with her teeth.

Miriam had a plan, and she needed to stick to it. She needed to get to the painting auction with everyone's clothes still on. Still, when their eyes met, and Noelle pushed off the wall she was leaning on, Miriam was ready for the sensible voice in her head to shut up. Her whole body flushed.

Miriam held her breath, watching Noelle stalk toward her gracefully, purposefully, unstoppably. When Noelle stood at the bottom of the stairs, they were eye level, and she beckoned for Miriam to lean in.

"You look unbelievable," Noelle whispered in her ear.

Miriam's heart leaped in hope. Noelle wanted her, and she was willing to admit it. Maybe, maybe, she would accept Miriam's apology, and they could start again. "You look like everything I've ever wanted," Miriam said honestly.

Noelle chewed on her lip, and Miriam squeezed her fingernails into her palms to stop herself from reaching out.

"Miri, I need to tell you . . ." Noelle's dark brown eyes were huge and full of some emotion Miriam couldn't read. She leaned forward, her whole body waiting.

Somewhere in the crowd, Ziva cleared her throat into a microphone. "If I can have everyone's attention, please."

"To be continued?" Miriam pleaded, dying to know what Noelle had been about to say.

Noelle grimaced, leaning back and sticking her hands in her back pockets. "Absolutely to be continued," she said gently. "Go sell your art. This is your big moment. You've got this. I'll be here when you're done."

Miriam nodded and went to the stage to introduce the auction items.

The first round of bidding was for the bespoke Miriam Blum pieces, and it was intense. Guests who'd known Miriam all her life went toe to toe with fanatical Instagram fans who were drooling to have her custom design a piece for them. The Bloomers had showed up in force and were committed to doing anything in their power to help Miriam save Carrigan's. Together, they raised more than Miriam had dared hope for—just short of $300,000.

But it wasn't nearly enough to stop her father.

"We've concluded the bidding for the pieces of personalized Miriam Blum art," Ziva announced, her iridescent black pantsuit shimmering under the lights. "It is now time to hold our live auction of one of the seven Mimi Roz paintings left in existence, only two of which were known to the public until a few days ago. I know this is the moment many of you came for, and I hope you have your checkbooks ready and your hearts open."

"What's a checkbook?" someone called from the crowd.

"We accept multiple forms of payment," Ziva volleyed back. "As you know, a developer has offered the bank five hundred thousand dollars to buy out the mortgage on Carrigan's Christmasland. He plans to bulldoze the whole farm and inn and turn it into luxury vacation homes."

The crowd booed loudly.

"If this happens, families will lose jobs. The town will lose tourist traffic. Many of you will lose a place you've thought of as a second home for generations. None of us want this outcome."

"Including me!" yelled out Mr. Rodriguez, the president of the bank. "I'm being overruled by the board of trustees!"

"I'd like to welcome my daughter, Miriam, to the stage, to tell you about this painting." Ziva had spoken with her usual flair, but Miriam could see the strain around her eyes. Being in front of this crowd—with cameras streaming, certainly, into her father's office—was burning a bridge her mom could never rebuild. This was an unmistakable message from Ziva about whose side she stood on. Miriam knew her mother must be terrified, even if she was hiding it well, and as she took the mic from her with one hand, she placed the other on Ziva's back.

They shared a little nod, and then her mother gave her the stage.

"Before tonight, there were only two Mimi Roz paintings known to the public—and five more no one realized had been placed in storage. I have displayed the five lost paintings behind me." She gestured to the easels set behind the podium. "Before we begin the bidding, I need to issue a correction. The materials for the auction state that there are only seven Mimi Roz paintings in existence. Until yesterday, that was true. Now, there are eight." She paused, trying to keep her voice steady.

The crowd went silent. Cole and Hannah were both grinning up at her as she locked eyes with Noelle, who looked frozen in place.

"Friends, family, Bloomers, Carrigan's isn't just a Christmas experience. It's a place to heal, to find yourself, to become," she started, trying to remember what she'd written earlier before deciding to wing it. "I was lost from Carrigan's for a long time, and also from myself. Being back here has given me the courage to face anything, even the things I'm most afraid of. I may never be able to make up for the hurt I caused by being trapped in my own past, but I can grow. I can be bigger, and brighter, and fiercer than my father's worst nightmare."

Cole whistled through his fingers, and Hannah hooted.

"To prove to myself and my loved ones that I'm done living in my father's cage, I did something I swore I would never do again as long as I lived. I painted."

Noelle's hands came up to cover her mouth, and Miriam

could see tears welling in her eyes. *Please, please let this work,* she prayed.

"This painting will not join tonight's sale, but I wanted all of you to be able to see it, because tonight is about hope and having faith in new beginnings."

Reaching behind her, she pulled the canvas out from where it had been hidden behind one of Cass's mannequins. Hannah materialized a stand, and together they set it up so the whole crowd could see the velvet-covered frame. Miriam took a deep breath, counted down silently, and pulled the velvet down in a dramatic swoop.

At the bottom of the canvas stood a pair of silver glitter-encrusted Doc Martens, from which roots were growing down into the soil below. Above the boots rose a spectral figure, white rags whipping around her and her face a mask of despair. Over one shoulder, she held a Christmas tree, slung like Paul Bunyan carrying an ax, and at her feet sat Kringle like Babe the Blue Ox. A circle of luminarias surrounded her, and her free hand pointed into the distance, at the North Star.

It was the most personal and most haunting painting Miriam had ever done.

"Who's the ghost?" called out Jason Green.

"It's La Llorona," Noelle said, her eyes never leaving Miriam's, her steady voice rising above the crowd. "She weeps for the family she lost, always trying to collect a new one."

"Someone I love has a thing for dangerous women," Miriam explained.

"Don't we all!" yelled Annie, her favorite immortal crone who owned the best junk shop in Boise.

"I'll give you seventy-five grand for it!" someone shouted.

"I'll give you free fries for life if you hang it at Ernie's," Ernie called.

"It's not for sale," Noelle said loudly, her tone brooking no argument.

Miriam and Noelle stared silently at each other for several beats, everyone else in the room disappearing from Miriam's awareness.

"Hey, we're still here to buy a painting!" one of the Old Ladies reminded them.

Noelle gave a tiny nod that Miriam couldn't interpret, then mouthed, "Later."

Miriam had done everything she could do for her love life. Now, she had to save her home.

She brought up the painting for auction and gave a brief overview, including some history of her inspiration while working.

The crowd cheered. "The bidding will start at thirty thousand dollars."

Miriam was nervous about whether or not anyone on Earth would want to pay $30,000 for one of her paintings, but she had to trust how much these old families loved this place, how far they would go for Cass's niece.

The bidding started flying, and Miriam suddenly wished her mother hadn't left her alone at the microphone. Hannah mouthed "breathe" to her, as paddles, and the price, went up and up and *up*. The scene in front of her was surreal, with the greenery and the glitter, the twinkling lights like tiny stars stretching the barn out into a galaxy. Everything was under a soft-focus lens, and time seemed to freeze.

Esther and Joshua ended up in a bidding war with the

president of the bank, Mr. Rodriguez, who had decided that if he could not save the farm at work, he was going to do so with his own money. Miriam shook her head the tiniest fraction at the twins, and they drove it to where they thought the president might break before bowing out.

"Sold! To Mr. Rodriguez for $232,500!" Ziva exclaimed triumphantly.

They were going to save Carrigan's.

With the funds from the online auction, and the GoFundMe when it was released, they might even be able to pay off the mortgage Cass had taken out. They could start their new vision with a clean slate.

But it wasn't over yet.

She walked into the celebrating crowd. Cole and Hannah surged forward to catch her up in a giant, ecstatic hug.

Hannah was sobbing, laughing, and screaming, over and over, "It's ours! We did it! It's ours!"

Someone snapped a photo that Miriam knew she would keep all her life, of her and Hannah holding each other and smiling as hard as they had ever smiled.

She labeled it: *The Heirs of Cassiopeia.*

Hannah kissed her cheek and whispered, "You saved the farm, Miri. Now go get her."

Miriam looked up to find Noelle watching them, standing still in a crowd of people going wild. She raised an eyebrow at Miriam, a little corner of her mouth turning up. Miriam took a deep breath, threw her shoulders back, and walked to her fate.

Chapter 25

Noelle

Noelle watched Miriam walk toward her and wondered when she'd become able to read every line of Miriam's body to divine her real feelings. Even from across the room, Noelle could tell—by the tilt of her chin, the set of her shoulders—that Miriam Blum was nervous. She hated that she'd put this uncertainty between them. Noelle wanted to be the person Miriam most trusted, to always be gentle with her heart, but she hadn't proven she could be.

She would, if she got another chance. She would prove it every day forever, if she was lucky enough for this magnetic, talented, fascinating, brave elf to forgive her.

And then Miriam was in front of her, holding her hands out, looking up with those huge sad eyes. All Noelle could think to say, suddenly, was "You painted for me."

"I did." Miriam nodded.

"You didn't have to do that."

Miriam just nodded again. "Yes, I did."

"No one's ever, in all my life, done anything even close to that for me. I can't—" She paused, holding Miriam's hands and gazing down into her face, trying to remember what breathing even was.

A microphone crackled.

"And now," Cole said in an old-timey radio announcer voice, "it's almost time to start the countdown to midnight. Grab your favorite partner. I've given the DJ instructions to play the most romantic slow dance song in the history of the world, 'I'd Do Anything for Love (But I Won't Do That)' by multiplatinum American treasure Marvin Lee 'Meat Loaf' Aday. Unfortunately, Hannah has paid him double to play you something else. But as long as you're in the arms of the one you love, your year will still end nearly as well as it possibly could."

The first notes of "Time After Time" played over the speakers.

"Dance with me?"

"Aren't you supposed to be spending this dance in the arms of the person you love?" Miriam replied even as she moved her hand to Noelle's waist and nestled her head under Noelle's chin.

Noelle started to answer, but Miriam kept talking.

"I know you're going to say my emotions are all over the map right now, and you don't trust me. I know I messed things up, and you're scared of making your heart vulnerable again. I know the feeling, because right now I'm more afraid than I've ever been, and I'm still walking through it. Maybe you'll choose to say we can't ever be together. It won't change anything for me, I'm still here. I'm so tired of running. This might be a once-in-a-lifetime kind of love. The kind Cass always told me to find—"

"Baby, stop for a minute," Noelle interrupted, "and let me tell you I love you."

This woman, this miraculous woman, whose mind and heart were so fascinating, who sparkled so brightly, who understood Noelle's worst impulses and her highest hopes, was in her arms declaring her love.

Noelle had been loved, and seen, in her life, but she'd never dared to dream about being loved like this. If she had ever lain in bed at night and asked the universe for a girl (not that she had, of course, at least not for a long time), never in her wildest imaginings would she have asked for a girl who painted La Llorona in silver Docs. She wouldn't have believed she could deserve this. But here this woman was, in a slinky dress smelling like heaven, and Noelle was going to love her so fiercely that Miriam never regretted choosing her.

"All I've been trying to do, all night, is find you and get on my knees to beg you to forgive me," Noelle said. "And then instead of being angry with me, you gave me the most beautiful gift, beyond anything I could imagine."

"You were going to apologize?" Miriam whispered.

Noelle nodded. "First, for even thinking in any universe that you would stay here if you suspected this would happen. It was an awful thing to say, and I will be lucky if you ever forgive me for it."

"Forgiven," Miriam whispered. "I would have wondered the same thing, and we both said things we shouldn't out of fear." Noelle's heart turned over.

"I've never felt for anybody what I feel for you," she continued, "and when you said you were leaving, I felt more fear than I ever wanted to feel again. I know where it came from. I know we don't always get to turn our trauma off. Once I calmed down, I knew that what you did in a panic wasn't your choice, and I'm so sorry I freaked out. I lost everything I loved, twice. I thought I didn't want to love anymore, but I was so wrong. I want you. I want to be your anchor, and I want to go on wild antiquing adventures with you. I want to fix your hot glue gun when it breaks, and make sure you eat while you're in your workshop. I want to go to therapy with you so we can both untangle our messes. Do you want that? Will you still have me?" Her breath caught in her throat, her heart trying to beat its way out of her tux.

"Noelle, even when you were telling me it was over, you were still fighting for me. You still believed that my art could save Carrigan's All Year, and that it was worth saving." Miriam's face beamed up at her, sparkling under the disco balls. "You threw me a lifeline and yelled at me until I grabbed on. How could I ever say no?"

The party started counting down. "Ten, nine, eight, seven—"

"I'm a superstitious girl," Noelle whispered. "Don't kiss me at midnight if you're not planning on spending the rest of your year by my side."

"Four, three, two, one! Happy New Year!"

Miriam yanked on Noelle's lapels and brought their lips together. She wrapped both arms around Noelle's neck and kissed her hard. Noelle picked her up, swinging her around and smiling against her lips before pulling back to rest her forehead against Miriam's.

"Wait," she said, as the chorus started up again, "is this our song, now? Is Cyndi Lauper our song?"

Miriam laughed. "I *was* lost, and you did find me."

"I did nothing of the sort!" Noelle protested. "You walked into my kitchen and demanded that I caffeinate you!"

Miriam shook her head and kissed Noelle again.

By two a.m., their voices were hoarse from thanking everyone profusely, and, in the case of the townies, ushering them home. Miriam had her head against Cole's shoulder as they sat together on the stairs.

Noelle walked up and offered Miriam her hand. "I promised your mother I would make sure you got into bed." Miriam grinned lasciviously at her. "And to sleep," Noelle clarified, as much for herself as for Miriam.

"But makeup sex," Miriam whined, fluttering her eyelashes.

"I'm not having sex with you when you're drunk," Noelle pointed out, as Miriam draped her body over Noelle's.

"I'm not drunk. I'm just so unbelievably tired." She waved a heel, which she was holding in her hand, over the sea of sleeping bags on the floor of the great room, where everyone who'd flown up and wouldn't fit in the guest rooms had set up anywhere they could find. "This was a lot."

When they reached Miriam's closed door, she leaned her head against it.

"I'm not ready for this day to be over," Miriam said, softly.

"I'm afraid I'm going to wake up and it will all be gone, like Peter in *The Snowy Day*."

"When Peter wakes up, the world is still covered in snow, remember. You're going to wake up and still have Carrigan's," Noelle reassured her, as she smoothed Miriam's curls away from her face. She couldn't help getting distracted and winding one around her finger.

"And you? Will I still have you?" Miriam looked at her with those giant eyes, and Noelle leaned down to kiss her forehead.

"You will still have me tomorrow."

She meant to brush her lips against Miriam's to say goodnight. Instead, the taste of Miriam's lips trapped her, the gentle pressure lingering. They wrapped themselves around each other, and kissed, tired and gentle, in the silence of the witching hour, for a very long time.

"Go. To. Bed," Noelle said, when she finally dragged her head up.

"Come with me," Miriam pleaded, and Noelle started to protest.

"Just to sleep. I was so scared you would never hold me again." Miriam tugged at her hand, and Noelle relented.

As long as they were in the same hotel, it seemed like a terrible waste of hours not to be holding each other.

"Sweet!" Miriam whispered. "Makeup sex in the morning."

The new year dawned earlier than any of them were ready for it to. The dining room had to be cleared of sleepers to make room to serve brunch, and people propped themselves up against walls and under tables, nursing hangovers and Bellinis. Mrs. Matthews set out a buffet on the sideboard before sitting down to chat with Jason's mother and Ziva, both regally perched in actual chairs, sipping coffee amid the chaos. Mr. Matthews brought his wife a plate, and they smiled at each other like they'd fallen in love yesterday.

Noelle watched them and thought that all of this had been worth it to see the weight lifted off their shoulders. Grant Matthews, the Big Kid of the current pack at age seven, was herding the Green twins away from the sugar bowls and coming up with endless new ideas to keep them occupied.

"That was us," Hannah said, sitting next to her at a back table. "I was the Responsible One, trying to keep Esther and Joshua out of the grown-ups' hair."

"Ah, so they're the reason you were a tiny adult even as a kid," Noelle nodded.

"Well, yes and no," Hannah said. "Miri or Blue were too busy making trouble to do it. The more things change..."

Noelle looked at Miriam, who was holding court over the now fully integrated group of Old Ladies, distinguishable only by who was drinking morning champagne versus strong coffee.

"Some things changed," Noelle observed. "And it's a new year. Who knows what miracles it holds? We already saved the farm. I fell in love. Levi Blue may yet grow up and start being responsible to the people he loves. Stranger things have happened."

She personally doubted this very much, and would be perfectly happy if Levi were mysteriously lost off the coast of

Easter Island or something, but all the people she loved best in the world would be devastated so, instead, she prayed for his (incredibly annoying) return home.

Hannah snorted in disbelief, throwing her arm around Noelle. "Thank you. For staying with me, through Levi leaving and Cass dying, and everything in between."

"You and me, Hannah. Ride or die. Besides, you made me fight for Miri. That's how we roll."

"What would I have done if you'd never shown up on my doorstep?" Hannah asked.

"Oh, I assume Cass would have gone out and found me," Noelle said, and Hannah laughed. Noelle couldn't bear to imagine a version of her life in which she hadn't ended up right here.

"Are you whispering about me?" Miriam asked, tucking herself up against Noelle's other side. Having her two best girls on her flanks felt pretty great.

"I wish," Hannah said. "We're talking about Blue."

"Gross. Stop. He's not even here, why do we keep talking about him? Talk about my artistic genius."

They both looked at Miri, and she grinned an impish little elf grin. It was a look Noelle had never seen, and she wondered, again, how much of Miriam was going to surface now that she was letting herself be.

She couldn't wait.

Chapter 26

Miriam

On Friday, Hannah threw a dress at Miriam and told her to get rabbi-ready.

"You live here now, you're going to services," she said, and then drove them to the synagogue in Lake Placid.

The longer she stayed at Carrigan's, the less everything felt like nostalgia and more like things she was doing for the first time. Parts like this, where she was singing Melissa Etheridge at the top of her lungs in the passenger seat while Hannah drove too fast, weren't new—they'd been doing it since they were too young to be driving. But heading out to shul, just the two of them, was new. For years, Miriam had been practicing her faith while removed from the rest of her life, two separate bubbles that never intersected. It tickled the part of her brain that still startled easily at any kind of real emotional connection, but she sat with the feeling instead of shooing it away.

Your roots are wide and strong, Miriam Blum, she reminded herself, *and love is being offered you every day, by family that spreads out as wide as the ocean.*

Rabbi Ruth led a beautiful service, and even if all the faces were new, hearing the Kabbalat Shabbat always felt like coming home. Miriam hadn't really thought what it would mean to her, to live in a home surrounded by people for whom Judaism was central to their daily lives. It was one more way she was going to be able to find herself here, and she was overcome with gratitude.

They'd invited Ziva to services, but she'd demurred, saying the girls needed time together. Miriam wasn't sure where her mom and G-d were currently standing, and certainly wasn't going to inquire. That was a conversation for when their relationship was much further repaired.

When they got back to Carrigan's, her mother was standing on the big front porch, beckoning her over insistently.

"Miri, come quick, look!" Her mom was pink-cheeked and bright-eyed. She pointed up, and there was the aurora borealis, huge and otherworldly and perfect. She clutched Miriam's hand, hard, and sighed. "I've had an epiphany," she said finally.

Miriam rolled her eyes at her mother's need for dramatic pronouncement, but she did it with some affection now.

"That's fitting, given the date," Noelle said, putting her arm around Miriam's shoulders. Miriam looked at her in confusion. "It's January sixth? Epiphany? No?" Ziva and Miriam both shook their heads.

"What's the epiphany, Mom?" Miriam asked, not sure she wanted to know. "Did the northern lights tell you what to do with your life?"

"I'll tell you, after I talk to Elijah." She bustled inside and grabbed her rental car keys.

"Mom, it's past the twins' bedtime," Miriam called after her. "It's probably past Elijah and Jason's bedtime. What are you doing? He's not our personal on-call attorney. Or our life coach! Let him live!"

"He just played a triple word score on Words with Friends two minutes ago. I know he's up," Ziva insisted. "This can't wait!" She waved merrily out the car window as she backed out of the long driveway.

"I'm kind of hurt that Elijah plays Words with Friends with your mom and not me," Hannah said, having come up behind them.

"Do you think Elijah is going to kill my mom?" Miriam wondered.

"I'm much more worried that he's going to fire us for being pains in his ass," Noelle answered.

Miriam nodded at this wisdom, and they all three stood together for a long time, watching the lights. Miriam wanted to be emotionally uninvested in her mom's journey, but in so many ways, their journeys were inextricable. They'd both been shaped by the same man, and now they were both trying to figure out how to shape themselves.

The next day, Elijah was back in their kitchen, with another mug of hot cocoa and another platter of Mrs. Matthews's cookies (pfeffernusse, today). This time, he looked much less anxious than he had the day after Christmas.

"As I'm sure you know, your mother came to visit me last night," he said to Miriam.

"We're sorry about that, by the way."

"Excuse me," Ziva protested.

"If I held you responsible for the actions of your parents, Miriam Blum, we would not be having this conversation," Elijah said, popping a cookie in his mouth.

Miriam nodded gratefully, and Elijah went on.

"She's been wondering what to do about your father, since she was certain he was already planning retaliation for her role in the auction," Elijah said. "I'm not a divorce lawyer, nor am I licensed to practice in the state of Arizona, but I am an estate lawyer, and I could act as your mother's counsel regarding some of her assets as she sets up a possible escape plan. These pfeffernusse are legendary, Mrs. M."

Mrs. Matthews grinned at him.

"Since Richard burned Miriam's paintings, I've been quietly transferring small amounts of money to an account in a Swiss bank," Ziva told them. "I wasn't ready to escape, then, but I knew I should have a plan."

"Elijah, is that legal?" Hannah asked.

"Legal, certainly," Elijah assured them. "They had joint bank accounts. Men have been siphoning off their wives' money and hiding it in offshore accounts since time immemorial. Is it ethical? I would say not usually, but in this case we'll call it hazard pay."

"So," Ziva said, "I had some savings, and, as you may or may not know, Arizona is a community property state. After Christmas, I began gathering evidence that I had been an integral part of growing and supporting your father's business ventures. I could get my hands on a lot, because the man has abysmal cybersecurity, and all his passwords are a variation on 'Big Dick' puns. Richard, Dick, he thinks he's very clever."

"As I said," Elijah continued, "I'm not a divorce lawyer in Arizona, but I know some really good sharks, and one of them had a killer recommendation for an attorney who was more than happy to take on your mother's case. We spoke to her this morning. I can't predict the future, but I know lawyers, and I would be shocked if your father ended up with even half his assets."

"I'm filing for divorce," Ziva announced. "And then I'm getting as far away from Phoenix fucking Arizona as a yacht will take me."

Miriam had known, as soon as her mom stood next to her on the livestream, that there was no way Ziva was going back to her old life, but she was surprised that her mom was doing it big, rather than slinking off quietly with her savings and hoping no one noticed.

"Mom, are you sure you want to do this?" Miriam asked. "It's going to look bad."

"It's going to look bad for Richard," Ziva said. "And I can't pretend anymore. Something broke inside me, and out flooded all the time I've wasted covering up for him and propping him up and losing my family, to keep up appearances. Besides, if it does get out, it will look a lot better if I've left in a blaze of glory."

Ah, there it was. Her mom might be bending toward her better impulses, but she was still choosing the path that reflected the best on her. It was sort of comforting, to know not everything had changed.

Ziva immediately went to start packing, and Miriam found her trying unsuccessfully to fit one of Cass's antique furs into a carry-on.

"Mom," she said in exasperation, "you're going to ruin that coat."

"Oh, love, I don't even need it," Ziva said. "I just had this moment of panic where I couldn't imagine anyone loving it as much as Cass did, and I was going to give it a good home."

"I'll keep it here for you, for the next time you visit," Miriam promised. "Were you planning on saying goodbye, or was your great epiphany scene as much emotion as you could muster?"

"I resemble that remark," her mother joked, an old Rosenstein pun for when someone saw too much of themselves in a criticism to argue with it. "I was, in fact, planning to come say goodbye. I know you don't particularly care if I'm here or not, and rightly so, as you're busy building a social circle and a business and a new relationship."

Miriam started to interrupt her, but Ziva waved her off. "Still, it's been so important to me to be here. To watch you stand up to your father and see you as the adult you've become. I don't have any right to be proud of you, but I am, very much."

Miriam rubbed her hand over her face and tried to be kind. Her mom's tendency to make everything as melodramatic as possible pushed all her buttons, but she was obviously trying to have a genuine, emotional mothering moment, only she was not very practiced at it.

Miriam knew she wasn't obligated to push their past under a rug out of any sense of family unity or to make her mother feel less guilty or uncomfortable. But she was starting to think that if they both looked the past unflinchingly in the eye, they might be able to cobble together some kind of relationship in the future. She wasn't sure she wanted that yet, but she wasn't sure she didn't.

"Are you coming back?" she asked, finally, and then added, in case it wasn't clear, "I'd like you to."

"I'll be back for the Fourth of July carnival," her mother said. "I promise, I won't miss it."

"You never do miss a chance for fireworks." Miriam smiled.

"Well," Cole said after hauling Ziva's various bags to the front door, "I think the party is officially over. I should probably also be going." He materialized a rolling suitcase from seemingly nowhere. Ziva looked both annoyed that he was stealing her dramatic exit and impressed by his flair.

Then Ziva and Cole were gone. Cole rode the train back to Manhattan with her, a trip Miriam wished she had hidden camera footage of. Cole swore they talked about *Middlemarch* the whole way.

Their guests were gone next, leaving them with an empty inn. It was eerily quiet after all the nonstop commotion of the past few weeks, a calm before the storm of upcoming Carrigan's All Year events. Miriam found herself wandering the hallways, feeling far too alone with her thoughts.

She should have known something was afoot when she hadn't heard from Cole for three days. It was, in retrospect, the longest she'd gone without hearing from him since the day they'd met. She was packing up more of Cass's belongings, systematically moving Kringle from one pile of laundry to another, when her phone buzzed itself off the bedside table. There were texts from her mom and Elijah.

Ziva The Great and Terrible: WTFFFFFFFFF
Best Lawyer in New York: HACKING PEOPLE'S FINANCIALS IS ILLEGAL also wow your dad is the actual worst???

She turned to find Hannah standing in her doorway. "Did your phone just blow up?"

"Yep. What's going on?" Hannah ushered her out into the landing, where Noelle and Mr. and Mrs. Matthews were sitting around a laptop. Noelle scooted over to make a space for Miriam and scrolled back to the top of the email they had been reading. It was from Cole's private email account, the one he never used with anyone he hadn't run an FBI background check on. Noelle, Miriam, Hannah, Mr. and Mrs. Matthews, Ziva, Elijah, and Mr. Rodriguez had all been cc'd.

My Carrigan's Family

I have attached some information I found particularly interesting from Richard's financials. As you'll see, the rumors Mimi alluded to are true—Big Dick was using his import business to smuggle cocaine into the country for years. Most recently, he's been close with some rather violent gentlemen who are helping him run product. He seems to have been dealing more in influence trading than actual cash, using the drugs to make very high up connections. He also seems, from his correspondence, to just kind of like hanging out with these guys.

Anyway, I knew that eventually he would come for Mimi and all of you again, and I wanted you to have what the kids these days call receipts (in this case, actual receipts). I almost leaked all of this to the media, to get back at him and ruin his life. But, it's not mine to leak. I didn't want to put you all in the path of that blowback. I still believe he needs to be taken down, so he doesn't have any power ever again, but that's not my call. Instead, I am providing copies to each person I think has a vested interest in keeping him in check, and one to Mr. Rodriguez as assurance. I trust his discretion; I hope I'm not wrong.

I have a standing job offer from a firm in New Zealand I've been putting off, as I couldn't imagine being separated from Miriam for that long. But now that she's trying to build a romance, I feel it would be timely for me to spend some time off the grid. Our lives can only be so entwined, after all. I have some recent emotional revelations of my own I need to process, and where better than the land of the hobbits?

I will probably be very difficult to reach for the next six months or so. I will send proof of life updates as possible, but I'll be working around the clock on a confidential project. Mimi, please feel free to ignore any and all calls from my mother.

Both my heart and my blackmail material remain yours,

Nicholas Jedediah Fraser IV

"Did he make us accessories to a crime?" Mrs. Matthews asked with annoyance.

"I don't think he would intentionally make us felons, no

matter how bad his other decisions were in this matter," Miriam said, "and if he had, I definitely think Elijah would have said so." *Oh, Cole.* What the hell was he doing, and how was she going to live without him for six months?

"I almost wish he'd taken your dad down, so we'd never have to worry about him again," Mr. Matthews huffed. "I hate that son of a bitch."

"We could always do it," Noelle reminded them. "We hold all the cards now."

"As long as these receipts are legal for us to possess, we're going to hold them as close to our chests as possible," Miriam said. "And we're going to buy Elijah and Jason the world's nicest belated Christmas gift for having to deal with all of this."

They all nodded. Eventually, inevitably, Richard Blum would again make himself a problem they would have to deal with. In the meantime, they had a team and ammunition and had bought themselves some time.

Miriam was miserable and whiny without daily access to Cole. For days, Miriam pulled out her phone reflexively, checked the text message notifications, and sighed.

When Hannah got sick of watching, she finally said, "Give me your phone."

"You can't put me on a phone moratorium," Miriam warned. "The Bloomers will riot, which no one wants. They are legion."

"I'm not taking your phone away, although it's honestly a good idea," Hannah assured her. "I'm making a call."

Miriam handed over her phone, skeptically. "If anyone knows where Cole is, and how he's doing, who would it be?" Hannah asked Miriam.

"*Me*?!" Miriam answered.

Hannah rolled her eyes and dialed.

It rang once and picked up.

"Miriam," Tara started over speaker. "This is a bad—"

"It's Hannah."

"Oh." Tara's voice thawed considerably. "Are you looking for Cole?"

Miriam threw her hands up in the air, exasperated. Hannah gave her a teacher look that said, *shut up.*

"Do you know where he is?" she asked Tara.

"Obviously," Tara said. "He is safe and doing remarkably well."

"Thank you. I would ask you to tell him he's making his best friend sad, but Miriam's feelings aren't your responsibility."

"They sure aren't," Tara said. "I know you have me on speaker but tell that ex of mine to come get her shit out of my garage." The phone clicked as Tara hung up.

"Well, fuck," Miriam said, and then added, "I didn't leave my stuff there on purpose—she wouldn't let anyone come get it!"

She wanted to sulk all over again that Tara and Cole had a whole secret life no one had ever bothered to tell her about, until she remembered that she'd never told Cole about most of her own life. So she went to bed early, the better to argue with Cole in her head. She felt Noelle join her, spooning her whole body into a cherished, protected ball, and she finally fell asleep.

"I have to go back to Charleston," she said the next morning, as they were lying in bed, staring at each other. "I have to figure out what to do with all my workshop stuff before

Tara sells it on eBay. And I want to say goodbye to the city, and my synagogue. I kind of ghosted my rabbi."

"How long is this trip?" Noelle asked skeptically.

"I'm not running," Miriam assured her, trailing a finger over Noelle's arm. "Carrigan's has a way of making you be honest with yourself, and feel all your feelings, for better or worse. It's magic, but it's dangerous for a girl trying to stay safe from her feelings. I'm not that girl anymore. I'm solidly Team Feelings, these days."

Noelle laughed at this description. "I blame Kringle, for the magic." Kringle meowed from somewhere, clearly accepting this as his due. "And I know you're not running."

Miriam's heart exploded at Noelle putting this trust in her. She sighed. "I don't want to leave right now, when things are finally perfect."

"I'll be here when you get back," Noelle told her, pulling on her pants.

"Where are you going?" Miriam pouted.

"To go get you coffee before you become a banshee," Noelle told her, and Miriam threw a pillow at her, before lying back against the bed in a happy sigh.

Chapter 27

Noelle

Miriam left for Charleston, and Noelle waited for her to come back, but not patiently. She was anxious, although it wasn't rational. Noelle knew, in her head, that Miriam wasn't running away again, and that she would always have to travel for work, but that didn't mean she wasn't coming back home.

Her head knew it, but her heart wanted Miriam where she could see her.

Without consciously deciding to, Noelle started going to the noon meeting regularly, having lunch with the ladies. Before long, they were showing up for brunch on Saturdays and had roped Mrs. Matthews into a weekly bridge game, and Noelle was rebuilding the wheelchair ramp to make it sturdier for them. They sat out on the back deck looking out into the back acreage, smoking long, thin cigarettes, complaining that the coffee was too weak, and giving her hell about her love life.

Two months ago, she'd thought Carrigan's could run fine without Miriam's interference, and now, without Miriam, it seemed absurd that everything would go on as normal. Hannah was sending out emails with spreadsheets. Mrs. Matthews was talking about produce deliveries. Collin was in and out from the cafe, bringing new recipes he wanted to collaborate on. When Noelle complained to Mrs. Matthews about the blasé attitude toward Miriam's absence, Mrs. Matthews looked at her like she'd grown a second head.

"If we shut down Carrigan's every time Miriam left, there wouldn't have been a Carrigan's for a decade."

When she tried to talk to Mr. Matthews about it, he rolled his eyes and told her to take up a hobby, like growing trees, perhaps. She pointed out that he and Mrs. Matthews had never spent more than a week apart, and he told her that was because he was smarter than she was.

She couldn't get comfortable in her skin, so she decided to build something. She went to the Greens with blueprints for a tree house for the twins, but Elijah shooed her off.

"It's bigger than the first apartment I had with Jason," he said, taking the hammer out of her hands. "No way."

"I just wanted to do something to thank you both for being so good to me when I moved here," Noelle explained. "You didn't have to take me in the way you did."

"I mean, there are slim pickings for friendship up here, honestly." Elijah winked at her.

She laughed. "I like to think I have some redeeming qualities."

"Sure, you're not terrible at trivia."

"Thanks? I guess?" She was totally mediocre at trivia.

"What brought on this sudden wave of sentimentality? Has falling in love made you full of good cheer?"

"Hey! I was always cheerful!" Noelle protested, and then laughed when Elijah raised his eyebrows at her skeptically. "I'm just trying to be more open about my appreciation for people. You've been a great friend. And a really good lawyer, in a situation that was a lot more complicated than you probably anticipated."

Elijah shrugged. "You pay me for the lawyer part. And the bill you're getting is going to be intense."

"Would you accept Carrigan's shares? You're welcome to Levi's." Noelle waggled her eyebrows.

He shook his head vehemently. "I do not need to be any more entangled in the operatic drama up there than I already am."

"A reasonable stance," she said. "Are you sure you don't need a tree house?"

"Go build something for Miriam," he told her. "I'm kicking you out."

This was brilliant. She started with a small renovation project to help Miriam get the Blum Again business settled in at the farm by doing a little bit of work on the carriage house. Then it escalated, as she kept adding on elements that might make Miriam smile when she came back.

"You're in serious danger of turning into a wife guy," Hannah laughed as Noelle pulled off her safety goggles and brushed wood chips out of her hair.

"I would be a great wife guy," Noelle said, her heart doing a little flip at the word "wife." She and Miriam hadn't talked about marriage, even in a general "do you believe in engaging in heteronormative cultural practices" kind of way. She would be okay with whatever version of forever made Miriam comfortable, but Noelle had to admit that she got more of a thrill than she would have expected out of the idea of calling Miriam her wife. But it was way too early for any of that.

"I'm glad, if I'm not going to be your person anymore, that your person is Miri," Hannah said, motioning for Noelle to put her head down before picking out a piece of wood she'd missed.

"What?" Noelle protested. "You're still my person. And Miriam is your person, and now somehow I'm Cole's person. We're all just each other's people. It's a big overly emotionally enmeshed club. If Cole falls in love, we'll probably fold them in, too."

"My life would have been so much easier if I could have fallen for Cole," Hannah lamented, hopping up to sit on a worktable. "We could have wrapped it all up in a neat little bow."

"Get your butt off my table! You know that's unsafe wood-working protocol." Noelle shooed her off. "I think Cole has his eye on someone else, and I *know* you're not ready to fall in love again. Believe me, I would be thrilled if you were."

"What if I'm never ready? What if I never fall in love with someone else?"

Noelle looked at Hannah, who was twisting a piece of wire nervously in her hands. She didn't want to lie to Hannah, to tell her that it would be okay eventually, to assure her that someday she'd be over Levi. Noelle couldn't imagine ever being over Miriam, and Hannah had loved Levi a hell of a lot longer.

"Well, you will ascend to your rightful place as the Carrigan, taking on the mantle to collect a new generation of misfit toys and lure them into the mountains."

"So in this scenario, Cass was the manifestation of some kind of ancient force, like the Morrigan?"

"Yes, but with tacky Christmas crap instead of ravens and death," Noelle nodded.

"Into every generation, a Carrigan is born," Hannah intoned. "I can live with that. I'll be the Carrigan, you be the wife guy, Miriam will be the artistic genius, Cole will be the...what does Cole actually do? Hacking isn't his official job, is it?"

Noelle shrugged. As far as she could tell, no one knew.

"We will be a happy family getting progressively weirder out here in the woods together," Hannah finished with satisfaction. "I'll learn to bake so that Mrs. Matthews can retire."

"I would love to see you try to learn to bake. Or we could maybe just hire a chef."

Hannah's face fell, and Noelle sighed. She wished she could erase all of Hannah's heartbreak, but she knew she wasn't the person who could fix this mess.

"Sorry!" Hannah said. "I don't mean for my face to do that. I'm working on it."

"Are you okay, really?" Noelle asked. "Not about Levi, but about sharing control, and having Miriam here full-time selling art out of your carriage house? I know you're thrilled about getting a chance to use all your galaxy brain brilliance on Carrigan's All Year, but you did still get bulldozed into it, a little."

"I'm thrilled about Miri being here, for the most part. I

may have some residual anger about her leaving, but now that I know the whole story, that's mostly gone. Plus, she showed up big, and her ideas are smart." Hannah paused, thinking. "I have absolutely no qualms about Carrigan's All Year; it's the absolute right next step. I did kind of get steamrolled into it, but by Cass and circumstances, and I can't really be mad at that."

"You can be mad at Cass. I still am, sort of, even if it worked out in the end, and I'm surviving the experience. You're allowed to be mad."

"I can't, NoNo." Hannah shook her head. "If I let myself feel how mad I am, at everything, all the time, I will burn up from the inside out, and I don't know who I'll be on the other side."

Noelle leaned next to her on the worktable, and Hannah rested her head on Noelle's shoulder. They stayed there, holding each other up as they had been for so long.

"Okay, well, you would be my rage ball, and I would still love you, just so you know. I am Team Hannah until the day I die. I'm the captain," Noelle told her.

"I know. Maybe someday I'll let myself burn up and we'll see who rises from the ashes. But not this week, because my schedule is extremely booked."

Noelle nodded in faux seriousness. "Oh yeah, we need to schedule your rage meltdown in your bullet journal at least three months in advance, so we can plan events around it."

"Stop mocking my preparedness! I am keeping this place afloat with only the power of my scheduling!" Hannah protested. "But speaking of, um, preparing for my rage, and also, everything else?"

Noelle's stomach dropped. She knew that hesitation. Hannah was about to say something about Levi, and she knew Noelle wasn't going to like it, which is why she was hemming around it. She raised her eyebrows at Hannah.

"I asked Cole if he could take a message to Blue for me, since he's on that half of the globe. I asked him to come home."

Noelle groaned, because she hated it, but she knew it was necessary.

"I had to," Hannah supplied. "We need to know about his shares. And I can't bar him from his home forever. His parents miss him, and I hate making them sad."

"I know. Ugh. I'm proud of you," Noelle said, grudgingly.

"I'm going to go now and leave you to . . . whatever you're doing. Trying to woo your girlfriend who already lives with you into loving you more, or something," Hannah said, kissing Noelle's cheek and ruffling her hair.

"I apologized but I don't feel like I did *enough*," Noelle said, pulling at her hands with her hair. "She made me a painting!"

"I don't think Miriam is keeping score of who's better at saying I'm sorry."

Noelle harrumphed. Hannah rolled her eyes but left her alone with her woodworking. She was going to build a space so perfect for Miriam that Miriam would always want to run toward home, instead of feeling driven away.

Chapter 28

Miriam

Tara opened the door to their—her—Single House and rolled her eyes, hard.

"Do you not have a functioning telephone, Miriam Blum?" she asked, a hand on her hip. "This is the kind of visit about which you forewarn a girl, so she can at least get a blowout."

Tara's hair was eerily perfect, as always.

"I came to get my stuff?" Miriam said, apologetically. This house was very beautiful, she noticed, now that she wasn't trying to live in it. "I wasn't sure if you'd be home if I warned you, or if you would clear out, and I was hoping to talk to you."

"That's the kind of sneaky move I would pull. Shady but smart. I'll allow it. Your clothes and whatnot are all ready to go, but I haven't touched your art stuff because I didn't want to break anything and face an army of angry Bloomers." She gestured toward the garage at the back of the house.

As Miriam passed through, she noticed a very familiar shadow box over the mantelpiece.

"Tara Chadwick, is that a Blum Again piece? On your wall?" She didn't think Tara could still surprise her, after all this time. "You hate my art."

"I never hated it, I just didn't always understand it," Tara clarified.

"How did you even get this?" Miriam asked, "Wasn't it part of the auction?"

"I bid on it," Tara said, defensively. "I liked it, and you needed the money."

"I would have given it to you," Miriam told her. "It pulls the room together. Makes it look homier."

Tara smoothed down her shirt primly. "I can afford to invest in up-and-coming artists once in a while. Go deal with your shit. I'll talk to you later."

Miriam smiled at her and disappeared into the back of the house.

Several hours later, Tara stuck her head in the workroom, where Miriam was carefully packing pieces for shipment to New York. "You look like you could use a cup of coffee and some fresh air. Do you want to walk down to the cafe? I'll give you that talk you ambushed me for."

Miriam looked down at herself. She was wearing a white tank top soaked with sweat under a pair of ripped-up, faded overalls, and a pair of Birkenstocks that predated college. Her hair was tied up, Rosie the Riveter style, in an ancient, stained handkerchief. "Do you really want to be seen, or smelled, in public with me?"

"Come on, you'll make me look great in comparison."

They walked down to the cafe on the corner in silence. The city around them buzzed with that dusk energy of business-people getting off work and looking for happy hour. Miriam realized she was going to miss feeling it in the background of her life. She let the heavy, damp air fill her lungs and tried to remember the smell of summer on the water. It was a city thick with stories, and she hadn't heard all the ones she'd thought she was going to have time to hear.

They'd taken this route a thousand times, even though they had an espresso machine at the house. Emma's was their neutral ground, where they went when they needed to hash something out that required French fries. The place was open all night, served a killer selection of cake, and poured decent, cheap coffee.

The staff all knew them by name and did a double take when they walked in together. Tara must have told them they were broken up. "I'm just packing up my stuff," Miriam called out to their favorite night waitress, Holly.

She turned to Tara. "Hey! Maybe now you can ask Holly out. Huh? Huh? You know you think she's cute."

"Holly is a million miles out of my league." There was a sigh in Tara's words that Miriam was certain she'd never heard directed at her. She was also certain that was exactly how she herself sounded when she talked about Noelle.

"I'm a little offended," Miriam said. "It's true, though, she is."

They settled in a booth facing each other. The vinyl creaked under Miriam comfortably, and she stored this away as another memory she was going to miss: the incandescent bulbs in sea green glass fixtures swinging from the ceiling, the old mural, lovingly preserved, of a doe leaping over a field of flowers, the perfect tater tots.

"Are you okay? Your eyeliner wings are crooked," she said to Tara, startled out of her reverie by this alarming incongruity.

"I left them that way on purpose when I messed them up." Tara winced. "I'm working on this whole living-with-small-imperfections thing. I mean, I don't leave wet towels on the floor or anything—"

"Of course not; it would ruin the hardwood," Miriam mocked, gently.

"Thank you! Exactly." This was a fight they'd had a hundred times, but now they smiled at each other about it, all the resentment gone. Miriam realized suddenly how many of their fights had really been them trying to say that they fit wrong. "But I'm trying to give myself an opportunity to practice being a little messy, so I don't get my whole world so twisted around when things don't go exactly as I planned them."

"Wow, that's huge emotional work for you," Miriam said, impressed. "I'm proud of you." She raised the mug of coffee that Holly had set down without their having to ask, and Tara tapped it with her own. "Cheers."

"You, on the other hand, have been working without stopping, even for caffeine, for ten hours. Are you okay?" Tara asked. "I've never seen you go without a cup of coffee for more than three hours."

"I'm both amazing and barely holding it together," Miriam said. "When I was up at Carrigan's, there was emergency after emergency, we were juggling the busy season, and I was navigating my mother."

Now she had breathing room, and she had never been good

at allowing herself to live inside of breathing room. But she'd meant what she said to Noelle about liking her new feelings. They were going to take a while to break in, but it was a good kind of discomfort, the growing kind. Miriam was grateful she was being given the chance to practice slowing down.

"You were falling in love," Tara said. "It was exciting and distracting." She winked, to show that she wasn't still upset.

"I'm sorry," Miriam said. "Yeah. I was. I didn't mean to be."

"I know that, sugar, or I wouldn't be buying you strawberry cake," Tara pointed out. She stirred an extra Splenda into her coffee, and then another, meticulously tearing the packages, tapping them three times against the side of the cup, and placing them exactly parallel with the edge of table.

"But now," Tara continued, having sipped her coffee to find it suitable, "you're here, and everything seems real, and final. It's a lot of endings in a very short time. You're feeling itchy and sentimental."

This might be, Miriam reflected, the most honest conversation they'd ever had about their feelings.

"I lost Cass, and you, and Charleston. Cole is AWOL for who knows how long. It's just so much." The words burst forth from Miriam unexpectedly, and she managed not to stamp her foot at the end, but it was a close thing.

"You hate when things end," Tara paraphrased *Breakfast at Tiffany's.*

"Oh my gosh, that song! It was playing in the bar the night we met. We both liked it, and we ended up talking all night. Shit, we met over a breakup song. What did we think was going to happen?" Miriam laughed.

"Well, you did lose Cass, that's true," Tara said, back

to enumerating her arguments. Miriam found it comforting now. "I'm right here though. Heck, someday, we might be real close, if we let ourselves be. Cole, well, I've known Cole as long as I've known myself, and I would bet my retirement stocks he's going to be knocking on one of our doors before the summer is out."

"You think so?" Miriam asked hopefully.

"Oh, he'll be here. Sleeping on my couch and eating my food, even though he has a perfectly good apartment," Tara assured her. "Charleston isn't going anywhere, except maybe into the ocean when the sea level rises. And, you also gained a whole damned Christmas tree farm."

"This is a weirdly good pep talk," Miriam said. She took a deep breath and felt the darkness of panic receding back into its corners, like the Nothing in *The NeverEnding Story*, driven back into its cave.

"I'm a really good ex-girlfriend," Tara said. "Now. Cake."

When they left Emma's, she stopped by the space that would have been Blum Again Vintage & Curios and peered through the windows. Seeing it empty was not as much a knife to the gut as Miriam had been expecting. It was hard, and it hurt, but it hurt because it was real.

She let the visions of all the things this space could have been wash over her: all the people who would have walked in off the street, all the Bloomers who would have made a pilgrimage here, all the friends from around the country she could have welcomed into her space, finally, and offered a cup of tea. She would have most of that at Carrigan's now, even if it would have a different flavor. More eggnog, less grits. She let all those visions float out into the Atlantic, setting them free.

And on Friday, when everything was on a truck and shipped off to New York, she made her last stop. She was going to services one last time at Kahal Kadosh Beth Elohim. When she first moved to Charleston, she wasn't sure if she'd find a spiritual home, but the oldest continuously operating synagogue in the United States had opened its arms to her. Charleston might always be here (pending global warming) but she would never be a part of it, in this particular way, ever again.

That night, Miriam was kicking off her Chucks when her phone buzzed. She had two text notifications.

True Blue: Are you going to call me? A very large, alarmingly beautiful blond man just showed up on my filming set to yell at me.

How did Cole...Never mind, she didn't want to know. The second text read:

Santa Baby: I miss you.

She pressed the video call button and braced for the physical jolt she got every time Noelle's face came on screen. Noelle was pushing the swoop of her undercut off her forehead like James freaking Dean when she answered, and Miriam bit her bottom lip to keep from screaming.

"What? What's happening? Why are you looking at me like I'm espresso?" Noelle looked behind her, like she was expecting to see something else Miriam would be salivating over.

"I miss touching you." She knew she was whining, but she figured it was better to be honest about what a schmoopy mess she was.

"Tell me about your day," Noelle said.

"I went to an Al-Anon meeting! It was good but weird."

"Wait, did you say you went to an Al-Anon meeting?"

"Well, I've never dated someone sober before, and it's for people who are in relationships with alcoholics, and I didn't handle my last relationship well..." Miriam sighed, staring up at the motel ceiling. "I have a lot of stuff that I haven't particularly dealt with."

"I noticed," Noelle said dryly.

Miriam flipped her off.

"Are you coming home soon?" Noelle asked, and Miriam nodded. *Home. Soon.*

She found she couldn't sleep, so she opened a box of mail Tara had been keeping for her. In among the cell phone bills she had on autopay and the requests from her alma mater for money, she recognized Cass's stationery.

Her heart stopped.

The handwriting was Cass's block letters, the date stamp a few days before she'd died. The letter and Miriam must have missed each other, one winging to Carrigan's, and one away.

She slipped open the glue, trying not to tear any part of this precious, unlooked-for last gift. Inside was a napkin, covered back and front in tiny writing.

My girl,

It won't be long. I need you to come run this place for me. Now, don't argue. I've found you the perfect girl, and you're going to make a life here. It's my last wish, and you owe me. You might have to convince her, but I know the two of you are going to make magic. And I need you to get Blue back here, your cousin is too stubborn to do it herself.

I love you.

That meddling old bat had been playing yenta from her deathbed, and they all fell for it. Miriam shook her head, and carefully moved the napkin so she wouldn't drop fat tears on it and smudge the ink.

Well, who was she to argue with Cassiopeia Carrigan's last wish?

Chapter 29

Miriam

Miriam stood in front of the doors to Carrigan's, with a better-packed suitcase than the last time, but without Cole. She brushed her fingers over the mezuzah again, this time without fear.

Hannah opened the door, and her eyes widened. Miriam gave a little wave. Hannah winked.

"Noelle," Hannah called, keeping her voice admirably normal, "the door's for you."

Noelle came bounding down the stairs, wrapped in approximately fifteen layers of cold-weather gear and pulling on her hat. "Can you tell whoever it is I need to get out to the back lot but I'll—"

She stopped when she saw Miriam. She leaped down the last three steps and barreled Miriam almost into the door as she hugged her.

Miriam was still wrapped entirely in a cocoon of Noelle

when Hannah said, "It's fitting that you came home on Tu B'Shevat."

"Oh, man, I did," Miriam said, peeking her head around Noelle's shoulder. "That's kind of perfect."

"What's Tu B'Shevat?" Noelle asked, letting her go.

"It's the Jewish holiday that marks the new harvest year," Miriam explained. "It's New Year's, for trees."

"Why have we not been celebrating this all along?" Noelle asked with delight. "Carrigan's All Year needs a big-ass Tu B'Shevat party. Someone write that down! Hannah, where's your clipboard?!"

The commotion brought Mr. and Mrs. Matthews, and then everyone was trying to get a hug and talk. The contrast between now and her old homecomings, slipping in and out of the house in Charleston like a sea breeze, unnoticed, was stark. She'd thought she loved being answerable to no one, but this made her want to weep with love.

All her childhood, she'd known she was an unwanted invader in her house. Now, she had been made to feel like an essential piece of the whole. She'd never wanted this because she never could have imagined it, but now that she had it, it was everything.

Noelle caught her eye, and they stared at each other, the air crackling between them, while Miriam tried not to look too much like she was desperate for Noelle to be kissing her. Suddenly, she found herself being thrown over Noelle's shoulder in one lift. She hadn't even seen Noelle *move*.

"What are you doing?!" Miriam asked, hanging upside down.

"We need privacy," Noelle said, as she carried Miriam out toward the carriage house.

"We'll have food ready for you later!" Mrs. Matthews called.

"Much later!" Noelle called back.

"Where are we going?" Miriam laughed. "It's cold outside. Also, all the blood is rushing to my head!" As Noelle set her down, she asked, "Wait, where are we?"

The carriage house looked completely new.

"This is the carriage house. It was built with the original house, so it's probably been here all your life," Noelle deadpanned.

Miriam stared at her.

"It's our house," Noelle told her, "I hope. I set up the front half of the house as a studio and workshop, because it gets better light."

Miriam clutched Noelle's hand as she looked around the room. The entire building had been redecorated, with an extensive studio setup ready in the front, including all the equipment she'd had shipped from Charleston and new blank canvases on easels. Baba Yaga and La Llorona were framed and hanging, looking at each other, over the fireplace. In the back of the main floor was an open-plan kitchen with a big farmhouse-style table, a professional KitchenAid mixer, a gas top stove—

"How did you do all this in two weeks? Are you magic?" Miriam was in awe.

"Mr. Matthews is. Do you like it?" Noelle asked, nervously.

Miriam needed a moment to find her voice, overwhelmed by the magnitude of such a gesture both from Noelle and from Ben Matthews, the man who'd shown her what a dad could be.

"I love it, but why?" Miriam asked. "What did I do to deserve this wildly elaborate gift?"

"Remodeling projects are how dykes say I love you," Noelle said sheepishly.

Miriam swung to look at her. "I know you love me. You said it forty-seven times yesterday alone. I can show you the text log."

Noelle shrugged. "I realize I tell you every day, but I needed to show you. I love you. I love your quixotic, unexpected mix of twee pop art and biting political commentary. I love that your hair is the size of the rest of your body. I love that you are the surrogate grandchild of an elaborate network of junkers across the country. I love that you come with a built-in fandom. I want to be the president of it, by the way. I want to be the head Bloomer and tag myself in Instagram stories where I gush about how smart and pretty you are. I want to rethink everything about my life and my future, with you at the center."

"You built me a house?" Miriam was trying to process everything Noelle had just said and also not start crying. "I was already in love with you!"

"I mean it was already built. I did build you the loft. And the staircase."

There was a spiral staircase leading up to a loft that Miriam hadn't noticed in everything else. The rails were beautiful carved wood spires.

"Is it safe?" Miriam was in awe.

Noelle pretended affront. "I would never risk your life with an unsafe staircase!" Then she looked down at her shoes, a little embarrassed. "It's Carrigan's pine. From my trees."

Miriam teared up. This was beyond her imagining. To be loved like this, that Noelle would cut her trees and shape them and build their home, so they could start their lives together sheltered in wood that Cass had planted.

"You didn't have to do this," Miriam started, but Noelle stopped her.

"I wanted to prove to you that I was ready for us. You did the biggest, bravest thing I've ever seen anyone do, and I wanted to be worthy of it."

"Is this the Adirondacks' version of the lesbian U-Haul?" Miriam asked. "I built you a cabin?" She had to joke, or she was going to sob.

Noelle laughed. "Will you live here with me? Can we build this life together?" She looked so nervous, and it was so damned cute.

"Were you really worried? Out here I can go get coffee in my underwear in the morning, I have my own middle-of-the-night-baking kitchen, and no one will get mad at us if we, um, get a little loud." Eventually, this house would be full of Bloomers all day, but for now it was just the two of them, and Miriam was going to take advantage of it. She was going to have to figure out how to balance having her space open to fans while keeping some privacy, being more herself on camera without losing healthy distance, but she didn't have to figure it out today.

"Were you planning on getting a little loud?" Noelle asked, her eyes lighting up.

"Do you think you can make me?" Miriam challenged her.

Noelle pulled her in for a hot, insistent kiss that was an entire seduction, a promise of filthy, beautiful things. Their mouths demanded and their hands grasped at each other's clothes.

"Is that a yes, Miri?" Noelle gasped, out of breath, her pupils blown out.

"Yes! Obviously yes. Where is the bed?" Miriam asked desperately.

Noelle grinned. "It's up in the loft."

"Well, get your ass up there and get out of those clothes," Miriam demanded.

They chased each other up the staircase, which did seem remarkably sturdy, and fell, laughing, on the mattress on the floor, piled with pillows. Noelle rolled to her side and propped her head on her hand.

"Do you like it?" she asked again, seriously.

"I love it," Miriam answered, sliding a hand up under the hem of Noelle's henley, so she could feel her skin. "I love you. Immensely. Overwhelmingly."

Noelle crawled over her and pinned her hands to the bed, looking down at the mass of curls spread out over the pillows. One of the body pillows yawned and moved out of the way with a huffy yowl.

"Oh yeah, Kringle is living with us, too," Noelle said. "He was disturbing the guests, and Hannah said she was going to ship him to Siberia if we didn't take him in."

"He can stay as long as he *goes downstairs*," Miriam said to him, sternly. He went, switching his tail in annoyance as he disappeared down the staircase.

"Is this it?" Miriam asked, her body bowing up to meet Noelle's. "Can we finally just get naked and enjoy each other, and live in our home surrounded by our family and be in love? Can we relax for ten minutes without a financial crisis, or some dude exploding our peace, or, I don't know, a roof caving in?"

"Well, we have a family reunion coming next week, so none of us is relaxing anytime soon," Noelle said. "And the roof in the cottage is in fact leaking, which we'll need to deal with ASAP. Probably at some point some dude is going to appear and make drama, even if it's just Cole. But all of it will happen in our home, surrounded by our family. And, in the meantime, we should very much get naked and enjoy each other. Finally."

They did, repeatedly.

In between they whispered about dreams they had. They talked about trips they wanted to take, to see Noelle's family in Santa Fe, and some of her old friends from her sustainable farming days, to antique markets around the world. They could, if they wanted, go through old napkins from Cass and then drink coffee in the same cafes she'd visited, see if anyone recognized Miriam's face and, if so, listen to their stories about the whirlwind of a woman in a turban who'd come through their lives for a season, years ago.

Miriam and Noelle held hands under the weight of a returned, and immoveable, Kringle, talking into the night about going to therapy together, about what they might do if, or more rightly when, Richard resurfaced, and how to face it together. They talked about their worries for Hannah and Cole, and how to keep themselves from interfering too badly in their best friends' love lives. They put Dolly on the Bluetooth speakers Noelle had installed and sang at the top of their lungs, because they weren't inside the inn and no one could complain.

In the witching hour, Miriam stole downstairs to the studio, running her hands over half-finished pieces she'd started in

Charleston and would finish here. She lovingly patted her chain saw and her industrial-size glue barrels. The eerie moonlight, under which she'd painted La Llorona, revealed something she hadn't seen before.

Blum Again Vintage & Curios: What You Never Knew You Always Needed

Noelle had stenciled on the giant windows. Miriam's knees gave out underneath her, and she sat on the floor, weeping.

She didn't know how long it would take her to get used to feeling this happy or being this open and present with the people she loved. She didn't know how long it would take for the voice in the back of her head to stop telling her to run away, shut down, and not risk all of this. She knew it was going to be a lot of work and being in love with Noelle wasn't going to cure everything that was broken inside her. Not even Carrigan's was that magical. But in the deepest part of her, in the marrow of her bones, Miriam believed she belonged here, that she deserved to be happy and home.

She was going to fight for this. To run Shenanigans with Hannah, to fight with Blue when he finally got here, to learn to braid challah from Mrs. Matthews and light Shabbos candles with Mr. Matthews. She was going to stay, be planted, and grow roots. She was going to make Noelle Northwood happy beyond her wildest dreams.

And she was going to cover so many Christmas trees in glitter.

Epilogue

T he week of Passover came to Carrigan's cold and bright.

Work on Carrigan's All Year had continued frantically. Every month had events that put Carrigan's front and center: writers' retreat weekends, summer camp field trips, collaborations with several town councils to host fundraisers. The wall-sized calendar in Hannah's office was color coded to within an inch of its life. All three women felt hopeful about the year, with the caveat that (a) one of their core group had disappeared down under and (b) their fourth shareholder was still unseen.

"Does anyone else notice that the men have conveniently disappeared in the middle of the real, sustained work?" Noelle asked during their weekly business meeting.

"Mr. Matthews is working his ass off on the plumbing in the cottage as we speak," Miriam told her.

"We pay him," Noelle said.

"Not enough," Miriam retorted.

Hannah was smiling at the two most important women in her life and feeling very satisfied about everything when she felt the hair rise on the back of her neck.

"I have to go," she said abruptly, startling Noelle and Miriam. She was never the person who ended business meetings before every agenda item had been crossed off.

They followed her down the hall.

She was standing in the kitchen, hands balled into fists, watching the door.

Miriam and Noelle came up from behind and flanked her. Noelle looked exasperated, and Miriam amused. The knob on the door turned, and Hannah took a deep breath. They all waited for the man who always came through the kitchen door, like "the help" he believed himself to be.

Although Miriam had spoken to Levi regularly, in her mind, he was the same kid she'd left: burning both ends of the night to work his way through culinary school, scruffy, overcaffeinated, a feral cat who kept walking into bad choices to see what would happen. He wore the same Black Flag shirt more days than not, he moved just a bit too fast all the time, and he was never quite settled in his own skin.

Noelle remembered an entitled, volatile man who never thought what he had was good enough, and left everyone who tried to love him scorched because he never bothered to stop himself from bursting into flame.

Hannah had thought about Levi every moment since she could remember, and she had every version of him tattooed into her consciousness. When she'd seen him last, he'd been angry, restless, and reckless, barreling out of her life and into the unknown.

The man who walked through the door was not the Levi any of them remembered.

He was bearded, still, but instead of looking like he'd forgotten to shave, it was full, well-tended, and thick black now. His hair was too long, his curls swooping up over his high brow with a life of their own. His face had thinned and hardened, and his eyebrows spread out over gray eyes the color of a cloudy sky, ringed in smudged kohl. That, at least, hadn't changed. He wore a gigantic scarf, beat-up boots, and a leather jacket that Hannah would know anywhere.

He was standing completely still, something Miriam wasn't sure she'd ever seen him do in her life. He looked at home in his own skin, which Hannah knew without a doubt he had never felt before.

He looked like an Adult. A traffic-stopping, smoking hot one.

He also didn't know Miriam or Noelle were in the room. He'd brushed his hair out of his eyes and looked up, scanning for his mom and finding Hannah instead. Now he was staring at her with such naked longing on his face that Miriam wished she could sink through the floor.

She watched as, in a blink, a mask of indifference shuttered his face. He dropped the bag he'd been carrying in one hand and crossed his arms, leaning his long body against the door frame.

"Hi." He half smiled, his eyes searching.

"It's about fucking time," Hannah said before turning on her heel and walking away.

Acknowledgments

Thank you to my editors, Sam Brody and Amy Pierpont, who believed in the magic at Carrigan's. To Becca Podos, the agent of my wildest dreams, I'm so glad you're on this adventure with me. Cathy Arnold made me a fat butch clinch cover, which I will never stop squeeing over. The team at Forever, from Estelle Hallick's genius marketing to every person who copyedited, formatted, and worked in production on this book, thank you so much for making my girls look so very good.

So many people read this book at some point, and offered encouragement, feedback, beta reads, and love. This would never have gone from an idea I had on Twitter to print without Rachel Fleming, Felicia Grossman, Kait Sudol, Anna Meriano, Ashley Herring Blake, or Skye Kilaen. Thank you to Sarah Sapperstein, Hannah Gaber, Tylar Zinn, Christina Hicks, Justin Williamson, and everyone else whose DMs I slipped into and asked to read a draft of a quirky queer romcom. My incredible sensitivity readers were Jennifer Rothschild and Melissa Blue. While I've worked to the best of my ability to ensure that this book is not harmful to anyone, I understand that I may have failed and, if I have, it is entirely my failing.

Making a debut happen is not just readers, but every-one in the author's karass. My kid, the absolute jackpot best funniest most interesting human being to ever live, who I'm so lucky to parent. I wanted to show you that, in our family, we live our dreams. My husband and my mom, both of whom did everything possible to support me, and kept my kid from interrupting me too often. Babe, thanks for fake dating me that one time so I could live out a romance trope. Mom, I know you've read more romance novels than anyone else on Earth, and I hope you like this one. My sister Jill, who let me borrow her Hebrew name and her hair for my main character. My Linda, for inspiring me to write a butch dreamboat. My best friend Aidinha, who talked me through at least one car panic attack where I tried to quit writing forever. Elizabeth Wrigley-Field, who wrote with me on Zoom through an entire pandemic summer. Joy Manesiotis, who made me promise I would never give up writing. I did give up, for twelve years, but I came back, because that promise wouldn't let me go. Bill McDonald, Dr. Bob Smith, and Lois Wilson (not you, Bill Wilson, you shut up), for building the institutions that built me.

Thank you to romance novels and novelists, for giving me a writing home I didn't think I'd ever find. And to four guys from West Virginia who inspired me to tell stories again, when I thought I was long done. You taught me to choose joy and do good recklessly, that I was a fully realized creation and I was going to be amazing.

And as always and forever, to my beloved Clytemnestra. Your turn is coming, I promise.

Reading Group Guide

A Letter from the Author

My Dear Reader,

This is my first novel, and as is perhaps often the case with first books, many of the themes in it are deeply personal to me. Among those, one of the most resonant is finding your home. My home, wherever I've made it, has never been complete without cats. While drafting *Season of Love*, my family lost our beloved tortoiseshell Manx. It was important to me to include a tortie in the book in some way, in her memory.

Most tortoiseshells are female, with boys accounting for only about one in three thousand. They're a genetic anomaly. As a lifelong parent to a parade of rescued tailless cats, I have a soft spot for feline mutants, and I was taken by the idea of a cat who was a good luck charm for Carrigan's Christmasland.

In my mind, Carrigan's always existed as a bit of a pocket dimension, slightly out of step with the normal passage of time, its edges a little fuzzier than real life. Miriam thinks of it similarly, comparing it to both Narnia and Christopher Robin's Hundred Acre Wood. Any good dimensional portal needs a magical guardian, and who better than a giant cat who mysteriously wanders out of the woods and makes himself at home?

Because of their rareness, many cultures have myths about male torties being magical. Various folklore holds that tortoise-shells originated from a goddess, can cure warts, bring prosperity, ward off ghosts, prevent shipwrecks. I would not rule any of these things out for Kringle.

Norwegian Forest Cats are significantly larger than most other breeds. My grumpy old lady domestic shorthair is twenty pounds, so I have to assume that Kringle is absolutely enormous. As Miriam barely clears five feet, I imagine him as almost reaching her shoulders with his front paws when he reaches up for a hug, which he certainly does.

It should be noted that, while male tortoiseshells in real life have a shortened lifespan due to health issues caused by their genetics, Kringle is immortal and will never die, either on the pages of one of my books or in our hearts.

I hope you, like Kringle, find a warm welcome at Carrigan's Christmasland.

Yours sincerely,
Helena

Questions for Discussion

1. Both Miriam and Noelle have best friends who are very important to them. How do those relationships impact their romance?

2. Miriam ends the novel in a cautious but hopeful place regarding her mother. Do you think Miriam should have forgiven her mother? Why or why not?

3. How does Miriam use art to keep her connected to the world even during her trauma?

4. Cass used her death as an opportunity to pressure her loved ones into doing things she thought would be good for them. Does the fact that she was right in the end mitigate her meddling? Is it, as Miriam believes, harmlessly charming, or is Noelle right that Cass should have intervened earlier rather than waiting?

5. Noelle is deeply loyal to her friends, sometimes coming to their defense without correctly judging the situation. What are some ways that this plays out throughout the novel?

6. When Noelle finds out about Richard's plans for Christmasland, she asks Miriam whether or not Miriam knowingly put them all in danger. Is this a reasonable fear? Or is Noelle being unfair to make that assumption about Miriam?

7. A large theme of the book is opening oneself up to emotional risk. What do you think Miriam and Noelle need to do to continue this theme past the end of the events of the novel?

8. Tara and Miriam agreed to, essentially, a marriage of convenience. How might Miriam's life have been different if they had stayed together? Do you think she would eventually have come back to Carrigan's in some capacity?

9. What movie have you watched so often you know every line?

Don't miss Hannah and Levi's story!

Available Fall 2023

About the Author

Helena Greer writes contemporary romance novels that answer the question: What if this beloved trope were gay? She was born in Tucson, and her heart still lives there, although she no longer does. After earning a BA in writing and mythology, and a master's in library science, she spent several years blogging about librarianship before returning to writing creatively.

Helena loves cheesy pop culture, cats without tails, and ancient Greek murderesses.